THE LOST

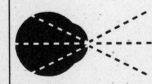 This Large Print Book carries the
Seal of Approval of N.A.V.H.

THE LOST

J. D. ROBB
PATRICIA GAFFNEY
MARY BLAYNEY
RUTH RYAN LANGAN

THORNDIKE PRESS
A part of Gale, Cengage Learning

GALE
CENGAGE Learning·

Detroit • New York • San Francisco • New Haven, Conn • Waterville, Maine • London

GALE
CENGAGE Learning

LIBRARY OF CONGRESS CATALOGING-IN-PUBLICATION DATA

The lost / by J..D. Robb . . . [et al.].
   p. cm. — (Thorndike Press large print basic)
ISBN-13: 978-1-4104-2398-6 (alk. paper)
ISBN-10: 1-4104-2398-0 (alk. paper)
   1. Detective and mystery stories, American. 2. Large type books. I. Robb, J. D., 1950–
PS648.D4L67 2010
813'.087208—dc22   2009046318

Published in 2010 by arrangement with The Berkley Publishing Group, a member of Penguin Group (USA) Inc.

CONTENTS

5

■ ■ ■ ■

MISSING IN DEATH
J. D. ROBB

■ ■ ■ ■

ONE

On a day kissed gently by summer, three thousand, seven hundred and sixty-one passengers cruised the New York Harbor on the Staten Island Ferry. Two of them had murder on their minds.

The other three thousand, seven hundred and fifty-nine aboard the bright orange ferry christened the *Hillary Rodham Clinton* were simply along for the ride. Most were tourists who happily took their vids and snaps of the retreating Manhattan skyline or that iconic symbol of freedom, the Statue of Liberty.

Even in 2060, nearly two centuries after she'd first greeted hopeful immigrants to a new world, nobody beat "The Lady."

Those who jockeyed for the best views munched on soy chips, sucked down tubes of soft drinks from the snack bars while the ferry chugged placidly along on calm waters under baby blue skies.

With the bold sun streaming, the scent of sunscreen mixed with the scent of water, many jammed the decks for the duration of the twenty-five-minute ride from Lower Manhattan to Staten Island. A turbo would have taken half the time, but the ferry wasn't about expediency. It was about tradition.

Most planned to get off at St. George, jam the terminal, then simply load back on again to complete the round trip. It was free, it was summer, it was a pretty way to spend an hour.

Some midday commuters, eschewing the bridges, the turbos, or the air trams, sat inside, out of the biggest crowds, and passed the time with their PPCs or 'links.

Summer meant more kids. Babies cried or slept, toddlers whined or giggled, and parents sought to distract the bored or fractious by pointing out the grand lady or a passing boat.

For Carolee Grogan of Springfield, Missouri, the ferry ride checked off another item on her Must Do list on the family vacation she'd lobbied for. Other Must Dos included the top of the Empire State Building, the Central Park Zoo, the Museum of Natural History, St. Pat's, the Metropolitan Museum of Art (though she wasn't sure she'd successfully harangue her husband and ten- and seven-year-old sons into that one), Ellis Island, Memorial Park, a Broadway show — she didn't care which one — and shopping on Fifth Avenue.

In the spirit of fairness, she'd added on a ballgame at Yankee Stadium, and fully accepted she would have to wander the cathedral of Tiffany's alone while her gang hit the video heaven of Times Square.

At forty-three, Carolee was living a long-cherished dream. She'd finally pushed, shoved and nagged her husband east of the Mississippi.

Could Europe be far behind?

When she started to take a snapshot of her "boys," as she called Steve and their sons, a man standing nearby offered to take one of the whole family. Carolee happily turned over her camera, posed with her boys with the dignified lady of liberty behind them.

"See." She gave her husband an elbow poke as they went back to looking out at the water. "He was nice. Not all New Yorkers are rude and nasty."

"Carolee, he was a tourist, just like us. He's probably from Toledo or somewhere." But he smiled when he said it. It was more fun to yank her chain than to admit he was

11

having a pretty good time.

"I'm going to ask him."

Steve only shook his head as his wife walked over to chat up the picture taker. It was so Carolee. She could — and did — talk to anyone anywhere about anything.

When she came back she offered Steve a smug smile. "He's from Maryland, *but,*" she added with a quick finger jab, "he's lived in New York for almost ten years. He's going over to Staten Island to visit his daughter. She just had a baby. A girl. His wife's been staying with them the past few days to help out, and she's meeting him at the terminal. It's their first grandchild."

"Did you find out how long he's been married, where and how he met his wife, who he voted for in the last election?"

She laughed and gave Steve another poke. "I'm thirsty."

She glanced down at her youngest. "You know, me, too. Why don't you and I go get some drinks for everybody." She grabbed his hand and snaked her way through the people crowded on deck. "Are you having a good time, Pete?"

"It's pretty neat, but I really want to go see the penguins."

"Tomorrow, first thing."

"Can we get a soy dog?"

"Where are you putting them? You had one an hour ago."

"They smell good."

Vacation meant indulgence, she decided. "Soy dogs it is."

"But I have to pee."

"Okay." As a veteran mother, she'd scoped out the restrooms when they'd boarded the ferry. Now she detoured to steer them toward the nearest facilities.

And, of course, since Pete mentioned it, now *she* had to pee. She pointed toward the men's room. "If you get out first, you stand right here. You remember what the ferry staff looks like, the uniforms? If you need help, go right to one of them."

"Mom, I'm just going to pee."

"Well, me, too. You wait for me *here* if you get out first."

She watched him go in, knowing full well he rolled his eyes the minute his back was to her. It amused her as she turned toward the women's room.

And saw the Out of Order sign.

"Shoot."

She weighed her options. Hold it until Pete came out, then hold it some more while they got the dogs and drinks — because he'd whine and sulk otherwise — then make her way to the other restroom.

13

Or . . . maybe she could just peek in. Surely not all the stalls were out of order. She only needed one.

She pushed open the door, hurried in. She didn't want to leave Pete alone for long.

She made the turn at the line of sinks, her mind on getting the provisions and squeezing back to the rail to watch Staten Island come into view.

She stopped dead, her limbs frozen in shock.

Blood, she thought, could only think, so much blood. The woman on the floor seemed bathed in it.

The man standing over the body held a still-dripping knife in one hand and a stunner in the other.

"I'm sorry," he said — and, to her shocked mind, sounded sincere.

Even as Carolee sucked in the air to scream, took the first stumbling step back, he triggered the stunner.

"Really very sorry," he said as Carolee fell to the floor.

Racing across New York Harbor in a turbo wasn't how Lieutenant Eve Dallas expected to spend her afternoon. She'd played second lead that morning to her partner's primary role in the unfortunate demise of Vickie

14

Trendor, the third wife of the unrepentant Alan Trendor, who'd smashed her skull with an inferior bottle of California chardonnay.

According to the new widower, it wasn't accurate to say he'd bashed her brains out when she simply hadn't had any brains to begin with.

While the prosecutor and the counsel for the defense hammered out a plea arrangement, Eve had made a dent in her paperwork, discussed strategy with two of her detectives on an ongoing case and congratulated another on closing one.

A pretty good day, in her estimation.

Now, she and Peabody, her partner, were speeding across the water in a boat she judged to be about the size of a surfboard toward the orange hulk of a ferry stalled halfway between Manhattan and Staten Island.

"This is absolutely mag!" Peabody stood near the bow, her square-jawed face lifted to the wind, her short, flippy hair flying.

"Why?"

"Jeez, Dallas!" Peabody lowered her shades down her nose, exposing delighted brown eyes. "We're getting a boat ride. We're on the water. Half the time you can forget Manhattan's an island."

"That's what I like about it. Out here, it

15

makes you wonder, how come it doesn't sink? All that weight — the buildings, the streets, the people. It should go down like a stone."

"Come on." With a laugh, Peabody pushed her shades back in place. "Statue of Liberty," she pointed out. "She's the best."

Eve wouldn't argue. She'd come close to dying inside the landmark, fighting radical terrorists bent on blowing it up. Even now, she could look at its lines, its grandeur, and see her husband, bleeding, clinging to a ledge outside the proud face.

They'd survived that one, she mused, and Roarke had diffused the bomb, saved the day. Symbols mattered, and because they'd fought and bled, people could chug by on the ferry every day and snap their pictures of freedom.

That was fine, that was the job. What she didn't get was why Homicide had to zip off the island because the Department of Transportation cops couldn't find a passenger.

Blood all over a bathroom and a missing woman. Interesting, sure, she decided, but not really her turf. In fact, it wasn't turf at all. It was water. It was a big orange boat on the water.

Why didn't boats sink? The errant thought

reminded her that sometimes they did, and she decided not to dwell on it.

When the turbo approached that big orange boat, she noted people ranged along the rail on the tiers of decks. Some of them waved.

Beside her, Peabody waved back.

"Cut it out," Eve ordered.

"Sorry. It's knee-jerk. Looks like DOT sent out backup," she commented, nodding toward the turbos at the base of the ferry with the Department of Transportation logo emblazoned on the hull. "I hope she didn't fall over. Or jump. But somebody would notice that, right?"

"More likely she wandered off from the passenger areas, got lost and is currently trying to wander back."

"Blood," Peabody reminded her, and Eve shrugged.

"Let's just wait and see."

That, too, was part of the job — the waiting and seeing. She'd been a cop for a dozen years and knew the dangers of jumping to conclusions.

She shifted her weight as the turbo slowed, bracing on long legs while she scanned the rails, the faces, the open areas. Her short hair fluttered around her face while those eyes — golden brown, long and cop-flat —

studied what might or might not be a crime scene.

When the turbo was secured, she stepped off.

She judged the man who stepped forward to offer his hand as late twenties. He wore the casual summer khakis and light blue shirt with its DOT emblem well. Sun-streaked hair waved around a face tanned by sun or design. Pale green eyes contrasted with the deeper tone, and added an intensity.

"Lieutenant, Detective, I'm Inspector Warren. I'm glad you're here."

"You haven't located your passenger, Inspector?"

"No. A search is still under way." He gestured for them to walk with him. "We've added a dozen officers to the DOT crew aboard to complete the search, and to secure the area where the missing woman was last seen."

They started up a set of stairs.

"How many passengers aboard?"

"The ticker counted three thousand, seven hundred and sixty-one boarding at White-hall."

"Inspector, it wouldn't be procedure to call Homicide on a missing passenger."

"No, but none of this is hitting SOP. I

18

have to tell you, Lieutenant, it doesn't make sense." He took the next set of stairs, glancing over at the people hugging the rail. "I don't mind admitting, this situation is above my pay grade. And right now, most of the passengers are being patient. It's mostly tourists, and this is kind of an adventure. But if we hold the ferry here much longer, it's not going to be pretty."

Eve stepped onto the next deck where DOT officials had cordoned off a path. "Why don't you give me a rundown, Inspector?"

"The missing woman is Carolee Grogan, tourist from Missouri, on board with her husband and two sons. Age forty-three. I've got her description and a photo taken aboard this afternoon. She and her youngest went to get drinks, hit the johns first. He went into the men's, and she was going into the women's. Told him to wait for her right outside if he got out first. He waited, and she didn't come out."

Warren paused outside the restroom area, nodded to another DOT official on the women's room door. "Nobody else went in or out either. After a few minutes, he called her on his 'link. She didn't answer. He called his father, and the father and the other son came over. The father, Steven

Grogan, asked a woman — ah, Sara Hunning — if she'd go in and check on his wife."

Warren opened the door. "And this is what she found inside."

Eve stepped in behind Warren. She smelled the blood immediately. A homicide cop gets a nose for it. It soured the citrusy/sterilized odor of the air in the black-and-white room with its steel sinks, and around the dividing wall, the white-doored stalls.

It washed over the floor, a spreading dark pool that snaked in trails across the white, slashed over the stall doors, the opposing wall, like abstract graffiti.

"If that's Grogan's," Eve said, "you're not looking for a missing passenger. You're looking for a dead one."

Two

"Record on, Peabody." Eve switched on her own. "Dallas, Lieutenant Eve; Peabody, Detective Delia; Warren, DOT Inspector . . ."

"Jake," he supplied.

"On scene aboard Staten Island Ferry."

"It's the *Hillary Rodham Clinton,*" he added. "Second deck, port side, women's restroom."

She cocked a brow, nodded. "Responding to report of missing passenger, Grogan, Carolee, last seen entering this area. Peabody, get a sample of the blood. We'll need to make sure it's human, then type it."

She opened the field kit she hadn't fully believed she'd need for Seal It. "How many people have been in and out of here since Grogan was missed?"

"Since I've been on board, just me. Prior, to the best of my knowledge, Sara Hunning,

Steven Grogan and two ferry officers on board."

"There's an Out of Order sign on the door."

"Yeah."

"But she came in anyway."

"Nobody we've spoken to can absolutely confirm. She told the kid she was going in."

Sealed, Eve stepped into the first of the four stalls, waved a hand over the sensor. The toilet flushed efficiently. She repeated the gesture in the other three stalls, with the same results.

"Appears to be in order."

"It's human," Peabody told her, holding up her gauge. "Type A Negative."

"Some smears, but no drag marks," Eve murmured. She gestured toward a narrow utility closet. "Who opened that?"

"I did," Jake told her. "On the chance she — or her body — was in there. It was locked."

"There's only one way in and out." Peabody walked around to the sink area. "No windows. If that's Carolee Grogan's blood, she didn't stand up and walk out of here."

Eve stood at the edge of the blood pool. "How do you get a dead body out of a public restroom, on a ferry in the middle of the harbor, under the noses of more than three thousand people? And why the hell don't you leave it where it dropped in the first place?"

"It's not an answer to that," Jake began, "but this is a tourist boat. It doesn't carry any vehicles, has extra concession areas. People tend to hug the rails and look out, or hang in a concession and snack as they watch out the windows. Still, it'd take a lot of luck and enormous *cojones* to cart a bleeding body along the deck."

"Balls maybe, but nobody's got that kind of luck. I'll need this room sealed, Inspector. And I want to talk to the missing woman's family, and the witness. Peabody, let's get the sweepers out here. I want every inch of this room covered."

Eve considered Jake's foresight in having the Grogan family sequestered in one of the canteen's solid. It kept them away from other passengers, gave them seats, and access to food and drink. That, she assumed, had kept the kids calm.

Calm enough, she noted, for the smaller of the two boys to curl on the narrow seat of the booth with his head in his father's lap.

The man continued to stroke the boy's hair, and his face was both pale and frightened when Eve crossed to him.

"Mr. Grogan, I'm Lieutenant Dallas, with the New York City Police and Security Department. This is Detective Peabody."

"You found her. You found Carolee. She's —"

"We haven't yet located your wife."

"She told me to wait." The boy with his head on Steve's lap opened his eyes. "I did. But she didn't come back."

"Did you see her go into the other bathroom?"

"Nuh-uh, but she said she was gonna, and then we were going to get dogs and drinks. And she gave me the routine."

"Routine?"

He sat up, but leaned against his father's side. "How I had to wait *right* there, and how if I needed anything, I was supposed to get one of the guys who work on the boat. The uniform guys."

"Okay. Then you went into the men's bathroom."

"It was only for a minute. I just had to . . . you know. Then I came out and waited like she said. It *always* takes girls longer. But it was really long, and I was thirsty. I used my 'link." He slid his eyes toward his father. "We're only allowed to use them if it's really important, but I was thirsty."

"It's okay, Pete. She didn't answer, so Pete

tagged me, and Will and I headed back to where he was waiting. They'd been gone at least ten minutes by then. There was the Out of Order sign on the door, so I thought she might've used another restroom. Except she wouldn't. She wouldn't have left Pete. So I asked this woman if she'd just take a look inside. And then . . ."

He shook his head.

"She said there was blood." The older boy swallowed hard. "The lady came running out, yelling there was blood."

"I went in." Steve rubbed his eyes. "I thought maybe she fell, hit her head, or . . . But she wasn't in there."

"There was blood," Will said again.

"Your mom wasn't in there," Steve said firmly. "She's somewhere else."

"Where?" Pete demanded in a voice perilously close to weeping. "Where did she go?"

"That's what we're going to find out." Peabody spoke with easy confidence. "Pete, Will, why don't you help me get drinks for everybody? Inspector Warren, is it okay if we forage in here?"

"You bet. I'll give you a hand." He added a warm smile. "And make it Jake."

Eve slid into the booth. "I need to ask you some questions."

"It was too much blood," he said in a soft

voice, a voice that wouldn't carry to his children. "A fatal loss of blood. I'm a doctor. I'm an ER doctor, and that much blood loss without immediate medical attention . . . For God's sake, what happened to Carolee?"

"Do you know her blood type, Dr. Grogan?"

"Yes, of course. She's O Positive."

"You're certain?"

"Yes, I'm certain. She and Pete are O Positive. I'm A Positive, so's Will."

"It wasn't her blood. The blood in the restroom wasn't hers."

"Not hers." He trembled, and she watched him struggle for composure, but his eyes teared. "Not her blood. Not Carolee's blood."

"Why were you going to Staten Island?"

"What? We weren't. I mean . . ." He pressed his hands to his face again, breathed, then lowered them. Steady nerves, Eve thought. She imagined an ER doc needed them. "We were taking the ride over, then we were going to ride back. Just for the experience. We're on vacation. It's our second day on vacation."

"Does she know anyone in New York?"

"No." He shook his head slowly. "She wasn't in there. But she wouldn't have left

Pete. It doesn't make sense. She doesn't answer her 'link. I've tried it over and over." He pushed his across the table. "She doesn't answer."

He glanced toward the concession where Peabody and Jake kept the kids busy, then leaned closer to Eve. "She would never have left our boy, not willingly. Something happened in that room. Somebody died in that room. If she saw what happened —"

"Let's not get ahead of ourselves. We're still searching. I'm going to check on the status."

Rising, she signaled to Peabody. "It's not her blood. It's the wrong type."

"That's something. They're really nice kids. They're scared."

"They're on vacation. Don't know anyone in New York according to the husband, and he comes off straight to me. What doesn't come off is how a body could disappear, a woman who we'll presume for the moment is alive could disappear, and potentially a killer/abductor could disappear. They're here somewhere. Get the wit statement, though I don't think that's going to add anything. I'm calling in more officers, ours and DOT's. We're going to need to get data, statements and do a search on every person on this damn ferry before we let anyone off."

"I'll take care of our end before I talk to the woman. Ah, he's kind of flirting with me."

"What? Who?"

"The adorable inspector."

"Please."

"No, seriously. I am spoken for," Peabody added with a flutter of lashes, "but it's still flattering to have cute guys flirt."

"Do the job, Peabody."

Shaking her head as her partner went out to do just that, Eve gestured to Jake. "We're going to need more men. I can't let anyone off until we've confirmed IDs, interviewed and searched."

"Over three thousand people?" He let out a low whistle. "You're going to have a revolt."

"What I've got is a missing woman, and very likely a dead body somewhere on this vessel. I've also got a killer. I want somebody in here with them," she added. "I want a look at all security discs, cams, monitors."

"That's no problem."

"We need an e-man to try to triangulate the signal with Grogan's 'link. If she's still got it, we may be able to locate her. What time did she go missing?"

"As close as we can determine, right about one thirty."

28

Eve glanced at her wrist unit. "More than an hour now. I want to —"

She heard the boom, the gunfire crackle, the shouts. Before the next blast, she was rushing through the door and out on deck.

Passengers whistled, stomped, cheered, as an impressive shower of color exploded into the sky.

"Fireworks? For Christ's sake. It's still daylight."

"There's nothing scheduled," Jake told her.

"Diversion," she muttered, and began to push and shove her way in the opposite direction of the show. "Get somebody to find the source, stop it."

"I'm already on it," Jake said and shouted into his communicator. "Where are we going?"

"The scene of the crime."

"What? I can't hear a freaking thing. Say again," he yelled into his communicator. "Say again."

Eve broke through the celebrating crowd, ducked under the barricade.

She stopped as she saw the woman arguing frantically with the DOT officer guarding the door of the restroom.

"Carolee!" she called out, and the woman whirled. Her face was deathly pale with high spots of color on the cheeks, and a purpling knot on her forehead.

"What? What is this? I can't find my boy. I can't find my son."

The eyes were wrong, Eve thought. A little glassy, a little shocky. "It's okay. I know where he is. I'll take you to him."

"He's okay? You . . . Who are you?"

"Lieutenant Dallas." Eve watched Carolee's eyes as she took out her badge. "I'm the police."

"Okay. Okay. He's a good boy, but he knows better than this. He was supposed to wait right here. I'm sorry to be so much trouble."

"Where did you go, Carolee?"

"I just . . ." She trailed off. "I went into the restroom. Didn't I? I'm sorry. I have a headache. I was so worried about Pete. Wait, just wait until I —" She stepped into the snack bar when Eve opened the door. Then slapped her hands on her hips.

"Peter James Grogan! You are in so much trouble."

The boy, his brother, his father, moved like one unit, bolting across the room. "Didn't I specifically tell you not to —"

This time the words were knocked back as her three boys grabbed her in frantic embraces. "Well, for heaven's sake. If you

30

think that's going to soften me up after you disobeyed me, it's not. Or only a little." She stroked the boy's hair as he clung to her legs. "Steve? Steve? You're shaking. What is it? What's wrong?"

He pulled back to kiss her, her mouth, her cheeks. "You — you're hurt. You've hit your head."

"I . . ." She lifted her fingers to touch the bump. "Ouch. How did I do that? I don't feel quite right."

"Sit down. Pete, Will, let your mother have some room. Sit down here, Carolee, let me take a look at you."

When she had, he took her hands, pressed them to his lips. "Everything's okay now. It's okay now."

But it wasn't, Eve thought, not for everyone.

Someone was dead. Someone had caused that death.

They were both missing.

THREE

"Inspector, I need you to locate the source of those explosives, then I want that area secured. I want a complete list of DOT and ferry employees, including any independent contractors, aboard at this time. I want those security discs. When NYPSD officers arrive, they will support those assignments. Peabody, make that happen. Now."

She glanced toward the Grogan family. She could give their reunion one more minute. "There are lifeboats, emergency evacuation devices on this boat?"

"Sure."

"They need to be checked, and they need to be guarded. If any have been used, I need to know. Immediately. I want to talk to the guard Mrs. Grogan talked to when she . . . came back. For now, get his statement."

"No problem. Lieutenant, we're going to have to deal with getting these people, at least some of these people, off."

"I'm working on it. Explosives, employees, discs, emergency evac, secured areas. Let's get on it."

She turned away, moved to where Carolee still sat surrounded by her family.

"Mrs. Grogan, I need to speak with you."

"I'd like to treat her head wound." Steve kept his arm protectively around his wife. "And check her out more thoroughly. If there's a medical kit, I could use it."

"I'll find one," Peabody told him, then glanced at Eve. "Our guys will be on board in a couple of minutes."

"Okay. Find the kit. Organize the team. I want another search, every square inch of this ferry. I want the sweepers in that bathroom. I want it scoured. See if you can find out if anyone else has been reported missing."

"Yes, sir."

As Peabody left, Carolee shook her head. "I'm sorry, I'm a little confused. Who are you again?"

"Lieutenant Dallas, NYPSD."

"The police," Carolee said slowly. "You need to talk to me? I know I got a little upset with the security man, but I was worried about Pete. I couldn't find my boy."

"Understood. Mrs. —"

"If you're police, do you have a zapper?"

Obviously content now that his mother was where she belonged, Pete gave Eve a curious squint.

"Don't interrupt," Carolee admonished.

"Mrs. Grogan," Eve began again, but lifted her jacket aside to reveal her sidearm — and the boy flashed her a grin. "Can you tell me what happened, after you and your son went to use the restrooms?"

"Actually, we were going to get drinks, then Pete needed to go, so we swung over that way. I told him to wait, to stay right there if he got out before I did."

"But, Mom —"

"We'll talk about *that* later," she said in a tone that warned of lecture, and the kid slumped down in his seat.

"And then," Eve prompted.

"Then, I waited a minute, watched Pete go in, and I . . ." Her face went blank for a moment. "That's funny." She offered a puzzled smile. "I'm not quite sure. I must've hit my head. Maybe I slipped?"

"Inside the bathroom?"

"I — It's silly, but I just don't remember."

"Don't remember hitting your head, or going into the bathroom?"

"Either," she admitted. "I must've really knocked it." She tapped her fingers to the bump, winced. "I could use a blocker."

"I don't want to give you anything until I check you out a little more," Steve told her.

"You're the doctor."

Eve thought of a case, not so long before, where memories had been lost. Or stolen. "How bad's the headache?"

"Between crappy and lousy."

"If you try to remember, does the pain increase?"

"Remember hitting it?" Carolee closed her eyes, squeezed them in concentration. "No. It stays between crappy and lousy."

"Any nausea, baby, or blurred vision?" Steve shined a penlight in her eyes to check pupil reaction.

"No. I feel like I walked into a wall or something and smacked my head. That's it."

"There was an Out of Order sign on the door," Eve reminded her.

"There . . . That's right!" Carolee's eyes brightened. "I do remember that. So I . . . but I wouldn't — I *know* I didn't go off to one of the other restrooms. I wouldn't leave Pete. I must've gone in. I must've, because I had to come out again, right? He wasn't there waiting. I must've slipped and hit my head, and I'm just a little shaky on the details. I'm not sure I understand why it matters to the police."

35

"Mrs. Grogan, you were missing for over an hour."

"Me? Missing? That's crazy. I just —" But she glanced at her wrist unit, and went sheet white. "But that can't be. That can't be the right time. We were only gone for a few minutes. The ferry ride takes less than a half hour, and we'd barely started. This can't be right."

"Nobody could find you. We couldn't find you," Steve said. "We were so scared."

"Well, God." She stared at her husband, shoved a hand through her hair as it started to sink in. "Did I wander off? Hit my head and wander off? Maybe I have a concussion. I wandered off." She looked down at Pete. "And then I yelled at you when I was the one. I'm sorry, kiddo. Really."

"We thought you were dead 'cause there was the blood." The boy pressed his face to Carolee's breast and started to cry.

"Blood?"

"Mrs. Grogan, the DOT officials notified the NYPSD not only because you were, apparently, missing, but because the facilities they believed you entered had a considerable amount of blood on the floor, as well as spatter on the walls and doors of the stalls."

"But . . ." Her breathing went shallow as

36

Carolee stared at Eve. "It's not mine. I'm okay."

"It's not yours. You went into the bathroom," Eve prompted, "despite the Out of Order sign."

"I can't remember. It's just blank. Like it's been erased. I remember watching Pete go into the boys' room, and I . . . I remember seeing the sign, but then, I can't. I would've gone in," she murmured. "Yes, that's what I would've done, just to check, because it was right there and why not look? I couldn't leave Pete. But I don't remember going in, or . . . coming out. But I couldn't have gone in, or I would've come out. Probably screaming if I saw blood all over the place. It doesn't make sense."

"No," Eve agreed, "it doesn't."

"I didn't hurt anyone. I wouldn't."

"I don't think you hurt anyone."

"An hour. I lost an hour. How can that be?"

"Have you ever lost time before?"

"No. Never. I mean, I've lost track of time, you know? But this is different."

"Will, how about getting your mom a drink?" Steve sent his older son an easy smile. "I bet she's a little dehydrated."

"Actually —" Carolee laughed a little weakly. "I could really use the restroom."

"Okay." Eve watched Peabody come back in with a med kit. "Just a second." She walked over to waylay her partner. "Go ahead and give the kit to Grogan, and take the woman to the john. Stick with her."

"Sure. We're on board, and we've got a deck-by-deck search going. I have to say, the natives are getting a little restless."

"Right. They'll have to hang on a little longer."

"I wonder if maybe this whole thing isn't some stupid prank. Somebody dumps a bunch of blood in that bathroom, hangs the sign, sits back and waits for somebody to go in."

"Then why hang the sign?"

"Okay, a flaw in the scenario, but —"

"And how did they transport a couple quarts of human blood? And where did Mrs. Grogan go for an hour?"

"Several flaws."

"Stick with her," Eve repeated. "Get their New York address. Let's arrange for them to be taken back so she can get a full check at a health center, and I want a watch on them." She glanced back. "If she saw something, someone, maybe whoever's responsible for the blood will start to worry about her."

"I'll make sure she's covered. Nice family," Peabody added, studying the group.

"Yeah. Welcome to New York."

Eve tracked down Jake.

"All emergency evac devices are accounted for." He passed her a file of security discs. "Those are from all cams on board. The list of employees, DOT officials, is labeled."

"Good. Where the hell did those fireworks come from?"

"Well." He scratched his head. "It looks like they were set off starboard side, probably the stern. That's from figuring the basic trajectory from witnesses. But we haven't got any physical evidence. No ash, no mechanism. Nothing so far, so I'm not sure they were set off from the boat."

"Hmm." Eve pondered and glanced out at the wide harbor.

"The NYPSD is crawling all over the place, and your CI team's covering the crime scene. If it is one," he added. "We've accounted for every DOT employee on board, and between your people and mine, we've been interviewing passengers, concentrating on those who are in the areas of the scene. So far, none of them saw anything. And you have to admit, hauling a body around would attract some attention."

"You'd think."

"What do we do now?"

As far as Eve could determine, there were two options. The killer — if indeed a murder had taken place — had somehow gotten off the ferry. Or the killer still needed to get off.

"Looks like we're going to Staten Island. Here's how we'll handle it."

It was going to take time, and a great deal of patience, but nearly four thousand passengers would be ID'd, searched and questioned before they were allowed to disembark at St. George terminal. Fortunately a good chunk of that number was kids. Eve didn't think — though kids were strange and often violent entities to her mind — that the pool of blood was the work of some maniac toddler.

"It's actually moving along okay," Peabody reported, and got a grunt from Eve.

"The search is ongoing," Peabody continued. "So far, no weapon, no body, no evil killer hiding in a storage closet."

Eve continued to review the security disc on boarding on her PPC. "The body's dumped by now."

"How?"

"I don't know how, but it's dumped or transported. Two searches, and this one with corpse detectors. He, or an accomplice, used the fireworks as a distraction. Get everyone's attention in one direction, do what you need to do in the other. Has to be."

"It doesn't explain how he got the DB out of the bathroom."

"No."

"Well, if it wasn't a prank, maybe it's a vortex."

Eve shifted her gaze up, gave Peabody a five-second pitiable stare.

"Free-Ager here, remember. I grew up on vortexes. It's a better theory than abracadabra." On a sigh, Peabody studied the bright, tropical fish swimming behind the glass of an enormous aquarium.

"He didn't toss the body overboard, then dive in and swim away," Peabody pointed out. "Like a fish." Noting Eve's considering expression, Peabody threw up her hands. "Come on, Dallas. There's no way out of the bathroom, not without walking in front of dozens and dozens of people."

"In back mostly, since they'd be looking out at the water. If the blood currently being rushed to the lab proves to have come from a warm body — one we hope to identify through DNA matching — there has to be a way out and a way off, because he used it."

"Parallel universe. There are some scientific theories that support the possibility."

"The same ones, I bet, that support sparkly winged fairies skipping around the woods."

"A mocker." Peabody wagged a finger. "That's what you are, Dallas. A mocker."

"In my world, we call it sane."

Jake joined them. "We're about halfway through. Maybe a little more."

"Find any vortexes, parallel universes or sparkly winged fairies?" Eve asked him.

"Mocker," Peabody repeated.

"Ah . . . not so far." He offered them both a go-cup of coffee. "No weapons, no blood, no dead body either, and so far everyone who's gone through the ticker and the interview station is alive."

"I'm going back on board," Eve told him. "If we get a hit — any kind of hit — contact me. Peabody, with me."

"Hey." Jake tapped Peabody's arm when she started to move off with Eve. "We're probably going to put in a long one here. Maybe we could get a drink after we're clear. You know, decompress."

Flustered, she felt heat rise to her cheeks that was a giddy mix of pleasure and embarrassment. "Oh, well. Um. That's nice — it's nice, I mean, to ask and all that. I live with somebody. A guy. An e-guy. We're . . . you know. Together."

"Lucky him," Jake said, and had her blush deepening. "Maybe, sometime, we can grab a brew, just on the friendly side."

"Sure. Maybe. Ah . . ." She flashed a smile, then shot off after Eve.

"Did you forget what 'with' means?"

"No. In fact, I remembered exactly, in that I'm *with* McNab. I remembered even when Jake hit on me."

"Oh, that's different." Eve shot out a sunny smile that had Peabody's stomach curdling. "Let me apologize for interrupting. Maybe the two of you want to take a break, go get a drink, get to know each other better. We can always puzzle out whether or not we have a missing DB and killer later. We wouldn't want a potential murder investigation to get in the way of a potential romance, would we?"

"I speak sarcasm fluently. He did ask me out for a drink though."

"Should I note that in my memo book, on today's date?"

"Jeez." Sulk warred with smug as Peabody boarded the ferry with Eve. "I'm just saying. Plus I get double credits. First I get the satisfaction credit of being hit on by the sexy

DOT inspector, and second I get loyal and true credit for turning him down because I have my personal sexy nerd. I hardly ever get hit on, unless you count McNab — which really doesn't since we cohab — so it *is* noteworthy."

"Fine, so noted. Can we move on?"

"I should get at least five minutes of *woo*. Okay," she mumbled under Eve's withering stare. "I'll put the rest of the *woo* time on my account."

With a shake of her head, Eve crossed the deck, now empty but for cops and sweepers, to speak to a crime scene investigator.

"Schuman, what've you got?"

She knew him to be a hard-bitten, seen-it-all type, as comfortable in the lab as on scene. He'd shed his protective suit and booties and stood unfolding a piece of gum from its wrapper. "What we've got is about two quarts of blood and body fluids, plenty of spatter. Got some flesh and fibers, and a virtual shit load of prints. We're gonna want to get it in for a full workup and analysis, but with the on-scene exam, we got your blood type — A Neg, and spot samples indicate it's all from the same person. Whoever that is would be dead as my uncle Bob, whose demise went unlamented by all who knew him."

He popped the gum, chewed for a thoughtful moment. "I can tell you what we ain't got. That would be a body or a blood trail, or at this point one freaking notion how said body got the hell out of that john." He smiled. "It's interesting."

"How soon can you tell me if the blood came out of a warm body, or came out of a damn bucket?"

"We'll look at that. Wouldn't be as fun, but the bucket'd make more sense. Problem being, the spatter's consistent with on-scene injuries." Obviously intrigued, he chewed and smiled. "Looks like a damn slasher vid in there. Whoever walked in living got sliced and diced, stuck and gutted. Then, you gotta say it's interesting, went *poof!*"

"Interesting," Eve repeated. "Is it clear to go in?"

"All swept. Help yourself."

He went in with her where a couple of sweepers examined the sinks, the pipes.

"We're looking at everything," he told Eve. "But you'd have to have a magic shrinking pill to get out of here through the plumbing. We're gonna take the vents, the floors, walls, ceilings."

She tipped her face up, studied the ceiling herself. "The killer would have had to transport himself, the body, and a grown

45

woman. Maybe more than one killer."

She shifted to study the spatter on the stalls, the walls. "The vic standing about there. Killer slices her throat first; that's what I'd do. She can't call out. We get that major spatter from the jugular wound, partially blocked by the killer's body."

Eve turned, slapped her hand to her throat. "She grabs her throat, the blood pumps through her fingers, more spatter there, but she doesn't go down, not yet. She falls toward the wall — we get the smears of blood — tries to turn around, more smears. He cuts her again, so we have the spatter on the next stall there, and lower on the wall here, so he probably stuck her, and she stumbled back this way." Eve eased back. "Maybe tries to make it to the door, but he's on her. Slice and dice, and down she goes. Bleeds out where she falls."

"We'll run it, like I said, but that's how I read it."

"He'd be covered in blood."

"If he washed up at any of the sinks," Schuman put in, "he didn't leave any trace, not in the bowls, not in the traps."

"Protective clothes? Gloves?" Peabody suggested.

"Maybe. Probably. But if he can get a DB out of here, I guess he could walk out covered in blood. No trail," Eve repeated. "No drag marks. Even if he just hauled it up and carried it out, there'd be a blood trail. He had to wrap it up. If we go with protective gear and a body bag or something along the line, he planned it out, came prepared, and he damn well had an exit plan. Carolee was a variable, but he didn't have too much trouble there either. He dealt with it."

"But he didn't kill her. He didn't really hurt her," Peabody pointed out.

"Yeah." That point was something Eve had puzzled over. "And he could have, easily enough. The door doesn't lock. Safety regs outlaw locks on public restroom doors with multiple stalls. He makes do with a sign, even though this had to take several minutes. The kill, the cleanup, the transport. And Carolee was missing for over an hour, so wherever he went, wherever he took her, he needed time."

"A lot of places on this boat. Vents, infrastructure, storage. You got big-ass ducts for heating and cooling the inside cabin deals," Schuman told her. "You got your sanitary tanks, your equipment storage, maintenance areas. We're going through here, but it doesn't show how the hell he got out of this room."

"So, let's find out where he went and work backward. And we need to find out who the vic was, and why she got sliced on the Staten Island Ferry. It had to be specific, or Carolee Grogan's blood would be all over this room, too."

For the moment, Eve thought, the best she could do was leave it to the sweepers.

FOUR

"Why didn't he kill Carolee?" Peabody wondered when they were back on deck. "It would've been easier. Just cut her throat, and get back to business. It wasn't as if he worried about covering up a crime. All the blood was a pretty big clue one had been committed."

Eve walked toward the stern, trying to reconstruct a scene that made no sense. "I'm looking forward to asking him. I don't think it's just his good luck she can't remember. Let's see what the medical exam concludes after she's done there. But the bigger question is, yeah, why bother to suppress her memory? And why would the killer have something on him that could?"

"Hypnosis?"

"I'm not ruling it out." She leaned back against the rail, looked up at the twin smokestacks. "They're not real. They're show. Just to keep the ferry looking old-timey. Big. Way big enough for somebody to hide a body and an unconscious woman."

"Sure, if he had sparkly fairy wings and an invisibility shield."

Eve had to laugh. "Point. Regardless, let's make sure they get checked out." She turned when Jake walked toward them.

"We let the last of the passengers through the ticker. Two short. We've accounted for everyone, passengers, crew, concession. Two people who got on didn't get off."

"They just got off before we made port," Eve corrected. "This ferry is out of service until further notice. It's sealed by order of the NYPSD. Guards on twenty-four/seven. Crime Scene hasn't finished, and will continue until they've covered every inch, including those," she added, pointing at the smokestacks.

Jake lifted his gaze to follow the gesture. "Well. That should be fun."

"Something this size, with this layout? There are places to hide, to conceal. He had to know the boat, the layout, at least to some extent."

"Having a place to hide doesn't explain getting out of that bathroom without anyone seeing him. Unless he has the cloak of invisibility."

Jake's remark got a quick laugh from

Peabody and a cool stare from Eve.

"We work the wit and the evidence. We'll be in touch, Inspector."

"You're leaving?"

"We'll be following up with the security discs, Carolee Grogan, and the lab. The sooner we identify the victim, if a victim there is, the sooner we can move on the killer. You may want some of your men backing up mine on guard duty. I don't want anyone on that ferry without authorization."

"All right."

"Let's move, Peabody."

"Ah, Detective? Should your situation change . . ."

Peabody felt the heat rise to her cheeks again. "It isn't likely to, but thanks." She scrambled to keep up with Eve's long strides. "He hit on me again."

"I'll mark it down, first chance."

"It's markable," Peabody mumbled. "Really." She risked a look over her shoulder before they boarded the turbo. "I figured we'd be staying, going over the boat again."

"We have enough people on that." Eve braced herself as the turbo shot across the water. "Here's a question — or a few. Why kill in a public restroom on a ferry in the middle of the water? No easy way off. Why not leave the body? Why, if interrupted by a bystander, spare that bystander's life? And go to the trouble, apparently, to secret her away for an hour?"

"Okay, but even if we find the answer to any of the whys, we don't answer the hows."

"Next column. How was the victim selected? How was the method of killing selected? How was Carolee Grogan moved from the crime scene to another location? And straddling columns, why doesn't she remember? How was the body — if there was one — removed? All of it comes back to one question. Who was the victim? That's the center. The rest rays out from there."

"The victim's probably female. Or the killer. One of them, at least, is probably female. It makes more sense, given the location of the murder."

"Agreed, and the computer agrees. I ran probability. Mid-eighties for female vic or killer." She pulled out her 'link when it signaled, saw Roarke's personal code on the readout. "Hey."

"Hey back." His face — that fallen-angel beauty — filled the screen as dark brows lifted over bold blue eyes. "You're out in the harbor? The ferry incident?"

"Shit. How much has leaked?"

"Not a great deal. Certainly nothing that

speaks of murder." His voice, Irish whispering through, cruised over the words as she rocketed back toward Manhattan. "Who's dead, then?"

"That's a question. I'm hoping the lab can tell me. I'm heading there, and depending on the answer, I might be late getting home."

"As it happens I'm downtown, and was hoping to ask my wife out to dinner. Why don't I meet you at the lab, then depending on the answer you get, we'll go from there?"

She couldn't think of a reason against it, and in fact, calculated the opportunity to run it all by him. A fresh perspective might give her some new angles. "Okay. It'll be handy to have you right there if I have to bribe Dickhead to push on the ID."

"Always happy to bribe local officials. I'll see you soon."

"It's nice, isn't it?" Peabody asked when Eve stuck her 'link back in her pocket. "Having a guy."

Eve started to shrug it off, then decided the turbo pilot couldn't hear them. Besides, there was no reason not to take a few minutes for nonsense. "It doesn't suck."

"It really doesn't. Having a really cute guy like Jake flirt with me has some frost, but knowing I'm going to be snuggled up with

McNab tonight? That's the ice."

"Why do you always have to put you and McNab and sex in my head? It brings pain no blocker can cure."

"Snuggling isn't sex. It's before or after sex. I especially like the after-sex snuggle when you're all warm and loose like a couple of sleepy puppies." She cocked her head. "I'm getting horny."

"So glad you shared that with me. Let's try to get this pesky investigation out of the way so you can go get your puppy snuggles."

"You know, I've got this new outfit I've been saving for a night when —"

"Do not go there. Do not," Eve warned. "I swear by all that's holy, I'll chuck you overboard, then order the turbo to run over you while you sputter in the water."

"Harsh. Anyway, maybe that's what the killers did, just chucked the victim in the water, then jumped in after the body wearing SCUBA gear."

"If he was going to chuck the body in, why move it in the first place? He didn't just want the kill, he wanted the body."

"Ewww. I know, a police detective's not supposed to say 'ewww.' But why would he want the body?"

"A trophy." Eve narrowed her eyes.

"I'm not saying 'ewww.' "

"You're thinking it. Proof," she added, "which strikes me as more likely than trophy. A body's unassailable proof of death. Which, at this point, we don't have. He does. Which brings us to another why. Why would he need proof?"

"Payment?" At Eve's nod, Peabody lifted her hands. "But for a hit, it was messy and complicated. It doesn't smell like a pro."

"No, it doesn't. Unless you add in the rest. Missing body, public arena, two people vanishing like smoke. That strikes me as very professional."

It kept her mind occupied on the drive to the lab. And at least she was navigating on solid ground instead of water. New York appeared to have burst open for summer, and out of its nooks and crannies poured tourists and the street thieves who depended on them. Glida carts did brisk business with cold drinks and ice pops, while portable knockoff vendors raked it in with cheap souvenirs, wrist units that might function until the buyer got back to his hotel, colorful "silk" scarves, fashion shades and handbags that could be mistaken for their designer counterparts if you were a half block away and had one eye closed.

But it also brought out the sidewalk florists with their bounty of color and scent and the alfresco diners taking in the sun over glasses of wine or thimbles of espresso.

It added to the street and air traffic, jammed the glides and sidewalks, and yet, Eve thought, it all rushed and roared exactly as it was meant to.

She spotted Roarke before she parked, standing outside the drab edifice that housed the busy hive of the lab and forensics. The dark charcoal suit fit the lean length of him perfectly, and showed a subtle flare with a tie nearly as bold a blue as his eyes.

Black hair fell in a mane around that striking face, shades shielded those stunning eyes as he slipped the PPC he'd been working on into a pocket and started toward her.

She thought he looked like some elegantly urban vid star with just a hit of edge. And she supposed it suited him as one of the wealthiest and most powerful men in the world — and on its satellites — who'd pulled himself by hook or — haha — crook out of the grime of the Dublin alleyways.

"Check on Carolee," she told Peabody. "See if they've finished the medical, have any results."

She watched Roarke's lips curve as they walked toward each other. She didn't need to see his eyes to know they mirrored that smile. And her heart gave a quick, giddy jump. She had to admit Peabody was right. It was nice to have a guy.

"Lieutenant." He took her hand and, though she lowered her eyebrows to discourage him, bent to brush those curved lips lightly over hers. "Hello, Peabody. You look fetchingly windblown."

"Yeah." She brushed ineffectually at her hair. "Boat ride."

"So I hear."

"Check on the wit, Peabody," Eve repeated as she led the way inside.

"What was witnessed?" Roarke wondered.

"Tell me what the media's saying. I haven't bothered to tune in."

"I caught bits and pieces on my way downtown to my meeting, then a bit more after. A woman apparently lost on the ferry, then found. Or not, depending on the report. A possibility someone was injured or fell overboard."

He continued as Eve led them through the maze, signed and badged them through security.

"The main thrust seems to be that DOT and NYPSD officials held up the ferry for over two hours, then additional time with a security search of passengers as they disembarked. A few of the passengers sent various media outlets some vids or statements. So, you can imagine, it's all over the board."

"Fine." Eve opted for a down glide rather than an elevator. "Better that way."

"Is someone missing? Or dead?"

"Someone was missing, but now she's not. Someone might be dead, but there's no body. Passenger count is off by two on disembarking."

"Which might equal victim and killer. How'd they get off the ferry?"

"That's another question." She stepped off the glide. "First, I've got a couple quarts of blood in a public restroom on the ferry. I need to find out who it belonged to."

FIVE

She wound through the labyrinth bisected by glass walls. Behind them techs worked with scopes and holos, forensic droids, tiny vials and mysterious solutions.

The air hummed in a blend of machine and human into a single voice Eve found just slightly creepy. She would never understand how people worked, day after day, in a vast space without a single window.

She found the chief lab tech, Dick Berenski, sliding his stool soundlessly along his long white counter as he commanded various comps. Dickhead was an irritant, a pebble in the shoe on a personal level, but she couldn't deny his almost preternatural skill with evidence.

He looked up, cocking his egg-shaped head as she approached, and she didn't miss the light in his eyes when he recognized Roarke.

"Got yourself an entourage today, Dallas."

"Don't think about trying to hit up the civilian for liquor, tickets to sporting events or cash."

"Hey." Dickhead couldn't quite pull off offended.

"Let's talk blood."

"Got enough of it. I got the initial sample a couple hours ago, and they're bringing in the rest. We'll run tests on samples of that, too. Could be more than one source. Got my blood guy reconstructing the scene, pool and spatter, from the record. That's a fucking beaucoup of blood."

"Fresh or frozen?"

He honked out a little laugh. "Fresh." He tapped some keys and had squiggles and swirls in bold reds, yellows, blues, filling a comp screen. "No indication the sample had been stored, cold-boxed, flash-frozen, thawed or rehydrated."

He tapped again, brought up another screen of shapes and colors. "Coagulation rate and temp says it hit the air about two hours — maybe a little more — before I tested it. That's consistent with the time it took to get here."

"Concluding the sample came out of a live human, and came out of said human between one and two this afternoon."

"What I said. A Neg, human blood,

healthy platelets, cholesterol, no STD. We filtered out trace portions of other body fluid and flesh. Double X chromosomes."

"Female."

"You bet. We'll keep separating other body fluids when we have the larger samples, and the sweepers tell me they've got some hair in there. We'll be able to tell you pretty much everything. Fluids, flesh and hair." He grinned widely. "I could freaking rebuild her with samples like that."

"Nice thought. DNA."

"I'm running it through. Takes some time, and there's no guarantee she's on the grid. Might get a relative. I programmed for full match and blood relations."

Thorough, Eve thought. When Dickhead got his weird little teeth into something, he was thorough. "There were fibers."

"Like I said, we'll separate and filter. I'll give hair and fiber to Harpo. She's the queen. But I can't pull the vic's ID out of my ass. She's either on the grid or — Hey!" He swiveled, scooted as the far comp beeped. "Son of a bitch, we got a match. I am so freaking good."

Eve came around the counter to study the ID photo and data herself. "Copy to my unit," she ordered. "And I want a printout. Dana Buckley, age forty-one, born in Sioux

City, why are you dead?"

"Nice-looking skirt," Berenski commented, and Eve ignored him.

Blue-eyed blonde, she thought, pale skin, pretty in a corn-fed sort of way. Five-six, a hundred thirty-eight, parents deceased, no sibs, no offspring, no marriage or cohab on record. "Current employment, freelance consultant. What does this personal data tell us smart investigators, Detective?"

"That the deceased has no family ties, no employer to verify identification or give further data on said deceased. Which makes a smart investigator go *hmmm*."

"It does indeed. She lists a home and office address here in New York. Park Avenue. Peabody, run this down."

"It's the Waldorf," Roarke said from behind her.

"As in Astoria?" Eve glanced back, caught his nod, and the look in his eyes when they met hers.

She thought, Crap, but said nothing. Not yet.

"Check and see if they have her registered," she told Peabody. "And get a copy of the ID print, show it to the desk staff to see if they make her. Quick work, Berenski."

"After quick work, I like to relax with a

good bottle or two of wine."

She took the printout and walked away without a second glance.

"Worth the shot," Berenski said at her back.

"There's nobody by the name of Dana Buckley registered at the Waldorf," Peabody told her as she caught up to Eve. "No make from the desk staff. This new data rates a second *hmmm*."

"Go back to Central, do a full run on her. You can start on the security discs. Send copies to my home unit. I'm going to swing by, reinterview Carolee, show her the print-out. Maybe she'll remember seeing the vic."

"We were lucky to get a DNA match that fast. I'll tag you if I dig up anything on her." She sent a quick smile to Roarke. "See you later."

Eve waited until she and Roarke were in her vehicle, with her taking the wheel. "You knew her."

"Not really. Of her, certainly. It's compli-cated."

"Is there any way you could be connected to this?"

"No. That is, I have no connection to her."

Eve felt the knot in her stomach begin to loosen. "How do you know her, or of her?"

"I first heard of her some years ago. We

were working on a prototype for some — at the time — new holo technology. It was very nearly stolen, or would have been if we hadn't implemented multiple layers of security. As it was, she got through several before the red flag."

"Corporate and/or technological espionage."

"Yes. I didn't know her as Dana Buckley, but as Catherine Delauter. I expect you'll find any number of IDs before you're done."

"Who does she work for?"

He lifted a shoulder in a dismissive if elegant shrug. "The highest bidder. She thought I might be interested in her services, and arranged to meet me. That's seven or eight years ago."

"Did you hire her?"

He glanced at Eve with mild exasperation. "Why would I? I don't need to steal — and if I did, I could do it myself, after all. I wasn't interested in her services, and made it plain. Not only because I don't — never did — steal ideas. It's low and common."

Eve shook her head. "Your moral compass continues to baffle me."

"As yours does me. Aren't we a pair? But I warned her off not only for that, but because she was known — and my own research confirmed — not only as a spy but an assassin."

Eve glanced over quickly before she pushed through traffic. "A corporate assassin?"

"That would depend on the highest bidder, from what I learned. She's for hire, or apparently was, and didn't quibble at getting her hands bloody. Peabody won't find any of this in her run. A large percentage of her work, if rumor holds, has been for various governments. The pay's quite good, particularly if you don't mind a bit of throat slitting."

"A techno spy, heavy into wet work, takes a ride on the ferry. And ends up not just dead, but missing. A competitor? Another kill for hire? It struck me as a pro job, even — maybe because — it was so damn messy and complicated. It's going to get buckets of media when the rest of the data leaks. Who would want that?"

"A point proven?" He shrugged again. "I couldn't say. Was the body dumped off the ferry?"

"I don't think so." She filled him in as she wound and bullied her way to the East Side. "So, as far as I can tell, he moved the body and the wit, in full view of dozens, maybe hundreds of people. And nobody saw anything. The wit doesn't remember anything."

"I'll have to ask the obvious. You're sure there were no escape routes in the room?"

"Unless we've got a killer who can shrink to rat size and slither down a pipe, we didn't find any. Maybe he popped into a vortex."

Roarke turned, grinned. "Really?"

Eve waved it away. "Peabody's Free-Agey suggestion. Hell, maybe he waved his magic wand and said, 'Hocus-pocus.' What?" she said when Roarke frowned.

"Something . . . in the back of my mind. Let me think about it."

"Before you think too hard?" She veered into the health center's lot. "Just let me point out there is no magic wand, or rabbit in the hat, or alternate reality."

"Well, in this reality, most people notice when a dead body's paraded around under their noses."

"Maybe it didn't look like one. They have a couple of maintenance hampers on board. The killer dumps the body in, wheels it out like it's just business as usual. And no, we haven't found any missing hampers, or any trace in the couple on board. But it's a logical angle."

"True enough." Once she'd parked, he got out of the car with her. "Then again, logic would say don't kill in a room with only one out, and a public one, don't take the body, and don't leave a witness. So, it may be hard to hold to one logical line when the others are badly frayed."

"They're only frayed logic until you find the reason and motive." Eve pulled out her badge as they walked into the health center.

The Grogans crowded into a tiny little room with Carolee sitting up in bed, a bouquet of cheerful flowers in her lap. She looked tired, Eve thought, and showed both strain and resignation when she saw Eve come in.

"Lieutenant. I've been poked and prodded, screened and scanned and scoped. All over a bump on the head. I know something bad happened, something awful, but it really doesn't have anything to do with me."

"You still don't remember anything?"

"No. Obviously I hit my head, and I must've been dazed for a while." Her hand snuck from under the flowers to reach for her husband's. "I'm fine now, really. I feel fine now. I don't want the boys to spend their vacation in a hospital room."

"It's just a few hours," Steve assured her. The youngest, whose name was Pete, Eve remembered, crawled onto the bed to sit at his mother's side.

"Still. I'm sorry someone was hurt. Someone must've been hurt, from what Steve said. I wish I could help, I really do. But I don't know anything."

"How's the head?"

"It pounds a little."

"I have a photo I'd like to show you." Eve offered the printout of Dana Buckley. "Do you recognize her? Someone you might've seen on the ferry."

"I don't think . . ." She lifted her hand to worry at the bandage on the forehead. "I don't think . . ."

"There were a lot of people." Steve angled his head to look at the photo. "We were looking out at the water most of the time." He glanced with concern toward the monitor as his wife's pulse rate jumped. "Okay, honey, take it easy."

"I don't remember. It scares me. Why does it scare me?"

"Don't look at it anymore." Will snatched the photo away. "Don't look at it, Mom. Don't scare her anymore." He thrust the photo back at Eve. "She was in the picture."

"Sorry?"

"The lady. Here." He pulled a camera out of his pocket. "We took pictures. Dad let me take some. She's in the picture." He turned the camera on, scrolled back through the frames. "We took a lot. I looked through them when they had Mom away for tests.

She's in the picture. See?"

Eve took the camera and looked at a crowd shot, poorly cropped, with Dana Buckley sitting on a bench sipping from a go-cup. With a briefcase in her lap.

"Yeah, I see. I need to keep this for a while, okay? I'll get it back to you."

"You can keep it, I don't care. Just don't scare my mom."

"I don't want to scare your mother. That's not why I'm here," Eve said, directly to Carolee.

"I know. I know. She — that's the one who was hurt?"

"Yes. It upsets you to see her photo."

"Terrifies me. I don't know why. There's a light," she said after a hesitation.

"A light?"

"A bright flash. White flash. After I see her picture, and I'm scared, so scared. There's a white flash, and I can't see anything. Blind, for a minute. I . . . It sounds crazy. I'm not crazy."

"Shh." Pete began to stroke her hair. "Shh."

"I'm going to speak to the doctor. If Carolee's clear, I want to get her and our boys back to the hotel. Away from this. We'll get room service." Steve winked over at Will. "In-room movies."

69

"God, yes," Carolee breathed. "I'll feel better once we're out of here."

"Let's go find the doctor," Eve suggested and sent a glance at Roarke. He nodded, and moved to the foot of the bed as Steve went out with Eve.

"So, Mrs. Grogan, where would you be staying here in New York?"

It took another thirty minutes, but Roarke asked no questions until they were out of the health center. "And so, how is the lady?"

"I had the doctor dumb it down for me. He was giving it to the husband — he's a doctor, too — in fancier terms."

"You can keep it dumbed down for me."

"She's good," Eve told him, "no serious or lasting damage. The contusion, mild concussion, and most interestingly what he dumbed down to a 'smudge' on her optic nerves — both eyes. He seemed to be pushing for another test, but he'd already done a recheck and as the smudge was already dissipating, I don't think Steve's going to go for it. Added to it, the brain scan showed something wonky in the memory section — a blip, but that's resolved, too, on retest. Her tox is clear," Eve added as she got back into the car. "No trace of anything, which is too damn bad, as that's where logic was leading me."

"A memory suppressor would've been logical. And may be yet." He shook his head at her look. "We'll have some things to check into when we get home. You'll likely have to follow up with the Grogans?"

"Yeah."

"Then you'll find them at the Palace. They'll be moving there tonight."

"Your hotel?"

"It seems they're a bit squeezed into a room at the moment, and it struck me they could use a bit of an upgrade for their troubles. Plus the security's better there. Considerably."

"I'm putting a watch on them," Eve began, then shrugged. "It is better." She engaged the 'link to update her men on the change. "Let's go home and start 'checking into.' "

Six

Summerset, Roarke's man about everything, wasn't lurking in the grand foyer when Eve walked in. She spied the fat cat, Galahad, perched on the newel post like a furry gargoyle. He blinked his bicolored eyes twice, then leaped down with a thud to saunter over and rub against her legs.

"Where's Mr. Macabre?" Eve asked as she scratched the cat between the ears.

"Stop." Roarke didn't bother to sigh. The pinching and poking between his wife and his surrogate father were not likely to end anytime soon. "Summerset's setting things up in my private office. We need to use the unregistered equipment," he continued when she frowned. "Any serious digging on your victim is going to send up flags to certain parties. And there's more."

He took her hand to lead her up the steps.

"If I don't dig into the vic through proper channels, it's going to look very strange."

"You have Peabody on that," he reminded her. "And you can do some of your own, for form. But you won't find what you're after through legitimate channels. Set up your runs, on Buckley, the Grogans, the possible causes of this optic smudge. All the things you'd routinely do. Then come up and meet me."

He lifted her hand to kiss her fingers. "And we'll do the real excavating. She's a freelance spy and assassin, Eve, who works for the highest bidder or on a whim. That work would definitely include certain areas of the U.S. government. You won't get far your way."

"What's the 'more'?" She *hated* the cloak-and-dagger crap. "You said there's more?"

But he shook his head. "Start your runs. We'll go over what I've heard, know, suspect."

Since there was no point in wasting time, Eve walked into her home office to set up the multiple runs and searches. She sent an e-mail to Dr. Mira, the NYPSD's top profiler and psychiatrist, to ask about the validity of mass hypnosis. It made her feel foolish, but she wanted a solid opinion from a source she respected.

Before compiling and updating her notes,

she checked in with Peabody, and read over all the initial lab and sweepers' reports. No witnesses had come forward to claim they'd seen anything unusual, including any individual transporting a dead body. Which was too bad, she mused. Also in the too-bad department was the report that the pipes and vents within the crime scene were just too damn small to have served as an escape route.

Solid walls, no windows, one door, she decided. And that meant, however improbably, both killer and victim had exited through the door.

He hadn't stepped into Peabody's vortex, hadn't employed an alien transporter beam or flourished a magic wand. He'd used the damn door. She just had to figure out how.

She made her way to Roarke's private office, used the palm pad and voice recognition to enter. He sat behind the U-shaped console with the jewel-toned buttons and controls winking over the slick black surface. The privacy screens shielded the windows and let the evening sunlight filter into the room in a pale gold wash. A small table stood by those windows, set with silver domed plates, an open bottle of wine, the sparkle of crystal.

His idea of a working dinner, she mused.

He'd already tied his hair back — serious work mode — and commanded keyboard and touch screens with rapid movements.

"What are you hacking into?" she asked.

"Various agencies. CIA, Homeland Security, Interpol, MI5, Global, EuroCom, and that sort."

"Is that all?" She pressed her fingers to her eyes. "I was going to stick with coffee, but now I think I need a drink."

"Pour me one. And after I get these to auto-search, I'll tell you a story over dinner."

She poured two, pleased the wine was red, which lowered the chances of something healthy like fish with steamed vegetables on the plates. She peeked under the silver cover and was instantly cheered. "Hey, lasagna!" Then, on closer study. "What's this green stuff in there?"

"Good for you."

"Why is good for you mostly green? Why can't they make it taste like candy or at least pizza?"

"I'm going to get my R and D right on that. And we're going to speak of R and D, as it happens. There now." He sat back, nodded at his screens. "We'll see what we see." He rose, crossed to her. Taking up his glass, he tapped it to hers, then smiled. "I think

I'll have another of these," he decided, and cupped her chin before taking her mouth with his.

"No distracting with wine and lip-locks," she ordered. "I want to get to the bottom of this. The whole thing is . . . irritating."

"I imagine it is, to someone of your logical bent." He gestured for her to sit, then settled across from her. "Your victim," he began, "was a dangerous woman. Not in an admirable way. Not like you, for instance. She fought for nothing, stood for nothing, save her own gain."

"You said you didn't really know her."

"This is what I know of her. It's not the first time I've looked into her, which will make tonight's work a bit easier on that score. Information on her is, naturally, sketchy, but I believe she was born in Albania, the result of a liaison between her American mother and an unknown father. Her mother served in the U.S. Diplomatic Corps. She traveled with her mother extensively, saw and learned quite a bit of the world. It seems she was recruited, at a young age, by a covert group, World Intelligence Network."

"WIN?"

"Which was exactly their goal. To win data, funds, territories, political positions —

however it was most expedient. They only lasted a decade. But in that decade, they trained her, and as she apparently showed considerable ability and no particular conscience, used her in their Black Moon sector."

"Wet work."

"Yes." He broke a hunk of bread in two, passed her a share. "Somewhere along the line, she opted to freelance. It's more lucrative, and she'd have seen WIN was fragmenting. She tends to take high-dollar jobs, private or government. As I said, I had a brush with her several years ago. I believe, two years after that, she killed three of my people in an attempt to acquire the data and research to new fusion fuel we had under development."

Eve ate slowly. "Did she target you? Have you been a target?"

"No. It's generally believed I'm more useful alive than dead, even to competitors or . . . interested parties. I'm able to fund the R and D, the science, the manufacturing, and others may hope to steal it. Nothing to steal if you cut off the head."

"That's a comfort."

He reached across for her hand. "I watch out for myself, Lieutenant. Now, depending on the source, your victim is given credit, so to speak, for anywhere from fifty to two hundred and fifty deaths. Some were in the game, some were just in the way."

"You couldn't find her." Eve watched him as she ate. "You thought she killed three of your people, so you'd have tried."

"No, I couldn't find her. She went under, considerably under. I thought she might be dead, having failed to secure what she was hired for." He studied the wine in his glass. "Apparently I was wrong."

"Until now. It's unlikely she was on that ferry to sightsee."

"Very. It might've been a meet or a target, but odds are it was business."

"Double cross. But someone like this, experienced, how does she get caught off guard and taken out? Someone she knew? Someone she trusted or underestimated maybe? Another spook? Another assassin?" She felt the frustration rising again, like flood water behind a dam. "Why so freaking public?"

"I couldn't begin to guess. Tell me what you think about this smudge, this flash of light."

She blew out a breath. "I left a message for Mira, asking her about the possibility of mass hypnosis. And that sounds crazy when I hear myself say it out loud. Not as crazy as vortexes or invisibility cloaks, but in that mix of nuts. Still, we've dealt with mind manipulation before. The tiny burn in the cortex found in autopsy after suicides, manipulated by your pal Reeanna Ott."

"Hardly my pal, as it turned out." But he nodded to show they were on the same page. "Manipulation, in that case, done through audio."

"So, a possible manipulation done optically," Eve finished. "One that affects memory. But it has to do more. I can almost swallow people wouldn't remember seeing someone haul out a dead body, but I have to figure they wouldn't just let him by in the first place. And Carolee, whether she was conscious or unconscious, her kid wouldn't have just stood where he was, would he, if he saw her come out? So, maybe we're dealing with a device that can manipulate behavior, or sight, and memory? That's a big jump. Mass hypnosis suddenly doesn't sound so crazy."

"There have been rumors, underground and through the tech world, of a device in development. A kind of stunner."

"Ah. Got one of those." Eve tapped the weapon at her side she'd yet to take off.

"Not your conventional stunner, but one that renders the target incapacitated through an optical signal rather than the nervous system. It sends a signal, through light, that shuts down certain basic functions. Essentially, in a theory not that far from your mass hypnosis, it puts the target into a kind of trance. Hocus Pocus." He lifted his wineglass in half salute. "It's often referred to as that, which made me think of it when you used the term. The rumors are largely dismissed, but not entirely."

"We're talking dozens of people," Eve argued. "Potentially hundreds."

"And the idea this device exists, and has a possibility for that sort of range, is . . . fascinating. And used as a weapon? Devastating."

Eve pushed up from the table to pace. "I hate this kind of shit. Why can't it just be regular bad guy crap? You've got money, I want it, I kill you. You've been screwing my wife, it pisses me off, I cut out your heart. No, I've got to worry about disappearing bodies and weapons designed to turn the lights out on masses of people. Crap."

"It's an ever-changing world," Roarke said lightly.

She snorted. "How much credence do you and your R and D people put into this device?"

"Enough to be working on something

similar — and a counter-device. Though both are still in the theoretical stages. I'm getting the data for you," he added, gesturing toward the console.

She sat again, drummed her fingers on the table. "Okay, say this device exists, and was used today. Say its existence speaks to why Buckley was on that ferry, either with the device in her possession or with the hopes to make that so. It still doesn't explain why she was murdered in the way she was, or why her body was taken off the ferry. Stealing or obtaining the device, even killing Buckley to get it, that's business. Basically exsanguinating her and taking what's left? That's personal."

"I wouldn't argue, but business and personal often overlap."

"Okay." She lifted her hands and swiped them in the air as if clearing a board. "Why remove the body? Maybe to prove the hit, if it's hired. Maybe because you're a sick fuck. Or maybe to buy time. I like that one because it's weirdly logical. It stalls the identification process. We have to depend on a DNA search and match. And then, we get what appears to be an innocuous vic, corn-fed Iowa-born female consultant. Maybe, given some time, we'd dig under that, have some questions. But the bigger puzzler would remain, at least initially, *how* rather than *who,* since we had the who."

"But, because I wanted to spend a bit more time with my wife, I happened to be there when she was identified."

"Yeah. You recognized her, and that's a variable the killer couldn't have factored in."

"Logical enough," Roarke agreed. "But buy time for what?"

"To get away, to deliver the device and/or the body. To destroy the body, certainly to get the hell away from the scene. This spy stuff doesn't work like the job. It's convoluted, covered with gray areas and underlying motivations. But when you wipe away all of that, you've still got a killer, a victim, a motive. We cross off random, because no possible way. It wasn't impulse."

"Because?" He knew the answer, or thought he did, but he loved watching her work.

"The sign on the door, the getaway. It was vicious — all that spatter. A pro wouldn't have wasted time with that. Cut the throat, skewer the heart, hit the big artery in the thigh. Pick one and move on. But blood doesn't lie, and the spatter clearly says this was slice, hack, rip."

The light softened as they spoke, and he

wondered how many couples might sit in the evening light over a meal and talk of blood spatter and exsanguination.

Precious few, he supposed.

"Are you sure none of the blood was the killer's?"

She nodded. It was a good question, she thought, and only one of the reasons she liked bouncing a case around with him. "Reports just in, taking samples of every area of spatter, and several from the pool, confirm it all belonged to Buckley."

"Then she was caught seriously off guard."

"I'll say. So, specific target, specific location and time, personal and professional connections. Add one more element, and I think it matters. Whoever killed Buckley didn't kill Carolee Grogan when it would've been easier, more expedient and even to his or her advantage to do so."

"Leaving her body behind. More confusion," Roarke agreed. "A longer identification time on the blood pool. A killer with a heart?"

She tossed back the rest of her wine. "It's more that a lot of people with a heart kill."

"My cynical darling."

She rolled her eyes. "Let's see what we've got so far." She jerked a thumb toward the console.

Roarke walked back behind the command center, sat. Then, smiling at Eve, patted his knee.

"Please."

"And thank you," he said, grabbing her and tugging her down. "There now, this is cozy."

"It's murder."

"Yes, yes, on a daily basis. Now, see here, we're through several levels on HSO, but then, I've been through that door before." He brushed his lips over her cheek. "And making some progress on the others. They'll have done some code shifting and house-keeping since my last visits, but see there, we're rerouting with them."

"I see a bunch of gibberish, numbers and symbols flashing by."

"Exactly. Let's see if we can nudge it along." He reached around her, began tapping keys. "There are all sorts of tricks," he continued as the codes zipped by on the screens. "Realignments, firewalls, fail-safes, trapdoors and backdoors. But we keep updating along with them."

"Why? Seriously, why do you need access to this stuff?"

"Everyone needs a hobby. What we want here are eyes-only personnel files, their black ops consultants. And verification if the device rumored to exist does indeed exist. Eyes-only again, but the trick would be to find where it might be tucked and by whom. Ah well, bugger it. Let's try this way."

Assuming from the oath and his increased tapping that he'd hit a snag, Eve wiggled away. "I'm getting coffee, and I'm going to run some data of my own."

When his answer was a grunt, she knew playtime was over. It was time for serious work.

SEVEN

Using an auxiliary computer, Eve initiated her own search for any mention of a device such as Roarke had described. She found several articles on medical sites detailing the memory suppressive drugs and tools used during routine surgeries, others edging toward hypnotherapy in both medical studies and gaming.

She also found a scattering of fringe blogs raging about government mind control, enslaving of the masses and the ever-popular doomsday warnings. A nation of human droids, forced experimentation, personality theft and human breeding farms were on their top-ten list of predicted abominations. This led her to others claiming to have been abducted by aliens in league with the shadow forces of government.

"I'm surprised the government has time to, you know, govern, when they're so busy working with aliens and their anal probes or pursuing their mission to turn the global population into mindless sex droids."

"Hmm," Roarke said, "there's government, then there's government."

She glanced over to where he sat, fingers flying, eyes intent. "You don't actually believe this crap? Alien invasions, secret bunkers in Antarctica for experimentation on human guinea pigs."

He flicked his glance up. "Icove."

"That was . . . Okay." Hard to argue when they'd both nearly been killed when dismantling a subversive and illegal human cloning organization. "But aliens?"

"It's a big universe. You should get out in it more often."

"I like one planet just fine."

"In any case, I have your victim. No, don't get up." He waved her back. "I'll put it onscreen. Data, wall screen one. This is from HSO, but the data matches what I've got from the other sources."

"Dana Buckley," Eve read. "With her three most common aliases. Same age as her current ID. But with the biographical data you had."

"Now it lists her assets. The languages she spoke, her e-skill level, the weaponry she was cleared for. Included in her dossier is this list." He scrolled down. "Names, nationalities, ranks if applicable, dates."

"Her hit list," Eve mumbled. "They know or believe she's killed these people, but they let her walk around."

"Undoubtedly she killed some of those people for these agencies. They let her walk around until now because she's useful to them."

Eve dealt with murder every day, yet this offended and disturbed her on some core level she wasn't sure she could articulate.

"That's not how it's supposed to be. You can't just kill or order someone's death because it's expedient. We've managed to virtually outlaw torture and executions; if a cop terminates in the line, he has to go through testing to ensure it was ultimate force that was necessary. But there are still people, supposedly on *our* side, who would use someone like her to do their dirty work."

"People who use someone like her rarely, if ever, get their hands dirty."

"She was a psychopath. Look at her psych profile, for God's sake." Eve swung an arm at the screen. "She should've been put away, just like the person who did her needs to be put away."

He watched her as she read the data on-screen. "You have less gray area than most."

"You think this is acceptable? Jesus, read

the list. Some of them are kids."

"Collateral damage, I expect. And no," he added as she swung around, her eyes firing. "I don't think it's acceptable to kill for money, for the thrill or for expedience. There may be more gray in my world than yours when it comes to killing for a cause, but that's not what she did. It was profit and, I believe, for fun. And I suspect, if it had been Buckley standing in that room when Carolee walked in, those boys would be grieving for their mother tonight instead of cuddled up with her watching in-room movies."

"Not all assassins are created equal?" Calmer, she angled her head as she studied the screen. "We need to look at this list, see if we can connect any of these names to someone in the same business. Someone skilled enough to get the drop on her."

"I'll set it up. Meanwhile, there's interesting data on the device. This memo was issued two days ago." Again, he ordered the data onscreen.

" 'The Lost delayed. Owl to commence new series of tests in Sector Twelve. Owl request for seventy-two and blackout approved.' " Eve puzzled over it a moment. "She's not Owl. Who'd code-name a female assassin — a young, attractive one — Owl?"

"We can go over the earlier memos, but I'd say Owl would be in charge of the development of the device."

"The Lost. You lose time, yourself, your memory of what happened when you're . . . gone. So, if this Owl or someone under him/ her had it, maybe it was an exchange. No, no, it was a setup. It was planned. He had to have a way off the damn ferry, so none of it was spontaneous. Delayed? But if it was used, it was complete."

"It wouldn't be the first time a member of the team decided to go free agent."

"Fake a delay so you could sell it, but you don't sell it. You walk away with whatever she had in that briefcase and the device. A twofer. If this is the last memo in the file, HSO isn't yet aware they have a problem."

"Still another reason to take the body," Roarke pointed out. "Buys that time you spoke of. Maybe he had another offer. Or wants to renegotiate the fee, from a safe location."

"It wasn't about money," Eve murmured. "not just about money. Buying time, yeah, that plays. She won't be identified, officially, to the media until tomorrow."

"There's more. Photos of some of her work. Images on-screen, slide-show method," he ordered.

She'd seen death, in all its forms, too many times to count. She watched it now, roll over the wall screen. Rent flesh, spilled blood, charred hulks.

"Some of these, of course, were very bad people. Others, very bad people wanted out of the way. It appears she didn't discriminate. She followed the money. Some might argue whoever killed her did the world a favor."

"And what makes him any better than her?" Eve demanded.

He only shrugged, knowing on some points they would never agree. "Some would argue otherwise."

"Yeah, some would. Let's find Owl." She pushed her hands through her hair. "And I have to figure out a logical way to explain how I came by anything we get out of this tonight."

"The ever-popular anonymous source."

"Yeah, that'll fool everybody who knows us."

He initiated a series of searches, then studied her as she stood still watching death scroll by. "It's harder when the victim is abhorrent to you."

Eve shook her head. "I'm not allowed to decide if a murder victim is worth standing for. I stand for them."

He rose, went to her. "But it's harder when that victim has so many victims. So much blood on her hands."

"It's harder," she admitted. "It can't always be an easy choice. It's just the only choice."

"For you." He kissed her brow, then cupped her face, lifted it and laid his lips gently, softly, over hers.

When she sighed and leaned into him, he hit the release on her weapon harness.

"Working," she said against his mouth.

"I certainly hope so."

She laughed when he tugged the harness off her shoulders. "No, I've got work."

"Searches will take a while." He circled her, reaching out to press a control on his console. The bed slid out of the panel in the wall.

"And you figure sex will cheer me up?"

"I'm hoping it's a side benefit to cheering me up."

He circled again, then launched them both toward the bed. She hit with a breathless thump, bounced and, what the hell, let herself be pinned under him.

"Rough stuff."

He grinned. "If you like."

He yanked her shirt over her head, let it fly as he lowered his mouth, with a hint of teeth to her breast.

She arched, urging him on. The violence here, so full of heat and hope, helped erase all those images of blood and loss. And helped her remember that no matter how they might differ on an issue, even an ideology, there was, always, love.

And lust.

She could take — a handful of that black silk hair, a ripple of muscle as she dragged at his shirt in turn. She could feel the pound of her heart and his as they rolled over the bed in a battle they would both win.

He made her laugh, made her breath catch. He made her skin shimmer and her blood swim. And when she wrapped around him, found his mouth with hers again, she could taste the flood of love and lust and longing.

So strong, so sweet. Her body moved under his, over his, agile and quick. The hum of the work that would draw them both back drowned under the thrum of his own pulse when his hands swept over her. Curve and angle, soft and firm. Wet and warm.

She arched again, rising up where he drove her, to break, then to gather again. Open for more, for him.

When he filled her, when they rose and fell, rose and fell, to break together, it gave her not only pleasure. It gave her peace.

Curled against him, warm and naked and replete, it occurred to her Peabody had been right again. After-sex snuggles were very, very good.

"You should sleep." He spoke quietly, stroking her back. "It's late, and there's no urgency on this one."

"I don't know. Isn't there?" She thought how lovely it would be to just close her eyes, to drift away with the scent of him all over her. "Closing the case, maybe that's not so urgent on a technical level. But if the killer did have this thing, this weapon, and still has it, ready to sell it to God knows, doesn't that make finding him, stopping him, part of the job, too?"

"Close the case, save the world?"

She tipped up her head until their eyes met. "You said you had people trying to develop this thing. Why?"

"Better you do it before the other one does. Self-preservation."

"I get that. It's always going to be that way. Bad guy has a stick, you get a knife. He has a knife, you get a stunner. The ante keeps going up. It's the way it is. So, there have to be rules and laws, and even when the line blurs, we have to be able to know who the good guys are. If I have the chance to find this guy, stop him before he sells this thing, maybe we hold all of it back for another day."

"The comp will signal when we have extrapolated data. Sleep awhile, then we'll see about saving the world."

It sounded reasonable.

The next thing she knew, the comp was beeping and she was springing up in bed — alone.

"What? Morning?"

"Nearly." Roarke stood behind the command center, shirtless, his trousers riding low on his hips. "And your Owl's come out."

"You found him — her?"

"Him," Roarke said as she leaped out of bed. He glanced over, smiled. "Come over here and I'll show you."

"I bet." She snatched at her shirt, her pants.

"Killjoy. Well, at least get us both some coffee."

"Who is he?" she demanded as she dragged on her clothes.

"That depends. He, like his victim, has gone by more than one name. This data claims him as Ivan Draski, age sixty-two, born in the Ukraine. Other data, which on the surface appears just as valid, has him as

Javis Drinkle, age sixty, born in Poland. As Draski, he worked for the Freedom Republic, the underground, at the end of the Urbans, in communications and technological development. He's a scientist."

She brought the coffee, gulping some down as she read the data.

"Recruited by European Watch Network, techno research and development," Eve continued. "A gadget guy."

"An inventor, yes. He makes the toys."

"An inside guy," Eve mused. "Sure there's some field time clocked here, but primarily during the Urbans. It's primarily science during and after that era."

"Nanotech," Roarke began. "Hyperdimensional science, bionics, psionics and so on. He's worked on all this. It looks to me, according to this data, you owe your stunner to his work, among other things. And yet I've never heard of him. They've kept him tightly wrapped for decades."

"Maybe he decided it was time for a raise and some credit." She tried to make sense of it. "So, he's lured away from EWN to HSO nearly twenty years ago. And still, I'm not seeing wet work here. He's a techno geek."

"A brilliant one. No. No black ops or wet work listed. But look there, his wife and daughter were killed twenty years ago in a brutal slaying."

"That's interesting timing," Eve said.

"Isn't it? Officially a home invasion. Unofficially, a fringe wing of EWN who'd targeted him for his knowledge and accessibility to sensitive material."

"They eat their own." When he switched to the crime scene photos, Eve hissed out a breath. "Jesus."

"Mutilated, hacked to pieces." Roarke's voice tightened in disgust. "The girl was just twelve. The wife was a low-level agent, hardly more than a clerk. You have higher clearance, I expect."

"The writing on the wall there. Did you translate?"

"The computer recognizes it as Ukrainian for 'traitor' and 'whore.' Neither EWN nor any other official file on the matter claims credit or responsibility for the killings."

"They were on her list. On Buckley's list of hits in HSO's data banks." She called for the computer to run the list on another screen to verify. "They're there, on her list, but no employer assigned. Nobody's taken credit."

"If there's data on that, it's in another area. If there's any more data on this hit, it's been wiped or boxed. Even I can't get at it from here, or certainly not quickly. You'd have to be inside to get at it."

"He's inside; he found it." There was motive, Eve thought. There was the personal. "Why the hell didn't they destroy the file if they continued to use her, and had him on the payroll?"

"Somebody fucked up, I'd say, but at the core HSO is a bureaucracy, and bureaucracies love their paperwork."

"Does he have a fixed address?"

"Right here in New York."

She looked back over her shoulder at him. "That's too fucking easy."

"Upper East Side, in a town house he owns under the name of Frank Plutz."

"Plutz? Seriously?"

"Frank J. Plutz, employed by HSO, who lists him as Supervisor, Tech R and D, U.S. Division, in their official file. Which of course is bollocks. He's a hell of a lot more."

Now Eve studied the ID shot of a middle-aged man with a thinning crop of gray hair, a round face, a bit heavy in the chin, and mild blue eyes who smiled soberly from the wall screen.

"God. He looks harmless."

"He survived the Urban Wars in the underground, has worked for at least two intelligence organizations, neither of which worries overmuch about spilled blood. I'd say appearances are deceiving."

"I need to put a team together and go visit the deceptively harmless Mr. Plutz."

"I want to play. And I very much want to meet this man."

"I guess you've earned it."

His eyes gleamed. "If you don't put him in a cage, I wonder what I can offer him to switch to the private sector."

Eight

As taking down a spy wasn't her usual job, Eve opted for a small, tight team. She had two officers in soft clothes stationed at the rear of the trim Upper East Side town house, McNab handling the com along with Roarke in the unmarked van. She, along with Peabody, would take the front.

It struck her as a bit of overkill for one man, but she had to factor in that one man had over forty years of espionage experience, and had managed to slip off a ferry of more than three thousand people with a dead body.

In the van, she cued up the security tape from the transpo station. "There he is, looking harmless. Computer, enhance segment six, thirty percent."

The man currently known as Frank J. Plutz enlarged onscreen as he shuffled his way through the ticker. "Anonymous businessman, complete with what looks like a battered briefcase and a small overnight bag. Slightly overweight, slightly balding, a little saggy in the jowls."

"And this is the guy who sliced up the high-level assassin, then poofed with her." McNab, his sunny hair slicked back in a sleek tail, his earlobes weighted with a half dozen colorful studs each, shook his head. "He looks a little like my uncle Jacko. He's famed in our family for growing enormous turnips."

"He does!" Peabody gave the love of her life a slap on the shoulder. "I met him last Thanksgiving when we went to Scotland. He's adorable."

"Yeah, I'm sure this one's just as adorable as Uncle Jacko. In a 'leaving a big, messy pool of blood behind' sort of way. He got a weapon — we assume — through the scanners without a hitch. Which, unfortunately, isn't as tough as it should be. More important, from my source, he's headed or been involved in the invention and development of all manner of high-tech gadgetry, weaponry and communications in particular."

"Love to meet him," McNab said and got a quick grin from Roarke.

"Right with you."

"Hopefully you geeks can have a real nice chat soon." Eve shifted her gaze to the other monitor. "I'm not seeing any heat source in there."

"That would be because there isn't." Roarke continued the scan of the house. "I've done three scans each on heat, on movement. There's no one in there."

"Takes the fun out of it. Well, we've got the warrant. Let's go, Peabody. McNab, keep your eye on the street. If he comes home, I want to know about it."

"Mind your back, Lieutenant," Roarke said as she climbed out. "They're called spooks for a reason."

"I don't believe in spooks."

"I bet they believe in you." Peabody jumped down beside her.

Scanning the building, Eve pulled out her master as they approached the door. "We go in the way we would if we had a suspect inside. And we clear the area, room by room."

Peabody nodded. "A guy who can disappear could probably beat a heat-and-motion sensor."

Eve only shook her head, then pounded a fist on the door. "This is the police." She used her master to unlock the door, noted the standard security went from locked red to open green. "He's got cams out here. I can't see them, but he's got them. Still, no backups set on the locks, and the palm plate's not activated."

"It's like an invitation."

"We're accepting. We're going in," Eve said to alert the rest of the team.

She pulled her weapon, nodded once to Peabody. They hit the door, Peabody high, Eve low. Swept the short foyer with its iron umbrella stand and coat tree, and the narrow hallway with its frayed blue runner. At Eve's gesture they peeled off, clearing the first floor, moving to the second, then the third.

"We're clear." Eve studied the data and communication equipment, the surveillance and security equipment ranged around the modest third-floor room. "Blue team, take the first floor. Roarke, McNab, we can use you on the third floor."

"Do you think he's coming back?" Peabody wondered.

"It's a lot to leave behind. I guarantee all this is unregistered, calibrated to duck under CompuGuard radar. But no, he's done here. He's finished."

"His wife and kid?" Peabody gestured to the framed photo on the console.

"Yeah." Eve moved over, opened a mini fridge. "Water and power drinks." She hit menu on the AutoChef. "Quick, easy meals." The sort, she thought, she'd have had in her own mini fridge — when she remembered to stock it — before she'd married Roarke. "Sofa, with a pillow, a blanket, wall screen, adjoining john. He spent most of his time up here. The rest of the house, it's just space."

"It all looks so tidy, kind of homey and neat."

Eve made a sound of agreement as she turned into the next room. "VirtualFit. It's a nice unit. He wanted to keep in shape. A weight machine, muscle balls, sparring droid. Female, and at a guess, just about the height and weight of Buckley."

Eve studied the attractive blonde droid currently disengaged and propped in a corner. "He practiced here." She moved across the room, opened the doors on a built-in cabinet. "Wow, toy chest."

"Holy shit." Peabody gaped at the display of weapons. "Not so much like Uncle Jacko after all."

Knives, bats, stunners, blasters, clubs, short swords, guns, throwing discs all gleamed in tidy formation.

"A couple missing," Eve noted, tapping empty holders. "From the shape, he took a couple of knives and a stunner. In one of his carry-ons, on his person."

"This is a lot to leave behind, too," Peabody commented.

"He did what he set out to do. He doesn't need them anymore." She turned as Roarke came in with McNab, and caught the gleam in Roarke's eyes as he crossed toward the weapons chest. "Don't touch."

The faintest line of irritation marred his brow, but he slipped his hands into his pockets. "A nice little collection."

"Don't get any ideas," she muttered under her breath. "It's next door you might be useful." She led the way and heard both Roarke and McNab hum in pleasure as some men would at the sight of a pretty woman.

"Geek heaven," she supposed. "Seal up, then see what you can find on all this. Peabody, let's take the second floor."

"Do you want me to get someone in to take over street surveillance?" McNab asked.

"He's not coming back. He hasn't been back since he took those weapons out of the chest. He doesn't need this place anymore."

"There are still clothes in the closet," Peabody pointed out when they started down. "I saw them when we cleared the bedroom."

"I'll tell you what we won't find. We won't

find any of his IDs, any of his emergency cash, any credit cards, passports."

She moved into the bedroom where the decor managed to be spartan in neatness and homey in its fat pillows and frayed fabrics. She opened the closet.

"Three suits — black, gray, brown. See the way they're arranged, spaces between? Probably had three more. Same with the shirts, the spare trousers. He took what he needed." She crouched, picked up a pair of sturdy black shoes, turned them over to reveal the worn-down heels, scuffed soles. "Frugal. Lived carefully, comfortably, but without any excess. I bet the neighbors are going to say what a nice, pleasant man he was. Quiet, but friendly."

"He's got drawer dividers. Cubbies for socks, boxers, undershirts. And yeah," Peabody added, "it looks like several pair are missing. Second drawer's athletic wear. T-shirts, sweats, gym socks."

"Keep at it. I'll take the second bedroom."

Across the hall in a smaller room fashioned into a kind of den, Eve opened another cabinet. She found wigs, trays of makeup, facial putty, clear boxes holding various styles of facial hair, body forms.

She saw herself reflected, front and back, in the mirror-backed doors.

She began a systematic search of the room, then the bathroom. He'd left plenty behind, she thought. Ordinary pieces of the man. Hairbrush, toothbrush, clothes, book and music discs, a pair of well-tended houseplants.

Everything well used, she thought, well tended. Very clean, ordered without being obsessive.

Food in the AutoChef, slippers by the bed. It all gave the appearance of a home someone would return to shortly. Until you noticed there was nothing important. Nothing that couldn't be easily replaced.

Except the photo over his work area, she mused. But he'd have copies of that. Certainly he'd have copies of that image that drove him. She studied the wigs and other enhancements again.

He'd left all this, and the weapons, the electronics. Left what he'd been all these years? she wondered. He'd done what he'd set out to do, so none of it mattered to him now.

Peabody came in. "I found a lock box, open and empty."

"One in here, too."

"And bits of adhesive behind drawers, behind the headboard."

Eve nodded. "Under the bathroom sinks,

behind the john. He's a careful guy. I'd say he kept weapons, escape documents, in several places around the house, in case he had to get out fast."

"We're not going to find him, Dallas. He's in the wind. It's what he does."

"What he *did.* I'd say he's finished, so it depends on what he's decided to do next. Check on the first floor, will you?"

Eve went upstairs to find both Roarke and McNab huddled with the electronics. On a quartet of small monitors she saw various spaces of the house — Peabody walking down the steps, her two men searching, an empty kitchen, the street view from the front of the house. Every ten seconds, the image changed to another location.

"Guy covered his ass double," McNab told her. "This place is hot-wired, not a trick missed. Motion, heat, light, weight. He's got bug sensors every fricking where. And check it."

He flipped a switch and a panel slid open in the wall beside her. She peered in, scanned the stairs and the weapon adhered to the wall. "Emergency evac."

"Icy. Plus, he could shut and bolt that door from right here."

"It's blast-proof," Roarke added. "He's got his C and D buried on here, but we're digging it out. I'd have to say it's not as well covered as I'd expect when you consider the rest of the security."

McNab shrugged. "Maybe he figured he didn't have to worry about anyone getting this far in."

"Or he didn't care particularly what they found at this point."

She glanced back up at the photo. "Possibly. It looks like he's finished, and with or without the cloak of invisibility, gone. No reason to stay in New York. He eliminated his target. We dig here, hoping we find some link to where he might go. If we don't find it, we're going to have to contact HSO."

Roarke gave her a long, cool look. "I don't see the value of that."

"It's not a matter of value. It's SOP. He's their operative. If he's gone rabbit or rogue, and has a device that's as dangerous as this one might be, we'll need their resources."

"Give us a moment, would you, Ian?"

McNab glanced over at Roarke, then at Eve. He didn't need a sensor to feel the blips of tension and trouble. "Ah, sure. I'll . . . ah, see if I can give She-Body a hand."

"This is my job," she began as soon as they were alone. "When I report in with what we have here, Whitney's going to order me to contact Homeland and give them what I have."

"You have nothing," he said evenly, "but the nebulous connection of one Frank Plutz, on the word of an 'anonymous source' connecting him to HSO and to Buckley."

"I have him getting on the ferry, and not getting off, which secured the warrant more than the source did. I have what we found here."

"And what have you found here that verifies he's an operative for HSO, or that he targeted and killed Buckley?"

She felt her stomach muscles quiver even as her spine stiffened. "We know he has a potentially dangerous weapon. He may intend to sell that weapon. In the wrong hands —"

"Homeland's aren't the wrong hands?" Roarke demanded. "Can you stand there and tell me they aren't every bit as ruthless and deadly as any foreign bogeyman you can name? After what they did to you? What they allowed to be done to you when you were a child? Standing by, listening, for Christ's sake, while your father beat you and raped you, all in the hopes they could use him to catch a bigger monster?"

The quivering in her gut became a roil. "One has nothing to do with the other."

"Bollocks. You tried to 'work' with them before, not so long ago. And when you found murder and corruption, they tried to ruin you. To kill you."

"I know what they did. Damn it, that wasn't the organization, as much as I despise it, but individuals inside it. Ivan Draski is probably thousands of miles away by now. I can't chase him outside New York. I don't *know* where he might try to sell this thing."

"I'll look into it."

"Roarke —"

"Goddamn it, Eve, you're not going to ask me to stand by a second time. I did what you asked before. I let it go. I let go the ones who'd had a part in letting you be abused and tormented."

Now it was her heart, squeezing inside a fist of tension. "I know what you did for me. I know what it cost you to do it. I'm not going to have a choice. It's national security. For God's sake, Roarke, I don't want to bring them in. I don't want anything to do with them. It makes me sick. But it's not about me, or you, or what happened when I was eight."

"You'll give me twenty-four hours. I'm not asking," he said before she could speak. "Not this time. You'll give me twenty-four hours to track him."

Here was the cold and the ruthless that lurked under the civilized. She knew it, understood it, even accepted it. "I can stall that long. At twenty-four and one minute, I have to turn it over."

"Then I'll be in touch." He started to walk by her, stopped, looked into her eyes. "I'll be sorry if we're at odds on this."

"Me, too."

But when he walked out she knew sorry was sometimes all you could be.

NINE

When a trail went cold, Eve's rule of thumb was go back to the beginning. For a second time she stood on the deck of the ferry under a blue summer sky.

"According to the security discs, the victim boarded first." Eve studied the route from the transport station to the deck. "He was easily a hundred passengers behind her. Several minutes behind her."

"It doesn't seem like he could've kept her in view," Peabody commented. "And from the recording, it didn't look like he tried to."

"Two likely scenarios. He'd managed to get a tracker on her, or had set up this meet in advance. Since I can't think of any reason he'd take chances or play the odds, my money is he did both."

"We haven't turned up a thing that points to her meeting a third party on Staten Island."

Eve huffed out a breath. "I'd say we haven't turned up a lot of things. Yet." She started up to the second deck. "She went up here. We've got that from the Grogan kid's camera. The ride over takes less than a half hour, so if she had a meet, and if she planned to make an exchange, she wouldn't have waited too long once they left port. The best we can gauge, Carolee went into the restroom less than halfway through the trip. About ten minutes in."

"But since she doesn't remember, and we've got no body to calculate TOD, we don't know if Buckley was already dead when Carolee went in."

"Odds are." Eve stood at the rail, imagining the roll and hum of the ferry, the crowds, the view. "Lots of excitement as people are boarding, right? Crowds, happy tourists off on an adventure. People would be securing their places at the rails, grabbing a snack, taking pictures. If I'm Buckley, I take my position, scope it out."

She took a seat on the bench. "Sitting here, and you can bet she sat here before or she'd never have picked or agreed to the location, she can judge the crowd, the traffic, the timing. If I'm Buckley, I move to the meet location as close as possible to leaving port."

Rising, Eve strolled off in the direction of the restroom. "That's around ten minutes before Grogan went in. Plenty of time for the kill. If Grogan had gone in before the attack, why not let her finish up, get out? If she'd gone in during, she should've been able to call out or get out and raise an alarm. She went down at the dividing point between stalls and sinks. That's where the sweepers found trace of her blood and skin from her head hitting the floor. She'd just turned at the wall. And got an eyeful."

"Do you think Mira can help her remember?"

"I think it's worth a shot. Meanwhile . . ." Eve detoured toward concession. "Before the eyeful, Carolee and the kid —"

"Pete."

"Right. They start toward the concession area, then swing to the restrooms." Eve followed the most logical route. "Stand here, discuss. Wait for me, blah blah. Carolee watches the kid go in, then notices the sign on the door. Debates, then decides to give it a try after all. And after that, doesn't remember. So we reconstruct. Going with the theory the meet was set in advance, and the murder was premeditation, Draski would go in first. It's a women's room; he's a guy."

"Right. Well, he might've slipped in when most people are focused on the view, but the Out of Order sign. He'd be smarter to go in looking like maintenance. A uniform."

"Which he could've slipped into right next door." Eve gestured toward the other restroom. "If we're dealing with premeditated, and a need to hide or transport the body, he'd need means. No one would question a maintenance guy going into an out-of-order bathroom pushing a hamper."

"None of the hampers were missing."

"He had an hour to put it back. He comes out of there" — Eve pointed toward the men's room — "goes in here. Who notices? Apparently nobody. Inside to wait for Buckley."

Eve pushed open the door. "I doubt he wasted much time once she came in."

"No way to lock the door from inside," Peabody began, "and no way to rig it shut because he needed Buckley to get in."

"Yeah, so he wouldn't waste much time. He'd want to make sure she had the payment, she'd want to make sure he had the device. Just business."

The congealed pool of blood, smeared now from several samplings, spoke to the nature of that business. As did the slight scent of chemicals, the faint layer of dust left by the sweepers spoke of the results of that business.

As did the long-bladed knife on the floor.

"Record on," Eve ordered, then, avoiding the blood still on the floor, approached the knife.

"But . . . how the hell did that get here?" Peabody demanded. "We've got the entire ferry covered with guards."

"Freaking invisibility cloak," Eve muttered, "answers that. So the first question is, why is it here?" She studied it where it lay. "Dagger style, about a six-inch blade. It looks like bone. That would explain how he got it through the security scanners. The natural material would pass, and it's likely he had a safe slot in that briefcase he carried on. Some protection against the scanner for shape, weight."

She coated her hands before lifting the knife. "Good weight. Good grip." Testing, she turned, swiped the air. "Good reach. You don't have to get close in. Arm's length plus six. Me, I'd use a wrist trigger. Click, it's in your hand, swipe, slice the throat."

Peabody rubbed her own. "Have you ever thought about going into the assassination game?"

"Killing for business, for profit, that was her line, not his. His was personal. Sure took him long enough though." She judged the spatter, the pool, swiped a second time, circled, jabbed, sliced.

"And now he goes to the trouble to put the weapon in our hand so we can see what and how."

"Bragging maybe."

Eve turned the blade, studied the blood smears. "It doesn't feel like bragging." She took out an evidence bag, sealed the weapon inside, tagged it. Holding it, she glanced toward the door. "If Carolee came in now, she'd see him, see the body as soon as she turned for the stalls. That puts, what, about ten feet between them, with her less than two from the door. What would most people do when they walk in on a murder?"

"Scream and run," Peabody provided. "And she should've made it, or at least gotten close. Plus, if he'd gone after her like that, you'd think he'd have stepped in some of the blood. She could've fainted. Just passed out cold. Smacked her head on the floor."

"Yeah, or he could've stunned her. Dropped her. A low setting. That would give him a little time to figure out how to handle the variable. He's got to get the body out, but he'd have prepped for that. Lined the hamper maybe, a body bag certainly. Load it up — along with the uniform. It had to be stained with blood."

"Then he'd use the memory blaster on Carolee as she came to."

Eve cocked her eyebrows at the term "memory blaster." "When she's under, he tells her she's going to give him a hand. He'd go out first."

"Mojo the people on this sector of the deck. He could do that as he made his way to wherever he wanted to go. It's one frosty toy."

"It's not a toy. It's lethal. If it does what it purports, it strips you of your will. You lose who and what you are." Worse than death to her mind was loss of self. "You're nothing but a droid until the effects wear off." She studied the knife again. "Sticks, stones, knives, guns, blasters, bombs. Somebody's always looking for something a little juicier. This." Through the evidence bag, she hefted the knife again. "It can take your life. This other thing, it takes your mind. I'd rather face the blade."

She glanced at her wrist unit. Roarke's twenty-four hours was down to twenty and counting. No matter what it cost her, she couldn't give him a minute more.

The little bakery with its sunny two-tops

and displays of glossy pastries might have seemed an odd place to meet with a weapons runner, but Roarke knew Julian Chamain's proclivities.

He knew, too, that the bakery, run by Chamain's niece, was swept twice daily for listening devices, and the walls and windows shielded against electronic eyes and ears.

What was said there, stayed there.

Chamain, a big man whose wide face and wide belly proclaimed his affection for his niece's culinary skills, shook Roarke's hand warmly, then gestured to the seat across the table.

"It's been some time," Chamain said, with a hint of his native country in the words. "Four, five years now."

"Yes. You look well."

Chamain laughed, a big, basso bark, as he patted his generous belly. "Well fed, indeed. Ah, here, my niece's daughter, Marianna." Chamain gave the young woman a smile as she served coffee and a plate of small pastries. "This is an old friend."

"Pleased to meet you. Only two, Uncle Julian." She wagged her finger. "Mama said. Enjoy," she added to Roarke as she bustled away.

"Try the éclair," Chamain told Roarke.

"Simple, but exquisite. So, marriage is good?"

"Very. And your wife, your children?"

"Thriving. I have six grandchildren now. The reward for growing old. You should start a family. Children are a man's truest legacy."

"Eventually." Understanding his role, Roarke sampled an éclair. "You're right. Excellent. It's a pretty space, Julian. Cheerful and well run. Another kind of legacy."

"It pleases me. The tangible, the every day, a bit of the sweet." Chamain popped a tiny cream puff in his mouth, closed his eyes in pleasure. "The love of a good woman. I think of retiring and enjoying it all more. You keep busy, I hear, but have also retired from some enterprises."

"The love of a good woman," Roarke repeated.

"So, we've both been lucky there. I wonder why you asked to meet me, and share pastries and coffee."

"We were occasionally associates, or friendly competitors. We dealt honestly with each other either way. We were always able to discuss business, and important commodities. I feel we've lost time."

He watched Chamain's eyebrows raise before the man lifted his coffee for a long, slow sip. "Time is a valuable commodity. If it could be bought and sold, the bidding would be very steep. Time wins wars as much as blood. What man wouldn't want his enemy to lose time?"

"If a weapon existed that could cause such a thing, it would be worth a great deal on the market."

"A very great deal. Such a weapon, and the technology to create others like it, would command billions. Blood would be shed as well as fortunes spent to possess it. Dangerous games played."

"How much might you be willing to pay, should such a thing exist?"

Chamain smiled, chose another pastry. "Me, I'm old-fashioned, and close to retirement. If I were younger, I would seek out partners, form alliances and enter the bidding. Perhaps a man of your age, of your position, has considered such a thing."

"No. It isn't a commodity that fits my current interests. In any case, I would think the bidding would be closed at this date."

"The window closes at midnight. Games, *mon ami,* dangerous games." He gave a long sigh. "It makes me wish I were younger, but some games are best watched from the sidelines, especially when the field is bloody."

"I wonder if the people at home are aware of the game, its current status."

"The people at home seem to have misjudged the game, and the players. Shortsighted, you could say, and their ears not as close to the ground as they might be. Women are ruthless creatures, and excellent in business. Persuasive."

Roarke said nothing for a moment. "If I were a betting man, and on the sidelines, I'd be interested to know a key player has been eliminated, and she's no longer on the field."

"Is that so?" Chamain pursed his lips at the information, then nodded. "Ah, well, as I said, a dangerous game. Try a napoleon."

Within the hour, armed with the cryptic pieces Chamain offered, Roarke sat in his private office. Clearly Buckley intended to make an exchange for the device — or more likely to kill the delivery boy and walk away with it. It was greed and arrogance that killed as much as the blade. Had it been self-defense all along, or a setup for revenge?

That wasn't his problem, but Eve's, he thought. His would be to track down Ivan Draski and the device. She'd keep her word on the twenty-four hours, just as he had kept his in not seeking revenge on the operatives who'd been a part of allowing her to be tormented and raped as a child, who'd allowed that child to wander the streets, broken and dazed, after she'd killed to save herself.

He'd destroyed the data on those men, for her sake. But their names were etched in his mind. So, he began the process of hacking his way through the agency, and to those men. On a secondary search he began the hunt for Ivan Draski, and Lost Time.

Well into his tasks, he glanced at the display of his pocket 'link when it signaled.

"Yes, Ian."

"As promised, I'm tagging you first, and praying Dallas doesn't skin my ass for it."

"I wouldn't worry."

"Not your ass," McNab replied. "I got through the shields and fail-safes. This guy's mega — more mega because it barely shows that he took down some of those shields and fail-safes so somebody with solid skills could get through."

"Is that so?" Roarke commented.

"That's my take. I'm saying I've got serious skills, but it should've taken me a couple days to get through, not a couple hours."

"Which means he wanted the information to be found." Roarke scanned his own data, jumbled the information and the theories together. "Interesting. What did you find?"

"He's got megabytes on this Dana Buckley, a massive file on her, complete with surveillance — eyes and ears. I did a skim, and if half this stuff is true, she was one bad bitch."

"And he was following her, and documenting."

"Keeping tabs for sure, back, it's looking like, around six months. The thing is, the data goes back years and from a variety of sources. But he didn't start to collect it here until about that six months ago. A lot of high-level stuff. I probably don't have the security clearance to skim, but, hey, just doing my job. But here's what's really the frost on the ice."

"He's running an auction."

"Shit." Onscreen, McNab's face fell. "Why have I worked my personal motherboard to the bone? But you only got it partly right. *She's* running the auction, which is a hell of a trick, seeing she's dead."

"Ah." Roarke sat back as it fell into place for him. "Yes, that's clever."

"It's running out of a remote location. It bounces all over hell and back, scrambling the signal. I wouldn't've found the source if I wasn't right at ground zero. And, well, gotta be on the straight, if he hadn't left the

125

bread crumbs. Upper East Side address. Swank. When I run it, I get it's owned by Dolores Gregory. That's one of Buckley's aliases."

"So it is. That's good data. Now you'd better call your lieutenant."

TEN

Using her master, Eve opened the locks and shut down the security on the Upper East Side apartment. "That was too easy," she told Peabody. "Just like the Plutz town house. We go in hot."

She drew her weapon, went through the door for a first sweep.

Quiet, she thought as she worked right and Peabody left. A lot of expensive space filled with expensive things. The wall of windows led to a terrace lofty enough to provide a river view. Inside, rich fabrics showcased gleaming wood, and art dominated the walls. The same held true in the master bedroom where the closet held a forest of clothes.

"Some digs," Peabody commented. "I think some of those paintings are originals. I guess assassins rate a high pay grade."

"It's the opposite of Draski. She lived high, he lived low. Easy to underestimate somebody who lives the quiet life."

"Easy to get cocky," Peabody added, "when you live the high."

"Yeah, it is." Eve gestured to the security pad on the second bedroom doorway. It blinked an open green.

"Boy, that was careless of her."

"Not her. He laid those bread crumbs, he lowered the security. We're exactly where he wants us to be." She pushed open the door, swept it, then holstered her weapon.

The room was cold, nearly frigid. A way to keep the body as fresh as possible, she thought as she studied Dana Buckley. He'd arranged the bloody shell of her in a chair angled to face a framed photo of his wife and daughter, and the single rose he'd placed by it.

"Well." Peabody hissed out a breath. "She's not lost anymore."

"Call it in. You'd better go get the field kits."

While she waited, Eve studied the room. Her lair, she thought. She expected they'd find the equipment unregistered, and much of the data on it illegally hacked. Not so different from her killer's, she thought, right down to the photograph.

On the wall screen the current status of the bidding was displayed. Up to four-point-four billion, she mused, with several hours yet to go.

He hadn't taken the body for proof. Not for a trophy, and only in part to gain that time. In the end he'd brought it here so while her greed ran behind her back she would stare sightlessly at the innocents she'd killed.

He'd taken the body, she thought, to pay homage to his family.

"We've got an e-team and sweepers on the way." Peabody opened a field kit, passed Eve the Seal It.

Eve nodded and thought they'd find nothing he hadn't wanted them to find. "I want all the data found copied. We'll have to turn it over to whatever agency the commander orders, but we'll have backup." She turned to her partner. "I think we've just spearheaded a breakdown on a whole bunch of really bad guys. The sort of thing that leaks to the media."

"I don't know whether to be happy or scared."

"Be satisfied. Now let's do the job and deal with her. Record on."

Roarke sat back, absorbing the data he'd just uncovered. Odd, he thought, the world was a very odd and ironically small place.

And the people in it were never completely predictable. He saved and copied the data, slipped the copy into his pocket.

He walked to the house monitor. "Where is Summerset?"

Summerset is in the parlor, main level.

"All right then, a fine place for a chat."

As he came downstairs he heard voices, and the roll of Summerset's amused laughter. It wasn't unprecedented for Summerset to have company in the house, but it certainly wasn't usual.

Curious, he stepped in. Then stopped and shook his head. "Aye, unpredictable."

"Roarke, I'm glad you've come down. I didn't want to disturb you, but I'm happy to introduce you to an old friend. Ivan Draski."

As the man rose, Roarke crossed the room to shake hands with his wife's current quarry.

"Ivan and I worked together in very dark times. He was hardly more than a boy, but made himself indispensable. We haven't seen each other in years, so we've been catching up on old times, and new."

"Really?" Roarke slid his hands into his pocket where the disc bumped up against the gray button he carried for luck, and for love. "How new?"

"We haven't quite caught up to the present." Ivan smiled a little. "I thought that should wait until your wife comes home. I believe she'll have an interest."

"I'll fetch more cups for coffee." Summerset laid a hand briefly on Ivan's shoulder before leaving the room.

"Are you armed?" Roarke asked.

"No." Ivan lifted his arms, inviting a search. "I'm not here to bring harm to anyone."

"Have a seat then, and maybe you should bring Summerset and myself up-to-date."

Ivan sat, and an instant later Galahad jumped into his lap. "He's a nice cat."

"We like him."

"I don't keep pets," Ivan continued as he stroked Galahad's length. "I couldn't handle the idea of having a living thing depending on me again. And droids, well, it's not the same, is it? I don't want to bring trouble into your home, or cause my old friend distress. If it had been anyone but your wife involved in this, I believe I would be somewhere else."

"Why my wife?"

"I'd like to tell her," Ivan said as Summerset came back.

"The lieutenant's come through the gate." He set the cup down to pour.

"This should be interesting," Roarke murmured. He waved off the coffee Summerset offered, deciding he might need both hands.

Eve walked into the house and frowned. It was rare not to find Summerset lurking in the foyer with the cat at his heels. She heard the rattle of china from the parlor, hesitated at the base of the stairs.

Roarke came to the doorway and said her name.

"Good, you're here. We need to talk. The situation's changed."

"Oh, it has, yes."

"We might as well have this out before I —" She broke off at the parlor doorway when she spotted the man she hunted sitting cozily in a chair with her cat on his lap. She drew her weapon. "Son of a bitch."

"Have you lost your mind!" Summerset exploded as she stormed across the room.

"Get out of the way or I'll stun you first."

He stood his ground while shock and fury radiated from him. "I won't have a guest, and a dear friend, threatened in our home."

"Friend?" She flicked a glance toward Roarke, a heated one.

"Don't waste your glares on me. I just got here myself." But he touched a hand to her arm. "You don't need that."

"My prime suspect is sitting in my house, petting my cat, and you're all having coffee? Move aside," she said coldly to Summerset, "or I swear to God —"

Ivan spoke in a language she didn't understand. Summerset turned sharply, stared. His answer was just as unintelligible, and with a tone of incredulity.

"I'm sorry, that's rude." Ivan kept his hands in plain sight. "I've just told my friend that I've killed a woman. He didn't know. I hope there's no trouble for him over this. I hope I can explain. Will you let me explain? Here, in an easy way, with a friend. After, I'll go with you if that's your decision."

Eve skirted around Summerset. She lowered her weapon, but kept it drawn. "What are you doing here?"

"Waiting for you."

"For me?"

"I feel you need an explanation. You need information. I won't try to harm you, any of you. This man?" He gestured to Summerset. "I owe him my life. What belongs to him is sacred to me."

"Brandy, I think." Roarke handed Summerset a snifter he'd filled. "Instead of coffee." And gave another to Ivan.

"Thank you. You're very kind. I killed the

woman calling herself Dana Buckley. You know this already, and, I think, some of the how. I read a great deal about you in the night, Lieutenant. You're smart and clever, good at your work. But the why matters, it must, when it's life and death. You know this," he said, searching her face. "I think you believe this."

"She killed your wife and daughter."

His eyes widened in surprise. "You work quickly. They were beautiful and innocent. I didn't protect them. I loved my work in my own homeland." He glanced at Summerset. "The purpose, the challenge, the deep belief in making a difference."

"You were — are — a scientist," Eve interrupted. "I read your file."

"Then you're very good indeed. Did you find the rest?"

"Yes. Just shortly ago," Roarke answered. "I'm very sorry. Homeland wanted to recruit him," he told Eve, "possibly use him as a mole or simply bring him over."

"I was happy where I was. I believed in what I was doing."

"They considered various options," Roarke continued. "Abducting him, torture, abducting his child, discrediting him. The decision was, as time was of some essence, to strip him of his ties, and offer him not only asylum but revenge."

"They sent that woman to murder my wife, my child, to make it seem like my own people had ordered it. They showed me documentation, gave me the name of the assassins, the orders to terminate me and my family. I should have been home, you see, but I had car trouble that delayed me. They'd rigged it, of course, but I believed them. I of all people should have known how these things can be faked, but I was grieving, I was wild with grief, and I believed. I betrayed good men and women because I believed the lie and was happy to take my pound of flesh. And I became one of them. Everything I've done for these twenty years has been on the blood of my wife and child. They killed them to use me."

"Why now?" Eve demanded. "Why execute her now, and with such theatrics?"

"Six months ago I found the file. I was searching for some old data, and found it. The man who'd ordered the murders is long dead, so perhaps there was carelessness. Or perhaps someone wanted me to find it. It's a slippery world we live in."

He stroked the cat methodically. "I thought of many ways to kill her." He sighed. "I've been one for the laboratory for a very long time, but I began to train. My body, with weapons. I trained every day, like the old days," he said with a smile for Summerset. "I had purpose again. I found my way with Lost Time. So apt, isn't it? All the time I'd lost. Time she'd cost me, had stolen from my wife, my baby."

"I'm sorry, Ivan." Summerset laid a comforting hand on his friend's arm. "I know what it is to lose a child."

"She was so bright, the light . . . the proof of light after all those dark times. And this woman snuffed her out, for money. If you've read her files, you know what she was."

He paused, sipped brandy, settled himself again. "I formed the plan. I was always good at tactics and strategy, you remember."

"Yes, I remember," Summerset concurred.

"I had to move quickly, to leak the data to her, to paint the picture that I was dissatisfied with my position, my pay, and might be willing to bargain for better."

"You let her make the approach, let her pick the time and the place so she believed she had the advantage."

Now he smiled at Eve. "She wasn't as smart as you. Once, perhaps, but she was arrogant and greedy. She never intended to pay me for the device and the files I'd stolen. She would kill me, have the device and all the records on it, while others

136

competed. She had no allegiance, you see, to any person, agency, any cause. She liked to kill. It's in her psych file."

Eve nodded. "I've read it."

Again his eyes widened before he glanced toward Roarke. "I think you may be better even than the rumors. How I'd enjoy talking with you."

"I've thought the same."

"In my business there's no law, as in yours," Ivan said to Eve. "No police, so to speak, where I could go and say this woman murdered my family. She was paid to do so. It's . . . business, so there's no punishment, no justice. I planned, I researched and I accessed her computers. I'm very good at my work, too. I knew before she arranged the meet what she intended. To take the money, disable or kill me, then —" He gestured to the case beside his chair. "May I?"

"No. She was carrying this," Eve said as she rose to retrieve the case, "when she got on the ferry."

"It's a bomb. Disabled," he said quickly. "It's configured inside the computer. It's rather small, but powerful. It would have done considerable damage to that section of the ferry. There were so many people there. Children. Their lives meant nothing to her. They would be a distraction."

"Like fireworks?"

"Harmless." He smiled again.

"Let me have that." Roarke glanced at Summerset, got a nod, as he took the case from Eve. And opened it.

"Wait. Jesus!"

"Disabled," he assured Eve after a glance. "I've seen this system before.

"You know, I think how we came to meet. The location was her choice," Ivan added. "She thought of me as old, harmless, someone who creates gadgets, we'll say, rather than one who would use them. But old skills can come back."

"Six months to refine your skills," Eve said, "and set the trap."

"Maybe there was a cold madness in the planning, in my dedication to it. Even so, I don't regret. I thought to do it quickly. Slit her throat. Put her in the hamper. I'd use the device to get away."

"How?" Eve demanded. "How did you get off the damn ferry?"

"Oh. I had with me a motorized inflatable." He shifted to Roarke as he spoke now, and his face became animated. "It's much smaller than anything used, as yet, in the military or private sectors. Inactivated, it's the size of a toiletry kit you might use for travel. And the motor itself —"

"Okay." Eve cut him off. "I get it."

"Yes, well." Ivan drew in a long breath. "I had thought I'd do what I'd set out to do quickly, then I'd disappear. But I . . . I can't even remember, not clearly, after I looked in her eyes, saw her shock, saw her death. I can't remember. I think I will someday, and it will be very hard."

Tears glinted in his eyes, and his hand trembled slightly as he drank more brandy. "But I looked down at what I'd done. So much blood. The way I'd found my wife and daughter, in so much blood. There was a stunner on the floor. She must have tried to stop me, I'm not sure. I picked it up. Then the woman came in."

"You didn't kill her when you had the chance."

He shot Eve a shocked stare. "No. No, of course not. She'd done nothing. Still, I couldn't let her just . . . It happened so quickly. I used the weapon on her, and she fell. I remember thinking, this is very unfortunate, a very unfortunate turn of events. In the old days, you thought on your feet or died. Or someone else did."

"You used the device on her when she came around, and took her with you," Eve supplied.

"Yes. I told her to hide. You can influence

people when they're under. She was to hide until she heard the alarm. I set it on her wrist unit. Then she was to go back where she came from. She wouldn't remember. She looked so frightened when she came in and saw what I'd done. I didn't want her to remember. I saw her with her children when we boarded. A lovely family. I hope she's all right."

"She's fine. Why the fireworks?"

"A good distraction. You'd think I used them to get away, and I'd already be away. And my little girl loved fireworks. You know the rest, I think. You've hacked into my system at home, and into hers. You have a very good e-team."

"Why did you come here?" Eve asked. "You could be thousands of miles away."

"To see an old friend." He glanced at Summerset. "Because you were involved."

"What difference does it make who led the investigation?"

"All," he said simply. "It was a kind of sign, a connection I couldn't ignore." He looked at Eve then with both understanding and sorrow. "I know what they did to you. They ignored the cries of a child being brutalized. They killed my child, who must have cried out for me in fear and pain. The same man ordered both. The slaughter of my family, and some years before the sacrifice of a child's body and mind."

He sighed when Eve said nothing. "I couldn't ignore that. It seemed too important. You and Mylia would be of an age now, had she lived. You lived, and you're part of the family of my old friend. How could I ignore that?"

"How did you come by that information?" Eve asked, her voice flat.

"I . . . accessed it when you married. Because of my friend. I couldn't contact you," he said to Summerset. "It might cause you trouble, but I wanted to know your family. So I looked, and I found. I'm sorry for what was done to you. He's dead, the one who ordered the listening post to do nothing to interfere. Years ago," Ivan added. "I don't know if that comforts you. It comforts me because I believe I would have killed him, killed again if he wasn't dead."

"It doesn't matter. It's done."

He nodded. "So is this. There are dirty pockets in the well of the organization. She, this woman, was one of the things that crawled around inside those pockets. But still, I took her life, and it doesn't, as I thought it would, balance the scales. Nothing can. These people shaped our lives, pieces of our lives, without giving us a

141

choice. They took something deeply personal from us. So, when I learned it was you looking for me, I had to come. If I may?"

He held up two fingers, pointed them at his jacket pocket. At her nod, he reached in carefully and slid out what looked like an oversized 'link.

"It's only the casing," he said when both Eve and Roarke lunged for it. "I dismantled and destroyed the rest. And all the data pertaining to it."

Roarke let out a breath. "Well, bugger it."

Ivan laughed, then blinked in surprise at the sound. "It needed to be done, though I admit it was difficult. So much work." He sighed over it. "If I'm arrested, they'll come for me. Or others like them will come. I have knowledge and skill. Your law, your rules, even your diligence won't stop them. I don't say this to save myself," he said gently. "But because I know they'll find a way to make me use my knowledge and skill for them."

"He saved lives, innocent lives, on that ferry," Summerset said. "He's certainly saved others, perhaps scores of others, by destroying that thing."

"That's not why I went there. I went to kill. The lieutenant knows that. The rest is circumstance. I'm content to leave this in her hands. Content to face justice."

"Justice?" Summerset snarled at the word. "How is this justice?" He rose, rounded on Eve. "How can you even consider —"

"Shut it down. Don't," she added to Roarke before he could speak. She paced away to stand at the window and wait for the war inside her to claim a victor.

"I saw her files, as I'm sure you wanted me to when we found her body. She kept reports and photos of her kills like a scrapbook. She's what I work against every day. So is what you did on that ferry."

"Yes," Ivan said quietly. "I know."

"They will come for you, and whatever obstacles I put in their way so you can face justice won't be enough to stop them. I consider this matter out of my jurisdiction, and will certainly be told the same when I contact HSO to report what I've learned up to the time I walked into this house."

She turned back, spoke briskly. "This is an internal HSO matter, involving one of their people and a freelance assassin they have previously employed. It's possible this is a matter of national security, and I'd be derelict in my duty if I didn't report what my investigation has turned up. I'm going to go up to my office, inform my com-

mander of my findings and follow his direc-
tive. You'd better say goodbye to your
friend," she told Summerset.

She turned to Ivan, his pleasant face and
mild eyes. "Disappear. You've probably got
an hour, two at the outside, to get lost.
Don't come back here."

"Lieutenant," Ivan began, but she turned
her back and walked out of the room.

EPILOGUE

Roarke found her in her office, pacing like a caged cat. "Eve."

"I don't want any damn coffee. I want a damn drink."

"I'll get us both one." He touched the wall panel and chose a bottle of wine from inside. "He was telling the truth. I got deep enough to find considerable data on him, on his work prior to Homeland, on the decision to kill his family and plant evidence that led to his own organization."

He drew the disc from his pocket. "I made you a copy." He handed her the wine, set the disc on her desk. "And he was telling the truth when he said they, or others like them, would come for him. He would have self-terminated before he worked for anyone like them again."

"I know that. I saw that."

"I know a decision like this is difficult for you. Painfully. Just as you know I stand across the line so it wouldn't be difficult for me. I'm sorry."

"It shouldn't be for me to decide. It's not my place, it's not my job. It's why there's a system, and mostly the system works."

"This isn't your system, Eve. These things have their own laws, their own system, and too many of those pockets inside them don't quibble about letting a child be tortured, don't lose sleep over ordering the death of a child to reach the goal of the moment."

She took a long sip. "I can justify it. I can justify what I just did because I know that's true. It's not my system. I can justify it by knowing if Buckley had gotten the upper hand yesterday, Carolee Grogan would be dead, and that kid waiting for his mother outside the door would be blown to pieces along with dozens of others. I can justify it knowing if I arrested him, I would be killing him."

She picked up the disc from her desk, and remembering what he'd once done for her, snapped it in two. "Don't let him come here again."

He shook his head, then framed her face and kissed her. "It takes more than skill and duty to make a good cop, to my way of thinking. It takes an unfailing sense of right and wrong."

"It's a hell of a lot easier when they don't overlap. I have to get my report together and contact the commander. And for God's sake, get that boomer out of the house. I don't care if it is diffused."

"I'll take care of it."

Alone, she sat down to organize her notes into a cohesive report. She glanced over when the cat padded in, with Summerset behind him.

"Working," she said briefly, then frowned when he set a plate with an enormous chocolate chip cookie on her desk. "What's this?"

"A cookie, as any fool could see. It'll spoil your dinner, but . . ." He shrugged, started out. He paused at the door without turning around. "He was a hero at a time when the world desperately needed them. He would be dead before the night was over if you'd taken him in. I want you to know that. To know you saved a life today."

She sat back, staring at the empty doorway, when he'd left her. Then she scanned her notes, the report on screen, the photographs of the dead. They were the lost, weren't they? All those lives taken. Maybe, in a way that nudged up against that line between right and wrong, she was standing for the lost.

She had to hope so.

Breaking off a hunk of cookie, she got back to work.

■ ■ ■ ■

THE DOG DAYS OF
LAURIE SUMMER
PATRICIA GAFFNEY

■ ■ ■ ■

For Jolene,
who's always allowed
on the furniture

BEFORE

I have a strange story to tell.

Too bad there's no one to tell it to. No real way to tell it, and by now, no compelling reason to, either. Still. I feel the need to get it off my chest. Already it's beginning to blur at the edges, fray in my mind like a dream in the morning. If I'm going to tell it at all, I'd better tell it quickly.

That's what I'll do, then: I'll tell the story to myself.

Where to begin? With my childhood? When I married Sam and we had Benny? When I landed the broker job at Shanahan & Lewis? But those were all normal stages, unremarkable. They followed acceptable patterns; they were *to be expected.*

Better to begin when things started to go off track. Faster, more interesting. Well, that's easy — that would be the day I drowned. The first time.

■ ■ ■ ■

Such a nice day, too. Early June, late afternoon, our first full weekend at Sam's cabin on the river. Our cabin, but I thought of it as Sam's — he was the one who'd found it, dreamed of restoring it, and generally yearned for it, until I surprised him on his thirty-eighth birthday and bought it for him. Us. It needed an enormous amount of work, but it was habitable, barely, and even though it wasn't my idea of paradise, I had to admit it did look charming that afternoon, with the windows blazing orange, the low sun casting tree shadows on the rough planks and the dirty white chinking. We were watching it from aluminum lawn chairs in the fast-moving shallows of the Shenandoah, Benny sprawled across my lap, half asleep after the long day. "To you," I toasted Sam with a last sip of wine. "To your project for the next ten or twenty years."

"To *us*," Sam toasted back with his beer, and I hoped that didn't mean he thought *I* was going to help with the renovation. I liked the idea of him and Benny spending weekends here being handymen together while Mom stayed in town and did her job. Which was to bring home the bacon.

Sam had looked handsome the night before in his magic-act tuxedo, but he looked even better now in faded cutoffs and a holey tee. Mmm, all that tan skin and soft blond hair. I was looking forward to later, after we put Benny to bed. Our first time in the new cabin.

"But mostly to you, Laurie," he said, "for being brilliant."

"Thank you," I said with mock modesty. Mock, yes. Last night I'd received the Shanahan & Lewis Mega Deal Maker of the Year award, and this morning Ronnie Lewis had promoted me to senior portfolio manager. You could say I was riding high. You could say I was *proud* of myself — except, of course, pride goeth before a fall, and what happened next just makes that too ridiculously literal.

Full of myself, then. I was pret-ty damn full of myself.

"Looks like somebody's ready for bed."

I thought Sam meant me and he'd been reading my mind, a skill he only *pretends* to have in his magic act. But then Benny squirmed on my lap and muttered that he wasn't sleepy. "Mom," he said clearly, out of the blue, "can we get a dog?"

Does that mean anything? Or my refusal — does that mean anything? I said, "No, honey, we can't," without hesitation, because it was completely out of the question. No way could we get a dog; we were all too busy, and besides, I had allergies.

But now I wonder. It was the last thing my sweet, five-year-old son asked me.

Then again, the last thing Sam asked me was to bring in my chair, and I didn't come back as a chaise longue.

My cell phone rang.

"Don't answer."

I checked the screen. "I have to. It's Ronnie."

Sam made a face, one I'd seen (and ignored) many times before, and started to get up, stretching his long arms over his head, splashing his bare feet in the water. "Okay, pal," he told Benny, and they reached for each other. He stuck his folded chair under one arm, hitched Benny onto his hip with the other. "What's this? You're *drinking* now?" With both arms full, somehow he'd plucked his empty beer can from behind Benny's ear.

And Benny snickered obligingly, always glad to be the dupe. Daddy's best audience.

"Hi, Ron," I said at the same time Sam said to me, for a joke, "Don't forget your chair." I smiled, watching him pick his way through the rippling, ankle-deep river toward shore. Then Ron mentioned the new Potomac Aerie development and I stopped watching. That was my last look at my family: Sam setting Benny down on terra firma and letting him run ahead, up the weedy path to the cabin. I got caught up in a preliminary design meeting coming up, the feasibility study, finance and development applications.

Something else I wish I could go back and redo.

Ron's a talker; our conversation went on for a good fifteen minutes. More or less — it's about now that things begin to blur. I remember deciding not to bother putting on my water sandals to make the twenty-yard trek to the riverbank. I remember standing up and folding my chair. I must've had my sandals, empty wineglass, and cell phone in one hand, chair in the other. Why didn't I put the phone in my pocket? My lifeline, my keystone, my — words fail me. The beating heart of my professional life. Why didn't I put it in my pocket?

I didn't, and it flipped out of my hand like a live fish.

I guess I lunged for it. Don't remember, but that's what I would have done. I probably threw everything else up in the air first, shoes, chair, glass. Who knows? If I'd been carrying Benny, I might've thrown *him* up in the air, too.

Okay, no.

I have one last tactile memory, quite vivid and distinct: the instant-long but somehow-forever feel of my foot sliding across a slick, slimy rock. After that, zero.

DURING

For how long? Two months, I've heard since, but that's not right. It was zero, literally *nothing,* for a time, but then — a week later? three weeks? five? — rips began to show in the matte black curtain, like the difference between a thick blindfold and a thin one. No, that's not right, either, because the first sense I got back was *hearing,* not seeing. So — the difference between a set of Bose headphones and Benny's flannel earmuffs.

Sound instead of silence. Such a blessing, like being saved. Word fragments at first. You know how, when you close your book, turn out the light, and prepare to go to sleep, bits of the author's syntax and rhythm float around in your mind for a while before you drop off? But if you ever wake up enough to concentrate on one of the bits you're remembering, it turns out to be nonsense? Like that.

Bits of music, too, jumbled, unrecognizable, like when you spin a radio dial too fast. And voices. Strangers', and then, mercifully, Sam's. That was the moment I began to heal. Or hope, which is the same thing. I didn't always know what he was saying, especially in the beginning when he might as well have been speaking Italian, but it didn't matter. Just his voice. A rope to the drowning woman.

Touch came next. The unutterable comfort of it. Skin on sentient skin, and it didn't matter whose then, just the nearly unbearable relief of not being alone anymore. To the nurses and aides and rehab people it must've felt like massaging a corpse, but I couldn't get enough bending, stroking, manipulating. I even liked it when they put drops in my eyes. Sam used to rub lotion into my hands and I'd drift off into something like nirvana . . .

Sight was last. "She can open her eyes," somebody marveled, and I remember feeling a surge of childlike pride, like a toddler praised for uttering her first complete sentence. It was narrow sight, just the thing I was looking at, everything else wavy as old glass.

The problem was, nobody knew any of this but me. And not that I was chugging along on all cylinders — it wasn't like in a movie when some guy gets injected with a drug that paralyzes his body but his brain still works fine. My brain was spongy, plagued with craters and holes, like the moon. But I progressed, is the point, and no one knew it except me. I couldn't tell them. The frustration! In hospitals they're big on asking you to rate your pain on a scale of one to ten. If they'd asked me to rate my loneliness, I'd have said a hundred and fifty.

Then came the day when I thought I might break through, finally jab a big enough hole in the veil to stick my head through and yell, "Look! It's me!"

That didn't happen, but something else did. The sort of thing that, shall we say, inspires incredulity. Ha-ha! I love understatement. Also the sort of thing that could get one returned to Neurology for evaluation if one were to reveal it to just anybody.

Another reason not to tell this story to anyone but myself.

"We'll have to bring her back inside now. BP's up. A little too much stimulation, I'm afraid."

God, how I hated those words. They meant my family was about to leave me.

The worst thing about being in a coma isn't the inability to speak, move, eat, make yourself understood — none of that. It's being left alone.

Benny was fidgeting at the foot of my geri-bed — a soft reclining chair I loved, because now they could wheel me outside for a few minutes on nice days, all my tubes and lines still attached to the beeping machines inside. Benny was out of my line of sight down there, but occasionally some part of his dear, jerky body would bump against my blanketed legs, and each time the careless touch would fill me with a warm, melting love. "She's skinny" was all he'd had to say to me today, and "Her hair's too long." When the nurse spoke, he jumped off the end of the chair like a racer who'd just been waiting for the starter gun. I could feel his heart lighten. I could feel mine sink.

"Let me do that." Sam's voice. A pull on the chair, and the precious blue sky began to swivel out of sight. A bump as we crossed the threshold, and there we were, back in the room, the dreaded room. My gray prison.

"She seemed better today." Sam had that desperate, hope-against-hope animation in his voice he used in front of Benny. I hated it. "I think there's been real progress."

The nurse that day was Hettie, my favorite. Very gentle hands, and she never over-enunciated like some of them, as if their patients were not only comatose but also idiots. "Well, no actual change, though, not on the test scale. But no, I know what you mean, she was pretty alert today," Hettie added quickly, kindly. "Tracking movements with her eyes sometimes —"

"She looked right *into* my eyes." My husband loomed over me, moving his head until we were gaze to gaze. He looked so tired, his eyes so sad. *Don't go,* I begged him. *Stay with me.* "She can't be completely unconscious if she can open her eyes. Right?"

"There are so many degrees of consciousness," Hettie started saying, and something about metabolic versus anatomic comas, every case is different, you have to balance hope with practicality — I gave up trying to follow. Too hard. I was a mummy, encased in gauze. If I could get out one feral grunt, raise one scary, wrapped arm . . . but everything was so exhausting. I only had the strength to look back into Sam's eyes.

He put his cheek next to mine. *Oh. Oh.* The scent of him. He whispered that he loved me. Was I crying? If I could cry — *he'd know.* I stared hard, hard, at the lock of his hair that tickled my face, concentrating, wide-eyed.

Dry-eyed.

"See ya, babe," he murmured. "Don't be scared. Everything's okay. See you soon, sweetheart."

I had no sense of time. *Soon.* It was the same to me as *later.* Or *never.*

"Benny? Come say bye to your mom. Ben? Come on, guy. Hey, Benny — !"

Sam disappeared.

If I couldn't cry now, I never would. What's the point of trying to get well if your son is afraid of you? You might as well be dead. As dead as I must look to Benny in this stupid chair, these stupid pipes and lines filling and draining me, keeping me in this ugly gray twilight jail I couldn't break free of, couldn't penetrate, couldn't smash my way out of —

"There you go, buddy. Give Mommy a kiss."

Oh, Sam, don't make him. He had his arms around Benny's waist, holding him up, pressing him toward me. Poor Benny! His face looked blotchy with distress. He squeezed his eyes shut.

"It's okay, it's just Mom. Come on, pal."

Don't, Sam. Oh, but I wanted it, too. If Benny would look at me, really *look,* I believed I could make it happen — the miracle. *Look, darling. It's Mommy. Please, honey, open your eyes.* He *had* to see me; otherwise I would truly be nothing. I would disappear. *Benny, look at me, see me! Open your eyes!*

That's when it happened.

What happened? At first, a period of pure nothing. So pure, if my brain had been working, I'd have thought I had disappeared. But there wasn't any "me" anymore, no one to think thoughts. No time, no space, and not even darkness this time. Sound, maybe, a low-pitched hum, a comforting whir or drone . . . but then again, maybe not. That would presuppose someone had ears to hear it, and I'm saying I was not there. Laurie Summer: gone.

"Daddy, is she dead? Please don't die. Is she dead?"

Benny! His beautiful, wide-open brown eyes were looking into mine. "I'm not dead," I tried to tell him, but nothing came out but a sort of . . . yip. But I could move my legs! It hurt, but they moved, and they . . . they . . .

They were covered with hair?

"Careful, don't touch her. She's hurt, she

might bite you."

I might what? Crouched over me, Sam had a pitying but distracted look on his face. This was not how I had pictured our miraculous reunion.

"We have to take her to the doctor, Daddy. We have to fix her up."

God, not more doctors. Where were we? My ears ached; everything was so *loud*. And the smell was amazing. Smells, rather, millions of them, all strong and incredibly interesting. Cars were whipping by — that's what was making all the noise. Why were we outside, in the street? A familiar-looking street, too. Weren't we on Old Georgetown Road? In Bethesda?

"Come on, buddy, back in the car. It's dangerous out here."

Sam and Benny got up and left me in the road.

A lot of bad things had happened to me lately, very bad things, but I can say without hesitation that that was the worst.

Then Sam came back. Happiness! Joy! He was carrying the smelly flannel blanket we kept in the back of the car to set plants on, or wet bathing suits, anything messy or unsavory, to protect the upholstery.

He wrapped me in the blanket and lifted

me up with a grunt and put me in the back-seat.

I had an inkling now, a sense, like glimpsing something from the corner of your eye that reveals everything but is too outlandish to credit. Maybe I should've figured it out sooner — the evidence was pretty much everywhere — but let's not forget I wasn't in my right mind. I had been in a near-drowning-induced coma for eight weeks. Then, too, if this was a cross-species metamorphosis, it made sense that my normally sharp, analytical mind was already being blunted by something softer and more accepting. I'm saying my retriever instincts were kicking in.

Sam started the car and pulled out into traffic. Benny, buckled up in front, craned around to look at me. His mop of chestnut curls needed cutting. I wanted to lick him all over his freckled face. Here we were, all together again. *The family.* "Sam, Benny, Sam, Benny!" I said, overwhelmed with the wonder of it. It came out "Arr! Urra! Arr! Urra!"

Another clue.

The car smelled wonderful, like Sam and Benny multiplied by a hundred. And lots of other things, especially McDonald's, that fabulous greasy-hamburger smell.

The ride was short. As soon as Sam parked, Benny unbuckled himself, shoved open the car door, and ran off. "Wait —" Sam called, halfhearted. He sighed, then hauled me out very gently and carried me toward a low brick building. Inside, the predominant smell was panic.

Benny was already jumping up and down in front of a counter, yelling, "We hit a dog! We hit a dog!"

Dog.

I was a dog.

As I said, the clues were abundant, but it wasn't until Benny said the actual word that the truth hit. I started to shake.

Nothing like a vet's exam on a cold metal table to knock the nonsense out of you. I credit it with shortening considerably what would otherwise have been a long and tedious period of *No, it's impossible! How can this be? I don't believe it! Is this a dream?* Et cetera, et cetera. I'm not saying I accepted what seemed to have happened to me in half an hour. But there's just something about having your temperature taken rectally that really *wakes you up* to reality.

Blood was drawn. X-rays were taken. I was poked, prodded, listened to, felt, and, in the end, the doctor, who smelled like tick poison, said what I could only partially agree with.

"It's a miracle."

"Nothing wrong with her?" Sam asked.

"Nothing serious. Bruises, mostly, and the scrapes you can see. But no broken bones or internal injuries, and that's pretty amazing if you were going as fast as you say."

"Can we keep her?"

"I was going the speed limit."

"And to hit her head-on and throw her as far as you did — that's just amazing."

"Can we keep her?"

"She must belong to somebody," Sam said. "What kind of dog is she?"

"No collar," said the vet, "no ID. Hmm . . . some sort of Lab-golden mix is my guess. And maybe something else smaller — she only weighs about sixty pounds. I'd say she's four or five years old."

This was helpful. All I'd seen of myself so far was my feet, basically. Good to know what I was. A big, middle-aged mutt.

"So can we keep her?"

"She must belong to someone," Sam tried again. "I'm sure somebody's —"

"No, Daddy, they'll put her in the pound, then they'll put her to sleep! They'll kill her!"

That's right. I read a story to Benny last spring about a dog with no collar who gets taken to the pound and is almost euthanized before a little boy comes in and saves him. You tell him, baby.

"They won't kill her," Sam said, putting his hand on top of Benny's head. "Um, what does happen here, Doctor? Do you put up flyers or something, keep the dog until she's claimed —"

"We don't have the facilities for that, unfortunately. No, she'll go to the humane rescue and they'll keep her there. As long as they can."

"Then they'll kill her!" Benny wriggled away from Sam and ran to me. I was still on the metal table — he had to stand on tiptoes to put his arms around my neck. *"Please* can we keep her? *Please?"*

"Benny, you know your mother never wanted . . ." Sam trailed off, looking pained.

Benny took the words out of my mouth. "But Dad — she's not *here."*

I don't know why I was worried. My heart was pounding, I was trembling uncontrollably, I had more saliva in my mouth than I could swallow. "The pound" was no abstract concept; I knew what would probably happen to me there. But that wasn't what I was afraid of. Abandonment was.

It's me, Sam! It's Laurie!

Everything hurt — miracle or not, get

170

thrown twenty feet in the air by a car, believe me, everything hurts — but when Benny let go of my neck, I gathered all four slipping, sliding paws under me and made a lunge for Sam.

Who has good reflexes. He stepped aside in shock.

The vet's were even better, luckily. He caught me — otherwise I'd have flown into the wall. "Whoa," he said without surprise, and calmly set me on the floor. "Looks like this one really wants to go home with you."

Sam never had a chance, I see now, but at the time it felt like touch and go. I had sense enough to hold still, not jump on him again, and let Benny wind his arms around me. What we must have looked like, cheek to cheek, four brown eyes yearning up at him. "Pleeeease, Daddy?" Beelzebub could not have resisted that plea. I echoed it with a warbly, "Arroooo?"

The vet laughed.

Sam put his hands on top of his head. "All right, all right, all right. But she's going to have to be spayed."

Home!

My house, oh, my house. I couldn't get enough of it. My muscles still ached, but I ran into every room; I sniffed everything; I peed in the foyer —

My God!

Nobody saw. Oh, thank goodness, they didn't see, and on the dark part of the Oriental it didn't even show. It was just a little pee, anyway, only a drop, really. From the excitement.

Behave, I thought, letting Benny catch me. We wrestled on the rug in the living room — "Gently," Sam kept saying — and it was pure bliss, utter contentment. As myself, I'd have been in a lot of pain from the accident, but as a dog I couldn't stay focused on my body long enough to care. There wasn't a thought in my head. Whenever Benny laughed, I wagged my tail — or rather, my tail wagged, a completely involuntary response, like crying when somebody else cries. We lay on our backs, panting and grinning up at Sam, whose cautious look slowly faded and turned into a smile.

He's making sure I'm not dangerous, I realized. *Making sure I won't hurt Benny.* Good; I'd do the same. I turned my head and licked Benny's face very gently, for Sam's benefit. *Play with us!* I thought, but he was already heading for the kitchen, mumbling about dinner.

"Hey, dog. Hey, girl. You like it here, don't you?" Benny patted me on top of the head, *pat pat pat,* making me blink. I yawned in agreement. "Want to see my room?"

We ran upstairs.

Fabulous room, I thought, and then, *Good Lord, where is the cleaning lady?* But so many things to smell and taste and roll around in, toys and clothes and food, a smorgasbord for the senses.

Except sight. Strangest thing, but it was like seeing sepia in blue instead of brown. I couldn't see red, and everything was muted, like the loveliest twilight. Except *blue.* With flashes of yellow. Hard to describe, but I liked it. I found it very . . . calming.

Benny showed me his dinosaur floor puzzle and his new Batmobile that lit up, made sounds, and shot out a weapon. He showed me all his dump trucks and bulldozers. I heard about his best friend, Mo, his second-best friend, Jenny; first grade was starting soon; Dad built him the coolest playhouse in the backyard; wait'll I saw it. He had a new bike; he could write the whole alphabet and count to "a billion." He had two loose teeth. "And my dad can throw his voice." Music to my ears, every word, even when my attention wandered. "And my mom's in the hospital" grabbed it back.

I worked my nose out of an old tennis shoe and joined Benny on top of the unmade bed.

"She fell in the river and hurt her head and she couldn't breathe. She didn't drown but now she's got a coma. It's like sleeping a really long, long time and not waking up."

I nudged him with my head until it was under his arm. We sat like that awhile.

"Dad says she'll wake up. He promised. We do prayers at night. We go look at her. He pretends like she can hear and reads stuff to her." He flopped down on his back. "She can't move or anything."

He stretched his arms up and played with his fingers. Dear, stubby, dirty, little-boy fingers. "She worked a lot, but we used to ride bikes. And run and stuff. We played games. She talked a lot. Spaghetti!" He bolted up and scrambled off the bed.

I'd been smelling it, too. "He makes it all the time," Benny said, "but it's good." His mood changed again and he stood still in his wreck of a room, staring into space. He'd grown in two months, or maybe it was all the curly hair making him look taller. But it was his face that broke my heart. Not as round, the bones more prominent. And this new silence. How many times I'd *wished* he would put a cork in it, my nonstop talker, my sweet If-I-think-it-I-must-say-it son.

"Benny!" I said. "Bruf!"

"Let's eat," he said, and we ran down to dinner.

"How about Gumball?"

"Gumball!" Hysterical laughter.

"Or . . . Falafel?"

Benny blew milk out of his nose.

"Easy," Sam said, chuckling, handing him his napkin. "Hey, I know. She sticks to you — we could call her Velcro."

Another laugh attack. "Or Glue!" Benny drummed his feet against his chair.

Under the table, I was having mixed feelings. On one hand, it was nice to be the center of attention, plus every now and then Benny dropped a piece of French bread on the floor; much better than Purina Dog Chow. But on the other hand, these name suggestions were ridiculous. Benny's were worse than Sam's — Jezebel, Caramba, Muffin, Baloney. *Be serious!* I wanted to tell them. *I don't* want *to go through life called Hairy-et.*

Benny got sidetracked and started telling Sam about school supplies he needed for the first day of first grade, which crayons, what kind of colored pencils. I'd been looking forward to that shopping trip since spring. Now I wouldn't even get to take him to *school.* Soon, though, the conversation swerved back to what to name the dog.

"Blunderbuss," Benny snorted, swaying in his seat, overcome with his cleverness. "Blinderbluss. Bladdabladda. Bliddablidda. Bliddabladdabliddabl—"

"Hey, I have an idea," Sam said seriously. About time he settled Benny down. If he got revved up this close to bedtime, he couldn't fall asleep for hours. "How about if we call her Sonoma?"

Sonoma. I crawled out from under the table. *That's not bad.*

"Sonoma?" Benny said. "Why?"

"Because that's where we were when we hit her. Georgetown and Sonoma Road."

They looked at me. I looked at them. "Sonoma," they said together. "Do you like it?" Sam asked.

"Yes," said Benny.

Me, too.

Good thing they didn't hit me on Roosevelt.

"One more, Daddy, please? Just one more, I promise."

That's what he said after the last story. This was new behavior; Benny was a pretty good sleeper, rarely had histrionics at bedtime, would often drift off in the middle of the first chapter. From my spot at the bottom of the bed, I could see he was exhausted, hear it in his croaky voice.

Sam sighed. "Hey, buddy," he said gently, closing the book. "We talked about this before, remember? What we said?"

"Yeah."

"What did we say?"

"I can go to sleep."

"You can go to sleep . . . and what?"

"Wake up."

"That's right."

"Not like Mom."

Oh, no.

"Right. You can let yourself fall asleep, and in the morning you'll wake up — what?"

"Bigger, better, and stronger."

"That's right. Brand-new day." He gave Benny a soft kiss on the forehead. "Okay?"

"Okay."

"Okay. You sleep tight, Benster. Love you."

"Love you. Can Sonoma stay with me?"

"Nope." Sam stood up and slapped his thigh — my cue to leave. I considered my options. Jumped off the bed.

"Leave the light on, okay? And the door open!"

"Don't I always?"

That ritual was familiar to me: hall light on, bedroom door ajar; Benny was afraid of the dark. Afraid of falling asleep because he might not wake up? That killed me. I wanted to cry, but all that came out was a high, whining sound in the back of my throat as I followed Sam down the steps. He thought it meant I had to go to the bathroom, and took me outside.

The red nylon leash not only annoyed me — where did he think I was going to go? — it also made it harder to do my business in private. Silly, maybe, but I was not going to squat in front of my husband. I managed by sidling around a gap in the Hortons' privet hedge next door, out of view. A particularly good spot because it was between two streetlights and therefore dark, or as dark as our suburban Bethesda neighborhood ever got.

How wonderful to be back, even under these, the most peculiar circumstances imaginable. I was feeling a kind of excitement that went beyond the fact that I was home again. The smells! I could even *see* better than usual, which was odd, considering that in daylight I saw slightly *less* well. Maybe it was because I had such big pupils. Whatever — everything was incredibly sharp and *interesting* and I could not get enough of the *smells.* Feral, musky, smoky, dusty — my vocabulary would run out before I could name them all. Anyway, it didn't matter if I was sniffing a "squirrel"; I could only concentrate on that spicy-dirty smell, the *essence* of "squirrel." I could flare my nostrils, inhale, and taste it on the roof of my mouth, the back of my tongue, all the way down my throat and into my vitals. And it was *fascinating*.

The phone was ringing when we got home.

"Hi, Delia," Sam said, and I skidded to a stop on my way to the kitchen for a drink of water. My sister! "We went this afternoon, yeah. Well . . . not much change, I guess. No. Although sometimes I swear she can hear me."

Sam carried the phone to the living room sofa and sat down. "Right. I know . . . Right."

These long pauses while Delia talked were driving me crazy. *What's she saying?* I jumped up next to Sam — who reacted as if I'd thrown up on him, leaping to his feet, sweeping me to the floor one-handed. *Sheesh.*

"Well, we just keep hoping. No change on the scale, the nurse said today. They call it the Glasgow Coma Scale. It evaluates . . . Right. So nothing new there, apparently, which you can look at . . . Right, exactly."

More silence on Sam's end. Frustration! I put my hands — I mean my front paws — on the arm of the sofa and slowly, slowly raised myself. He had the phone to his other ear, though; I could hear Delia's voice but not her words.

"I played it for her today. Well . . ." He laughed. "Not, uh, not to the naked eye. I'm sure, though, deep inside she was boogying."

Delia's mix tape. I remembered now; I'd heard snatches of it, but thought I was dreaming. Our favorites from high school — "Love Shack," "Vogue," "Losing My Religion." Sweet Delia.

She lives in Philadelphia with her growing family. She must've visited me in the hospital and rehab, and yet I couldn't quite remember it. So much of that time passed in a dream state, some gray twilight zone between being and not being. I saw myself as if from a great height, and the connection between the two me's would be strong one moment, tenuous as a paper-clip chain the next.

"Hey, that would be great. Sure, either weekend is fine. Whichever's better for you guys. You can always stay here, you know. Plenty of room; it's just . . . the two of us. Well, whatever's easier. That's fine."

More talk on her end. *When* was she coming?

"I'm okay. You know. Yeah. Well, that, too. I've put the cabin on the market."

What? Oh, no.

"Yeah, it's a terrible time, but I couldn't see a choice. The bills . . . you can't believe. Insurance, sure, but not enough. Nowhere near. Thanks. Thanks, but we're okay."

Oh, Sam. Not the cabin. And not *now,* right after we *bought* it. You'll lose all the closing costs, the mortgage fee — thank goodness there was no prepayment penalty — and you'll have to pay them *again,* the buyer's *and* the seller's closing costs. Oh, this was terrible.

"I'm looking now. I've already started," Sam was saying. Looking for what? "Tomorrow, in fact, I've got a . . . Yeah. Oh, something will turn up. Um, he's all right, basically. No, I don't tell him that. No, I keep it . . . Right, very hopeful. But the longer this goes on, the less chance . . ." Sam rubbed his eyes with his free hand. "He starts school in three weeks, so that's . . . Yeah. A good distraction. Oh, he'd love that, thanks, Delia. And how are you? And Jerry and the kids . . . ?"

More frustrating pauses. I padded around the room, unable to settle, until Sam hung

181

up. Then I sat at his feet, the perfect dog. Minutes passed before he even saw me. "I forgot to tell her about you."

I noticed.

Half smiling, he put his hand under my chin. I turned my head and pressed my cheek into his palm. With my eyes closed, it felt as if I were absorbing his sadness, taking it into a place in myself where it couldn't hurt him as much. Was this what dogs did? And what I gave back, what I exchanged his sadness for, was simply love.

He took his hand away and stared. His eyes were alert, puzzled.

Sam. Sam, it's me, Laurie. I put a paw on his knee, not letting him look away. *Do you see me? Help me. Rescue me.* For an instant, I swear he knew.

But then time moved, "reality" returned, and he laughed — uneasily — and gave a tug on my ear. "Come on, Sonoma. Bedtime."

In the kitchen? I couldn't believe it. He wanted me to lie down on the brand-new, corduroy-covered dog bed he'd bought on the way home from the vet's that still smelled of the plastic wrap it came in. Pew. He gave me a few perfunctory pats and stood up. So did I. We went through that a few times — "No, lie down, *lie down.* That's it. Good girl" — until I gave up. And then, *then,* he turned out the light and closed the swinging kitchen door. Didn't even leave a radio on for me.

I waited for about half an hour, listening to Sam upstairs in the bathroom, then the creaks and cracks of the house settling, the next-door neighbor smoking his last ciga-rette on his screen porch, the occasional car purring by. I even heard Sam turn his bedside lamp off — amazing. He's a good sleeper and he conks out fast; I waited ten more minutes. Then I nosed the door open and escaped.

Treading quickly on the rugs, carefully on the hardwood so my toenails wouldn't clack. New instincts were kicking in. I felt like a huntress.

That earthy, humid, little-boy smell in Benny's room was stronger than ever, as if it had been fermenting in the dark. Bath time must be in the morning under Sam's regime. I went to the source, creeping onto my son's low bed with such grace and preci-sion, he never stirred. As usual, he'd thrown his covers off. He lay on his stomach, arms flung out as if he were flying. The soft, quick sound of his breathing kept time with my heartbeat. I wanted to taste him, lick all the skin his hiked-up pjs exposed, but settled for discreet snuffling, deep, silent inhales of his calves, his feet, the delicious back of his neck. I settled myself along the length of his leg, touching as much of him with as much of me as possible. And guarded him.

Time passed — I didn't know how much. The numbers on Benny's Spider-Man clock ran together; I couldn't make sense of them. Sometime deep in the night, I gave him a last nose caress and crept out of his room.

Into Sam's. Where the smells were much subtler but equally intriguing. More so, in their way. Our bed was higher than Benny's. I put my front paws on the foot of the mattress and cautiously raised myself so I could see Sam. For a long time I just watched him, asleep on his back, one arm over his eyes. The sheet covered half of his bare chest; under it he'd have on his running shorts — his summer pajamas. In the light from the streetlamp his skin looked hard and bluish pale, like marble. God, I'd missed him. I missed him right now. Quiet as a ninja, I got all four feet on the bed and curled up on my wide, empty side of it in the smallest ball I could manage. And fell into the second-deepest sleep of my life.

I'm sealed in icy water, trying not to breathe. If I breathe, I'll die. Darkness is closing in. I can see only through a narrowing tunnel. I flail my limbs, knowing it's useless, unwise, but the fear is too strong. Help me! (Did this happen? Is it real?) *When I can't bear it any longer, my mouth opens and I suck in — water. Panic devours me. I scream, but there's no sound because there's no breath. I have one last clear thought:* This is so stupid. *The last emotion is fury — I kick, I punch, I push —*

"What the hell?"

I wake up.

Back to the kitchen. I didn't protest. Bad dog, caught in the act. Sam was so groggy, I couldn't tell if he was mad or amused because his new dog had kicked him awake. Except for "What the hell?" he had nothing to say. But he made his point when, after closing the kitchen door on me, he pulled a dining room chair in front of it.

I see now that there was still a part of me that believed this whole thing was a hallucination. It died a tragic death when Sam dragged that chair in front of the door. *This isn't funny anymore,* I thought. *I have got to get out of this.* The fact that I had no idea what "this" was didn't daunt me. I had spent my first and last day as a dog. Tomorrow: liberation.

I figured out where we were going on our walk when we got to the bottom of York Lane and turned right on Custer Road. Monica Carr's house. Benny and her twins were the same age, and they played well together. When I had been working (which was most of the time) and Sam had had something urgent to do (which was not very often), Monica was good about taking Benny, even on short notice. Monica was pretty good about everything, truthfully. I would hate to think that's why I had never much liked her.

"Morning!" she called from the doorway of the renovated two-story brick colonial she got to keep in the divorce, waving, wiping her hands on a dish towel. "My goodness, who's *that?*" Me, she meant. Benny dropped Sam's hand and ran toward her, already launched on a complicated explanation of the origins of his new dog. "Ethan, Justin, Benny's here!" Monica called back into the house. And then she squatted down in her skintight biking shorts and put her arms around Benny and kissed him, and he stopped talking long enough to hug her back.

What? What?

Ethan and Justin were adorable, two blond-haired angels with mischievous senses of humor and hilarious laughs. When they saw me, they fell all over me, thrilled and fearless. What *fun* children were! Human toys. Benny started the Sonoma saga over again for their benefit. Ethan and Justin always made me soften toward Monica; she must be doing *something* right, I'd think, usually after some less charitable assessment. But the truth was, Monica did almost everything right, and I was just never saintly enough to find that endearing.

"Hi."

"Hi."

Their tones, Sam's and Monica's, pulled me up short. I stopped roughhousing with the boys and moved closer on my leash.

"How have you been, Sam?" Such sympathy she put in the simple question; it sounded like a caress. An extra caress, to go with the solicitous hand she had on his arm. "How are you holding up?" She tossed her head to shake the glossy black bangs out of her eyes. She smelled of delicate sweat, if there was such a thing, and also of cinnamon, yeast, something fruity . . . Raisin muffins, that was it. From scratch, of course, probably very high in fiber, and she'd made them either before or after her five-mile morning jog. What time was it, *eight?* "Have you got a minute to come in? I have a coffee cake ready to come out of the oven."

Coffee cake, same thing. Sam said he wished he could, but he was in a bit of a hurry, didn't want to be late for his appointment. No, no, she agreed, it wouldn't do to be late for *that.* What appointment? Nobody told me anything.

Monica offered to keep me as well as Benny, but Sam said no, thanks; that was nice of her, but Benny would be enough for her to handle. All three boys groaned their disappointment. I felt let down, too; I'd been looking forward to some time alone with Sam, but if he was going out anyway, I'd much rather have stayed at Monica's with Benny. So much for what I wanted, though. "It's a dog's life" — I was never sure if that meant you had it hard or you had it easy. But it's neither. It means you're a slave, with no rights, no privileges. Why don't dogs rise up and rebel? Instead they love us — that's all they do. It's a mystery.

I couldn't believe it when Sam shut me out of the bathroom while he took his shower. Something else I'd been looking forward to was seeing him naked, although I hadn't quite realized it until the opportunity was snatched away. At least he came out in his shorts, all clean skin and wet hair, smelling of soap, shaving cream, deodorant, toothpaste. And at least he let me watch him get dressed. Ten years ago, when we were first married, he had lots of suits, and he wore them to his job as an actuary in a large downtown insurance company. These days he was down to one suit and a few sport coats, and he rarely wore any of them. No need when his main job was to take care of Benny and his other job called for a tux.

He pulled on a T-shirt, then stepped into the pants of his dark blue suit and zipped up. Light blue shirt next (I assumed; it looked gray to me), followed by his navy paisley tie. His best black belt. What was this "appointment" he needed to get dressed up for? He combed a side part in his longish, streaky-blond hair, and that was a tip-off that wherever he was going, it had nothing to do with magic. Milo Marvelle wore his hair straight back from his handsome forehead, accentuating his sharp, dramatic features. Sam Summer was a good-looking man, but Milo Marvelle was a Master of Mystery.

He kept glancing at his watch. When he was nervous, he had a habit of pursing his lips and blowing air in and out of his cheeks. He stowed his wallet, change, comb, and handkerchief in various pockets, then took a long, scowling look at himself in the mirror over the bureau. "Million bucks," I wanted so much to tell him. It was what we said to each other whenever we dressed up for something special. "Honey, you look like a million bucks." Sam inhaled deeply, said, "Okay," into the mirror, a one-word pep talk, and went out.

He closed me up in the kitchen again. "Just until we're sure she's housebroken," he'd explained last night to Benny. What, I hadn't proven myself yet? What did I have to do? Explode? "Be good," he said, ruffling the hair behind my ear. *You, too.* I licked his wrist. *Good luck. Drive carefully.* I had the stupid dining room chair out of the way and the door open before I heard his car start.

I'd never noticed before, but there wasn't a comfortable chair in my living room. Not one. I'd gone for modern when we bought the house, pleased with the new sleekness of leather, metal, and glass. Modern was sophisticated; modern meant professional, in control, and on the way up. Maybe so, but where do you sprawl out? No wonder Sam and Benny liked the den best (or the "away room" as we say in real estate). I used to keep the door to the den closed when we had company, as if hiding a mad relative. Now it was where I went after sampling all the slippery leather sectionals and the scary Eames recliner in the living room. The den even smelled better. Like people.

Over in the corner, my computer was humming. In sleep mode, but it was on, which was a relief; the button that activated it was in back, flush with the monitor, and I wasn't sure I could've punched it in with my nose. All I had to do was press the space bar and . . . voila. The blue screen.

Now what? How could I write a message to Sam? First thing, get myself settled in the office chair so I could reach the keys. That took more time than I'd expected, owing to the fact that the chair revolved and sat on castors. I reminded myself of a seal balancing on a beach ball. But that was nothing compared to trying to get the computer into word-processing mode. I fell on the floor an embarrassing number of times, and failed in the end anyway because I simply could not push the mouse up to Word and keep it there while left-clicking with my chin.

Even if I had been able to, how would I have typed letters? My feet were too big. And my tongue — I'd noticed this already

— was really clumsy and inefficient; it wouldn't go sideways, couldn't point or flatten; all it could do was go in and out, in and out.

Discouraged, I jumped off the chair and onto the sofa. Sam's sofa; I'd never liked it, but that was because I hadn't known how great the nubby fabric would be for scratching the sides of my face. And the top of my nose, between my eyes, those places I couldn't reach very well myself. I curled up in the patch of sunshine coming through the window, resting my chin on the sofa arm. So I could think better.

The phone woke me. Charlie, Sam's father, left a message on the machine saying he'd be over Saturday night about eight thirty, if that was okay, in time to say good night to Benny.

Maybe I could write a message to Sam in longhand. Of course! Getting the legal pad off the desk was simple; I just swiped it sideways with my nose. Ditto the cup full of ballpoints and pencils. Too bad there was writing on the top sheet of the legal pad. I couldn't tell what it said; my eyes wouldn't focus that close. Well, whatever it was, I had something much more important to write. Using tongue, teeth, and my bottom lip, I tore that page off and spit it on the floor in pieces.

I won't recount how many times I tried to click on a ballpoint pen, just that I was unsuccessful. There were three pencils, and the first two broke in half in my mouth. I got the last one clamped between my molars, no easy feat since I only had about two-thirds the number of teeth I used to have. Now, what to write? Words were out of the question, I'd realized a pencil and a half ago. A symbol, then. A heart.

Crap, crap, crap. I couldn't control the pressure. I pierced a hole in the paper with the pencil, and in the end all I got was a trembly rhomboid with drool on it.

I needed bigger media. *Think.* If I were the kind of woman who kept a lot of throw pillows on the furniture — someone like Monica Carr, say — I could spell something out with them on the floor. But I wasn't, so I couldn't.

Upstairs, I finally found a box of crayons in the rubble of Benny's room. No sense figuring a way to use them up here; I could write the Gettysburg Address on the wall in finger paints and no one would notice for days. Back to the den.

Like the tongue, a dog's toes extend and retract. That's it. I gave up trying to write something with Benny's crayons and concentrated instead on arranging them in some kind of shape. My initials! If I could make *LS* out of crayons, wouldn't that tell Sam something?

I had to eat part of the box to get the crayons out, but that was okay. Cardboard had a pleasant woody taste; I wouldn't have minded eating the whole thing, actually. How many crayons were in this box? Eight, ten, something like that; precise counting was no longer one of my strong suits. I nosed two crayons into an *L,* but that looked random, meaningless. Two on a side, that was better, a big *L.* Good. Now for the *S.*

It's hard to make curves with straight edges. I kept getting a 5 when I wasn't getting a swastika. (I could just hear Sam: "You're *Hitler?* I know — Eva Braun!") I did the best I could until hunger distracted me. That cardboard, it was like an hors d'oeuvre. I trotted into the kitchen.

Sam had served a mix of canned and dry dog food last night — surprisingly tasty — but today it was just a bowl of kibble. Boring but not bad, and the crunch was satisfying. I ate the whole thing.

I was sitting in the hall, scratching an itch under my collar, when a noise on the front porch brought me to full alert. Footsteps. I gave a low, warning bark, but it sounded self-conscious, rehearsed. Like what I was *supposed* to do. Then the screen door squealed open. *Bark!* That felt better. A cascade of envelopes and magazines pushed through the slot in the door. *Bark bark! Bark bark bark bark bark!*

I used to like the postman, a nice guy named Brian, but now I hated him. What fun! Barking was so invigorating, pure self-expression, like singing at the top of your lungs. I kept it up till Brian was barely a memory; then I went back to the den and took a nap.

The key in the front door woke me. Sam! I ran to the door, heart soaring. Sam was home! Joy! Bliss! I jumped up high, trying to lick his face, tail flying, barking, spinning, *not* peeing, *not* peeing —

"Down!"

Where had he been? I could smell plastic . . . car exhaust, people . . . some chemical-ly smell, like a new carpet —

"Down! Damn it, dog." He wasn't as glad to see me as I was to see him. He looked tired and tense at the same time. *Oh, baby,* I thought, sobering fast, and followed him into the kitchen. He saw the chair, the door. "Oh, for the love of . . . How the hell did you . . ." His shoulders drooped. Mine, too.

He got a beer out of the refrigerator and took it into the den.

A beer? What time was it? Clocks didn't tell me anything anymore. Too early for a beer, though, I knew that from the sun. When had Sam started drinking during the day?

"Oh, jeez. What did you do?"

Stop! Don't, don't —

Too late. He didn't even read it. He just bent over, swept up all my carefully placed crayons, along with the broken pencils and ballpoints, the torn paper and the crayon box remains. *Damn it, Sam, do you know how hard I worked on that?*

"Bad dog! Bad Sonoma!" He shoved the evidence under my nose. "*Shame* on you. *Bad* dog."

Okay, okay, I get it. I lay down and put my paws over my ears. I've always hated criticism.

I heard the heavy, hopeless sound of Sam dropping down on the couch. A sigh. A gulp of beer. When I sneaked a glance, he was shaking his head at me. But smiling. Just a tiny bit.

I meant to be subtle, but my heart turned inside out with gladness and I pounced to him instead of slinking. I didn't jump up next to him — I had enough self-control to stop short of that. I sat at his feet, and after a few minutes Sam put his hand on top of my head and just rested it there, heavy and trusting, and we stayed that way until it was time to go get Benny.

By week's end, I had the run of the house. Sam decided the incident with the pencils and papers was an anomaly brought on by separation anxiety. Since then I'd behaved like Perfect Dog, and on the third night he moved my bed to the upstairs hall. No more closed kitchen doors for me. It didn't matter, though; as soon as they were asleep, I'd sneak into Benny's room, then Sam's. I slept lightly, and never got caught again.

Saturday was housecleaning day. It used to be Tuesday, when the cleaning lady came, but evidently those days were over. Now it was just Sam, with Benny's "help," trying to bring order to a week's worth of laissez-faire living — that's putting it charitably. Benny's room was beyond shoveling out; what they needed was a backhoe. How could one five-year-old boy make such a mess in only seven days?

I wasn't completely blameless, mess creation–wise. I should have felt guilty, but it wasn't in me anymore. And to think, I used to be such a fastidious person. "Persnickety," Sam called me. I'd had food aversions, too; I was picky about textures, smells, certain flavors. Ha! Now I'd eat anything. Anything. If I was thirsty enough, the toilet bowl was not off-limits. When my butt itched, I dragged it across the carpet. Dog hair everywhere? Pfft, life was too short to obsess about such trifles.

Benny and I went outside when Sam started vacuuming. What a diabolical machine; the noise alone was painful, but there was something menacing about the moves it made, that predatory back and forth. I wanted to get away from it as much as I wanted to shred it into metallic pieces.

Sam had started to build a fort for Benny last spring. When I'd seen it last, before the accident, it was a three-sided plywood lean-to abutting the oak tree at the bottom of our backyard. In the past two months, Sam had enclosed the fourth side, put in a door and a window, and painted it gray-blue with white trim. A dream playhouse and, needless to say, Benny's favorite place. I wasn't surprised when he headed straight for it after Sam said, "Thanks, buddy, good job," and released him from his chores.

"Look, Sonoma. This is where I keep stuff."

The fort was roughly a five-foot cube,

smelling of wood and earth. Benny opened a plastic chest in a corner of the cube and showed me his toys. "Brontosaurus puzzle. See, look. I can do it fast." Indeed; he had the dinosaur assembled in about one minute. "Then it goes back in this egg, see?" He took it apart and put it away in its plastic cup. "I got a preying mantis one in my room, but it goes back in a box, not an egg. Look at this." He showed me his plastic bulldozer and his magic deck of cards. His special marble, his lion mask.

"Okay, now," he said in a different voice, bending into the toy box and pulling out a smaller one, metal: an old cookie tin. I went closer.

He whispered, "See this, Sonoma?" He held out an item I didn't recognize at first. "My mom owned it. It's a secret. I took it out of her car. It's for coffee, you put coffee in and then you drink it when you're driving. Going to your job in your car, and it won't spill." He demonstrated how to drink from my old coffee cup.

"It says the name of her job right here." SHANAHAN & LEWIS REALTORS. "She went every day. They sell houses to people. She got rewards because she was good. She was the best."

Well. I was, but I didn't know Benny knew

it. I felt proud, but also as if I might've been caught doing something slightly embarrassing. Bragging.

"This is her mouse pad." He was whispering again. He did that adorable thing he did with his face when he was thinking hard: He scowled and pursed his mouth and wrinkled his nose. I knew exactly what he was thinking: *How do I explain a mouse pad to my dog?* In the end he decided not to bother. "It has a picture of us Dad took, me and Mom, then he had it put on this thing. It's us sledding down York Lane. I was a little boy. I couldn't go on my own yet. This is Mom and this is me."

I loved that picture. Benny, three years old, sat in front of me on the sled, both of us red-faced from the cold and laughing like loons. He had on his silver snowsuit, the same outfit he'd worn at Christmastime that year to sit on Santa's lap. Outgrown long ago.

He held the mouse pad photo closer to my face. "It looks like we have the same color hair, but we don't." No, we did — he'd forgotten. His hair had darkened in the past two years, and mine stayed the same. He'd just forgotten.

The mouse pad went back in the box; out came something wrapped in a piece of cloth. Something special, I could tell by the way he held it.

"Look," he said, and opened the last treasure.

Earrings. Cheap metal hearts with MOM engraved on each one — he and Sam had bought them last Mother's Day at a kiosk in the mall. "She liked them a lot. She said they were *beautiful.* When she wakes up, I'm giving them to her again. As soon as she wakes up." I leaned my weight against him; he put his arm around my neck. "I told Dad, and he said she might not remember. That I gave 'em to her before, but I think she will. Don't you?"

He wasn't crying, but I licked his cheek. *I know she will.*

I'd always liked Sam's father, even though he was as unlike his only son as could be. Where Sam was a quiet man, unassuming and kind, often reserved around strangers, Charlie was the kind of guy the phrase "good time" was invented for. He sold insurance before he retired a few years ago, and I used to like to imagine what a nice surprise people were in for who invited him over to discuss premiums on their whole life. What I hadn't known was how much fun he was if you happened to be a dog.

201

Pretend-growling was great fun, too, sort of like constant gargling. Charlie played tug-of-war with me and my toy pheasant almost as long as I wanted. Almost. We played in the kitchen until he dragged me out of the house by his half of the toy and collapsed on the front porch step. I let him pry my mouth open, hoping he would heave the bird out into the dark front yard. He did; then he did it again, and then again, but not *enough*. He tired out — they always do. I could've retrieved that pheasant all night.

Sam came out with a couple of beers, handed one to his father. "Hot," he said. "We can sit inside if you'd rather. Cooler in the air-conditioning."

"Not me, I like it. The dog days. Benny go to sleep?"

"Finally."

"Seems to me like he's doing pretty well."

"You cheer him up, Pop. I think he's too quiet."

"You were like that." Charlie took a sip of beer and then belched a few times, softly. He still had a full head of sandy hair, but he was going soft and round in all the places Sam was hard and angular. "Quiet kid, you were. Always figured that's why you took up magic."

"But Benny's a talker."

"That's for sure. Nonstop. But he'll be okay. He will be, Sam."

"Sure, I know."

"Hey, getting that dog was a great idea."

"Well . . ."

Well, what?

"No leash — you're not worried she'll run off?"

"No way. She sticks to us like a shadow."

"What about when you and Benny are gone all day? Him in school, you at work?"

I stopped sniffing around in the grass and trotted over. What work? Sam had work?

"She's housebroken," Sam said.

"Yeah, but cooped up in the house all day, that's no life for a big dog."

I thought of myself as medium.

"I'd take her for you myself, but they've got a weight limit on pets." Charlie lived in a retirement community in Silver Spring. But what a sweet offer. I nuzzled his hand in gratitude.

"I'm more worried about Benny than the dog." Sam set his beer on the step and pulled out the deck of cards he always kept in his pocket. "I hate it that I won't be here when he gets home from school."

"So what'll you do?"

"There's a neighbor who's offered to keep him. She's got two boys his age, so it should work out."

Monica? "Mupf?"

"Hush, not now," Sam said, thinking I wanted to play.

"Well, that's good. Yeah, that sounds like it'll work out all right. Kids adjust," Charlie started saying. "When they're little, they can adapt to almost anything . . ." So on and so on. I quit listening. Monica Carr was going to take my child after school every day? Why? Where was Sam going to be?

"Queen of spades."

"So tell me about your new job," Charlie said, pulling a random card from the flared deck Sam held out to him. "Queen of spades," he confirmed without surprise, and handed it back.

"It's not what I wanted. I was hoping for something part-time, but that was a dead end. There's been a lot of downsizing and merging since I got out of the field. I had to take what I could get. Two of clubs."

Charlie picked a card and nodded. "Two of clubs. But you hate this job."

"No, Pop. Don't say that." He gave a weak laugh and concentrated on his overhand shuffle. "Anyway, it's irrelevant. I have to make some money."

"I was real sorry to hear about the cabin."

Sam nodded, shrugged.

"I know you had high hopes," Charlie said gently. "Spend more time with Laurie and all."

Really? I tried to read Sam's face in the dimness. That wasn't why he'd wanted the cabin. Was it?

Charlie patted his knee. When I came over, he started ruffling my ears and blowing into my face. I wagged my tail, ready for a game. "Kinda ironic," he said.

"How so?"

"Laurie always wanted you to go back to work."

I wheeled away, out of Charlie's reach. *That's not true.* Even if it was, Charlie never knew it. *Sam* never knew it — because I never *said* it. Not out loud. I looked at Sam, waiting for him to deny it.

"Laurie . . ." he said and stopped.

Yes? What?

"She thought she was marrying an actuary. It's not her fault she ended up with a part-time magician."

"Oh, yeah?" Charlie sat up straight. "Well, the way I remember it, you didn't think *you* were marrying —"

"Hey, now, Pop."

"— a type-A workaholic go-getter who —"

"Pop."

"— lived for making dough and setting

205

sales records. Okay, okay. Sorry. But if she was disappointed in you, I say that went two ways."

Charlie! I thought you loved me!

Oh, this was so unfair. I slunk farther out into the yard, beyond the circle of the porch light. If only I could disappear. I found a patch of dusty-smelling ivy and burrowed down in it.

What was wrong with liking your job? I was *not* a workaholic. Charlie was right about one thing — when I met Sam he was working in one of the biggest insurance companies in the country, climbing the actuary ladder, taking the competency exams, passing with freakish ease. A math geek. As it turned out, he hated math, but I didn't know that. But it didn't matter! We were *glad* to switch gender roles, especially when my salary tripled and quadrupled during the real estate boom. When it went bust — okay, that was when I *might* have said something to Sam. Not nagging, though; more pointing out the obvious. Tactfully. Lovingly and supportively.

Then I got the O Street property in Georgetown and sold it to a Chinese businessman who paid the asking price in cash. Huge commission, Mega Deal Maker of the Year, promotion — Sam's cabin on the river. In the worst housing market slump in recent history, I was *invincible*.

Then I drowned.

Now Sam had to go back to a job he hated. Benny had to face first grade without a mother, and after school he had to go to Monica Carr's house. Sam had to sell his beautiful cabin to pay the insurance bills. Everything was going to hell, and it was my fault.

I might as well lie down in the street and get hit by another car.

I would have, except just then Sam said, "Delia's coming down tomorrow and we're all going to Hope Springs to visit Laurie. You can come along, Pop, but you don't have to. I know it's hard to —"

"No, I'd like to come. Thanks, Sam. For including me. I feel bad that I haven't gone to see her more often."

I couldn't remember Charlie visiting me at all. But this was great! "All" must mean the whole family — Sam would take me, too. They encouraged pets at places like Hope Springs — we were therapeutic!

My God, this was it. The answer, the key. Tomorrow would change everything. I didn't know how — I just knew it would. All I'd wanted was my family back, and in a way, a most peculiar way, I'd gotten it. It was time to get myself back.

They didn't take me.

It took me until the last second to figure it out, when Sam stuck his foot across my chest, said, "No, Sonoma, you stay here. Stay, girl, we'll be back. Guard the house," and shut the front door in my face.

Unbelievable. All my hopes, dashed in an instant. The capriciousness, the absolute *tyranny* of humans over dogs had never hit me before. If I hadn't known it would make everything worse, I'd have hurled my sixty-pound body over and over against that obstinate closed door until one of us broke. Now I wouldn't even see my sister!

But worse, much worse, I wouldn't see myself. And after conceiving the idea, I'd only grown more certain that that was the only way out. How it would work, exactly, I had no idea — how could I, when I didn't know how this bizarre business had started in the first place? — I just knew I had to try. To reconnect. To reclaim myself.

Which meant I had to escape.

Stratford Road, our one-block-long street in suburban Bethesda, was such a safe, sweet neighborhood, sometimes we didn't even lock the doors. Sam and I used to say we ought to do something about the basement windows, which were small, old-fashioned casements set high in the walls, grimy and cobwebby, most of them *rusted* shut if nothing else — but we never got around to it. I knew which one was the most vulnerable: the one in the furnace room over the fuel tank. Last spring two oil company guys had come to service the furnace, and in the process they'd opened that window to pass tools back and forth.

The hardest part was getting up on top of the fuel tank, slippery, stinky, rusty, dusty metal, four feet high, but where there's a will there's a way. What a godsend that the window opened *outward* on its hinges. All I had to do was pull the lever down with my teeth and push against the glass with my head. "All," I say; I almost broke a tooth, and the gap I finally pushed open was so narrow, I scraped my backbone scrambling through it. But I got out. I stood on the hot driveway pavement, triumphant, and shook myself. *Call me MacGyver.*

Hope Springs was in Olney, technically another Washington suburb but a really faraway one, twenty miles or so up Georgia Avenue from the district line. My best bet would be to take Georgetown Road to I-270, get off at the Beltway, follow it to Georgia, head north. In a car, that's probably half an hour. On foot . . .

Well, no point in thinking about it. Just put one paw in front of the other. Dogs can travel amazing distances — you hear that all the time — and they only have their senses to rely on. I had senses *and* an extremely clear and vivid mental map of Montgomery County, acquired from years of driving clients around to look at properties. Talk about a head start. I set off at a confident lope.

At the corner of York and Custer, though, I paused. A car coming down the hill honked; I scuttled over to the right, into the Givens' side yard. Something kept me idling there instead of heading left — my route, my way out. Some nagging little thing I couldn't identify. Not until I turned right and trotted down the sidewalk a little ways and found myself — *hey, how did this happen?* — in front of Monica Carr's house.

And speak of the devil. Wouldn't you know? Sunday was the day Gilbert, the ex-husband, got the twins, so what did Monica do on her one day off, the single childless day of the week she could've done anything she liked? Did she go shopping? Take a drive, go to a museum, a movie, visit friends, *go on a date?* No. She stayed home and perfected her already perfect front-yard perennial garden. It was all flowers, no grass — she grew an emerald green carpet of that in the *back*yard — and it was beautiful. I would like to say Monica's garden was precious and too planned, or too artificially rustic, or too self-conscious and full of itself, but it was none of those. It was magazine-lovely eleven months of the year, and in its off-month it had "winter interest."

There she was, deadheading the rudbeckia. In khaki shorts and a sleeveless top that showed off her tan and her tight runner's body. I sat on the sidewalk and watched her through the spokes of the wrought-iron fence surrounding the garden, surprised when a growl, low but definite, vibrated in the back of my throat. Could I be a *violent* dog? How interesting. I lifted my lips and bared my teeth, experimenting. *Whoa.* Rush of aggression!

I heard the phone ring in the house before Monica did. She tossed her clippers down and ran inside, and that's when I decided this was my chance. To do what? A dog's strong suit isn't planning ahead.

Simple to get in — the gate was open. Inside, nothing smelled very interesting; squirrels and chipmunks probably took one look at all the pristine gorgeousness and went next door. Monica had everything: the flowers you'd expect in late August, gaillardia, daisies, asters, salvia, cosmos, and then dozens more you had no name for, everything beautifully banked and clumped and color-coordinated, all of it lush and alive. I was drawn to a perfect side-by-side harmonization of low verbena and feathery coreopsis, deep purple and butter yellow. So simple, so lovely. I had to kill it.

The weed-free soil was, as you'd expect, rich and soft and loamy, and *digging* — I'd been a dog for almost a week now: How had the peerless, inimitable joys of digging in dirt eluded me? It was an all-encompassing feeling once you got going, once you figured out how much more efficient and satisfying it was to use *all* your appendages, all four feet *and* your snout. Thrilling, really, and so satisfying to see how high the piles of earth, stalks, stems, and flowers rose behind me, littering the brick walk, obscuring its tasteful herringbone pattern. Why stop at the verbena-coreopsis combo? Right beside it was a swath of ferns and hostas for green relief, and then came a spray of tall fountain grass — *that* would be a challenge. Excitement filled me. The first hosta plant came out so easily, I made the mistake of barking at it. *Take that!* Dead as a doornail. I started on its neighbor, one of the variegated kinds I've never liked anyway. *And that! Die, you stupid plant, die like a — like a —*

"Hey!"

Where did *she* come from? Monica had the phone in her hand. She stuck it to her ear, said, "I'll call you back. There's a dog in my yard, it —" She squinted. *"Sonoma?"*

Busted.

She made a run for me — I jumped out of reach. She tried another off-balance lunge; I dodged the other way. Great fun. She looked so silly, and I was grace on four legs, shifting and feinting at the last second. *Loser,* I taunted, juking out of reach just before she could grab my collar. She tried stalking me next, hand out, voice coaxing. "Here, girl, it's okay, c'mon, Sonoma, c'mon, girl." *Up yours.*

We circled each other around the debris on the sidewalk. Then — too late — I saw that she'd gotten between me and the gate. A second later, she reached back and slammed it shut.

Trapped.

Screw you, I'll jump over the fence. Watch this.

But it was four feet high, and it had arrow-shaped uprights, *sharp* arrow-shaped uprights, between each iron post. I pictured myself half inside, half out, impaled in the middle.

Okay, you got me, I told Monica, and lay down on the hot brick walk. *Now what are you going to do with me?*

She put me in the bathroom. I don't know why I let her. Exhaustion, partly, but also the growing suspicion that I wasn't a violent dog at all, that growling was my whole arsenal, after which I had nothing. Well, barking, and some fast footwork, but that was it. I even kept an eye on Monica's calf while she guided me into the house, imagining my teeth sinking into its tan firmness — her shriek of pain — the taste of blood. But I couldn't do it. What was I, a vampire? No, I was a retriever.

"Sam? It's Monica." She was out in the kitchen, but I could hear her plainly through the closed bathroom door. "I just tried you at home, but I guess you're . . . Oh. Oh, I'm sorry. I won't keep you; I just wanted you to know Sonoma's here. Sonoma. No, *here.* Well, I guess she got out." Light laughter.

I waited for the ax to fall.

"I have no idea; maybe you left a . . . Oh, she's fine, none the worse for wear. I don't *know.* I know, it's so . . . No problem, I'm here all day, just pick her up whenever you . . . Sure, that's fine. Okay, Sam, we'll — You're welcome, see you soon. Oh, please, don't give it a thought. Bye-bye."

She brought me a bowl of water. She brought me half a piece of toast with peanut butter. After an hour, she let me out.

Oh, such transparent manipulation. I wasn't fooled for a second. I snooped around the house awhile, then lay down on the comfy couch in the living room, dirty paws and all. *What are you going to do about it?* She put her hands on her hips and shook her head in a cute, exasperated way. Uncharmed, I curled into a ball and took a nap.

When I woke up, she was all sweet-smelling in clean clothes and fresh makeup, running a feather duster over the furniture. A *feather duster.* I rest my case. One whole living room wall was covered with framed photographs, mostly of the twins. She was a photographer, too? She looked at her watch just as the doorbell rang. I jumped off the couch.

Benny! Sam! Benny! Sam! Joyful squeaking, ecstatic circling. They smelled like Hope Springs, but also like Delia. And pizza! I sat when Sam said, "Sit," though, and didn't shove my nose in his crotch, and I didn't lick Benny on the mouth, another

215

no-no. It probably made no sense to be on best behavior now, but it was the only defense I had. I'd figured it out in the bathroom: Monica hadn't told Sam on the phone about my adventures in the garden because she didn't want to upset him while he was visiting his comatose wife. She'd tell him now, though.

But it was Sam, not Monica, who said, "Benny, why don't you take Sonoma out to the car? Monica and I have to talk about something."

"Okay," Benny chirped, and patted his thigh for me to come, the way his dad did. "Come on, Sonoma!"

I didn't want to go. Instinct told me it would be better to be there when Monica lowered the boom. On the other hand, prompt, willing obedience was all I had left, so I trotted outside after Benny.

A neat, empty rectangle of sour-smelling mulch had replaced the massacred flowers and hosta, and the brick walk had been swept clean, neat as one of Monica's countertops. Nice of her to tidy up the scene of the crime, I thought sullenly. She probably had OCD.

I wanted to hear all about the visit to Hope Springs. How was I? What was my prognosis this week? Did Benny cry? Was he sad? But for once my son was in a quiet mood. We sat in the backseat of the car with the door open for a breeze. Hot as it was, Benny didn't mind when I sidled close and rested my cheek on his chest. *Blub-blub* went his heart, the best sound. Love filled me up. How wonderful to be back with my family again.

But what was taking Sam and Monica so long? I didn't like the look of them, standing too close in the doorway, talking in earnest voices too low to hear. Although at one point Monica clapped her hands at some comment of Sam's and said distinctly, "Oh, that would be *great*." What would? Having me put to sleep?

At last Sam turned and started toward the car. Well, this was it. The moment of truth. I searched his face for anger, indignation, but he was smiling, no doubt savoring some bon mot of Monica's. Who, just then, thought of something else she must say to him and jogged out to the car, too.

"Oh, Sam, don't forget the, um . . ." Suddenly she was tongue-tied. Sam finished buckling Benny's seat belt, backed out, and closed the door. "The, um, you know." She made a gesture with her hands, but Sam moved and his body blocked her. I couldn't decipher it.

"I won't," he said.

"Don't forget what?" alert Benny asked through the open window.

"Don't forget . . . to tell me how Sonoma got out," Monica said, clearly improvising. She reached in to ruffle Benny's hair. "Pretty smart dog you got there."

"She is really, really smart," he agreed.

Monica looked at me and lifted one eyebrow. She wasn't trying to communicate — sending ironic signals to a dog was the last thing on her mind. But to me, that private, raised brow was as good as a wink.

She hadn't ratted on me.

Well, great. Just great. What was I supposed to do, thank her? And for a second, actual gratitude welled up in my retriever heart. I yawned at her. I grinned. I licked my lips.

Then I got a grip on myself. What naïveté. How could I fall for such a slick trick? I wasn't one of those dogs you could smack around and then give a bone to and everything was hunky-dory. Forgive and forget — that's what dogs do, but I was still *Laurie.* If I wanted to keep my family, I had to hang on to what I knew: Monica Carr was not my friend.

"I wonder why she came over to your house," Sam said, settling in behind the wheel. "Although I'm glad she did — she could've gotten run over on Wilson Lane."

"Maybe she's in heat," Monica suggested. "You should think about having her spayed."

"I'm going to. I've just been too busy. I'll call and make an appointment tomorrow."

"Ah-roooooo!" *Oh, noooooo!*

Monica thought that was a riot. "Ha ha ha! It's like she heard you!"

At home, somebody had stuffed a large white envelope through the mail slot in the door. I got a whiff of a familiar smell, and just before Sam snatched it up, I recognized the preprinted logo in the return address: S&L. Of course — the familiar smell was Ron, my boss at Shanahan & Lewis. Funny, until now I hadn't even known Ron had a smell.

Normally I'd have gone with Benny when he ran upstairs to his room, but something about Sam, a new dejection I could sense even though he didn't say a word, didn't even sigh, made me want to stay with him. When he went into the den, I followed.

He was pulling paper-clipped pages out of the envelope when his eye caught the blink of the answering machine light. He tossed the papers on the couch and punched the button.

Ron's voice. "Hey, Sam, it's Ronnie. Sorry I missed you this afternoon. I should've called first, but you were right on my way home, so I took a chance and stopped by. Anyway, good news — we got a bid on the cabin. As you can see from the offer there, it's not the asking price, but it's close. It's no insult. So you think about it and let me know. We can go up ten or fifteen percent with our counter, I'm thinking. This guy's a lobbyist. He lives in D.C., wants the cabin for hunting on weekends with clients. He says he'd hire someone for the rehab, wouldn't do it himself — not the way you would have, and that's a shame, but . . . Anyway, he seems like a pretty sure thing, no, uh, financial liabilities or anything like that, obviously. So, you've got the bid and the deposit check there, so now you think about it and just let me know. Hope you're keeping well, you and Benny. We're thinking about you. Everybody in the office — well, we just miss her like hell. Okay, talk to you soon."

What a mensch. At the end, Ronnie's voice wavered a tiny bit, and that put a lump in my throat, too. Sam dropped down in the desk chair and put his head in his hand. I couldn't see his face, but I didn't need to. Whatever had happened today at Hope Springs, which couldn't have been good, this just made it worse. Sam's beautiful cabin, going to some rich guy who wanted to use it as a base for shooting our deer, our birds.

I put my head on his knee. *Sam*. I nudged his elbow so he had to uncover his face and look at me. *Oh, Sam, I'm so sorry.* He gave me a twisted smile of affection, absent-minded at first but gradually focusing. "You," he said — and my heart stopped. Did he see me? Did he know me? *Sam*. He leaned closer, stared harder. "How the hell did you get out?"

They say you don't know what you have until you lose it. I found out in that moment that that includes the ability to cry.

Sam gave my head a pat and stood up slowly, his shoulders slumped. "Hungry?" he said, and headed for the kitchen to start dinner.

I followed a few minutes later. Not quite as hungry as I had been.

"Daddy, what does 'spayed' mean?"

We were in my favorite place, at my favorite time of day: on the couch after dinner, when Sam read the paper and Benny got to watch TV for half an hour if anything suitable was on. Tonight was Sunday, so it was *The Simpsons.* Which may or may not have been suitable, but since I didn't have a vote anymore, I tried not to make judgments. I just enjoyed.

Funny, when I was myself, I usually grabbed this interval between dinner and Benny's bedtime to get some work done, phone clients, schedule appointments, do a little paperwork. I'd thought of it as Sam's time with Benny. Which didn't make much sense, I saw now, since Sam had Benny all day while I went to work.

I wasn't technically allowed on the couch, but I had perfected the art of the stealthy creep, the discreet, painfully slow advance whose key element is patience. It almost always worked, and sometimes, when he noticed it in progress, it even made Sam laugh. Tonight I'd been especially successful by ending up *between* him and Benny, not curled in the smallest ball I could make on Benny's far side, for invisibility. Ahh. This was the life. Everybody touching. Fidgety Benny on one side, warm, steady Sam on the other.

Sam let a lot of time go by without answering Benny's question. Something in the newspaper seemed to have him enthralled.

Did he think Benny would forget? What a dreamer.

"Daddy, what does 'spayed' mean?"

Sam put the paper down. "Spay. It's an operation they perform on a girl dog so she can't have any babies. Any puppies."

"Why?"

"Why what?"

"Why can't she have any puppies?"

"Because they fix her so she can't. They tie things up in her stomach. No puppies can come out. Say, how many more days till your birthday?"

"Does it hurt?"

"No."

"But Sonoma would make *good* puppies. She'd make *great* puppies. How did she get out?" Benny veered, dropping the puppy question. "How'd she get out of the house?"

"I guess she got out while we were leaving this morning. That's all I can figure — she slipped out the door and we didn't notice. We'll have to be more careful from now on."

Sam had checked every window and door in the house — I went with him. He found the open casement window over the oil tank and closed it, but not once did it cross his mind that it might've been my escape route. No dog could be that clever or that dexterous, he was thinking. I felt so proud.

Back to puppies. "What if Sonoma got so many puppies inside her stomach and they couldn't come out and she exploded! She could blow up. She could — *pwow!*"

"No, that wouldn't happen. Are you getting excited? The big six is next Sunday."

"Why not?"

"Because it just wouldn't. They tie things up so she doesn't even *make* puppies."

Whoa, edging over into dangerous territory there. I perked up my ears.

But for a change, Benny missed a grown-up reference and went back to "Why?"

"Because . . . it's better to have just one dog than six or seven dogs."

"Why? No, it isn't."

"Because six or seven dogs would be too hard to take care of."

"I would take care of them!"

"So we have to fix Sonoma so she's our one and only dog, our main dog. She gets *all* the love and attention." Oh, very nice. But then Sam went too far. "Like an only child."

"Like me?"

"Right."

"But I don't want to be an only child!"

Sam blanched, but I don't know who that hurt worse, him or me. "It's different for

224

dogs," he tried. "Sonoma will be happiest with just us. She'll have a good life, a much better life, if she's our one and only dog."

"How old will she get?"

"I don't know. Pretty old, though. We hope."

"Will she die?"

"Someday. A long time from now, we hope."

My son put a very gentle hand on my neck. Sam rubbed my back softly. At least talk of my eventual demise had gotten them off the puppy subject. I imagined Sam's relief.

I lay my head on his thigh. We used to talk about having another child. We both wanted one, and then . . . I don't know what happened. He'd bring it up every once in a while, and I'd stall. "Oh, I can't take off work right now to have a baby, the market's too good" or "the market's too bad." I'd say, "Don't you like things the way they are right now? I'm only thirty-two," or thirty-three, or thirty-four. Well, now I'm thirty-five (five in dog years). What would I say to Sam if he brought up the baby question today? My reasons always sounded sensible, but maybe I was just being selfish. I knew it was there, but I never let myself *feel* Sam's disappointment. And now it was so much clearer — as if I could see him through his skin. Or as if I'd taken *myself* out of the picture, so I could see Sam in perfect focus. Unbiased. My motives and ambitions and vanities no longer in the way.

This must be how dogs saw us all the time.

What had I been thinking? Of course I wanted more children! I *loved* babies. In a flash — this was very peculiar, and powerful for the instant it lasted — I pictured myself lying on my side, nursing six or seven at the same time. Not nearly as disturbing an image as it might've been, and it cleared my head.

Getting myself back was more vital than ever now, and it had to be soon. Soon, before Sam made an appointment with the vet.

After he put Benny to bed, Sam went into the den and called Ronnie Lewis.

"I'm looking at the bid, Ron, and I think we should take it."

I knew it! He's so naïve about money. He's a dreamer, not a schemer. Fine, I love that about him — but Sam, for Pete's sake, don't take the first offer!

Ron told him the same thing.

"I know, Ron, but I don't want the hassle. I can't deal with it right now. Let's just take it and get it over with. I've thought about it, and that's what I want to do."

Ronnie talked for a while.

"Okay, that all sounds fine. One thing, Ron — you said there was a check with this stuff? Hand money?" He fanned out the envelope and papers in front of him on the desk. "Um, well, no, I've looked and it's not here." Ron's voice got higher; I could almost hear his words. I didn't need to, of course; I could easily imagine them. "No, I've looked," Sam said again. "Well, I guess, I don't know; maybe it got — maybe you . . . Nope, not here. Yeah, I guess you'd better call him and see if . . . Okay. I'm here. I'll sit tight."

Sam hung up. I felt his eyes on me, and pretended to be asleep.

May I just say, escaping through a high basement window is child's play compared to sliding a check out of a paper clip on a three-page stapled document without disarranging the papers or leaving any drool. Eating the check was even harder because for some reason it tasted like gasoline. But a dog does what she has to do.

I felt bad for Ron. You couldn't lose a ten-thousand-dollar deposit check without seriously queering the deal, even if the buyer was reasonable, and this one didn't sound like he was. How did I know? Instinct and experience. Luckily Ron was the boss, so at least no one could fire him.

He called back faster than I expected. Spoke very softly; I couldn't hear a thing. Sam kept apologizing, trying to make him feel better. "Geez, I'm sorry. I don't know how it could've happened. So even though he could put a stop-payment on it, he doesn't . . . ? Honest to God, it's not here. I've looked several times, gone through the whole . . . Well, hell, it's not your fault. Don't worry about it, seriously. It's okay, we'll just start over. Forget it, Ron, I mean it. It's just one of those things. It's a mystery."

Maybe it was my guilty conscience, but after he hung up I thought Sam looked at me strangely. Suspiciously. I thunked my tail and grinned at him. We had a staring contest, Sam's gaze squinted and searching, mine blinky-sleepy and innocent. I won.

"Let's go for a *walk,*" he said, standing up. "Want to go for a *walk?*"

Outside, I noticed a new spring in his step, a lightness on his end of the leash. It wouldn't last forever — Ron Lewis was too good a salesman — but for the time being, there would be one less thing for Sam to feel sad about. Because of me.

228

Good dog.

In the week that followed, escape was the last thing on my mind. Instead I was a model of courtesy and decorum. I sat, lay down, and shook on command, I came when called, and at all open doors I halted, ostentatiously waiting for an invitation to proceed. Butter would not melt in my mouth. By Sunday, Sam's trust had rebounded so completely, without a second thought he granted me the thing I wanted most: permission to attend Benny's birthday party. Free, untied, walking around in the yard just like another guest. Only furry and better behaved.

The afternoon was perfect. Good thing, because eight sugar-saturated six-year-olds stuck in our small living room on a rainy day would've been a disaster. (We learned that last year, on Benny's *fifth* birthday.) The theme was crazy hats — everybody had to wear a crazy hat, and sweet Benny's was the red and white striped stovepipe from Dr. Seuss. He looked adorably goofy. He was — and I was not one bit prejudiced — absolutely the cutest, most adorable child at the party. But strangely — I liked them, of course, but I'd never been indiscriminately *wild* about other people's children —

strangely, on this day I found myself in love with all of them. I can say I've never had as much fun in my life as I did running and chasing and romping and playing with Benny and his friends. I loved being mauled, tackled, yanked on, ridden. It was as if we were all six. Or all dogs. I don't know, but I've never felt such a sheer blending of — of creatures, just species-less beings intent on nothing but delight.

Lunch at the picnic table was a judicious mix of healthy foods disguised as junk and junk, and the games afterward were fun but also thoughtful and creative, the kind you read about in parenting magazines but never quite pull off in real life. Sam deserved some of the credit, but it was clear to me who the real brain behind this party was. Not that it took a genius to figure it out. Monica had arrived an hour early with bags of tasteful party decorations and a homemade — what else? — three-layer yellow cake with chocolate ganache and toffee chips spelling out BENNY. Sam set the table, and Brian Kimmel's mother stayed to help out with the present-opening, but at my son's sixth birthday party Monica Carr was obviously the co-host. And official photographer.

"Boys and girls! May I have your attention? Let's come to order, people!" That didn't work, so she picked up the whistle around her neck and blew it. "Everybody, we need to take our seats at the table again! So the show can begin!"

The show? Ah, so that's what that curtain thing was — I thought it was for some new educational game. It was a circular, upright contraption, like a very small shower enclosure, surrounded by a colorful patterned curtain made from a sheet. Was Sam in there? I couldn't smell him, but my senses were overloaded. He'd disappeared into the house a few minutes ago, so I really should've known.

Hmm. Was this a good idea? Benny wasn't five anymore. What if, instead of making him proud, his magician father embarrassed him? And Sam always said magic was 10 percent technique, 90 percent presentation — how was he going to *present* himself as anything other than the neighborhood guy most of these children had known all their lives? How could he make magic out of what he'd always been to them: Benny's dad?

Monica was the emcee. After she got everybody settled, a magic trick in itself, she launched into a rousing introduction to whip up excitement, winding up with, "And now . . . I present to you . . . the amazing . . . the incredible . . . The Great Sambini!"

She pulled the curtain back with a flourish to reveal — nothing. She gasped, looked horrified, tried it again. "The Great . . . Sambini!" Nothing. Third time's the charm, and I had to admit she had the kids going by now — worried but not too worried. "The Great . . . *Sambini!*"

A puff of smoke, and Sam appeared — from behind a *second* colorful patterned sheet, I assumed, but the effect was too fast to see. Out he strode, coughing, waving his hands at the smoke. He didn't look like himself. He'd moussed his hair into alarming tufts and spikes that shot out all over, making him look beyond eccentric, possibly insane. He wore turquoise and gold striped pants and a gold vest, high-top sneakers, a polka-dot tie. One shirttail hung out under the vest, and a pair of horn-rimmed glasses kept slipping down his nose. Okay, he was a sort of wizard-nerd, but the image didn't gel. He was still Sam, until he started talking.

"Mmm, good afternoon, ladies and germs," came out in a nasal, adenoidal drone, followed by more coughing and silly noises like "Bleh! Haw. Brak." "Allergies," he explained, pulling a yellow handkerchief from his pocket and waving it at the smoke. "I mmunderstand it's somebody's birthday? Who would that beee? Who is the birthday mmperson today?" he wondered in the tenor nerd voice, nervous and sweet, a sound I'd never heard come from his mouth before.

"Me." Benny raised his hand, grinning, blushing.

"Me? No, oh, no, mine's in April, I'm almost sure."

"No!" said Benny, laughing with the others. "It's *my* birthday."

"Oh, *you*. Well, I knew that — I am, mmm, the Great Sambini! Now, don't tell me — your name is mmm . . ."

"Benny!" the kids shouted.

"No, no, starts with a *Q*. Mmm, I mean *J*, starts with a *J*. It's . . . Joaquin?"

"No, Benny!"

"No, no, that's not it. Don't tell me; the Great Sambini knows all. Mmm, your name is . . ." He pressed his fist to his forehead. "Montague."

"No," they shouted, "it's *Benny!*" giggling but spellbound. Like me, they knew it was Sam, and yet it wasn't Sam. It didn't hurt that while he talked he kept making wild efforts to get rid of the scarf, but it seemed to be glued first to one hand, then to the other.

233

"Benny? Really? Mmm, if you say so. Happy birthday, Benny. How does it feel to be thirty-nine?"

"Six."

"Six!" The Great Sambini went closer, squinting at Benny through the horn-rims. "Here, hold this." Benny took one end of the scarf, and when Sam backed up, a dozen more came with him, like a string of yellow sausages between their two hands. "Hey," Sam exclaimed, "how'd you do that?"

"*You* did it!" the children shouted.

"I did it? Oh, I seriously doubt that. Here, I'll, mmm, take those." He reeled the silks back, stuffing them into one closed hand and opening it to discover, in more apparent amazement, they were gone. "Why, you, you scarf thief," he blustered. "Luckily the Great Sambini knows where you hid them. A*ha!*" Little Justin Carr jumped in delight when Sam yanked another long parade of scarves out of his ear. "Thieves and pickpockets, mmm, tsk tsk tsk, what are they teaching our young people these days?" He kept stuffing scarves into his pants pocket — but of course, the more he stuffed, the longer the string grew. "Quit it," he ordered Justin. "Quit that, I say," which cracked the kids up. His fussbudgety irritation tickled them, and they loved being in on the joke that his incompetence was feigned. They knew they were, literally, in good hands.

Sam made more scarves appear and disappear, multiply and divide, he made a blue and white scarf turn into a blue and white striped scarf, on and on, and somehow each trick was a conspiracy against him. The kids were doing them, not the Great Sambini, who was getting more and more steamed. Suddenly his aggravated face cleared. "No wonder! Of course!" He slapped his forehead. "I forgot my magic hat! Can't do a thing without it."

Out came a flat red disc from an inside pocket. He took a deep breath. "Magic air," he peeped in a squeaky voice, then blew on the disc. It inflated into a red felt homburg. Which fell off his spiky-haired head as soon as he stuck it on. Much hilarious hat schtick ensued, Chaplin-inspired, and tricks with a wand-cane I'd never seen him do before.

In fact, this whole act was new to me. Sam had done gigs at trade shows, adult parties, once a cruise ship, where he appeared variously as Sam Summer, Magician; Milo Marvelle, Master of Mystery; The Prodigious Presto, Prince of Prestidigitation ("but you can just call me Your Excellency"). I'd seen bits and pieces of all of them, and occasionally the whole act in front of a live audience. And I never really got it. Magic was silly, wasn't it? Because there's no such thing. Not that Sam wasn't good. Prospero the Prince of Magic was smooth, suave, sexy, confident, everything you could want in a magician — if you wanted a magician. I never had.

Now I was starting to get it. He hadn't picked the persona of a blowhard or a clown or a doofus for these kids. He was more of a disgruntled Peter Pan, a grown-up child as enchanted, under the aggravation, with the wonderful things he could do as they were. As the act went on even his face changed, lost years, lost strain, and his body seemed to grow suppler and more agile. As a result, eight six-year-olds became rapt and obedient, no jeering or mouthing off, not a single wise guy. Just laughter and wonderment.

I couldn't laugh, but I could wag my tail when Sam botched the coin vanish, and especially the disappearing egg. The kids laughed so hard, Kayla Logan fell out of her seat. I stopped wagging, though, when Sam pulled two yard-long pieces of cord from a pocket and announced he needed two volunteers for his final and extremely difficult trick, Magic Handcuffs.

He picked Allen Hansen and Ethan Carr,

Justin's twin. "Watch carefully! Don't blink!" he instructed as he tied knots with the cords around four little wrists, stringing the cords together in the process so that, when he finished, Allen's rope hung in a loose loop around Ethan's.

"Are you stuck? Try to get away from each other. Nope, they're stuck. But! Mmm. *If* they've got magic, mmm, mojo, they will miraculously break free! We'll give them one minute! You have *one minute* to get free. You can do anything but *you cannot* untie the knots. Ready? One minute, starting . . . *now.* Go!"

They started out self-consciously, testing the ropes with tentative moves like putting their arms around each other from the back, the front. But frustration, crowd laughter, and Sam's constant countdown — "Thirty more seconds! Twenty-five! Twenty-four!" — soon had them in a heap on the ground, thrashing and wrestling like kittens, arms and legs tangled. Allen lost a shoe. Everybody thought it was a riot, everybody but me. I knew where this was heading.

"Time!"

Spent, the boys lay flat in the grass, red-faced and still giggling, while Sam undid the knots around their wrists.

"Too bad, nice try, but now I, the Great

Sambini, shall demonstrate, before your *wondering eyes,* the mystery of Magic Handcuffs. For this difficult trick I will need a mmm partner. A *magic* partner, it goes without mmm saying. Anyone?" All hands shot up. Sam covered his eyes and pointed to, surprise, surprise, Monica. "Monica the Marvelous!"

"Me?" Such pretty modesty. The kids weren't even disappointed at not being chosen. They loved Mrs. Carr. And they sensed this trick, the Great Sambini's last, required an assistant in the know.

It certainly did. Sam had never asked outright, but once or twice, years ago, he'd *hinted* that he would love it if I'd assist him in his act. Of course I'd said no. Without a second thought. How absurd. Ridiculous and unthinkable, like asking him to hold a real estate closing for me. Still, just for fun, sometimes he enlisted me to help with tricks that needed two people, tricks he couldn't do onstage — no assistant — but that he just liked and wanted to try out. Like Magic Handcuffs.

So I knew how to do it. You let people from the audience tie the knots, as many or as complicated as they want — just not too tight. "Don't cut off my blood!" you say (if you're the assistant), because it's vital that *one* wrist rope have a little slack in it. Just a little. So the magician can slip his cord under it and then over the top of your hand. Ta-da, you're free.

The rest is acting. *Over*acting, as you both writhe and wrestle and struggle and contort, accomplishing the magic part on the ground and out of view — underneath yourselves, ideally. So it's like Twister, only more intimate. The one or two times Sam talked me into trying it with him, we enjoyed it very much. Very much.

No way was he going to play Magic Handcuffs with Monica Carr.

Maybe if she'd had on more clothes, not a sleeveless sundress and strappy sandals. Maybe if she hadn't looked so cute, or smelled so sweet. Maybe if she'd been a little less perfect. Maybe if she was in this country on a visa about to run out. Then I might've behaved myself.

Eager volunteers got one of Monica's wrists tied before I made my move. I was still *trying* to be good. But my best intentions were undermined by the persistent vision of Sam and Monica locked in an indecent embrace. And then when it hit me — my God! — they must have *practiced* this trick before, I lost all restraint.

Rowrrr!

Not all restraint; I didn't bite anybody. But I was in the grip of the most primitive anger I'd ever felt, and Monica wasn't the only target. Sam infuriated me, too. I wanted to, but I didn't bite them, only because of the proximity of so many children. One stray fang — it didn't bear thinking about. I jumped between Sam and Monica and did everything else, though — I growled, threatened, herded, head-butted. Monica I body-slammed to the ground on her behind.

Sam couldn't believe his eyes. "Sonoma!" he kept shouting, lunging time after time for my collar. "What the hell? No! Sonoma, *no!*" He still had one end of his rope in his hand. I let him get close, closer — then I sprang, snatched the rope in my teeth, and whirled away.

Now what? Another damn fenced yard, the bane of my life. I ran around and around the perimeter pursued by two adults and eight children. When it looked like they had me cornered, I dashed into Benny's play-house. Hide the rope, hide the rope. Where? In his toy chest?

Too late, no time. I hadn't escaped. I was trapped. At least the trick was ruined — the Great Sambini could hardly start over after all this mayhem. I'd broken the spell. Mission accomplished.

"Great party, Sam."

"It was. Goes without saying, I couldn't have done it without you."

"Oh, sure you could've. Wow, the magic show was *fantastic.*"

"Until it went to hell." Sam and Monica made the same disgusted face as they glanced through the kitchen door at me. Benny and the twins were upstairs playing with Benny's new rainbow-making machine; Sam and Monica were finishing the cleanup. I was trying for a low profile in the safest place I could think of: under the dining room table.

"What do you think set her off?" Sam took a handful of washed glasses from Monica and set them on the top cabinet shelf — too high for her to reach.

"I can't imagine."

Did he hear the same note in her voice I did? Was it my imagination, or did Monica just send me a *look?* No, ridiculous; she didn't know anything. She couldn't. Except that I didn't like her — that had to be pretty clear by now.

"I had no idea you were so *good,*" she told Sam. "I should have. I mean, you do it professionally —"

"Did."

"But I just never realized. *You'd* never say, and from what I've always gathered from Laurie . . ."

"What?"

"Nothing, I just — assumed it was more of a hobby, is all. But, Sam, you're *good. Really* good."

Oh, shut up. She wasn't flattering him, though; she meant it. And Sam beamed with pleasure. So unfair — *I* wanted to say it to him. *I* wanted to make him smile and blush and look tickled.

Why hadn't I ever told Sam he was good?

They finished in the kitchen and moved past me — I watched their legs — into the hall. "Ustin and Jethan!" Monica called; a family joke. "Time to go home!"

Sam started thanking her again. She cut him off to ask, "How are you doing, Sam? I haven't had a chance with all the birthday business to really *talk* to you, not in days."

Days, big deal.

"We're all right," Sam said. "We're fine. Day at a time."

"But you. How are *you* doing?"

He hadn't combed out his Great Sambini hair yet. Backlit in the open door, he looked like a punk angel. "Starting the new job will be good," he said, with no enthusiasm. "Get my mind off things."

"Is anything new with Laurie?" Monica asked gently. Speaking of things.

"Not really. We'll go see her tomorrow night. I usually take Benny on Sundays, but . . ."

Since it was his birthday, he got a reprieve. I put my paws over my eyes, wishing I could disappear. Cease to exist. Think how much better off everybody would be.

When I looked up, Monica had her hand on Sam's arm, rubbing it in a comforting way while her melty eyes shone with sympathy. Instantly I was on my feet, snarling, slinking forward, low to the ground like a wolf.

Who knows what might've happened if Benny and the twins hadn't come bouncing down the steps just then, quarreling and overstimulated, minutes away from a meltdown. Everybody's attention shifted to them, including mine. Good thing, because at that moment Monica's pert little butt had never looked more, how shall I say, toothsome.

I was allowed to go, too, when everyone went outside to the car — Monica had driven over instead of walking. Piling the twins and the birthday paraphernalia in took a while. When it was done, she cupped the back of Benny's head and kissed his forehead. "Happy birthday, mister."

He reached his arms around her waist — she squatted down in front of him. "Tell Monica —" Sam began, but Benny didn't need reminding. "Thank you," he said, and she said, "You are *so* welcome," and pulled him into a close hug. I took two steps toward them, stiff-legged, hair standing on end. My mouth watered.

Monica patted Benny's shoulders and started to sit back on her heels, but he hung on. He hung on. I saw his tight-shut eyes, his wrinkled lips. The need and the blank satisfaction on his face.

I could've eaten a whole family — I could've mauled a playground full of children. God! I wanted something between my teeth to grind and shake until it was dead. But I couldn't lift a paw to interrupt a few seconds of happiness for Benny, even if it came in the arms of my mortal enemy.

I walked around to the side of the house and threw up.

After that, things went downhill.

The day after the party, Benny started first grade and Sam started his new job. Sam dropped Benny off at school on his way to work, and in the afternoons Monica kept

Benny at her house until Sam picked him up. I never met Benny's teacher. I never saw his classroom. Sam dropped the first week's lunch menu on the floor and I made out "teriyaki beef bites" and "café burger with baked beans" before he picked it up. In the evenings, I might hear a precious tidbit about a new friend of Benny's, a confusing assignment, a funny thing that happened that day. But he told Sam all the good stuff as soon as he saw him; by the time they came home, all I got was leftovers.

As for Sam's job, he never mentioned it.

A day lasted a year. I know why dogs sleep so much — there's nothing else to do. The highlight for me was when Mr. Horton, the next-door neighbor, came over at noon to let me out in the backyard for ten minutes. Sam had told him to be sure to change my water and leave me a rawhide chewy, but more often than not Mr. Horton, who was ninety, forgot.

The only way I had ever found out anything important, meaning grown-up, was by listening to Sam's side of telephone conversations, especially with my sister, Delia. Now that he worked every day in an office, those occasions had petered out. One night, though, Ronnie Lewis called and I got to hear the bad news: He had another buyer for the cabin.

He thought the offer was too low and wanted Sam to counter. I held my breath while they argued, Sam saying no, let's take it, Ron trying to talk him out of it. *Are you crazy?* I wanted so badly to say to my husband. I never heard actual figures, but I didn't need to. Even in this lousy market, only a putz would take the first offer. But that wasn't even the point. *Sam, hold out! Don't sell!* When would it end? How many dreams was he going to have to give up for my sake?

But the following Sunday afternoon: a miracle. It happened so fast — one minute I was sulking under the piano, preparing myself for the weekly Hope Springs abandonment; the next Sam was snapping my leash on and saying, "C'mon, girl, wanna go for a ride? Wanna go in the car?" They were taking me with them!

Such a *beautiful* day. The last day of August but clear and blue for a change, not muggy, even a taste of fall in the air. It filled me with new hope, the kind I hadn't felt in so long, it made me euphoric. Sam kept telling me to settle, settle, but it was impossible not to dash from one backseat window to the other, taking in deep gulps of air and watching the world fly past.

And yet, the closer we got, the calmer I grew. Or if not calmer, more thoughtful. I still had no plan, no real idea of what I would *do* once I saw myself — rejoined myself. It didn't seem necessary; some strange faith told me it would just happen. Whatever needed to happen would happen. Whatever force or mutation or reality glitch that had changed me into Sonoma would, just as suddenly and inexplicably, turn me back into Laurie. Because, if nothing else, the universe was still an orderly place — so I had always believed — and it liked balance. Weird anomalies eventually got fixed. Yin and yang. Today was the day I got to do my part to set things right.

Poor Benny. He slumped in his seat, as excited about visiting Mom as he'd be about visiting the pediatrician. Less so. Sam had made him bring along one of his books from school, to show me how well he could read. *It'll be okay,* I told Benny, nuzzling the salty-sweet back of his neck. Except for dog feet (mine, anyway), nothing smelled better than Benny's hair. I licked his ear, which got a laugh out of him. *Don't worry, baby. Mommy's coming home.* He rubbed my muzzle and kissed me on the nose.

So this was Hope Springs from the outside. Pretty. A long, winding drive through

247

woods to a sprawling complex of old, new, and middle-aged buildings. HOPE SPRINGS NURSING AND REHABILITATION CENTER one sign read; another, HOPE SPRINGS ASSISTED LIVING. A multipurpose place, then; something for everybody. Everybody who was infirm. But it was pretty, I had to admit, and clean and quiet, well tended, all you could ask for. It must be costing Sam a fortune.

He parked in a shady spot in one of the enormous parking lots.

"We don't have to stay long," Benny mumbled, fiddling with his seat belt. "I'm hungry."

"You just ate."

"My stomach hurts. I don't feel good. I have a condition."

"Ben."

"I have a disease, Daddy. I'm not well."

Sam scowled. Then sighed. Then ruffled Benny's hair. "Okay, pal, we won't stay long."

Well, wait, now.

"You can tell Mom all about your birthday party — how's that? They'll probably have her outside today. If you like, you can play around by the lily pond —"

"Okay!"

"*After* you talk to her and tell her you love

her and everything."

"Okay." He slumped again. *Not for much longer, sweetheart,* I told him as he opened his door and slammed it. Sam got out and slammed his door. I waited by mine, tail up, shuddering with anticipation.

"Be good," Sam said through the four-inch crack in my window. "We'll be back. Be a good girl."

What? What was this? Incredulous, I watched Sam and Benny walk up a wide, yew-bordered path to a low brick building with glass doors. And disappear inside.

No. No. I howled it, but nobody heard. I raged until my throat hurt, but nobody cared. What had I been thinking? The universe was not an orderly place. Ghastly miscarriages of justice were allowed to persist, and no wise hand balanced horrible, unnatural inequities. I was lost.

I never thought things could get worse.

"Hi, yes, I'd like to make an appointment to have my dog spayed."

Behind Sam's chair, I choked on a piece of empty cottage cheese carton from the garbage.

"Tuesday? Is that as soon as you can do it? Right, the holiday weekend . . . Okay, next Tuesday, then. Eight a.m., that's fine."

I ran around the chair, put my paws on his knees. *No!* I shook my head so hard, I hit myself in the eye with an ear. He kept talking — I started barking. *No! No!*

He *laughed.* "Yeah, that's Sonoma," he said into the phone. "I know. It's like she heard us."

The days that followed were peculiar. I would lie at the top of the stairs at night, guarding the house, and think, Well, another day gone and I didn't run away. I could have: the basement window was still unlocked. Home alone every day, there was nothing to stop me from making a break for it. But I didn't go. The human world was falling apart around me. Running away and reconnecting — somehow — with the real me was my only chance, but I stayed.

Why? The chances of actually making it were tiny — that was one thing. The time Sam let me go with them to Hope Springs had opened my eyes to what would really be involved, the distance, the danger, cars going sixty-five miles an hour. It might take *weeks,* not days. I was scared.

Also, it's hard to describe how seductive being a dog is. How tempting it was to give up. Forget who I used to be and sink into this new self, a self whose boundaries seemed to be nothing but love. To give love and get love — that was what my needs were narrowing down to. I could feel it intensifying every day. Friendship, sweetness, play, companionship — with the exception of evil Monica, that was all I cared about. Going, going, almost gone were any feelings about justice, fairness, tit for tat — and never *mind* anger, disappointment, umbrage, pride, ego, disapproval. Jealousy — I still had that. I wanted *all* the love my loved ones had. And that was a failing, but one I knew I'd never overcome. It came too naturally.

And it's just so damn *nice* to be a dog. I can't overstate the pleasures of sinking into a light doze about five times an hour. Drifting off . . . waking up . . . drifting off . . . dreaming . . . waking up . . . You fall into a pattern of sleeping and waking that, over time, averages out to almost constant half-asleepness (or half-awakeness) and it's very . . . nice.

Another example, just a small thing, but — the game of sock. Tug-of-war, I should say, but Sam and Benny called it "sock," as in "Want to play sock? Sonoma! Get the sock!" I tried to remind myself that *tennis* was the best game — *Tennis, Laurie! You're good at it, remember? Tennis is the best!* —

but it was hard. And face it: I got so much more joy out of sock than I ever got out of tennis.

Anyway, I didn't leave. The days drifted by in a pleasant haze, long periods of comfortable idleness punctuated by bursts of extreme excitement — *They're home!* — and profound contentment. I worried, and sometimes I had bad dreams, but time passed and it became increasingly clearer that the dog side of me was winning.

On Thursday, the principal at Benny's school left a message on the machine that he'd been in a fight. She was sending a note home with him. She wanted to talk to Sam about it as soon as possible.

Benny in a fight? Impossible. What kind of fight? Was he hurt? No, or she'd have said, or there would've been something in her voice besides calm professionalism. I paced instead of napping the rest of the afternoon.

Mr. Horton came over twice to let me out, the second time in late afternoon, five or six, something like that. An amazing number of people talk out loud to dogs — you can't believe the things they'll say — but Mr. Horton wasn't one of them. *Where's Sam? Where's Benny? Why are they so late?* I asked him with my best supplicant face, but all I got was the usual, "Come on, dog," and, "Get busy."

It was getting dark when the car pulled up. Of course the engine didn't sound any different, and of course the doors slamming were just doors slamming — but I knew before I heard Sam and Benny's slow, draggy footsteps that something was wrong. My sixth sense. And as soon as I smelled them, I knew what it was. Me. The scent of Hope Springs was all over them.

Sam let Benny have a glass of milk in the kitchen. I thought they'd talk, but they didn't. *How was I?* Worse — I must be. Or exactly the same; that would be just as bad. So this mutual dejection that hung in the air like smoke from a grease fire was only because they'd seen me. That was all. No change. Just another soul-eroding visit to Laurie.

Benny dawdled over his milk, but didn't argue when Sam told him to go up and get ready for bed, it was late. I usually went with Benny at those times, because of the intimacy. My little boy was never more my little boy than when he was getting into his wonderful-smelling pjs or peeing in the toilet (and on the floor) or standing at the sink on tiptoe to brush his teeth. But now I stayed with Sam, followed him when he

went into the den. I wanted to see his reaction to the principal's message.

He played it twice. His face was turned
away, but everything else about him answered my question. This was the first he'd
heard.

His feet on the stairs sounded like doom
to me; I could imagine what they sounded
like to Benny. I wanted to trip Sam, block
him at the door, do something to protect
Benny — but the instinct to confront him
was just as strong. Sam and I went into our
son's room side by side.

He was sitting on his bed, working a
puzzle. He didn't look up, even when Sam
sat next to him. "Ben."

No answer. Intense scrutiny of puzzle.

"Is there something you have to tell me?"

Head shake.

"Benny."

Silence.

"Is there something you have to show
me?"

Long pause, then Benny got out of bed,
found his book bag on the floor, rummaged
through it for about an hour, withdrew a
sealed envelope. Handed it to Sam word-
lessly and got back in bed.

Sam looked at the envelope for a while
before opening it. Not to prolong the

suspense, just to put things off a few seconds longer. I sympathized.

Leaning in, I tried to read over his shoulder, but the type was too small. The letter wasn't very long, one or two paragraphs, signed in ink. Sam sighed when he folded it and put it back in the envelope. "Okay. Tell me about this."

Wordless and sullen, Benny clacked wooden puzzle pieces together hard.

"We've never talked about fighting before, not much, you and me. Were you angry at this boy, this — Doug? It's okay to get mad at people, you know that. It's what you do about —"

"He's a poop head. He's a dummy. He's —" Benny looked up from the puzzle, right into Sam's eyes. "He's an asshole."

"Hey, now —"

"He is."

"Why?"

Benny wouldn't answer.

"What did he do? Did he hit you first? That's —"

"No."

"Okay."

"I hit him."

"Okay. Why? Did he say something?"

"He said — he said —" Tears welled and spilled over. "He s-said . . ."

"What did he say?" Very gently, Sam folded Benny in his arms. I sidled close, leaning my flank against both of them.

"He said Mommy . . ."

"What?"

"Is a . . ."

"What?"

"Vegetable."

I made a choking sound, the closest to a sob I could come. They didn't hear me; Benny was crying and Sam was crooning consolation. They were a tangle of arms and pressed-together faces, and all I could do was shove my snout into the places I could find skin.

"All right, listen. That kid was wrong." He lifted Benny's chin so he could look at him. "And you were right — he's an asshole."

"I know." Benny wiped his slimy face on the sheet. "I told you."

"But we don't use that word, right? Well, except us, you and me. On rare occasions. We can say it to each other, but nobody else. How about that?"

"Okay." A smile broke through. How cool to have a secret dirty word with Dad. I wasn't sure I approved.

"And we don't hit people when they say stupid things. Because they're allowed to, it's not against the law. People can be as stupid as they want, and we just ignore them. We can say, 'You're wrong,' or maybe, 'You're an idiot,' but that's it. We don't hit 'em, we just ignore 'em. Right?"

"Okay." But then Benny's face crumpled again. "Is she?" he asked in a small voice, head down, playing with a button on Sam's shirt. "Is Mommy a . . ."

"No, Ben, no. She's not."

"But she just lies there."

"She's asleep."

"But what if she never gets up?"

"She will."

"But what if she doesn't? What if she stays like that forever? I wish she would come home! Why can't she wake up? Why!"

"I think she will." He took Benny's shoulders before the tears could start again. "I really think she will, but it might take some more time."

"How long?"

"I don't know. But we're her family, you and me —"

"And Aunt Delia."

"And Aunt Delia, and all we can do is keep thinking about her, and praying for her, and going to see her, and telling her we love her. Because she can't help it — you know she'd come back if she could, right? You know that, don't you?"

"Yes."

"She's trying, but it's very hard. She wants to be with us as much as we want her to be. We just have to keep waiting. And hoping, and not losing faith. And meanwhile, we've got each other."

"I know."

"You know." Sam hugged him for a long time. "We'll be okay," he whispered over and over, until Benny's body finally began to sag from sleepiness. "You and me, pal. We'll be okay."

So I knew what I had to do. And not tomorrow: tonight. No more stalling. I felt as if I'd woken up from an embarrassingly long nap. Why had I waited so long? Laziness, denial, cowardice — some retriever I'd been. But no more. Tonight I would begin the journey back. To myself. If I didn't make it — and all the obstacles between me and Hope Springs had never looked so daunting — at least I'd have taken the chance. At least I'd have tried to put my family back together.

I stayed with Benny after he fell asleep, stretched out alongside him, my head on his shoulder. The sound of his heart and the rhythm of his breathing came right inside me, merged with my heart and breath. It was difficult to leave him, the hardest thing I've ever done. I didn't want to wake him, so I didn't kiss him good-bye. I put my warm nose in the hollow of his throat and breathed him in.

Downstairs, it was dead quiet. I found Sam by smell — on the sofa in the den, grasping something, looking down at it in his lap. I didn't want to, but it was time to say good-bye to him, too.

When I jumped up next to him, he barely noticed, and his "Down" was so halfhearted, we both ignored it.

My picture. That was what he was holding.

Oh, Sam. Don't be sad.

And then I saw something I'd never seen before. Sam crying.

It was worse than anything. I licked his cheek, and when he turned his face away I howled. Softly; more of a whine, a really tragic sound. It got his attention. He did something he never had before: He put both arms around me and buried his face in my neck.

And I raised up on my back legs and embraced him back. It was . . . divine. We'd never been so close, not since I changed. I'd have stayed there all night, but too soon

Sam pulled himself together and pushed me away.

Incomplete again, bereft, I watched him dig a ratty Kleenex from his pocket and scrub his face. His crooked smile was the saddest thing I ever saw. He rarely talked to me, but now he said, "Funny dog. You're a funny old dog. What's up with you?" So many times I'd tried to answer that. Now I just shook my head. When he petted me, I closed my eyes and reveled in it, although my heart was cracking. *Bye, Sam. Don't worry anymore. I'm going to fix it. I love you so much.*

The phone rang.

"Hello? Oh, hi, Monica."

I almost left then. What would have happened if I had? I've often wondered.

"We got back about an hour ago, hour and a half. Fine. I mean, you know, it was the same. No, no change."

Blah blah. I didn't want to hear this.

"Listen — Benny didn't say anything to you about a fight, did he? At school? When he was over there this afternoon, he didn't . . . I didn't think so. I wouldn't have known myself if . . . No, he's okay; he's fine. Some kid named Doug. Apparently he said something —"

Don't tell her! Don't you dare tell her!

"Kid stuff, nothing really . . . Yeah. I know. Right, I'm sure he's bottling up a lot of anger and frustration . . . Right. Right."

Right, right. Shut up, Monica, nobody wants to hear your amateur child psychology.

Finally she got to the point. "A picnic?" Sam said, brightening a bit. "Sounds good, we're free all weekend. Which is better for you? Sunday, then, fewer people than on Labor Day, yeah. Good. Sonoma, too? Great, she'll love it."

Thanks for thinking of me.

"Okay, you bring that. I can do — Right, drinks, snacks . . ."

More blah blah about the portable grill, whose cooler was bigger, did they want lemonade or pop or both. I made myself not imagine it, not romping around with Benny and the twins in some beautiful woodsy, meadowy place, some sylvan spot alive with squirrels and chipmunks, maybe a lake or a stream. *Have a great time. Without me.* In a negative way, self-pity is very motivating. *So long.* I slunk toward the door.

"Patuxent Hills Park? No, we've never been there. Sounds good."

Patuxent Hills Park? Patuxent Hills Park? I sold a house near there, in Brookville, south a little ways on Route 97. The park is

261

only a mile from Hope Springs! As the crow flies — as the dog walks, it's probably two. Two miles! Through woods and rural lanes and sleepy, high-end housing developments. With sidewalks!

Oh, thank God, thank God, thank God, thank God. I collapsed at Sam's feet — my knees were too weak to hold me up. Gratitude turned my bones to jelly. I rolled over and showed him my belly.

All I had to do was wait till Sunday. Reunion day.

DOGS MUST BE LEASHED AT ALL TIMES

Why couldn't things ever be easy? No alcoholic beverages, no dumping, no loud music, we close at sundown — I could live with those, but LEASHED AT ALL TIMES was going to be a problem.

So was mud, although not for me. The sun was peeping out between clouds now, but it had rained every day since Thursday and the park was saturated, even the picnic tables under the wooden pavilions. They could've postponed until tomorrow — I was afraid they would — but the kids were so wound up, they'd have exploded if the grownups had canceled. Sam said a little rain never hurt anybody, and here we were.

The first order of business, after claiming one of the many empty tables and setting up all the picnic stuff, was a walk. This was my chance — except the person on the other end of the leash was Sam, not Benny or one of the twins. Or best, Monica, whom I'd have had zero guilt about bolting from, preferably with violence. Sam was another story. He was strong, for one thing, but also — this is hard to explain — as *pack leader* he was someone I had a hard time disobeying. Believe it or not. I'd always thought of us as equals, or if one of us was a tiny bit ascendant, it was me. Not true as man and dog. Sam was alpha.

The river was narrow here, really more of a stream, and swollen from all the rain. This little park fit in an inlet the river made on its way northwest, bisecting two counties. A main trail to the left and a rougher, secondary one to the right followed the water's twists and turns. We took the main one because it was wider and not as mushy, but even so, sometimes we had to detour into the woods around puddles or stretches of mud. I wanted to run ahead with the children, but I was stuck with Sam and Monica. Plod, plod, stop and look at this, plod some more, shout at the kids to quit doing something or other, plod, plod, stop and look at that. Absolutely no fun at all. Once we ran into two guys coming the other way, and I had to *sit down* to avoid the rude attentions of their irritating male Shih Tzu. Sometimes, frankly, I didn't mind that sort of thing, but today was not one of those times.

A moment came when I thought I had a chance.

"Look!" Monica said, stopping, pointing up. "See it? A redheaded woodpecker."

"Where?"

"Right there. Three, four — five branches up, left side, that maple tree."

Sam knew birds; they'd become his hobby when we bought the cabin. "I think that's a red-bellied woodpecker."

"But it's got a red head."

"It's got a red *crown*. A redheaded woodpecker's head is completely red."

"But where's its red belly?"

"It's hard to see; you have to be closer." His hand went slack during this fascinating conversation, his attention focused completely on the bird. I let the leash go loose to soften him up even more, then gathered my feet under me and leapt.

And almost pulled Sam's arm out of the socket.

"Hey!"

I'd almost strangled myself, too, but I had the wit to go into a bedlam of barking, pretending I'd seen something incredibly exciting, a rabbit, a deer, an elephant. When Sam told me to cool it, calm down, I obeyed instantly. "Good girl," he had to admit.

"She is," Monica agreed, surprised.

"I really think she's starting to get it."

Escape-wise, lunchtime was a bust because Sam looped the leash around one leg of the picnic table. Nothing to do but lie down and be good, and munch on tidbits Benny and the twins let fall from time to time.

Sam asked Monica if Benny could stay late at her house on Thursday, and I learned something I didn't know. "We're moving up the closing on the cabin," Sam said. "Guy decided to pay cash, so there's no reason to wait."

"Oh," Monica said. "Well." And then, when the kids were talking, she said, "I'm sorry," just loud enough for Sam (and me) to hear.

"No, it's good. Really. The money's coming just in the nick."

Well, didn't that just tie it. Another reason, as if there weren't enough already, to act fast. What else could possibly go wrong in the human world?

After lunch, Sam did his disappearing saltshaker trick. I always knew it had to end up in his lap somehow, but I could never figure out how. A new perspective changes everything.

"Have you been doing any magic shows lately?" Monica asked, cutting big pieces of layer cake for everybody. Homemade, naturally. What a perfect family we must have looked like to everybody else in the park. Mom, Dad, three kids, the faithful dog.

"No, no." I recognized Sam's fake-careless voice. "That's all . . . I don't do that anymore. No time."

"Ah," Monica said softly. "Too bad. But I guess with the new job and all . . ."

"Right."

"Do you still . . ." *Hate it,* she was going to say. But she changed it to "Is it getting any better?" even though Benny wasn't listening — too busy comparing his loose tooth to Ethan's.

"It's a job. I'm in no position to complain."

"You don't complain."

"It's just . . . well, you know."

"It is what it is."

So profound.

But a little later, I wondered if maybe

Benny had been paying attention, at least to his father's tone of voice — upbeat but tight, a world of discontent just beneath the surface. Because Benny pulled on Sam's sleeve, interrupting something Monica was saying, and told him about troodon dinosaurs. "The male sits on the eggs and guards the nest, Dad. I read about it. He's the mom. She goes out and does stuff and he stays and makes the nest safe and keeps the babies warm."

All Sam said was, "How about that," but he put his arm around Benny's waist and pressed him close.

Oh, Benny. Light of my life.

Monica decreed the grass was now dry enough to play games on, so that was what the boys did, with Sam. I got to stay where I was and watch Monica clean up.

Desperation was creeping in. How in the world was I going to pull this off? To be *this close* and still fail — I couldn't think about it. Maybe if I . . .

"What, Sonoma? Do you have to go? Do you have to do *business?*"

Bingo. It was partly the high whine, partly the soulful-eyes thing. They never let me down.

"I'm taking Sonoma for a walk," Monica called over to Sam, who waved and went back to swinging the kids around in a game of statue.

She picked the secondary trail this time, the one that wound east, under a cement bridge and around a bend — out of sight. Perfect, perfect. Nobody was here; the path was too narrow and boggy for hikers today, and too close to the clattering river. That sound and the smell of wet earth filled my head, intoxicating. Sunlight made blue crystals on the damp tree leaves. Everything was beautiful, but lost on me. I'd remember it later — or not.

Monica went at an excruciatingly slow pace when she wasn't stopped dead, admiring nature. She'd brought along an expensive-looking camera. She halted on the bank to snap a picture of dappled light on water. Was this my chance? I would only get one. If I failed, she'd be on guard from then on. I preferred nonviolence, but only as a first resort. I would fight if I had to.

I braced. *Don't make me have to hurt you.*

She had the leash looped around her wrist, though. Better to wait till it was loose in her hand. Then I could just snap it and run.

"Come on, Sonoma. Don't you have to pee? *I* do," she said, laughing, and I hoped she would, right then and there. Talk about

268

a distraction. But no, too much of a lady. We slogged on.

A thick pine tree had snapped at the base and half fallen in the river, years ago from the look of it. "How pretty," Monica said, turning the camera on again. It did look picturesque, the sparse, rain-dark branches stretched out over churning water. She took a few shots. Then, "Oh, look, Sonoma, a spiderweb. See it?"

I saw it, in the crotch of a dead branch at the end of the tree, just before it dipped into the river. It would've been invisible if it hadn't been shiny with drying raindrops. *Yes, very pretty. Why don't you go out there and take a picture of it?*

And that's exactly what she did.

What a moron. *Are you crazy?* I thought, before I recollected myself. *Be* that stupid; go *farther* out there with a camera in one hand, a dog leash in the other, the racing brown river beneath you. Please, after you.

But she was so athletic and surefooted, she never even tottered. And she wasn't stupid enough to go to the end, only half-way, with me about four feet away, the length of the leash, just one long leap to shore. The expensive camera had a telephoto lens. I heard it whir into action, watched Monica sight her spiderweb picture, one-

269

handed, through the LCD. I started to shake. From anticipation, I thought, but then I realized — *I* was the one who was scared. The chopping sound of the river, the potent smell of water, and the humid air were the last good memories I had of my human self. What came next was all a nightmare. I *hated* rivers.

Still one-handed, Monica snapped off a couple of shots, then tilted the camera ninety degrees for a vertical. Now or never. I dug my toenails into the bark and jerked my head, my whole body, to the side as hard as I could.

She yelped as the leash flew out of her hand, and I spun and leapt to the bank.

A splash, hard to hear over the chop. I looked back. Oh, for the love of —

Monica lay flat out in the water, gripping a branch in one hand, camera high in the other, trying to keep it above the drink. *Let it go, you idiot* — but I saw myself in another river, leaping cartoonishly after a slippery cell phone, and I knew she wouldn't.

The current was strong enough that her feet were bobbing at the top behind her. I didn't know I was barking until I had to stop to hear what she was yelling. "Help! I can't swim!" She gave an angry wail and dropped the camera — so she could grab for the branch with that hand, too. *Crack.* The branch broke and the water took her.

It was supposed to be the other way around, but in that moment *my* life passed before my eyes. I saw it all in fine detail, a Technicolor highlight film, the ups and downs of Laurie Summer's life. Glimpsed as a whole like that, I could see it came up short in an important department, the very one Sonoma the dog excelled in. The love-and-be-loved department. The only one that mattered to her, and really the only one that mattered — I saw it in this extreme instant with perfect clarity — period.

No point jumping in the water here — I'd catch Monica faster if I ran. Mud flew behind my feet as I tore along the bank, dodging rocks, trees, bushes, brush. Monica sailed downriver like a kayak, her dark head bobbing in and out of sight. I caught up when she slammed into a tangle of wood and debris swirling in the middle of the stream. She flailed for a branch, but her grip slipped. I made a running jump from an outcrop of bank and landed in the same roaring surge that took her down again.

Rocks! One sheared my side; another cracked me in the forehead. I *recognized* the pain more than felt it. The current flipped me over; I swallowed water. Over the tumult, I heard shouting, a man's voice. Sam's? Had he heard me barking? Monica saw me for the first time and reached out — to save herself or me, I'll never know. She missed, but we flailed side by side long enough so that I could snatch up the shoulder of her blouse in my teeth. We smacked violently into something hard and stationary. Another fallen tree, anchored to shore. *Grab it,* I told her, but she was too dazed; she just hung there between me and the tree, limp.

Yes, it was Sam; I recognized his voice yelling her name. All that was keeping me afloat was the force of the water battering me against Monica. *Grab something,* I begged her, shaking the glob of wet cotton in my mouth. It was hard to breathe. I shook her again. Her eyes stayed closed, but she reached out for the log and hung on.

Now I could spit out the cloth and get a breath. Sam was forty feet away, sprinting for us along the muddy bank. "Hang on!" he kept shouting. Except I couldn't — no hands. Monica began to cough and retch, reviving. The one paw I could keep on the tree trunk suddenly felt it vibrate. Sam was trying to walk on it, arms out for balance. He slipped and fell to his knees. But he kept coming at a crawl.

At the last, he stretched out full length, slapped his hand over Monica's hand, and she was safe.

I couldn't hold on to anything anymore. I slipped under the log, resurfaced on the other side. The drag of the current felt like heavy, coaxing hands pulling me down. I fought the temptation to let go as long as I could. *Good-bye. Good-bye.* It wasn't so much sad as inevitable. The last I saw of Sam, he had one arm around Monica, the other stretched out to me. *This is so stupid* was my final thought the first time this happened to me. This time it was *I love you so much.*

Same sky, different trees. Where was I? This upward view looked familiar, painfully so, but when I turned my head to the side, I didn't recognize anything. Scattered benches, tidy walks, trimmed hedges. Brick building. Institutional neatness.

Wait a minute.

"What did she say?" asked a tense female voice behind me.

A different tense female voice answered. "I think she said — I think she said — 'I love you.' "

That voice I recognized. "Hettie?" I asked in a croak.

The nurse loomed over me, gaping, the whites of her eyes eclipsing the irises. "Laurie?"

I nodded. "I do love you, but" — I had to clear my throat — "I was thinking of Sam. Would you call him? On his cell — he's not home."

The other woman must be an aide; her name tag read "Victoria." She and Hettie grabbed each other's hands and started to cry. So of course I did, too.

Hettie pulled herself together first. "Yes, call," she told Victoria. "Call the husband. And go get Dr. Lazenby. And Dr. Pei. Hurry!"

Not much time for reflection after that. Nursing homes for the incurably comatose don't experience miracle awakenings very often, I guess. For mine, Hope Springs went quietly wild. Doctors and nurses surrounded me, then aides, staff, social workers, custodians, even other patients — you'd think there would be a protocol for times like this, rare though they might be. But nobody seemed to be in charge, and everybody was so *happy.* Dr. Lazenby himself wheeled me back into my room, so then the crowd had to disperse. "Keep talking," he told me, passing a file or something up and down the soles of my feet. "How do you feel? What's your full name?"

"Laura Claire Marie O'Dunne. Summer. I feel . . . awake. Where's Sam? And Benny? Did you call?"

"On their way." He peered into my right eye with a lighted scope. "Count backward from twenty, please."

In a lull in the excitement, I had a little cry myself. "It's natural," Hettie assured me. "Strong emotion can very often follow a prolonged period of semi- or unconsciousness. It's relief, confusion, the stress — or nothing at all. You just go ahead and cry."

Such a nice woman. I *did* love her. But I wasn't weeping from relief or stress or confusion; I was weeping for Sonoma.

She gave up her life for me. That was how it felt, although in another sense you could say *I* gave up my life for me. Some sort of better me. And Monica was almost irrelevant, just a vehicle, you could also say — but then again, trying to save her was the very thing that had restored me to myself, that act. Wasn't it?

So confusing. Hettie might be right — these tears were just from stress.

No, they were for Sonoma. When she drowned, I lost the best of myself. But I would spend the rest of my life trying to find her again. In me.

■ ■ ■ ■

Sam saw me before I saw him. Hettie was raising the bed and punching up the pillows when I heard a sound and looked behind her. He stood in the doorway with his arms held out a little from his sides, knees flexed. His face looked tender and dumbstruck, his body poised as if to fly.

"Hey," said Hettie with a huge smile. "Well, I'll just finish this up later, won't I?" I bet she was Sam's favorite nurse, too. "They're getting set up to do a lot of tests, so this visit will have to be quick. Plenty of time later, though. Plenty of time."

She hugged Sam on her way out, but I'm not sure he noticed. He didn't seem to be able to move. Even when I held out my hand, he only came a step closer. It took my voice to uproot him.

"It's me, Sam. I'm back. I've come back to you."

Then I had him, tight in my arms, holding me, warm and breathing and alive. My Sam. Both of us laughing, crying, saying, "Thank God," and "I love you," and "I *missed* you," and things that made sense only to us. We started to kiss everywhere, as if welcoming each other back in pieces.

Then we rested, just holding on and breathing together. Then we kissed again.

"Benny?" I said, and Sam said, "He's here." And there he was, shy as a fawn, holding Hettie's hand in the door. But unlike his dad, he came to me on his own.

"Hi, Mom," he said, comically matter-of-fact; I thought he might shake hands. But something, maybe my tears and gluey-voiced "Oh, Benny!" cracked his bashful shell, and he landed beside me in a bound, all arms and nuzzling head and sharp shoulders. Just under my joy and the intense need to hold him closer, tighter, an odd thought drifted: *I can't* smell *him.* Even when I buried my nose in his hair, I couldn't completely *get* that smoky-sweet scent I loved so much. Oh, well. I had Benny.

"You woke up! I knew you would. Daddy said and said, and at first I thought you might not, but then I knew you would."

"That was clever of you."

"What were you *doing?* What were you *thinking?*"

"Umm . . ."

"Where *were* you? Did you know when I was here? I came a *lot.*"

"I did know. Sometimes, anyway."

"But you couldn't wake up until now?"

"Not till now."

"Because it was hard."

"It was so hard."

"And your head hurt."

"Well, at first. But then it didn't, and I was just sleeping."

"Could you hear us talking? We did. We talked all the time. Dad . . . Dad, mostly. Sometimes, Mommy." He mumbled this against my neck. "Sometimes . . . I just played."

"Oh, but that's okay — I always knew you were here. I *wanted* you to just play."

Exactly the right thing to say, because Benny heaved the deepest sigh and laid his head on my chest, his relief heavy as a winter blanket.

Sam was kissing my hand, each of my fingers. "You're still wet," I noticed, patting his damp sleeve. His lifted brows told me he thought that was an odd sentence construction. That was the moment it first hit me: *I have a strange story to tell.* And this probably wasn't the time to tell it.

"That's because we've had a bit of an adventure," Sam began. "We —"

"We went on a picnic and Monica almost drowned! But Dad got her in time and she's okay, and she's in the lounge with Justin and Ethan. They came with us, but they have to go back and get all our stuff because

278

it's still there, because we didn't pick anything up. We just ran! Daddy speeded."

Sam and I smiled at each other, and I felt the world shift a fraction. Go back to normal. I was definitely home.

I stroked Benny's dear, bumpy back, comforting him. Lovely for him to get his mom back, sure, but how terribly, terribly sad to lose his dog. "We'll get another one, sweetheart," was on the tip of my tongue when he suddenly sat up straight and said, "Mom! We got a dog!"

"Oh, baby, I'm so —"

"She's a girl — Sonoma — she's really good, and smart, she can shake hands and open doors and everything. We ran over her! But then we saved her and now she's ours. You'll like her, Mom, she's really, really good."

I looked at Sam in alarm. Didn't Benny *know?*

Sam made a wry face. "Well, I don't know how good she is, but she's definitely our dog. She's out in the car. Maybe they'll let you see her later, tomorrow or —"

"Sonoma's in the car? Sonoma is *here?*"

"Yeah." Sam looked at me strangely again. "She's a mess right now, though, been in the river, got some scrapes and bruises —"

"Monica said she saved her! Monica said

she jumped in and got her by the shirt! Then *she* almost drowned, but she ended up on a rock and now she's okay except a bump on her head. Monica said we should take her to the vet."

"Don't spay her," I said. In case I wasn't home by Tuesday.

They *both* looked at me strangely.

"I mean, if you were going to, you know. Just hold off till we talk about it, is all. 'Kay?"

"Sure," said Sam. He looked bewildered. "No problem."

"So we can keep her?" Benny asked in a very soft voice, also garbled because of the two fingers he had in his mouth. As if he didn't really want me to hear. As if no answer would equal permission.

The fact that he was worried at all just killed me. "Hey, are you kidding? Of *course* we can keep her. She's our *dog*."

At least.

I couldn't wait to meet her.

AFTER

"Crap!" Sam makes a graceful grab for his jack of spades, but the river is too swift. The card floats away before he can catch it.

"I was wondering when that would happen," I rouse myself to say. He's been doing flawless fancy shuffling for five minutes straight. Something had to give.

"You said crap."

"I was provoked."

"Crap, crap, crap, crap —."

"Benny. Stifle."

My son cackles and goes back to pitching a rubber ball to Sonoma in the shallows. Underhand lobs, up high and right into her mouth. Being in the river was supposed to add a new layer of difficulty, but they perfected this game a long time ago.

So here we are, back where we started. Looking at us, if you didn't know, you'd think we were the same Summer family as before, just a year older and with a dog.

You'd be right, except for all the ways in which you'd be wrong.

"What time are they coming tomorrow?" Sam asks, stashing his deck of cards in his pocket.

"Two-ish. Which means two on the dot," I say in the middle of a wide-mouthed yawn. Time for my nap. I love naps.

That's a difference — old Laurie would've suspected some horrible health crisis if she'd ever wanted anything so pointless and wasteful as a nap.

Another difference is my friendship with Miss Punctuality: Monica Carr. She and the twins are coming down to the cabin for the afternoon tomorrow. Sam will take the boys fishing or hiking while Monica and I sit in chairs in the river — like now — and talk and talk, and then we'll all go in and eat whatever delicious but healthful meal she's prepared ahead and brought down with her. I won't feel an ounce of resentment. I'll *notice* all the ways in which she's a better mother, friend, and general human being than I am, but instead of feeling cynical or superior, I'll just be grateful. That she likes me as much as I like her.

She'll probably bring her new camera and take lots of pictures. She never told old Laurie her secret ambition was to be a nature photographer — Why would she? I wouldn't have been interested anyway — but she was afraid to try. What if she wasn't any good? she worried. What if it took too much time away from Justin and Ethan? What if it was impractical or, horrors, *self-ish?*

I like to think I helped set her straight there. If you can find a way to make a living doing what you love, welcome to the elite group of the most blessed people in the world. I'm in that group — I started back at Shanahan & Lewis full-time in January. Sam's in that group — he quit the hated actuary job in February, and now he's doing magic gigs almost every weekend. Why shouldn't Monica be in that group? I'm glad she took my advice and enrolled in photography courses at the Maryland Institute at night. We keep the twins.

I think of that spiderweb picture she took on the log. Bet it was great. Too bad it's lying at the bottom of the Patuxent.

The Shenandoah is bright blue today, reflecting the June sky. "Say, pard," Sam calls over to Benny, "wanna head up to the bunkhouse and rustle some grub for the old lady?"

Who could resist such an invitation. "What'll we make?" Benny asks, splashing

283

over to our chairs. He's grown an inch since school ended, I swear. In two months he'll be seven. I want to slow time down, make this summer last forever. Benny at six is too precious to lose, so I hold on tight.

"How 'bout a side o' beef, a mess o' beans, and a hank o' jerky?" I say. Benny's in his cowboy phase; it's between spaceman and what I predict will be all soccer all the time.

He puts his arms around me, getting my shirt soaked. This is a good hug, though, spontaneous and fun. For a while last year, Benny's hugs were needy and clingy and he was my too-constant companion. I'd wake at night with a feeling of being watched, open my eyes, and see Benny's, two inches away. "Hi," he'd say, stare until I said "Hi" back, and go back to bed.

We let it go, didn't take him to a psychiatrist or anything. I let him have all of his mother that he wanted, every last second I could spare, all my attention and all my love — sometimes I thought I'd go nuts — and after a while he quit shadowing me. Of course, now I miss him.

"Or we could just heat up a boot." Sam bends down to kiss me. "Got any ol' boots, pard?"

"Just you, Hopalong."

"Sure you don't want to come on up to the ranch and help out? Me and Ben, we got a hankerin' fer yer grits."

"Why does that sound —"

"Can we just make some sandwiches?" Benny says with adult impatience. Sam and I look at each other and sigh. We feel bad. Nothing shoots Benny out of a phase faster than our embrace of it.

"So you're okay?" Sam asks, sliding his fingers through my hair. Thank goodness the question is only rhetorical, but it took many weekends to get to this point — leaving Mom by herself in the river. After I woke up I went through a long period of dizziness, completely gone now, and a shorter period of "confusion." I'd say something strange, something only Sonoma could know, for example, then get in trouble backtracking.

Like the night I told Benny, "Don't feed her that; she can't handle rich food," as he was about to smuggle the rest of his dessert to Sonoma under the table.

"Yes, she can."

"No, she can't. Remember that time she threw up all over the dining room after . . ." Oops. "No, wait, that was some other dog."

"What dog?" Sam asked, interested. "Because Sonoma did that —"

"No, no, some other dog. Hettie's dog, she told me about her once. She has a big —"

"Nuh-uh, Hettie has cats."

"Not Hettie. Did I say Hettie? *Carla,* the other one, she's got some big dog who threw up in the —"

"When did she tell you this?"

"Well, not when I was *asleep,* obviously, ha-ha!"

"So —"

"Afterward, I guess, I mean, when else? Unless it wasn't Carla — wait, no, it was Mrs. Speakman, the lady across from Monica. She's got a German shepherd, Trudi, *she* threw up in the dining room. After she ate a — pie. She ate a pie off the — kitchen window, like in a story, and — Who wants coffee? Sam? I mean, *Sam,* do you want coffee?"

I wanted to tell them the truth. A dozen times I started to tell them, or at least Sam, but I'd listen to the sentence about to come out of my mouth and have second thoughts. "You'll never guess where I really was all that time you thought I was in a coma." Or "I know you guys think you hit Sonoma that day on Georgetown Road, but guess what, you really hit me!"

Let's face it, even Benny wouldn't believe

me. Even if I told Sam everything that happened, things only he and the dog could
possibly know, he'd find a way to rationalize
it. So would I — who wouldn't? "Oh, you're
just remembering something I told you
while you were sleeping," he'd say. He'd
find an excuse, the way we do with people
who've seen ghosts or UFOs or religious
miracles. Whatever they say, somehow we
always find a way to explain it.

Besides, sometimes *I* think it couldn't have
happened; it must've been a dream. People
do not come back as dogs. I can't even
prove it anymore, because Benny gave me
back the hoarded treasures that were going
to be my ace in the hole, the secret I
couldn't have known because no one knew
it except him and Sonoma. But I wasn't fast
enough. The day I came home from Hope
Springs, Benny piled my coffee mug, mouse
pad, and earrings on the bed. "Look,
Mommy. I was saving them for you." After I
had a good cry, we had a long snuggle.

"Come up soon," Sam says, and I say, "I
will, five more minutes," as he and Benny
gather their stuff and start for the cabin.
Sonoma used to follow Benny everywhere, I
happen to know, when she wasn't following
Sam everywhere, but now she sticks with
me. She's my dog. Benny's feelings weren't

hurt — he took it as a matter of course. Sam, too. The only one who had a problem with her instant devotion was me.

She splashes over and sits next to me, her rump in the water, chin on the arm of my lawn chair. "Hey, babe," I say, gently squeezing one thick, silky ear. She's smaller than I thought. Smaller than I *felt,* rather. She comes to just above my knee, perfect stroking height as she winds gracefully by. She has soft, soulful, light brown eyes. She likes to cross her legs in front when she lies down, very ladylike. We have the same color hair, tawny reddish tan, but hers is straighter. I admire her trim waistline. When I take her to the ball field in the park and let her off the leash (illegally), she chases the low-flying barn swallows until she's so tired her tongue hangs out. I could watch her run forever.

Now she puts her paw on my lap for me to shake, which I do, but it's never enough. She switches paws, I shake that one, she switches back. It's almost a tic. "What do you *want,* honey?" She never answers, but sometimes I think it's to put her arms around me. Just get *closer.*

She scared me at first. I was, of course, ecstatic when I heard she hadn't drowned, but when they brought me home and the first thing she did was leap up beside me on the bed and gaze deeply into my eyes, I was, frankly, weirded out. "Who are you?" I whispered — when we were alone. "Are you me? Nod your head for yes."

Nothing.

Since then I've tried lots of other ways to communicate ("Blink your eyes." "Lift one paw." "Wag your tail." "Bark twice."), but nothing's worked. Either I haven't found the key yet, which seems increasingly unlikely, or Sonoma is simply a dog ("simply"; not "just"). A delightful, handsome, intelligent, affectionate dog, yes, but nothing more, no one hidden or trapped inside trying to get out. Apparently.

So I don't know what happened to me. Sometimes I imagine *all* dogs are, from time to time, secretly people, and there's this global conspiracy to keep it under wraps so those of us who've experienced it aren't carted off to asylums. Other times I think, well, why just dogs? Why not cats, too? Or birds? Squirrels, whales, hedgehogs? Maybe there's constant species body-swapping going on, but nobody talks about it except in children's books and science fiction.

Other times, I'm pretty sure I dreamed the whole thing.

One thing is true: Being a dog changed

me. I've become a pack animal. Family's everything — Sam and Benny not only complete me; in some bone-deep way they *are* me. And not just them. The whole concept of family stretches out farther, farther, planets around the sun. It includes all my friends, Delia and her family, Charlie, and Monica, Ronnie Lewis, neighbors, the community, anybody I love, even Mr. Horton — we're all a pack. With my little, *immediate* pack, Sam and Benny, I still have a faint but undeniable urge to roll around on the floor, but with the secondary and tertiary members, I mostly just want to have constant goodwill and cooperation. Which, believe it or not, works out well in the real estate business. Ronnie says I'm *better* than I used to be and, in all modesty, that's saying something. It turns out that honesty, reliability, transparency, and kindness not only make good retrievers; they make good house sellers, too. News to me. I thought my profession was dog-eat-dog.

"Shall we go in?"

Sonoma backs up in the water, tail wagging. She loves transitions, anything new. I was the same way. I fold my chair, tuck my phone in my pocket, the real estate contract I was reading under my arm. Put on my water sandals. It's such a pretty day. Maybe we'll go on a hike this afternoon — Shenandoah National Park is our backyard. "Ready?" Sonoma and I set off across the rocky shallows, and of course I'm extra alert, setting each foot down with care, wary of slipperiness. We reach the shore without mishap.

Sometimes I try to catch her off guard.

"Who saved Monica, Sonoma? Hmm? Who saved her, girl, you or me?"

Her ears twitch at her name and my questioning tone. She looks at me in happy blankness.

We start the climb to the cabin. I think of another trick.

"Hey, Sonoma! How would you like to be *spayed*? Huh? Do you wanna be *spayed*?"

I can't believe my eyes! Her tail sags — her ears flatten.

"No?" My heart skips a beat or two. "You don't want to be *spayed*?"

She shakes her head so violently, her ears sound like cards shuffling.

"Okay," I say, shaky-voiced. "Okay, then. Don't worry; we won't."

Now what? Did that just *happen*?

"I'm actually having the same dilemma," I tell her as we proceed up the path. "Not getting spayed — getting pregnant. Sam and I, we're talking about it. He's for it, but, you know, trying to sound neutral. What do you think?"

But she's through communicating. She's got her nose buried in something stinky on the ferny wood floor. When she finishes smelling it, she pees on it.

So I am left, once again, to imagine what my dog thinks. It's not as satisfying as knowing for sure, but since she's the best of me I can never go far wrong — in ethical quandaries, tough decisions, tricky situations. I just ask myself, "What would Sonoma do?"

■ ■ ■ ■

LOST IN PARADISE
MARY BLAYNEY

■ ■ ■ ■

ONE

Summer 2009
Isla Perdida
Lesser Antilles

"We should not have come. The curse will never die." Father Joubay blessed himself as he spoke.

"A curse? What curse?" *Why in the world would he say that?* Isabelle wondered. It was a gorgeous day. The boat chugged its way through calm water clear to the seabed, filled with fish and sea grass.

The sky ahead was as blue as a sky could be, the island they were headed to as lush as one expected in the Caribbean. The air was warm. The old fort that loomed over the bay was the only thing that kept the shore from looking like a postcard picture of a tropical paradise. The home of the mysterious Sebastian Dushayne. A man who owned an island and lived in luxury. But a man Google had never heard of.

When Isabelle Reynaud turned to question Father Joubay, she saw that he was not looking at their destination, but was mesmerized by something behind them.

Isabelle looked toward the wake of the boat and drew in a sharp breath of shock. The sky on the far horizon was darkening with astonishing speed. Even as she watched, the rapidly building clouds eclipsed the late-afternoon light.

"How can there be a storm from the west? The weather never comes from the west here." Isabelle folded her hands in front of her heart. "It's only a squall."

The boat lost its smooth momentum. The engine still ran steadily but the increasingly choppy waves made the going rough.

"Squalls pass quickly." *Please God.* Isabelle breathed the prayer as the waves around them grew.

"We will outrun it," the captain called back to them as the small boat sped up noticeably. Lightning lit the storm clouds, and a dozen prongs of light chased after them.

"We cannot outrun this," Father Joubay said, and Isabelle agreed with him. It was true that neither of them was a weather expert. They were, however, realists.

Isabelle turned from the storm to look

toward the land, grabbing on to the strut that supported the canopy over the engine house.

The waves had grown from choppy to malicious. Not only was it a challenge to stand but the waves were so high Isabelle could not see the shoreline or the trees, only the fort rising over the harbor. It was more threat than comfort despite the lights that flickered through the dark.

The rain began, pushed by the wind, so that it fell like needles. Isabelle and Father Joubay moved to the partial shelter of the windowless cabin, bracing themselves against the wooden walls that gave scant protection.

Were there any life jackets? she wondered.

The captain yelled back to them, "Life jackets are in the covered bin."

Isabelle found only two. The orange kapok was older than she was and bug infested, but better than nothing. "You take it. You and the captain. I can swim."

"No!" Joubay shouted and pushed the life vest back to her as if it were too hot to handle. "I will make the right choice this time. This is my salvation!" Father Joubay threw the other life jacket to the captain, who ignored it.

A strong wave poured more water on them

and they were thrown to the other side of the shelter. Father Joubay fell to the deck and Isabelle slid down to sit beside him.

"Are you hurt?"

"No, no, Isabelle." He reached for his hat but the water swept it away. "May God help you, child. For me, I welcome death, but I pray, with all my heart, that you survive even if this place is cursed."

"What curse?" she asked again, pointedly. "Father, you know there is no such thing as a curse."

"My dear, do you think that only God can work wonders? So can the devil, for that's what a curse is. The devil's miracle."

Isabelle saw no fear in his eyes even as the rain and wind grew stronger, whitecaps crowning the waves that were now taller than the boat.

"Tell me what you mean," she insisted and did her best to ignore the fear. She would put her faith in God's wisdom and her own ingenuity.

"You will learn eventually, Isabelle. There is not enough time now."

She stood up to see if the boat could possibly reach shore before it fell apart, but she could not see to the shore. The waves and the rain defined their world.

The boat rode up high, very high, and

before it slammed into the trough of the wave, she saw lights above them, much closer now, but still too far away for the boat to make landfall before the worst of the storm overtook them.

The wooden trawler rose and fell, shuddering and rattling as the boards loosened and water seeped through the seams. Isabelle struggled to her feet, and helped Father Joubay stand as water pooled around their legs.

Another shudder and the roof of the cabin flew off. *When* the storm broke the boat apart, they could ride out the waves on one of the bigger pieces. The water was warm enough for them to survive for hours.

"Isabelle, listen," Father Joubay shouted over the storm. He took her hand, pulling her down below the side of the wheelhouse so she could hear him. "When Sebastian Dushayne gave us permission to come to his island for a year of medical and missionary care?"

"Yes?" *Hurry,* she thought. *We don't have much time.*

"There are two things you should know, Isabelle. One is rather odd."

"Odd?" she prompted, worried that he would not finish before the waves swamped the boat.

"The first is that the island healer will not cooperate with you, and Dushayne insisted that I bring a doctor who could sing."

Sing? A doctor who could sing? That was absurd. And besides, "I can't sing and I'm a nurse, not a doctor."

"You are as good as a doctor, Isabelle, and you have a lovely voice."

"But that's only in church. I only know hymns."

He shook his head sharply as the waves took control of their lives. He shouted, "Sebastian loves music, especially music that is sung. It did not seem too much to ask. And if it was meant to be, I knew a singing doctor would appear, and you did. I do not think that will matter now. Kneel down."

Father Joubay put his hand on her head and began to pray over her. "God keep you safe, Isabelle. Show Him that your love is true and pure and free."

Show Him that your love is true. Is that what Father Joubay had said? God knew her heart better than anyone.

Isabelle felt the boat turn into the waves again, but this time instead of climbing over the mountain of water, it wallowed in the troughs.

The screeching wind made any more conversation impossible. His lips moved,

300

but Isabelle could not hear what he said. Prayers surely. They held on to each other and, as the giant wall of water broke over them, she whispered, "God bless you too, Father."

The storm came with such force that Sebastian Dushayne had to brace his body to stand at the open window and watch the harbor, his narrowed eyes the only concession to the rain that bit into him.

Anger pulsed through him, his rage matching the weather around him. Sebastian knew the boat would be lost the moment that the clouds dimmed the sun and the servants began to light candles.

The curse would not allow those on board the island trawler to reach the shore. Joubay and the doctor would die along with the fool who let money convince him that his boat could beat the curse's fury.

The storm brought an early twilight, but Sebastian could see the boat as it struggled in the waves with a desperation that he could feel even this far away.

Joubay would pray. Sebastian knew better than to try that. God had no place here. This was the devil's playground. The sounds of the revelry in the next room proved that. God's minions were not welcome and lasted only as long as it took to seduce them with life's pleasures.

The boat disappeared from sight and the words of the curse crawled through Sebastian's memory as clearly as if it had been yesterday. *Joubay, because you love this island, I cast you out. If you dare to return, you will die.*

Even if Joubay was coming back with a solution to the curse, it would die with him. Sebastian wished he had never trusted, even for a moment, that there was a chance he could escape this island, his prison. He continued to stare at the roiling harbor. Suddenly, quiet settled around him as though a shield of silence held him between his world and some other place.

Two ephemeral shapes rose from the water, shrouded in the rain, but rising, rising, rising out of sight as a song echoed, sung in a lovely voice more than alto but not quite a soprano. *"I will be with you always in light and in love. My light surrounds you with love from above."* The song ended, the cocoon vanished and the wind came back with renewed strength.

Cursing, Sebastian pushed the shutters closed, pressing with all his strength against the east wind that battered them.

He returned to the grand salon where the

others partied, all of them unaware that people were dying within sight of this room. Why tell them, he thought. They were tourists, here for entertainment, for the taste of another time as if man had lived better or more fully in 1810.

If he told this group what was happening, they would be shocked and it would ruin the mood.

Sebastian had watched people die for so long he had grown used to it. He would take one of the women to bed and let her help him forget what he had witnessed.

The prettiest in this group, he was fairly certain her name was Genetta, reached for the one remaining cream cake and drank the last of the champagne with drunken greed.

No one complained. The group was already bored with the illusion of nineteenth-century life conjured for their entertainment and were well into the carnal pleasures that transcended time and place.

Genetta looked at him with a provocative pout and he nodded. She would be the one. Her gold blond hair was natural; her body was not too muscular, like so many other women these days. But Sebastian already knew what sex with her would be like.

She would be less entertaining than most.

Not evil, not at all, but shallow and self-indulgent. And not very creative.

With a promise to bring back more champagne, Sebastian left the salon, found his way to the open courtyard, the inner ward of this onetime fortress.

As he crossed the wet stone, the squall was already passing. The last of the rain fell as a soft mist.

Sebastian opened the small door in the giant iron gate facing the sea. He saw the wreckage floating, random pieces of wood, the ship's wheel, and among the debris a body in black, arms outstretched.

Sebastian Dushayne lived a curse of his own making. He had no doubt that he would spend eternity living it, but the least he could do was send word to the village and order a decent burial.

TWO

Isabelle wondered if this was heaven and she was resting on a cloud. Impossible. She was sure heaven would be more than her idea of a perfect bed.

Besides, Isabelle knew she was alive. Her chest rose and fell with each breath as aches and pains marched over every inch of her body.

Where were Father Joubay and the trawler's captain? Opening her eyes, Isabelle hoped to find them lying beside her, but all she could see was the crown of a massive canopied bed and the soft light of the candles on the table nearby.

Isabelle turned her head toward the light, and the illusion of well-being disappeared. A man stood beside the bed, surrounded by darkness. How could he be in shadow when so many candles lit the room? Her heart began to race and anxiety twisted in her stomach.

He was not tall, but powerful in build, but that was all of him she could see. Isabelle wished he would say something. Even as she had the thought, she realized his body spoke a language all its own. Anger radiated from him.

Maybe I'm the one who should say something. But she was too tired to speak; too tired to do anything but stare at him and wish for comfort.

"Sleep for now. You were almost dead but you will live."

Isabelle gave a little nod and closed her eyes. As she fell asleep she gave the man a name. Sebastian Dushayne.

Sleep was the perfect escape at first. Then the nightmare of the shipwreck overwhelmed her. She was in the water, being tossed by the waves like a piece of driftwood, held under by some current until her lungs would burst, then freed and allowed one more breath.

Fighting, fighting to reach the shore until it became too much of an effort, giving in and floating until finally she was washed up onto the beach like flotsam.

She felt a hand on her head, heard a voice whispering. "You will live. You are safe. You survived."

He must have spoken the words. She most

definitely heard them, but the comfort of his hand smoothing her hair was what convinced her. If she had a drink of water, maybe she could speak, could ask him if the others had survived.

The next thing she knew he was smoothing her hair off her face, sliding his arm under her neck, raising her as though he knew how much even that small movement would hurt.

His hands were cool, but they sent a shock of warmth through her. A shock that overrode the discomfort of her bruised body. A feeling so welcome that she turned her face into his shoulder.

"Drink a little." Sebastian Dushayne held the glass at her lips and she drank, her eyes on his, though he watched the glass and the water and nothing more.

He was handsome and unsmiling, with a straight nose, a rather fine mouth and a dent in his chin. She thought he might have dimples when he smiled. If he ever did smile.

Settling her back on the pillows, he poured more water. "You can have another drink in a few minutes."

Sebastian Dushayne knew something about trauma care, she thought. Sometimes even a little water was more than the stomach could tolerate.

He pulled up a chair and sat down. Now he did look her in the eye. His brown eyes were not at all friendly. She saw none of the warmth or comfort she had felt when he touched her. She braced herself.

"Joubay is missing. As is the boat and its owner."

Isabelle's throat clogged with tears. She knew it was true, though her heart begged for their lives.

He gave her a handkerchief and stood up.

"Are you a doctor?"

"A nurse," she answered in a rusty voice.

"It hardly matters which. You are a woman. Joubay knows I will not allow a woman to live here. Now neither one of us can ask him what he was thinking."

"I want a phone. I need to arrange for their funerals."

"First you must rebuild your strength. Then we will talk about what you can and cannot do."

Where had the kindness gone? she wondered.

"I want answers." She cleared her throat and hoped she sounded determined.

"You will not have them today." He stood up as if he was going to leave without another word.

"Father said there was a curse. What did he mean?"

"Joubay lived a fool and died one." Now Sebastian Dushayne did walk away, but stopped at the door and asked, "Can you sing?"

If Father Joubay had not warned her, she would have thought him mad to ask such a question. "I can only sing hymns." The way her throat felt now, she doubted she could sing "Row, Row, Row Your Boat."

His laugh was cynical and not at all appealing. "Of course you sing hymns. Next you will tell me that you are a virgin with a heart as pure as snow."

Isabelle wanted to know where the cynicism came from, but he did not give her a chance to speak. "I don't care what you sing. It has been years since I heard a new voice, new songs. Perhaps your hymns will convert me."

Before Isabelle could agree, argue or ask for more water, he left the room.

She fell asleep almost immediately, her dreams such a mix of nightmare and grief that it was a relief to wake up.

Dushayne was there again and she wasted no time, determined to move, to speak and to find some answers. She struggled upright in bed, then realized she was naked and pulled the sheet up to cover her breasts. He did not turn away but watched her with a disinterest that told her she was the only one who was embarrassed.

Isabelle reached for the water and groaned as the pain of damaged muscles spread from her fingers to her neck. Forcing herself to drink the water, she thanked God for the feel of it sliding down her throat, freeing her voice.

"You are Sebastian Dushayne."

"Yes, and you are?"

"Isabelle Reynaud."

He bowed with old-world courtliness. "How do you do, Mistress Reynaud."

"I am not married."

"Yes, I know, but *mistress* is a term we use for every grown woman."

"Where am I?"

"You are in the Castillo de Guerreros on the Isla Perdida."

"The Castle of Warriors on the Lost Island?"

Dushayne nodded and Isabelle wondered what it would take to get more than basic answers from him.

"The village healer sent some of her salve to ease your bruises and sore muscles. Sit up and I will put some on your back, where you cannot reach."

Isabelle wanted to say no, but she also knew that to reject his help would send all the wrong messages, to him, to the healer, even to the servants. She could see one peeking around the corner of the door. "Let the servant do it."

"Are you afraid I will seduce you?" Genuine humor made her blush. "Believe me, Mistress Reynaud, I am not the slightest bit interested in a woman with a body that is no more than bruises and hair still filled with sand and seaweed."

Even though her arm blazed with pain at the action, Isabelle raised her hand to her head. Her hair felt like lengths of used raffia. Who knew what was in it besides sand. "I need to wash it. I hate the sand. I want to wash it right now."

"Yes, I will send my housekeeper to help you. But first the salve. It will make it much easier to move." He added, "Please," as though it was a password of some kind, and Isabelle gave a half nod and looked away from his smile. He did have dimples.

She leaned forward. Even that hurt. She held back the groan and kept the sheet in front of her. The air felt warm on her back and she waited for the even warmer touch of his hand.

Isabelle could not see his face, but

watched him scoop a portion of the salve from a stone dish, and rub his hands together. They were strong, well-shaped hands, tanned, with long fingers and blunt-cut nails, with a pronounced curve of white cuticle. There was a scar on one knuckle, the white of it in contrast to the warm tan of his skin. The scar did not look very old.

He raised his hands to her back and Isabelle stared out the window at the water, today looking as benign as a baby's bathtub.

Sebastian Dushayne smoothed the cream, warmed by his hands, from the back of her neck all the way down her spine, then began to rub it in with the most sensual of pressure, not too soft and not hard enough to hurt, but just firmly enough to make her feel wonderful. He might not be interested in seducing her, but that did not mean she was oblivious to it.

Dushayne ran his hands very slowly down the outsides of her arms and then, even more slowly, up the insides of her arms so that his fingertips brushed the edge of her breasts.

She straightened instinctively but said nothing, wondering if she was overreacting, deciding she was when he stepped back a moment for more salve.

Dushayne used both hands to massage the

cream into her lower back, the feeling so relaxing that Isabelle dropped her head, her long hair falling around her face, loosened crystals of sand spilling onto the sheet.

Moving his hands over her hips, he cupped her buttocks and she wondered whether the magic was in the salve or in his hands.

"That is quite enough." Isabelle used as firm a voice as she could command, the kind she used to the children who were using markers to make tattoos on one another.

Dushayne ended the treatment abruptly. The next thing she felt was his breath near her ear. "No," he whispered. "Do not lie. It is not nearly enough and we both know it."

Isabelle wasn't lying. It wasn't nearly enough *pleasure,* but it was quite enough temptation. She turned around to tell him that and saw the door closing.

How could she even be thinking about something so physical when she still ached, when her friend was dead, when Sebastian Dushayne himself was such an unknown?

For now, all she wanted was sleep. The scent of the ointment was part of its power, she was sure, so soothing.

She pulled the sheet up to her neck and prayed for strength to resist and tried to recall all the questions still unanswered.

■ ■ ■ ■

Sebastian closed the door quietly.

"Sit here," he told the servant, indicating the chair near the door. "Come to me for help if she is upset or has nightmares." The servant nodded and Sebastian headed for the beach. He needed a woman or a swim in cold water, and right now there was only one woman he wanted.

Isabelle Reynaud was a sweet confection. Tiny, not so much short as fine boned and perfectly proportioned, what a Regency man would have called a "Pocket Venus." Her hair was so dark and so long that he wondered how her neck could bear the weight of it. He could hardly wait to feel that hair once it had been washed, to taste her, to make himself part of her.

But the woman would need to grieve awhile. He understood that, even if death no longer moved him.

Anticipation would make her surrender all the more satisfying. He could spend weeks tutoring her in the finer points of erotic pleasure.

What a lovely surprise Joubay had brought for him. Sebastian decided she was meant as a consolation if Joubay's idea for ending the curse did not work.

Damn, damn, damn. The old man was free now. Even worse, without him in the world searching for the solution, there was no hope of ending it. A dozen women were not consolation enough.

Shedding his clothes, Sebastian walked into the water, dove into a small wave and swam out to the deeper, cooler part of the harbor.

THREE

Isabelle closed her eyes and prayed, for Father Joubay, the ship's owner, herself and Sebastian Dushayne. She was not sure which one of them needed it more.

Her dreams were filled with grief this time, the dead, bloated bodies of Father Joubay and the captain and a Sebastian Dushayne who did not care if the birds feasted on them. Just as the dream verged on a nightmare, Father Joubay rose from the water and walked through it to the shore, looking like his mortal self. "Do not grieve. We are buried and our souls have gone to God."

She fell more deeply asleep, sure she could feel Father Joubay's hand comforting her.

"Do you remember that moment in New Orleans?" he asked. "How I threw out my prepared sermon and talked about how much help was needed on this little Caribbean island?"

"Of course I do. How no one had the most routine vaccinations, and health care was centuries out of date."

"The Church of Lost Souls was filled with people who understood, who'd been through Katrina."

Their eyes met as Isabelle remembered, as Joubay announced he was looking for someone trained in medicine willing to accompany him and volunteer for a year. Isabelle had smiled and Father Joubay had smiled back, and their pact was made.

"Dearest Isabelle," Father Joubay spoke with some urgency as his body began to fade and drift upward. "Do not abandon your commitment. Do not grieve, or better yet, let grief fuel your good deeds. There is so much need here and you are the key."

All right, Isabelle decided as Father disappeared into the clouds. *Let her grief fuel her good deeds.* She would stay for the year she had promised. She would sing hymns as Sebastian Dushayne demanded. She would do her best to update the medical care, introduce routine inoculations and set a standard that could save lives. It was what Father Joubay had asked her to do. It was why she had come.

From her own experience she knew that if God wanted her to do something else, she would know.

Finally, at last, Isabelle's sleep was as pure as her body and as sweet as her heart.

When she woke the third time, Isabelle had no idea what time of day it was or even if it was the same day. She did feel one hundred percent better and decided that the healer's salve was worth investigating.

The sun shone, so she pushed up from bed, wrapped a sheet around her nakedness and went to the window.

The opening looked out onto a village that was a few hundred yards from the castle, or was this a fort? The one main street was quiet, only a woman and a girl walking its length.

That meant it was probably noontime. This part of the world still understood the merits of a siesta, though more sleep was the last thing Isabelle needed right now.

If she could find some clothes and dress, she would ask someone to show her to the cottage that was going to be her clinic and her home.

There was a shy knock at the door and Isabelle turned back from the window just as a woman came into the room, carrying a bundle of neatly folded clothes.

"Good afternoon, Mistress Doctor. It is a surprise to see that you are up and about.

Are you feeling that much better?"

"Yes, thank you, amazingly better. What is that ointment that Mr. Dushayne gave me?"

"Ointment?" She seemed uncertain for a moment. "Oh, yes, it is the curing cream that the healer makes. It is all most of us need."

Isabelle heard the defensive tone in that last sentence and recalled Father Joubay's *They do not want you.* Well, she had faced that before in so many different guises that she was not surprised.

"I can see why you find the cream essential. It really worked. I am so looking forward to meeting the honored healer."

The woman cackled. "She is no more honored than a witch doctor. She drinks too much, demands the finest pieces of fish and gives the best care to those who bring her anything that shines." The woman raised her index finger, making the final point. "But she does know how to heal almost everything and that makes us tolerate her shortcomings."

"Thank you for the insight." She gave the woman, most likely the housekeeper, a deferential nod. Isabelle would judge for herself, but every piece of information was useful, so she told herself this was not gossip. "My name is Isabelle Reynaud. And I am not a fully trained doctor but a physician's assistant."

The woman shrugged as if that made no difference. "I am Vermille, Mistress Housekeeper of the *castillo*. You may call me Mistress Vermille. I will take you to the bathing room and give you these clothes." She held up the folded clothes. "All your things were lost or ruined in the storm but these will fit you. The master sent to the hotel for them and he is very good at estimating the size a woman wears."

"Thank you, Mistress Housekeeper," Isabelle said, even as she cringed at the use of the word "master" to describe Sebastian Dushayne. His was a small world but he did control all of it.

"I would love to wash my hair. After I bathe and dress, could you spare someone to show me to the cottage in the village where my clinic will be?"

"Yes," she said bluntly. "Come with me." Mistress Vermille did not wait but left the room. Isabelle followed her, feeling silly using the sheet as a bathrobe, but the passageway was empty so it really didn't matter.

"When you are dressed, follow the passage and turn right at every opportunity."

With that, Mistress Vermille left her at the

door of what she called "the bathing chamber."

The bath defied conventional description. The toilet was no more than a hole in rock and there was no shower or sink, but the bath was more like a small swimming pool, big enough to float freely in. There were hooks on the wall, a very comfortable-looking chaise longue and a mirror that was bigger than she was.

The room had three windows, the shutters were pulled closed at the moment and the space was lit with candles. A sybarite's delight. Isabelle had never been a hedonist, could never afford to live like one, but thought the adjustment would not be hard to make.

She walked around the bath and found some steps at the far end. The water was warm, comfortable, but not as hot as she would have liked. It felt like silk, liquid silk, and she enjoyed the sensuality of it as much as the feeling of being clean.

There were five elegant stone containers with various soaps, all the fragrances different. She chose the one that smelled like jasmine. It was heaven to wash her hair.

The experience would have been perfect if the door had a lock on it. It did not, and the whole time she was bathing she was aware that anyone could come in. The only "anyone" she worried about was the master, Sebastian Dushayne. This bath was definitely big enough for two and she suspected that he would not hesitate to invite himself to share it with her.

And, because honesty was such a fundamental part of her, Isabelle admitted she might enjoy it. Her imagination headed down that wayward path and it was not hard to imagine him naked. Too easy, in fact. Broad shoulders, strong arms, powerful legs. She hurried out of the bath before she could visualize any more of his body and left the image behind, swirling in the deep end of the water.

The toweling was different from the kind she was used to. More like an absorbent linen than fluffy cotton.

With her hair wrapped in one of the lengths, she dressed as quickly as she could. Isabelle had never worn a thong before and found it more comfortable than she thought it would be. The bra was a stretch of lace that was more sexy than useful. She had never been able to decide if it was fortunate or unfortunate that she did not need much support, but in this case it was a good thing.

Add to that a sleeveless cotton shirt and some capris in a blue and white print, and she was dressed perfectly for the warm weather. The shoes were not what she would have chosen. Some kind of close-toed, sneakerlike synthetic material, similar to the old well-worn Diesels she wore at the clinic in New Orleans.

It felt very strange to know she owned nothing but what she wore, and even that was a gift. Isabelle comforted herself with Jesus' admonition to his disciples to take nothing but the clothes on their backs. She thought that was the phrasing. If she could find a Bible somewhere, she would look it up.

Untwisting the linen, she picked up the comb and worked it through her hair. There were lengths of ribbon in a basket near the entrance, and Isabelle took one and tied her hair back.

With a deep breath and a prayer for wisdom, Isabelle opened the door, walked down the passage, turning right at every opportunity.

The castle was huge and still seemed deserted. Making her way down an enclosed set of winding stairs, Isabelle came out onto what looked like the inner courtyard, surrounded on all four sides by a covered passageway supported by elegant arches that ran in a square. The only break was where the great iron doors stood closed tightly against the pitiful village just outside the gate.

Doors and windows set in smaller arches lined the walls on the other side of the passageway. Benches in some dark, worn wood gave evidence that there were times when the courtyard held a crowd.

Isabelle crossed to the giant door, at least twenty feet high and almost as wide, and was in front of it when she saw a small door set in the wall nearby open from the other side.

A boy, no more than ten, came into the courtyard, all confidence and good nature. "Good day to you, mistress. Mistress Vermille says I am to take you to Mistress Esmé, the healer."

"Thank you. But I need to see where my cottage is first."

"No, no. I am sorry, mistress, but you must see the healer first. You have no choice."

Isabelle was not surprised and only a little irritated at this command performance. Clearly power plays existed on little islands in the Caribbean too. There was no other reason she could think of for the healer to insist on seeing her before she had even set foot in her cottage.

324

Isabelle followed the boy who said his name was Cortez. He pointed out the village's most significant sites, which were cottages that all looked the same to Isabelle.

Whitewashed with palm-leaf roofs, well kept and so small it was hard to believe that one housed a barbershop and a beauty shop, another a dry goods store and a third the produce shop. She could smell bananas and realized that she had not eaten anything since she had arrived here.

"Cortez, can we stop here so I can buy a banana, please?"

"No, no, you cannot buy."

Just before she lost a hold on her temper, the boy produced a coin. "I will buy you the best and biggest banana there is." He popped into the store and a minute later came out with a lovely, firm, yellow banana big enough for two. Indeed, Isabelle broke off a quarter and shared it with him and they continued down the street in companionable silence.

Cortez took the peel and Isabelle brushed her hands on her pants just as they reached a house that was set back from the street. Larger than the rest, it had an actual door and two windows.

Cortez did not have to tell her that this was the home of the healer, Mistress Esmé.

A woman came to the entrance when Cortez pulled the bell. She gave Isabelle a long look that made her feel dirty and uneducated.

"I am Esmé, the healer, and you are the nurse."

"Isabelle Reynaud," Isabelle answered even though Esmé made the word "nurse" sound like a lower life-form.

"I told you, master, she will not do at all," Esmé called over her shoulder. "There is no place for a nurse in our village. What can she do that I cannot?"

Isabelle stepped past the woman and into the entry hall, having faced this prejudice before and determined to prove her worth. She stopped short when she realized that Sebastian Dushayne was stretched out on a bed, his shirt off, his arms up against the headboard.

FOUR

Sebastian Dushayne laughed at the dismay he saw on Mistress Isabelle Reynaud's face. This woman must have come from a convent to be so shocked by the sight of a man without his shirt on. He hoped seducing her, introducing her to the world of carnal pleasure, took a very long time. It was hard to tell with the innocent. For some their naiveté was only skin deep; for others it was a way of life.

Letting go of the bedposts, he sat upright. "For God's sake, Healer, finish this or I will be in misery all day."

"You should not have gone swimming today. You know that after a storm the fire worms are found in unexpected places."

"Yes, yes, now come and finish taking the bristles out. They hurt like hell."

"How do you treat them?" Isabelle asked, walking closer to him, her expression now very serious. She no longer saw him as a man, he thought, but as a patient.

"I remove bristles with tweezers and then rub the area with papaya to ease the discomfort. With stings from sea life it is wisest to stay still for a while to be sure that the sickness has not reached other parts of the body. There have been deaths from the worst stings. Of course, Sebastian does not have to worry about that, though I tell him he could lose an arm. I can usually find a way to keep him in bed."

Now Esmé was trying to shock the girl. They were closer to enemies than lovers, and her idea of a cure for any of his ills usually involved as much pain as she could possibly induce.

"It sounds like an excellent treatment, Healer."

Sebastian watched Isabelle's demeanor, standing back, behaving as if she were in training and not the one who should be teaching. He could tell that it was not easy for her to be so subservient. Somewhere she had learned self-discipline.

The burning along the right side of his rib cage made him swear. "Give me the papaya if you two are going to talk all day."

It took less than five minutes to finish the treatment. He pulled his cotton shirt over his head but left the buttons undone. He could tell by the healer's stony expression that she was going to dismiss Isabelle the moment he left. "I know what you are thinking, Esmé, and I tell you that you must work with her."

Before he could walk out the door, Isabelle objected. "Mr. Dushayne, the healer will work with me when she can trust me and not one moment before. She is established here and I am the newcomer. Why should she believe that my ways are superior? Indeed, that is not always true."

Sebastian shook his head. "As you wish. But that behavior will be seen as a weakness. Do not forget you are here to sing as well. Come to the courtyard of the *castillo* before the last meal of the day." This time he left before either one of them could object.

Isabelle made a nasty face at his departing back and then closed her eyes and prayed for self-control. Her temper was one of her greatest weaknesses. One of many.

Now she had to decide which was more important, to convince the woman, Esmé, she had no interest in Sebastian Dushayne or to convince the healer, Esmé, that she was not going to compete with her.

"The master wants you."

Isabelle could get really tired of that term

for their boss, but Esmé's statement did choose the subject for her. "Maybe so, but I do not want him."

"You lie."

"No," she said, understanding the misunderstanding. "I can see that it sounds like it. He's very appealing. Who wouldn't want him? His eyes demand everything you have and he has a weary way with the world that makes a woman think he needs her. Of course I want him."

"Then why say you do not?"

"Because, Mistress Healer, I do not want him on his terms. I want love too. I want to receive as much as I give. I want true sharing. And it's clear that he does not know the meaning of the word."

"Hmm. I think you want too much."

"I've been told that before." Isabelle shrugged, undaunted.

"Call me Esmé or simply Healer. And I will call you Isabelle. The next person who walks through the door, you will treat and I will decide if you stay."

No sooner were the words spoken than a boy came hopping through the door, doing his best not to cry.

Isabelle turned to Esmé for permission. The woman nodded with a smile that Isabelle hoped was pleasure at her fawning but feared was satisfaction at Isabelle's likely failure.

Patience, she reminded herself. *Pretend that Esmé is this island's version of the nun in charge.*

After his own questioning glance at the healer and a second nod, the boy plopped down in a chair and put his foot up on a stool.

"I see you have a splinter," Isabelle said after examining the foot without actually touching it. Beyond filthy, the soles of his feet looked calloused. Did none of the children wear shoes?

"A splinter. Yes." The boy nodded.

"Tell us how it happened." The boy explained and with her usual prayer for guidance, Isabelle went through the process of removal. She never once looked to Esmé for help but always included her in the explanation of what she was doing. It did not take long to remove the splinter. It was set rather deeply but was in one good-sized piece. The boy bit his lip and did not show that he felt pain.

With the splinter out, his toe began to bleed.

"Stop the bleeding," Esmé demanded.

"No, I think not, Mistress Healer." Isabelle thought she deserved points for her model behavior. "The blood cleans the site of the wound and pushes out anything that might cause infection. We should keep him here until it stops, which will be any moment now."

Even as she said the words the bleeding stopped and a scab began to form.

They all stared at the spot and then Isabelle said, "As a rule, I prefer to let the air reach it, but since it is on his toe and he does not wear shoes, I think it should be covered."

"I agree." Esmé handed her a large bandage and Isabelle completed the work and the boy trotted off with a smile and a piece of some sweet that Esmé gave him for "not crying like an infant."

Isabelle cleaned up the work area and did her best to estimate where everything went when not in use.

Esmé circled the room with her arms behind her back, which tested Isabelle's pride to the limit. "Very good, Isabelle. You may stay for the rest of the day and then I will decide."

"No, Mistress Healer," Isabelle spoke firmly but with respect and thanked her years of experience. "You must decide now. I know that I am good at this work. You have the advantage of years more experience with the illnesses here, but I can give the islanders protection against illnesses that you know nothing about. We are evenly matched and could complement each other. I am willing. It is up to you."

"All right." The healer shrugged her shoulders, which made Isabelle feel that she had given an ultimatum where none was necessary, which meant that the healer still had the upper hand. *The islanders' health is why you are here.* Isabelle pushed the prideful vanity out of her head.

Esmé might drink too much, be vain and greedy, but she was true to her word. By midafternoon they had treated another simple wound and talked to two pregnant women, girls really. They obviously had children young here.

By the time Esmé showed Isabelle to her cottage, "with two hours to rest before you sing," they had established a cordial working relationship. Despite that, Isabelle doubted they would ever be friends.

It had been a very mundane afternoon. Her calling here might be to help the villagers, but Isabelle did not think they needed her medical expertise. They had excellent care in the Mistress Healer, and her ability as a midwife was impressive.

Isabelle hoped she would feel more useful

when she began the inoculation program, though the chance of the children being exposed to measles and mumps was amazingly limited. According to Esmé, you could leave the island, but once a person did, he never came back. And any visitors who came from the hotel came in the evening and never saw anyone but the master and a few of the servants who lived at the *castillo*. Exposure to illness was limited but, remembering the boy's bare feet, tetanus inoculations were essential.

Her cottage looked like the others, with the same palm-woven door and roof. Inside she found one large room with a very primitive bathroom and no way to cook anything. The room was loaded with boxes that she recognized as supplies she had sent from New Orleans.

In a little space, bumped out from the side of the cottage, was a sleeping alcove surrounded on three sides by walls. Small openings circled the room where the wall met the ceiling, a clever way to welcome a breeze and light and still maintain privacy.

The bed was freshly made. There was a curtain that could be pulled across the space during the day so the room looked more like a living room or a work space than a bedroom, or could be used at night for privacy.

As always, work had energized her all day, but as soon as she saw the bed, exhaustion enveloped her.

She would have fallen on the sheets fully clothed, if Esmé had not insisted she undress and put on the nightgown that hung on the hook nearest the bed. Isabelle complied, too tired to be embarrassed by her ridiculous bra and thong.

She was aware of Esmé putting her clothes on the hooks but was asleep before the healer left the cottage. Her sleep was spared nightmares, though the dream she did have, of Dushayne watching her bathe, left her feeling restless. It wasn't hard to guess why.

"Mistress Nurse, the master wants you."

She heard the voice and in her dream, it became very clear that the master wanted her. He pulled her from the water, laid her on the chaise lounge and began to dry her with one of the lengths of linen. His touch on her breasts, her stomach and between her legs made her writhe in her sleep, both frustrated and eager for more.

"Mistress Nurse." The voice was closer and more urgent. "You must sing."

Isabelle opened her eyes and saw Cortez's worried eyes.

"You were moaning. Are you sick?"

"No, no. Just very tired." Isabelle closed her eyes. It was not a lie. She wasn't sick and she was tired.

"Yes, mistress. It's late. I will be outside while you dress."

Isabelle hurried into her clothes, determined never to call Sebastian Dushayne "master." It was a demeaning, demoralizing title. It reminded her of everything awful about the way a man treated women and servants, as if he was superior by his very masculinity. It was an antiquated, outdated concept, everywhere but here in Sebastian Dushayne's corner of the world.

She pushed open the palm door and fell into step beside Cortez. No matter what Sebastian Dushayne was called, she had promised Father Joubay that she would sing for him.

By the time she reached the street, her annoyance at the demands of Sebastian Dushayne had died. By the time she reached the door to the *castillo,* nerves made her legs shaky. By the time she reached the center of the castle courtyard, she prayed for help and inspiration.

Both came in the song she began to sing. The courtyard amplified her words, making her sound like a diva on a stage, and she relaxed enough to enjoy herself and think about the words as she sang them. *"Be not afraid, I go before you always. Come follow me and I will give you life."*

As the words of the familiar hymn floated upward, Isabelle turned around and around, singing to the empty doors and windows that overlooked the courtyard, and then looked up to the heavens. The thin slice of a new moon lit its corner of the western sky and some planet sent a bold light out into the universe.

Isabelle loved the night sky and smiled as she came to the last of the hymn. That was when she saw Sebastian Dushayne, shadowed in one of the upper windows, lit from behind so that she could not read his expression. She tilted her head slightly, waiting for a comment. He did not move, but once again his body spoke for him. He looked wounded, as though her presence was more than he could bear.

Her heart sped to double time as the truth struck her.

Sebastian Dushayne is why I am here.

The realization came to her so suddenly and with such certainty, Isabelle had no doubt that this was a cosmic truth and not her ego.

It was this man who needed her, not the

villagers. His dark presence was as powerful as the storm that had changed her life.

The curse. The dark shadow around him reminded Isabelle that she had completely forgotten to ask about it. Ask who, a boy or a healer who did not like her? Or Sebastian Dushayne.

As she thought his name, he left the window and disappeared into the darkness behind him.

Yes, he would just as soon keep the curse, whatever it was, a secret. Who knew how long she would have stared at the closed window if a voice had not distracted her?

"Dinner is ready. Mistress Esmé says you must eat."

Isabelle's stomach rumbled and she knew Esmé was right. She raised her eyes to the empty window, gave a deep bow and left, wondering if Father Joubay had known why Sebastian Dushayne needed her and had died before he could tell her.

Sebastian stepped back into the room, and slumped against the wall. The pain in his heart would have made him fear an apoplexy if it was possible for him to suffer from something so human. He closed his eyes and a kaleidoscope of pictures tumbled out of his mind as if his memory had been

338

unlocked for the first time in two hundred years.

Sebastian saw his wife, his anger, her stubbornness, his insistence and the storm that took her life as she did her best to obey him and come home.

Those dreams, even daydreams, were nothing new. But the pain that came with them was as tortured as anything a sadistic man could devise. Rage, guilt, heartache drove him to his knees even as he remembered how much he had loved Angelique, how much he could not stand for them to be apart, how he wanted her sleeping beside him every night.

How could the inane words of that hymn have done this to him? He was no more afraid of God or of life, whichever it was, than he was afraid of the waif of a woman singing from the courtyard as if her life depended on it.

Sebastian had thought it would be entertaining to have someone new to sing. That a year would be just long enough to enjoy a new voice before boredom set in. He was already bored. He would send for the singer from the hotel even though her voice was failing and her songs were too modern for his taste. Then he would tell this amateur that he never wanted to see her again.

FIVE

Isabelle was not surprised when Esmé missed work for the next three days without explanation. Whether the healer's absence was another test or the result of too much liquor hardly mattered.

What did surprise Isabelle was the message Cortez brought telling her that she was not expected to sing anymore. She was brushing her teeth on the second evening when she realized that her voice must have disappointed Dushayne and that was why he had no desire to hear her again. She cringed with embarrassment even though she was alone.

The third day was the busiest of all, and then Isabelle realized it was curiosity that brought so many with hard-to-diagnose headaches and upset stomachs.

It was almost dusk when Cortez came running to her. "You must come. You must come. One of the master's servants is hurt and needs help. It is Riono and he is bleeding badly. You must come now, Mistress Nurse."

Isabelle grabbed her bag and ran.

Riono lay on the kitchen floor, a bloody gash on his arm, a kitchen knife still in his hand. The radial artery, Isabelle decided instantly. She pulled a cord from her bag and made a tourniquet.

"Will he live?"

She sat back on her knees and looked up at the cluster of people, trying to find the one who had asked the question. Sebastian Dushayne stood among them, the servants having left a space between them and him.

He watched with a detached interest that reminded her of the doctor who had supervised her clinical work. Isabelle hated the man until she realized that after years of seeing students come and go his disinterest was the only way to protect his emotions. It was too hard to say good-bye over and over again. Did Sebastian Dushayne's servants come and go with as much regularity?

"Riono will be all right in time." She nodded to Dushayne but spoke to everyone gathered around them. "I will have to clean and stitch the wound. The healer is not well today, but there is no time to waste."

"Not well?" Sebastian folded his arms and

did not hide his cynicism. "That did not take long."

Without answering Dushayne, Isabelle asked for help moving the man. Finally they settled Riono on a table moved near the sink.

She explained the procedure to the patient and to Dushayne, who had insisted on observing even though she had asked everyone to leave. "I will have to wash the wound for at least twenty minutes and it will hurt, but it is essential to remove any dirt from the knife blade. After that I have some medicine, a spray, that will block the pain, but you will still feel the stitches going through your skin."

Riono's eyes were wide with shock but he nodded. "I heard you sing the other night and cannot forget how beautiful it was. Can you sing while you wash my arm, Mistress Nurse? It will help me think of other things."

"Yes, if you wish," Isabelle answered without looking to Dushayne for approval. If the man did not want to hear her, he could go away.

Isabelle started the pump and let the water rinse the wound. Riono gasped and Dushayne took his hand. "Think of your woman in childbirth." Riono's grimace might have been a smile.

Isabelle did not look up, but was struck by the contradictions in the man. As she supervised the cleaning she let her mind wander.

Sebastian Dushayne's ill humor kept company with an essential kindness that left her off-kilter, uncertain whether to allow herself to like him or keep him at a distance, and then she realized that uncertainty was exactly what he wanted.

When the wound was clean, she sprayed the area with lidocaine and, as she took the first stitch, began to sing. *"I live to serve, I live to love, I live to care as Christ once showed."*

Sebastian winced as the needle pierced Riono's arm but the man lay there watching Isabelle, not flinching or seeming even to notice anything but the insipid words she sang.

"Let me share your pain. Let me share your joy. Let us share the sun and rain, Till our lives are soon fulfilled and we pass to God again."

When she sang the last sentence, Isabelle raised her eyes to his, sincerity echoing in every word. Her goodness was more than Sebastian could stand. It tore into him like a double-edged sword. It was all he could do not to beg for forgiveness, and she was not even the one he had hurt.

It was time to show her how overrated virtue was. Once goodness did not shine from her, his pain would ease. "Tomorrow, come back to the *castillo* after dark, Isabelle. Dress for a party. I am hosting one for the tourists and I think you will enjoy it."

"Thank you." She did not smile but seemed pleased.

Oh, you will thank me, he thought. Tomorrow night he would know how bone deep her virtue was.

Of course the perfect dress hung on the hook in her bedroom. It was a gauzy floral print with filmy sleeves and a swirling skirt that made her feel fairylike and feminine. The man certainly did know how to choose clothes a woman would like.

The shoes were not quite as successful. There was no way she could walk to the castle on the four-inch heels that were the only possible choice.

She had almost decided to go barefoot when someone pulled the string on the bell at her door.

Esmé stood there holding a pair of sandals, much, much better than the towering heels Isabelle had in her hand. The healer pushed them at her and then stood with her hands on her hips. "I tell you, girl, I will know if your soul is corrupted by Sebastian Dushayne or any of his guests. You will not be welcome here when that happens."

"You can tell even that. How intriguing. Do you think my corruption is inevitable?"

"Yes," Esmé said firmly.

Isabelle considered a debate, but suspected it would be pointless. "Thank you for the shoes. They're perfect."

"Of course they are." She left without further explanation.

Isabelle walked slowly up toward the castle. She really had no idea what to expect. Cortez told her that the master had company at least once a week and that some of the guests stayed longer. Never the same group and none ever stayed more than a week. It was, by Cortez's definition, a noisy party with endless drinking and dancing until the people began to play games with one another or wander off to a bedroom to sleep.

Isabelle walked into a party well begun. The men and women were dressed in clothes that were very twenty-first century, but everything else about the gathering had an old-world feel. Even the music was played by a three-piece combo.

The food was not the typical island fare

but looked as though it would be better suited to a European dining room. There were tables for cards and other sorts of gambling, but right now most everyone was gathered around a woman dressed as a gypsy, who was telling fortunes accompanied by much laughter and rude comments.

"People of all ages love to hear stories about themselves."

She had felt him beside her before he spoke. Dushayne was dressed in a fabulous costume and she smiled at him, thoroughly entranced by the picture he made in early-nineteenth-century garb. He reminded her of a rakish Darcy, not in looks but in style, and definitely in the way he showed both pride and prejudice.

"What fun this is. It's like a step back in time. I wish I had a dress that matched what you're wearing. Something with a high waist and embroidery around the edges."

"Next time," he said with a smile of satisfaction. And yes, there were the dimples. "Everything will be better next time, Isabelle."

"I hope that's a promise." She really wasn't much of a flirt, but she had a desperate longing to know this man better, to understand him, to keep him smiling.

"Indeed it is." Dushayne raised her hand

and kissed it and then tucked her arm through his. "Let's see what the fortune-teller has to say about you."

"Will you ask her to tell your fortune? Or is 'the master' " — she made the words sound as pretentious as they were — "above such things?"

"I never would have guessed that you were such a tease. A temptress, yes, but not a tease."

"And I would never have guessed that you would not enjoy a little flirtation." Isabelle refused to be embarrassed by his insulting tone, almost positive that he was trying to make her feel uncomfortable so that he would have the upper hand. Or, she thought, was he the one who was uncomfortable?

Neither one of them spoke as they made their way across the salon. Isabelle wondered why he would feel even a little threatened by her presence. He was the one who had given permission for her to come, along with Father Joubay. So it was not her presence as a medical person that upset him, but something about Isabelle Reynaud herself that bothered him.

Could it be the same thing that bothered her: attraction to a person he was not even sure he liked?

The crowd clustered around the fortune-teller made room for their host and eyed Isabelle curiously. The fortune-teller sat at a round table. The seat across from her was empty and she gestured for Isabelle to take it.

"May I hold your hands, please?" the fortune-teller asked.

The woman was heavily made up and dressed in traditional gypsy garb, but her voice identified her as one of the islanders.

Isabelle smiled and put her hands on the table. The woman took them; then she jerked her head up to look in Isabelle's eyes. Between their touching hands and staring eyes, the connection between them was so strong that it was an effort to keep smiling.

The woman grinned at her and let her hands go. "You will live a long and happy life, for you have been blessed with optimism and a sense of adventure. You will find love; you will know its deepest meaning but you will also know pain and loss."

The fortune-teller pressed her lips together as if she wanted to say more but then thought better of it. Leaning forward, she whispered, "Be careful. More than your heart is at risk."

Isabelle closed her eyes. Yes, she knew that. Had known it from the first time she had sung to Sebastian Dushayne. Isabelle pressed the woman's hand. "Thank you. I do understand."

When she stood up, another woman took her place instantly. "Tell me something useful," she demanded.

The fortune-teller laughed. "If you are not careful, you will lose more than your money on this trip."

"What does that mean?" the woman demanded.

Isabelle moved away from the group before the gypsy answered. She had no idea what the fortune-teller meant but was equally certain that the woman would not like the details. Sebastian was nowhere to be found, so she accepted a glass of champagne from one of the servants and began to circle the room.

The next hour passed in a haze of names and amusing conversation. Several men and one woman tried their best to corner her for more than talk. Isabelle might look like an innocent, might actually be one, but she had dated enough and worked in some hard places. A party flirtation was easy enough to handle.

Sebastian Dushayne found her in the corner with one of the men who would not take no for an answer. Isabelle had just poured her glass of champagne down the man's shirtfront when Sebastian pulled her from the nook and propelled her to the dance floor.

"This is a reel. A popular Regency dance. Follow the lead of the people in costume. It is not difficult to learn."

It was fun. It reminded Isabelle of square dancing but was more elegantly done. By the time the dancers made their last bows to one another, all were a little out of breath and laughing.

The next tune changed the mood completely. "A waltz," Sebastian told her, "but a Regency waltz. Much more decorous than a Viennese waltz, but for the people of the early nineteenth century it was very risqué."

Holding her at arm's length, Sebastian put a hand at her shoulder and one at her waist. They began to move through the steps and within a minute Isabelle felt as though there were nothing around them, only the two of them in each other's arms.

Stepping closer to Sebastian, Isabelle used her body to tell him that she was going nowhere, that here was exactly where she wanted to be. She saw the pleased surprise in Sebastian's eyes, but he still held her as if he were afraid she would run.

Finally he relaxed and sighed, a small sigh

that she understood as appreciation for the sweetest of pleasures. Closing her eyes, she drew a mental picture of the two of them alone, dancing through clouds set in a dark velvet sky strewn with diamondlike stars glittering around them. A peek at heaven, she decided, or as close as she could imagine. Yes, she could go on like this forever.

"Forever?" Sebastian said, and Isabelle realized she had said that last out loud. "Not forever, only for as long as the thrill of it lasts. Let me show you."

Isabelle opened her eyes just as Sebastian kissed her. *Oh, this is paradise.* To be so closely connected to someone you love, or could love. Like an invitation to the best party imaginable.

Then all thoughts evaporated in a rush of emotion, sensation that bound her to him more completely than the touch of his mouth on hers. Her soul opened to him, her heart begged his and she gave herself to him as fully as she could with her mouth and her hands, and every part of her body that touched him. It was not a branding, but a gift, happily given.

Sebastian did not give as easily. Isabelle realized that as the kiss ended. He straightened, his look of shock changing to fear, or was it pain? He pushed her into the arms of one of the other men.

"Take her, Leo. This one is more than ready for a quick fuck. You won't even need to take your clothes off."

Leo grabbed Isabelle from behind, his hands settling on her breasts, his arousal pressing into her buttocks. She could smell the scotch on his breath when he nuzzled her ear. Freeing her arms, she used her elbows to pound into his gut and was more than satisfied when he staggered back, cursing.

"A quick fuck? Is that what you said?" Isabelle could feel her temper cut loose. "You are a disgusting excuse for a gentleman."

"And you are courting trouble."

"You don't scare me." She proved it by closing the distance between them. She could feel anger, passion, even fear shimmering around him. What was he afraid of?

He grabbed her shoulders and shook her a little. "I should terrify you."

"But you don't," she said gently, her anger fading as she realized what he was worried about. "Not at all."

"If I took you, you would never be the same." He was pleading with her. She heard no pride in his voice. "You would be no more than a whore because you would never find as much satisfaction with anyone else."

"But then, neither would you because what is between us is about more than sex. If you are afraid —" She emphasized the word and paused. "If you are afraid to give more than your body, then we will never be together."

Sebastian Dushayne had nothing to say. In the silence she could feel his fear disappear, along with his anger and almost all his passion. "Time will tell, my little nun."

"Why do you call me that?" The description made her more defensive than anything else he had said, which, she realized, was exactly why he had used the word.

"Who else but a nun would know nothing but hymns and wear her virtue like it was her proudest possession?"

"What a waste. She has sky-high tart potential and she's a nun?"

The words of the man nearest reminded Isabelle that they had an audience.

"No, she's not a nun now," Sebastian said, looking into her eyes as if he could read her soul. "I imagine they dismissed her for flirting with a priest."

Isabelle could feel the color drain from her face. "And you are filled with disdain because you're afraid that if you care for another woman, she will leave you just like the first did."

If it was possible to wound a person with words, Isabelle realized that they had each dealt a near mortal blow to the other.

She was not sure how Sebastian felt about revealing someone's deepest secret, but his shock and distress at her accusation made her feel as sinful as Judas when he betrayed Jesus. "I'm sorry," she whispered and ran from the room before they hurt each other any more than they already had.

Six

Once she was outside of the *castillo*, Isabelle slowed her steps and tried to calm herself. Tears trickled down her cheeks. She was sorry that she had not been able to control her temper, that his insult had made her retaliate in kind. It was so mean-spirited of her, the worst of all her failings as far as she was concerned. An apology would not change anything, but it was more than he had offered her.

The streets were quiet. The healer's home the only one still with light. The open door showed people inside. Thinking that there had been an accident, Isabelle pushed her heartache aside, ran up the short path and went inside.

The people gathered were not patients. They were playing some sort of game with dominos and while it may not have required alcohol, every one of the five players took a sip of something after their turn at play.

"Aha!" Esmé called out. "The one we have been waiting for. Come over here."

Isabelle did as asked, sure that Esmé was drunk and would remember none of this tomorrow. But Esmé surprised her. Her mug held the distinct smell of Earl Grey tea that appeared to have nothing in it but sugar.

"And milk if I had any," Esmé agreed as if Isabelle had spoken aloud. "But the island has no milk until tomorrow so I make do with extra honey." She pointed to a chair and then clapped her hands.

"My friends, you have drunk enough of my spirits. I appreciate your keeping the evening with me and will see you tomorrow if you need a headache cure."

No one objected. All finished the last of their drinks and staggered out of the house with a chorus of "Best wishes to the mistress of this house."

Esmé stared at Isabelle for almost a minute. "You come back to me with a pure spirit. I will not ask how that can be or doubt my insight. If I had been drinking with my friends, I would not be so certain, but I refrained, intent on discrediting you. Now it appears it was a waste of restraint."

"I cannot say that I am sorry I disappointed you," Isabelle answered, "only relieved that you are so perceptive. And honest."

"Few appreciate how expensive honesty can be."

"I respect your work, Healer, and will never do anything to undermine your wisdom, unless I know that someone's life is in danger." Isabelle paused and when Esmé gave a grudging nod went on. "Yes, I do know how expensive honesty can be."

Esmé stood up and poured more tea for herself and a mug for Isabelle. To each she added a dollop of spirits from a clay jug and set both on the table.

"He hurt your heart," Esmé stated.

"Why is he so hard? Why is he so alone? There is immense kindness in him. I have seen it, felt it. Why, if he has a good heart, does he think that lust and drunkenness and drugs are the answer to anything? Why does he stay here when he is so obviously unhappy?"

"Sip your tea and wrap yourself in a shawl. It is a long story and one that will test your faith in my honesty."

Isabelle took the shawl Esmé handed her and, though the evening was not particularly cool, wrapped the gossamer-light piece around her shoulders.

"Sebastian Dushayne was assigned here

as a soldier when the *castillo* still housed warriors, though they were English soldiers and not the Spaniards who had first built it. Captain Dushayne fell in love with a local girl. Her mother was the village healer. Not me," Esmé hastened to add. "Despite the mother's misgivings, which were far more insightful than most people's, she allowed her daughter, Angelique, to marry Sebastian."

Esmé sipped her tea and added more spirits.

"Sebastian Dushayne wanted Angelique. He said he loved her, but he wanted her beauty, her sweetness, her pure heart. And it was a fine match. Her goodness tempered his carnal wants and his commanding presence made Angelique aware of the value of a forceful personality."

Isabelle settled back into the cushions of the sofa to find comfort where she could. This story was not going to have a happy ending.

"After a great storm swept the region, Angelique told her husband that she must go to help her sister on another island. Sebastian allowed it but insisted that she come back quickly, afraid that separation would be too great a test of his vows. Can you see that his love was mixed with too great a need to control?"

Isabelle saw that in him still. The way he told people what to do, never asked a question, demanded rather than suggested.

"Finally, when she had been gone too long, Sebastian Dushayne insisted his wife return. Despite the fact it was the month of the worst storms of the year, Angelique tried to obey him and was lost at sea. Of forty people, only three women survived and one man of God."

"Man of God?" Isabelle straightened.

"Yes." Esmé nodded. "Father Joubay took a place in the dinghy. If he'd given the spot to Angelique, she would have lived."

"Oh, dear God." Isabelle raised her hand to her mouth.

"The healer cursed both Joubay and Sebastian Dushayne to an eternity of suffering for causing the death of her beloved child. Joubay was forbidden on the island, the one place he wanted to live more than anyplace else, until he could undo his wrong. Dushayne was given total control of this island, but only this island. He was condemned to live here, unable to leave the island, for as long as it took for him to win the love of another woman as pure of heart as Angelique."

"This is true? You swear it?" Even if Esmé

swore, Isabelle was not sure she would believe it.

"Yes, Isabelle, I swear on my skill as a healer. And what I have told you is not even the hardest part to believe." Esmé pushed her tea away and closed her eyes for a moment.

"This happened in the fall of 1810. Sebastian has been living here, frozen in age and time, for almost two hundred years."

Isabelle stood up, knocking over the mug. "That cannot be."

"Yes, it is. I swear it on Angelique's grave. Sebastian can use the modern version of anything already invented in 1810. He can read any book he chooses and wear any style clothing he prefers, but he cannot use electricity or the telephone or any other modern convenience."

"What happens if he tries?"

"Whatever it is does not work, or bursts into flame, or disintegrates."

Isabelle allowed herself to believe it for a moment. The *castillo* was lit by candles. She had seen no sign of a computer or a telephone. There were no battery-operated radios or even an old-fashioned boom box, and that was odd for a man who loved singing.

"But worst of all, Isabelle, Sebastian

Dushayne cannot leave this island for even a moment. Over the years the strip of land that connects the fort here to the main part of the island has been eroded by storms, so now even the islanders can only leave at low tide."

"But people can come here from the big hotel on the main island?"

"Yes, Sebastian holds his version of a nineteenth-century soiree, which draws tourists to the *castillo* and they are only too happy to fill his needs. He is a man of broad sexual tastes and greatly interested in experimentation."

"Stop!" Isabelle insisted. "I do not want to hear any more. I do not believe you. You're insane or trying to manipulate me."

"Think what you will, innocent," Esmé said with a shrug. "But you cannot stay pure of heart around someone like the man he has become, and that is what you must be to save him. A conundrum, is it not?"

Standing up, Esmé ignored the spilled tea and took Isabelle's arm. "Think about it, dear girl; sleep and pray to your God. Joubay found his answer in you. Who knows? It could be that I am mistaken. If that is so, and I am wrong, we will become enemies. My mission in life, as the healer's descendant, is to see that Sebastian Dushayne is punished into eternity."

Isabelle must have looked as stunned as she felt. "You would murder me?"

"Murder you?" Esmé's shock was sincere. "Never. But there are other ways to make you unwelcome here. Please, don't let it come to that. Avoid him. He deserves his misery." The healer patted her arm as she showed her to the door. "For two hundred years. This has been going on for two hundred years. You are not the first innocent and you will not be the last." Esmé pushed her out the door with a gentle shove and clicked it shut.

Home was five doors down, and even though Isabelle walked very slowly it was not nearly a long enough walk to sift out the truth of the healer's story.

Hanging her dress on one of the hooks, she brushed her teeth halfheartedly and climbed into bed. Sleep was impossible, but Isabelle felt safest in her snug bed tucked into the alcove.

The sheets were soft with many washings and as white as island sun and lemon could make them.

Relaxing a little, Isabelle began to pray. If she did not actually fall asleep, she did begin to dream. Father Joubay came to her and sat on the edge of her bed, which was, suddenly, aboard a ship being tossed about in an insane sea.

"We are safe," he assured her. "He is the one in danger."

In the way of dreams she could see a man swimming, struggling against the waves, but swimming away from them and not to them.

"It really should not be hard to believe that a devil's curse could hold this man and this curve of land in thrall." He picked up a wooden cross from the shelf at the head of her bed and held it to his heart. "Isabelle, you believe in the miracles that are in the Bible."

She nodded and Father Joubay went on, pressing his advantage. "You have seen miracles in your work. Why is it more difficult to believe in the curse of evil?"

"You called it the devil's miracle."

"Yes. Like the planes that destroyed the World Trade Center. Like the nightmare of slavery in America or the children who destroyed innocence at Columbine High School. Those were calamitous events and millions of people felt their impact.

"But there are many other curses like the one that Sebastian must endure, curses that do not impact the whole world." He took her hand. "We could have been spared every one of those events, great and small, if one person had done the right thing."

"What right thing?"

"Only God knows who or what would have led to a different ending to those tragedies, but there is always someone who could have changed what happened."

"But no one stopped the Oklahoma City bombing or the Holocaust."

"That's true. But someone changed the heart of the man who would have destroyed the San Francisco Bay Bridge and the men set on destroying the Tokyo water supply. A beautiful sunrise convinced your mother not to abort you."

"Yes, I know that story but not the others."

"No one knows of those others because they never happened and never will. Goodness in some form changed a heart and drove all thought of hatred from them. And, you, Isabelle, are the one who can change Sebastian Dushayne's life."

"You ask too much of me."

Father Joubay stayed silent, and Isabelle knew what he was waiting for.

"I've lived such a sheltered life, at least it was sheltered until I became a nurse. And even since then I have never had a serious boyfriend. How can I help a man as mired in dissipation as Sebastian Dushayne?" Isabelle asked as she pulled her hand from his and folded her arms.

"Because, despite his lifestyle, you can see the good in him. Because you freed me from the curse. Because your heart has love to spare. When our eyes met in church that day I had never felt so hopeful. It was as though you understood."

"It's absurd and this is just a dream." She took the cross away from him and put it back on the shelf. "It's my mind's way of making sense of this."

"Isabelle, do not let the scientist in you reject what the woman of faith believes. Look around you and see that the healer tells the truth." Father Joubay spoke with a doggedness that belied the gentle way he patted her hand.

A cock crowed and Isabelle woke up, the image of the man disappearing along with the storm and the furious seas.

The sky was leaden today as if rain was inevitable. Taking a page from the healer's book, Isabelle left a note under her door saying that she was taking the day off. Then she walked on to the *castillo*, allowing the scientist in her to rule the day.

She visited the kitchen, a massive vault of a room kept cool because it was mostly be-lowground. A line of windows ringed the ceiling to let in light.

All the household work was done by hand and even in the morning there were already five people busy preparing the main meal of the day. The staff was welcoming, the chef annoyed by the distraction. The mix of twenty-first-century life with nineteenth-century ways was disconcerting.

There were contemporary clocks but no timers. Spoons of all kinds, except plastic, but no wire whisks or eggbeaters. The fireplace had a baking oven to the side but there was no sign of a microwave or a conventional cooking range. Huge porcelain sinks looked contemporary but the hand pump was not.

Isabelle wandered around the *castillo,* finally getting a sense of the place as it was before it became one man's prison. It must have housed hundreds of soldiers once and the construction of the time was impressive.

The Castillo de Guerreros was hundreds of years old but showed little sign of deterioration.

Isabelle found the room she had woken up in after the shipwreck. The curtained bed and candles made more sense now.

The window overlooking the harbor was open and she could hear shouting from the beach.

A group of men and older boys were playing some kind of game. But it was Sebastian who caught her attention. Stripped
down to an odd undergarment, a cross
between boxers and briefs, he was a magnifi-
cent contrast to the darker, shorter islanders with whom he was playing.

The game involved running and kicking,
some combined version of soccer and kick-
ball, apparently of island origin. Periodically
play would stop, they would all drink something from various mugs, laugh and joke
and then begin again.

Sebastian was in such good humor that
Isabelle hardly recognized the man who had
been so awful to her the night before. She
loved watching the way he controlled his
body, the ripple of muscles, the flex of his
buttocks as he kicked the ball, his agility in
avoiding opponents who wanted to stop his
progress, the way he bent over, putting his
hands on his knees to catch his breath.

The game grew more heated and one of
the younger players broke ranks and took a
punch at a boy on the opposing side.

The game stopped and Sebastian switched
roles, from player to coach. With an arm
around the young man's shoulder he took
him to a spot in the shade and they talked.
Well, it appeared Sebastian mostly listened

while the boy talked.

The others ignored the discussion, drank or found a shady spot to cool down. A few minutes later Sebastian and the boy returned to the team, the boy said something to the guy he'd punched and the game resumed, all ill will gone.

The competition ended a few minutes later with much cheering and back slapping. Then the men stripped off their clothes and ran into the water. When he was waist deep, Sebastian looked up and waved to her.

Isabelle raised her hand to him, but ducked out of sight when the others tried to figure out to whom he was waving.

Those few minutes told her as much about Sebastian Dushayne as she had learned in all their conversations. He was a natural leader, respected by his fellow islanders, capable of being a team player or a peacemaker as needed. He found pleasure in the physical and that meant more than sex. And, oh, yes, he had a fabulous body.

It was a shame that the man's talents had been limited to this little world for so long. If there were any chance she could free him, she would. With that thought Isabelle realized she did believe that Sebastian Dushayne and Father Joubay had been cursed. For two hundred years.

There was no scientific proof. It was the man and the place, the aura that surrounded both. Despite his youth and good health, the way everyone referred to him as "the master" epitomized the feeling that Sebastian Dushayne was not a part of this world.

But wanting to help him and acting on it without debasing herself were two different things. Isabelle had no idea how she could do it and prayed with all her heart that there was a way.

There is. The two words came to her in a whisper as quiet as a raindrop.

She prayed again that Sebastian would believe. No quiet word reassured her that he would.

SEVEN

As days turned into weeks, Isabelle wondered if she might have been wrong about her reason for being on Isla Perdida. Had her fascination with Sebastian Dushayne misled her? His tortured world, his wounded heart, his compelling sexuality haunted her but she had seen no sign of him for almost three weeks.

Her work with Esmé and the villagers was rewarding. The healer was open to the idea that Isabelle begin a process of inoculation of both children and adults against the most common diseases.

Isabelle initiated the prototype program used by most world health organizations. Part of the process was a record-keeping initiative that would identify and track the routine treatment as well as the emergency needs of the village.

Recording a medical history was its own massive chore, as big as convincing the villagers that inoculations would discourage, not encourage, illness. Isabelle found the villagers unwilling to help her with the written work for a dozen reasons down to the fact that they had never kept records before.

Esmé was a superb midwife and the neonatal health of the village women was impressive. Most girls were matched with mates by the time they were sixteen and mothers within the year.

The village was run much like a classic commune with little interference from the outside. Meals were shared in a common dining room and those few who did not work for Sebastian Dushayne fished and raised fruits and vegetables for the whole village.

No one crossed the tidal-submerged strip of land to work at the hotel on a daily basis. Those who did never returned. There was nothing mystical about that. The twenty-first century was too strong a draw.

While Isabelle's work with the villagers was rewarding, her contact with the castle was nonexistent. Each evening she went to sing and each evening was turned away by one of the servants who told her that Sebastian was entertaining privately and did not wish to hear her.

The fourth week into her work, Sebastian

came to the village right after breakfast as Isabelle was walking back to her cottage.

The villagers' excitement was palpable as the master stopped at the dining area, now empty except for the children dawdling over their fruit and porridge.

The boys and girls mobbed him as he took a seat on one of the benches just outside the dining room. Isabelle watched Sebastian listen to stories, admire toys and suggest that they meet at the beach later.

"Yes! Yes!" the children chorused. "Let's go now!"

"After school," he insisted.

"Oooooh," they moaned.

"It could be that if you work hard today, Mistress Teacher will let you out early. I will be waiting, no matter where the sun is, when you are free."

As one, the group of children — Isabelle guessed there were fifteen in all — jumped up and raced to the schoolroom, where the Mistress Teacher waited. She waved at Sebastian, shaking her head as she did, then followed the children inside.

The street was quiet.

"I suspect this will be a difficult day for her to hold their attention." Isabelle came up beside him and, at his start of surprise, she reached out and touched his shoulder.

"I'm sorry I —" Isabelle began but stopped at the anger she saw. "What is it?"

"You made an agreement, Mistress Nurse. You are to come sing at the castle every night. And you have not visited for three weeks. Do you think to punish me because I am not interested in taking any pleasure from your body?"

"You make it sound as though my body exists for your use." She did her best to sound reasonable even as her temper seethed. "Men are not that sexist these days and it's not how I see sex. It's a way to express affection, to share love in a physical way. It is about the mind and heart as much as the body."

"Isabelle, we each exist for the other's 'use' as you call it. Let me demonstrate." He pulled her into the dining room entry hall, pinned her against the wall and kissed her. His lips touched her neck below her ear. Isabelle raised her arms to push him away, but the kiss enchanted her and she encircled his neck instead.

This is more than lust, more than wanting; this is the deepest of feeling. Isabelle tried to convince him as his mouth met hers and she opened to him. Opened more than her lips, opened her body, her mind, her heart as she had the first time Sebastian had kissed her.

He ended the kiss abruptly. His hardness pressed against her, arousing her even though they were both fully clothed.

"This is not the mind and heart, you simpleminded virgin. This is lust at its most powerful. If you think this is the ultimate sharing, then you are amazingly uneducated. This is only the beginning, though I wonder if you will ever free the wanton that is hiding inside you."

Isabelle's cheeks burned, and not only because she knew what she was capable of, had dreamed of the two of them together in ways that were very creative and slightly shocking.

It hurt physically to push him away, to deny herself what she wanted to give and he wanted to take — for all the wrong reasons.

"You do have a way with words, Sebastian. Were all men this insulting in 1810? Or have you become so used to being called 'the master' that you think of yourself as above everyone else?"

"You annoy me."

That was stating the obvious, Isabelle thought. He looked like a chastened schoolboy pretending not to have a crush on a girl, but she reminded herself he was definitely not a schoolboy, and the depth of his feelings on the subject of lust and love made the idea of a crush laughable.

"Your talk of love and union is a fantasy." He stood with his hands on his hips, not angry with her, she saw, but very, very frustrated. That made two of them.

"No, love is not a fantasy," Isabelle insisted. "I know I will be yours as well as I know what day this is, but you will be mine, Sebastian Dushayne, and that makes all the difference in the world."

Isabelle smoothed her pants and shirt into place and stepped away from him. "I have come to the *castillo* every evening since I last saw you and am told every evening that you are 'entertaining privately' and have no wish for me to sing."

Sebastian did not answer her with any more than narrowed eyes, so she left the dining room and began a brisk walk to her clinic to gather the supplies for the day.

"Wait!"

"I am already late," she said, without breaking stride.

Sebastian fell into step beside her, smiling now. "You have been very busy. Cortez tells me that the immunization program has started."

"Yes, I was very pleased that Mistress

Esmé was so receptive to the idea."

"I'm sure she was."

At his cynical tone, Isabelle slowed and looked at him. "Why do you say it that way?"

"Isabelle, my sweet, I never left word that you should be turned away from the *castillo*."

Now she stopped walking completely. "You didn't? But then why would they tell me to leave?" She had a niggling feeling she knew the answer.

"You know why. Because Esmé does not want us to be together. I can guess that she told the gatekeeper to send you away. She is keeping you busy and me distracted."

"Then you are entertaining privately?" Isabelle did not want to sound coy, but it was such a gentle way to ask if he was having sex with someone else.

"Every night," he said with rueful nod. "Esmé has a long and deep connection with the concierge at the hotel. The woman on the desk is her cousin and the man is her grandson. They are always on the lookout for guests who suit my taste."

Isabelle tried not to show her disgust.

He laughed. "Your striving for sainthood is as amusing as it is obvious. Make up your mind, Isabelle. You can be a saint or a woman. Not both."

"Then you do not understand faith or God at all."

"Oh, it will be a joy to have you educate me."

"Yes, it will." Isabelle had never once heard him use the word "joy." It was the smallest, tiniest step in the right direction.

"Come tonight, Isabelle."

"Yes, I will."

Sebastian watched her leave. Her joie de vivre was endearing. Her honesty amazing and amusing. He was not in a hurry to have sex with her. The dance they were sharing was so much less predictable than what happened in bed.

By the time he visited all the villagers, the noon bell rang for the midday meal, as he was walking through the castle gate. While he had no need for food, he did like the afternoon rest that was a part of island life. He would sleep a little and then head to the beach for his time with the children.

While he dozed, Joubay came to him, sitting beside him on the huge rock that was the shadiest spot on the west-facing beach. They did not look at each other, but watched a sailboat approach, both of them afraid, both of them pretending they were not.

"So Esmé is up to her old tricks," Joubay began.

Sebastian had not heard his voice in two hundred years but recognized the gravelly sound that came from too much tobacco.

"Doing her best to keep Isabelle Reynaud away from me." Sebastian threw a rock into the water gently slapping the outcropping beneath their feet. "Does the healer actually think the girl is a threat to the curse?"

"Yes, I do believe so."

"There could never be another as pure of heart, as generous, as compliant as Angelique was." He felt the breeze stiffen and the fear became dread. "My love for her caused her death and I deserve every year of this curse. It is not all bad, you know."

"Nonsense. You cannot lie to me. Sex is an endless seeking for what is lost. You know as well as I do that sex alone is not the answer."

"Don't preach to me. You have not been celibate for two hundred years."

"For more of it than you think. The difference between us is that I knew it was not the answer." Joubay raised his head as the breeze became a wind and the first of the clouds crept up from the west. "And I had faith that I could find redemption. I have, and I am at rest at last. Need I remind you that Isabelle was the key?"

"I am not going to watch this again, Joubay." The sky was darkening. Sebastian could feel the rain in the air.

"Then wake up and stop torturing yourself." Joubay had to shout now as the wind whipped around them. "Sebastian, give the woman what she gives to you and see what happens. It cannot hurt more than you are hurting now."

Sebastian woke up to the sound of something crashing to the floor and the muffled curse of a servant. Standing up, he shook off the last of the dream and readied himself for an afternoon with the only true innocents on the island.

EIGHT

The children always refreshed Sebastian in body and spirit. Their teacher was a truly gifted woman, and they had learned from the first that sharing was its own reward. The one little blind girl never lacked for someone to help her down the walkways or to read her the arithmetic problems.

By the time dusk settled on the *castillo,* he had rinsed off the salt and sand and dressed, ready for his next guest. Sitting in the chair near the fireplace with the smallest of fires, totally unnecessary but very comforting, Sebastian thought about what Joubay had said in his dream. Or it could be that some of the children's innocence touched his heart. Before he could decide, he heard Isabelle's voice and walked to the door and out onto the passage that overlooked the inner bailey.

"I will come to you when you need me. I will free you from all your fear. All you must do is accept me and believe that I am always near."

380

He felt wet on his hand and brushed another tear from his face. As she finished the song, the words that touched him echoed through his head. *"I will free you from all your fear. All you must do is accept me."*

No one had ever named it "fear" before. Sebastian realized that he had not even thought of it that way until the moment the words were out of Isabelle's mouth.

Fear. He was afraid, afraid of a hundred things.

Afraid that if he loved again, he would die. Not that death frightened him, but it would mean that there was so much that he would never have a chance to do.

He would like a chance to give back to more than his island home. To see the world denied him for so long. To meet men and women like his villagers. People who thought more of others than of themselves.

Fear hounded him. Fear that he did not know how to love. Love was as imperfect as the lover. His way of loving had cost Angelique her life. Was the fear of losing another lover what had kept him from finding someone in two hundred years? He'd never been able to decide if that was part of the curse or his own failing.

The biggest fear of all was that Isabelle would die if he even tried to love again. He put his head in his hand and let the tears fall. Fear weakened him so completely that Sebastian put his head in his hands and cried like a child.

Isabelle left the *castillo,* annoyed that the master had not shown himself when she had finished her song. He took time to encourage everyone else in the world, everyone but her.

She searched out the spot she called her own, a small grove of very old palms that had the feel of a holy place. She sat on one of the stumps and wished for someone to talk to.

The palms clacked in the light evening breeze. Isabelle did not think that was a divine message. No more than the surf or the sound of the night was. But it did inspire her to sit in silence, and lift her heart in prayer, to be part of nature as nature was part of her. She tried to convince herself that she was not lonely.

An amazingly bright shooting star lit the sky and Isabelle laughed. "Yes, I know I have only to speak from my heart and I am heard. I know some hymn that teaches that truth. But at this particular moment I would like someone to talk with."

"You could talk to me, Isabelle." Sebastian emerged from the shadows and sat across from her on the trunk of a palm tree that had fallen in some storm ages ago.

"Where were you tonight?" she asked with an edge to her voice.

"You sang 'Be Still and Know I Am Here.' Doesn't that apply to you too?"

"Yes," she said, which showed how good she was at preaching but not at living what she preached. "It's one thing to say the words and another to live them."

"It took me a while to deal with my fear."

"What fear?"

"The list would take too long. But the biggest fear is that I will lose what I love the most."

"It's inevitable, Sebastian. We all face that fear."

"Yes, but we don't all cause death like I did."

"You do think of yourself as 'the master,' don't you? It happened for a hundred reasons, dear man, and one of them was to bring the two of us together. How else to match two destined souls born almost two hundred years apart?"

"Now, that is a fantasy."

She laughed. "No more than being lost in paradise for two hundred years."

"So you think predestination brought us

together?"

"Not for a minute. I think a hundred things could have kept us apart. But by some miracle I came here and you listened." Tears filled her eyes and tracked down her cheeks, not tears of sadness but an overflow of such profound belief she could not hold them back.

"Father Joubay called your curse a miracle of the devil's making. I think he is wrong. This is a miracle of the highest order."

"Miracle as torture?" he asked, and she had to agree that it had not been easy for him.

"Maybe all heartache is a gift in disguise. Maybe all good events have some darkness shadowing them."

She came to him, the tears gone, and looked up into his face, overwhelmed in the best possible way by his physical power and presence. "Sebastian, maybe there is no pure good and bad in the world, but one grand invitation for us to live life to the fullest."

He smiled, not quite showing his dimples, and kissed her as if it was the only answer he could give. That kiss, filled with a sweetness she had never felt before, gave her hope. He leaned back and now there were dimples showing. "This is too much theology for me. I came to invite you to watch the moon rise with me."

"All right." Indeed she had said quite enough. "I imagine you know the perfect spot."

"I do." He bowed a little and offered his arm.

She took his hand. It startled him and she decided it would be an evening of discovery for both of them. "Is it far?"

"On the top of the fort."

"Let's hurry. I don't want to miss a moment."

Isabelle held tight to his hand as they hurried up a ramp, to move guns, he said. They dashed around the outer wall where the gun mounts stood empty and up three sets of stairs. At the very top of the *castillo* there was a long line of guardhouses that marked the side of the fortress that faced the harbor.

All the while they held hands. His hold was awkward and she loved him all the more for it.

Isabelle let go of his hand, walked over to the wall and looked out to the harbor.

She loved him.

Of course she did. Stupid girl, she chided herself. How else was this story to play out? She could hardly give herself to a man without love. Had actually worried about it a little, knowing how much she wanted him. Now she did not have to worry about it anymore. This was living life to the fullest for her. She had no doubt.

Isabelle twirled around and leaned back on the rock and instantly felt the rock give way. She choked out a scream as she fell, the backs of her knees hitting the broken part of the wall and sending her into the black night.

"No!" Sebastian roared. He grabbed her hand, pulling her into his arms. They fell to their knees. Isabelle held on to him as if he were the only real safety in her world. She buried her face in his chest as she heard the broken chunk of the wall bounce off another rampart and fall into the sea.

"I was going to tell you how perfect that spot was," Isabelle whispered. "But this spot with your arms around me is even better."

Sebastian leaned back and took her face in his hands. "Do not die, do you hear me? I cannot have another life on my conscience."

"I'm fine."

Sebastian kissed her as if the touch of his lips would make her safe. She felt the sweetness again, and desire. On their knees, his lips begged for acceptance and when she gave it to him, he deepened the kiss. It was everything she wanted. The kiss ended, or at least he moved his lips to her hair and the way he rocked as he cradled her against him was as exciting as it was soothing.

She touched the spot below his ear with her lips and whispered, "Have we missed the moonrise or do you think the moon will wait for us?" Isabelle hoped he would laugh, but when she raised her head to look at his face, she saw that she would have to settle for a smile.

Sebastian stood and took her hand. "Come this way. And do not go too close to the wall."

"All right," she said and let him lead the way. Isabelle looked up to see that the stars seemed only just above her reach. "This is one of the most perfect places on earth."

Sebastian pressed her fingers to his lips and turned her to face the east where the moon had just popped up over the horizon. With his arms wrapped around her and her hands over his, they watched the moon make its graceful climb. It was lemony yellow and huge, though it grew smaller in size as it found its place in the heavens, surrounded by the stars that beckoned and twinkled.

What did the moon see in them? Isabelle wondered. Two people from completely opposite times and places, who found each other. Who, together, were going to end a curse with the miracle of love that was God's gift to humankind.

Sebastian led her to a bench just like the ones that lined the walls in the castle's courtyard. This one was more weathered, still comfortable enough if they sat very close together.

Sebastian played with her hair. "Your hair is so thick I cannot believe you can hold your head up. But when I touch it, it feels like the finest-spun silk." They kissed, and kissed again.

"Tell me about the convent, Isabelle."

Tears filled her eyes as she squeezed his hand before pulling hers away. She closed her eyes but nodded, and Sebastian sat back, folding his arms, waiting with the patience of a man who had tested that virtue to its limits.

This was how trust began. Isabelle knew she would have to be the first to give. It was about more than the way a man was made. This man had forgotten how to trust a long time ago.

But he had actually asked, cared enough to want to know how she became who she was.

With her eyes closed, Isabelle pictured the

huge convent, now much too big for its small community, with echoing halls and the sound of hymns at all hours. The memory still touched that part of her that longed to be closer to God.

"I went into the convent right after high school. I'm from Nebraska." She glanced at him. "Do you know where Nebraska is?"

"Somewhere in the American midsection," he suggested without much confidence.

"The Midwest, yes. My parents had a farm that was fifty miles from everyone else. So they sent me to a girls' boarding school run by a very progressive order of nuns. Then my mom and dad died my second year of high school and I spent vacations for the next two years with relations who really did not want me."

"I am so sorry, though I find it hard to imagine anyone not wanting you." He kissed the top of her head. "That would never have happened here."

"Yes, Cortez explained your way of caring for children," Isabelle said, pretending not to understand his meaning. "Your community here is impressive, Sebastian, but it only works on a small scale with an enlightened man at the head."

"Yes, I think the term is 'despot.' "

She fisted her right hand and gently punched his left arm.

"You try so hard to make me see you as a dissipated, ruined man." She straightened and raised one finger so he would know she was serious. "I tell you, Sebastian, the man I am getting to know is the one I saw on the beach today with the children. The one who took the blind girl up on his back and made her the leader of the group. The one who let himself be buried in sand." She folded her hands in her lap and waited pointedly for him to answer.

"Yes, Mistress Nurse, I know you want to think well of me and I am sorry to have to explain to one as high-minded as you that I play with the children so that when they grow up they will be loyal to me; they will stay and serve me as their parents have."

"Oh, nonsense. You play with them because they remind you of what you miss the most."

He laughed. "There is no discouraging you."

"Oh, yes, there is. I have faced my share of disappointments in my life."

"And convent life was one of them?"

"Yes." She sighed and took his hand. "I was so very lucky to have a Mother Superior who understood me. When I was accused, more than once, of inappropriate behavior, she took me aside and counseled me."

Isabelle rested her head against the wall and wondered what Mother would make of her now. "She knew that I was not flirting in a sexual way, but the priests were men after all. In the end she made me see that I did not want to be a nun so much as I wanted a sense of community, a place where I could belong, a place where I mattered to people as I had to my parents."

Oh, it still hurt to talk about it and remember the day she had taken her one little suitcase and walked out of yet another home. A tear splashed onto her hand and Sebastian wiped it away with one of his fingers.

"We all want to belong, Isabelle."

"I suppose so, and I was looking for it in the wrong place. We have something in common that way, Sebastian."

He did not rise to the bait but asked, "How long were you in the convent?"

"Three years. The order helped me find a scholarship for nursing school, which is what I had an aptitude and inclination for. I finished my training as a nurse, went to work and found an organization that would train me as a physician's assistant if I would work for their relief group for two years. I finished that work with the clinic in New Orleans after Katrina.

"Two weeks later I was in church when Father Joubay asked for a volunteer to come here for a year and here I am, sitting beside you on a gorgeous night wishing I was talking about anything but my past."

"Such a colorful life it is."

"I'm not sure if you're joking or not. But since I left Nebraska it has been one adventure after another." Isabella straightened and made sure she had his attention.

Oh, she certainly did.

Sebastian was watching her the way a child stared at a treat just out of reach or a shark biding its time until it could pounce. She looked away before the list of comparisons grew even more threatening.

"I've worked with prostitutes in Mexico and with the homeless in Thailand after the tsunami. I've treated child soldiers in Africa and seen a saint martyred."

Tears threatened again, but Isabelle had had enough of them and she prayed, not for Joseph, her martyred friend, but for the lost souls, the men who had killed him.

"I have seen people die for lack of the simplest things and seen amazing recoveries. God works around us, through us and in us all the time. I know that as well as I know the hymns I sing."

When Isabelle stopped talking, she was afraid he had fallen asleep. "I'm sorry, but you did ask."

"And through all that you are still a virgin?"

"Yes, and if that is the only thing you care about, then I am sorry I told you the story." She was more than a little peeved by his question. "I think you have some kind of sex addiction. It's considered a disease now, you know."

"Oh, what I have is worse than that. Much worse." He scooped her up into his arms and set her on her feet. "I do not see how any man in his right mind could not pursue you."

"They have. But I decided that I would wait until it meant more to me than another way to feel good." She thought of something else. "Sebastian, in 2009, a woman has a right to say no and be respected for that decision."

They watched each other in silence. Finally Sebastian said, "But you are not saying no to me. You would not have told me your story if you did not want to be closer, would you? And I would not have asked if I did not want to be closer to you."

Exactly, she thought.

"It's growing cool here, Isabelle. Come and have some tea or wine." He started toward the stairs.

"Sebastian, it is hardly ever cool here."

He looked over his shoulder and showed his dimples. "Pretend, Isabelle."

When they reached his sitting room, he paused before he opened the door.

"Yes," Isabelle said, looking at him with her heart in her eyes. "Tea, I think."

His smile disappeared and he bowed to her as though she had just given him the greatest gift.

NINE

Sebastian could tell by her smile that Isabelle had just given him the greatest gift she could bestow. Not her virginity, but her heart. Her smile said it all. How he loved that smile. Ignoring the dread that came with the word "love," he bowed to her, following her into his bedroom.

Isabelle ignored the long settee and walked over to the bed. "Tea, later." She half asked, half suggested, and he knew for a fact she was a mind reader.

Sebastian watched her take off her shoes, brush sand from her feet. Her toes were as sweet as the rest of her, and he realized she did not know the first thing about seduction.

"Isabelle, I'm supposed to help you take your clothes off."

She wriggled out of her pants and thong and was naked from the waist down. "Oh, no, really?" she said with a tone that told him she knew exactly what she was doing. "Let me help you undress first."

She climbed up on the bed, giving him an arousing view of her backside, from the waist down, and then turned to face him, kneeling up on her knees, so that they were of the same height.

"I was hoping you would be wearing that Regency costume from the other night. Untangling that cravat would be fun, and we could use it for so many other things."

She unbuttoned his shirt. The placket ended in the middle, so she pulled it up over his head. When they were face-to-face again, she pressed her lips to his.

That kiss was more than Sebastian could stand. He pushed her back on the bed and she let him, laughing and tugging at the fly on the cotton pants he wore. They wrestled like puppies as they undressed, helping, hindering and teasing. They came together as though the other was all the covering they would ever need.

He should go slow, Sebastian reminded himself. She was unschooled, untouched.

When he moved from her lips to kiss her neck and caress her breast, she sighed with such anticipation that he knew slow was not what she wanted. In a wordless communication he had never experienced before, Sebastian knew what she wanted, when, where, how. Her first orgasm came when he touched her between the legs, using his hand to cup and caress her silkiness.

She threw her arms out and then around him, pulling him closer so that his manhood could feel her warmth. "Don't stop."

Obeying her, Sebastian pushed himself into her, not as gently as he might have, and she arched up under him. They moved together and when his seed spilled into her, she held herself tight against him as if she needed every bit he had to give.

They played and slept and made love as the moon passed their window and the night waned. When the sun began to lighten the sky, the bed was a tangle of linen, the pillows long gone. Sebastian pulled the curtains around the bed while Isabelle slept, to give them some privacy when the servants brought hot water.

Sebastian watched the dawn and wondered what love meant.

He felt her hand on his back and then her lips where her fingers had touched. "I feel like we are in our own Eden. Come, my Adam" — she held up her arms offering herself to him — "help your Eve greet the day."

Lovemaking gave her a glow that made

her more womanly than she had been twelve hours before, but Isabelle Reynaud was as fresh and sweet as ever.

His world had not changed either. The battery-operated clock on his nightstand still pointed to midnight as it had for fifty years. If he had harbored the tiniest hope that truly *making love* with someone so generous and untouched would change his life, then he was disappointed. He did not dare hope that Isabelle would spend her life with him. There were too many forces who would not allow him that kind of happiness, that "living life to the fullest," as she said.

As he leaned down to kiss her, Sebastian wondered if he was Adam to her Eve, who was going to play the serpent?

When Sebastian invited her to share breakfast with him, Isabelle accepted, hoping, praying that this was the beginning of a lifetime of days and nights together, but first she had to tell him the truth.

"Sebastian, I know about the curse. Esmé gave me the details weeks ago."

He answered with no more than a slow, considering nod as he poured her coffee. Isabelle could not tell how he felt about her announcement.

She tasted her coffee and found the brew

too strong for her taste. After adding enough milk to temper the flavor, the coffee was more white than brown.

"Angelique drank hers the same way." Sebastian's eyes burned into her as he spoke. "But that is the only way the two of you are alike."

"Good," Isabelle said, "because I do not believe in reincarnation."

"Angelique was tall and I guess you would say buxom, but in 1810, her size meant she was healthy and well-to-do. Her skin was a creamy brown and she was beautiful in that way that mixed-race children can be. Her blue eyes were startling and her teeth so white and healthy they did not look real. She was perfect."

"You have no portrait of her?" Isabelle reminded herself that Angelique was a memory two hundred years old and did her best to ignore the sting of jealousy.

"No, I have no painting." His voice was filled with regret. "The artists here were not very skilled. I did not want to waste my money on a second-rate image when I had the real woman beside me all the time."

They sipped more coffee, and Isabelle ate some of the bread if only to pretend that everything was all right.

"What version of the story did Esmé tell you?"

Isabelle recounted the conversation as accurately as she could recall.

"Esmé is honest; I will give her that. It's the truth or as close as makes no difference." He shrugged, not very successful in hiding the misery the story recalled. "To this day I can dream of Angelique drowning, her heavy cloak and skirts dragging her down, fighting, fighting to stay afloat, to stay alive."

"Stop. Stop it, Sebastian. It does you no good to relive something that you had no control over." What kind of love had they shared that he could still feel this pain two hundred years later?

"You think I had no control? I could have told her to wait until the storm season was ended. I could have tried harder to control my lust. I could have prayed instead of cursed when she told me she wanted to stay longer."

"You missed her." She swallowed hard. "You loved her. It is perfectly understandable."

"I do not know if it is. I didn't miss her so much as I missed the comfort of her body, the way she worshipped me and everything I did. Does that sound like love to you?"

Isabelle didn't answer.

"No, Isabelle, it was no more love than what you feel for me."

"And how would you define that?"

"Curiosity. You are a normal, healthy woman and much too old to be a virgin. You are a generous woman and think that if you share yourself with me enough, then all my problems will be solved. You are wrong."

"No," she said slowly, "what I think is that if *you* love *me* enough, then all your problems will be solved."

"After two hundred years of trying, I suspect that love is beyond me."

"Only because you confuse lust with love." Her hand shook as she put her cup down.

"Do not play with the words," he said, showing the first anger since the discussion began. "Love and lust are not the same and I know the difference."

"But they are not exclusive," she said with heat in her voice. Not that anger would make him listen to her. "I think lust is the body's longing for love. Lust and love combined are as perfect an intimacy as a man and woman are capable of."

With a jerk of his hand he dismissed the subject, standing. He looked away from her, his expression more frustrated than annoyed.

Isabelle stood up too. It took a lot of trust to argue, and they had pushed trust to the limit for today. She wrapped her arms around him and pressed her cheek into his back.

"I have to work. I will come back to sing this evening."

She felt him relax. Because she had stopped questioning him? Because she had said she would come back? Because she left the choice about their future up to him? Because she had not said "I love you"? Probably all of them.

"I will walk you as far as the gate." This time he took her hand and wrapped it around his arm. "Holding hands is for children. This is much more intimate." The way his arm brushed against the side of her breast was proof enough.

They walked halfway across the courtyard in silence. Isabelle breathed in the morning air, living in the moment, knowing there was more to come. "It's so lovely not to be in a hurry. Life in the States is lived at a running pace. I prefer this."

"Two hundred years of this much quiet is more than anyone needs."

"Do you wish you could die?" The question popped out before Isabelle remembered she was not going to pester him with any more soul-searching.

"Isabelle, if I knew the answer to that, I am not sure I would tell you." He was quiet a moment more and then told her, "I don't think I can. I tried to drown myself before I had been cursed for six months. But someone rescued me. I paid someone to run me through with a sword, but he fell and killed himself instead. I ran into a burning cottage to rescue a child, hoping I would die. I wound up miserably burned on my hands and arms. It took two years to recover completely."

"I imagine that you gave up after that."

"Yes. And before you can ask, I tried to leave for the last time about twenty years ago. I cannot. There is no way to explain the force that keeps me here, but it is not human or man-made. And at this point there is a whole village of people who depend on me for their livelihood."

He was nobler than he gave himself credit for.

"Woman, stop looking at me as though I belong with your martyred saints. Go now. I will see you this evening."

She kissed him, a quick kiss of promise and parting. If she had known what was coming, she would have made the kiss a farewell embrace he would never forget.

Isabelle was committed to her work. It had always been what came first in her life. Last night had changed that. She could hardly wait to see Sebastian again, to do whatever he wanted to do up to and including making love all night long again.

She was not sure if Sebastian loved her beyond amused affection and passion, but she loved him. Their future was uncertain at best, but their present was filled with hope.

Isabelle changed and washed up as quickly as she could and hurried to the healer's house. Esmé looked awful, as though she had drank and smoked everything she could think of. Why was she at work if she felt so bad?

"You bitch!" The healer wailed and tried to slap her. Isabelle knew how to defend herself and, in less than a minute, Esmé was on the floor, with Isabelle sitting on her back.

"Why are you calling me names?"

"You slept with him." With that, Esmé's rage disappeared. It felt as though she were a balloon that had lost all its air. Isabelle moved off her back and sat on the floor beside her.

"Yes, I stayed the night. Why does that upset you?"

"You are still as pure as you were yesterday. He loves you?"

"I don't know!" Isabelle's uncertainty came out as anger, and she took a deep breath and tried again. "He hasn't said the words, but I love him and I think that's what matters."

"How can you love someone you hardly know?"

"I have never thought loving someone was about time, but about the connection you feel with them. You know what I'm talking about if only because you and I do not have it."

"You hate me."

A hangover-induced pity party was imminent. Isabelle got up and went to find the teapot. "I like you and respect your work immensely, Esmé. But there is something missing. Or something so important to you that it will keep us from being any closer than professional colleagues. If friendship is important to you, then you will tell me what it is."

"No." Esmé struggled to her feet. "But I can tell you that I can no longer work with you. Leave this house and find some other

405

way to amuse yourself." Esmé grabbed the teacup from Isabella and pushed her toward the door. "And stop being a fool. Of course it matters if he loves you. If he doesn't, you will be sent away the moment he grows tired of you or when you begin to demand too much. He is just a man after all."

TEN

Before Isabelle could answer, argue or leave, a man and woman came through the door carrying a boy whose foot was covered with blood-soaked linen. She could not recall their names but did remember that they had been among the first to come for inoculations.

"He was playing with his brother," his mother began but started to cry.

The boy's father patted her awkwardly on the shoulder and took up the story. "They were supposed to be harvesting coconuts, but they grew tired of that and began to use the machete as a toy. Herreo cut his foot and I think he cut off his toes."

The boy was in shock. As Esmé unwrapped the linen and exposed the wound, it was a relief to see that Herreo still had his toes, though they looked seriously damaged. What a relief that one of the shots they had agreed to had been against tetanus.

The healer began the process of cleaning the wound. Isabelle stayed in the corner of the room, observing. She bit her lip to keep quiet but when Esmé stopped running water over the injury after less than five minutes, Isabelle had to speak. "Healer, I will collect more water if you will wash it out for at least forty minutes."

"Nonsense. Fresh water is too precious here. The wound is clean."

"Esmé —" Isabelle began.

The healer cut her off with a look of pure hatred. "I have been cleaning wounds longer than you have been alive. Leave now. You are not welcome here."

To argue would only upset everyone so Isabelle did as ordered, determined to visit the family later to see if she could convince them to let her treat the boy further. Really the wound should be treated in a sterile environment. In a hospital.

Back in her cottage Isabelle considered the paperwork that was part of any bureaucracy no matter how remote. Her funding hinged on filling out the forms, and she tackled the project even though she was distracted by her worry for the boy. Occasionally she found herself staring off into space with a sappy smile. The smile had nothing to do with her concern for Herreo.

Mother Superior had always insisted that God's will was for each man and woman to be happy and fulfilled. Well, if that was true, then Isabelle knew she was on the right path, no matter what Esmé said. Her journey was not complete, but from where she sat, even surrounded by annoying forms, she was sure she was headed in the right direction.

After wrestling with the paperwork for most of the afternoon, Isabelle put it away, freshened up and walked to the edge of the village to see the boy. The family welcomed her. Fortunately, they were some of the early adapters you could find in every culture, the kind of natural leaders who were receptive to new ideas.

Herreo was in his bunk, a cup of juice at hand and the healer's salve nearby. Isabelle raised the bed linen to look at the wound and felt physically ill. Esmé had stitched it closed, not the right course of action for a "dirty" cut.

"What do you think, Mistress Nurse?" Herreo's mother asked.

"Please let me cut the stitches open. The wound should be cleaned. Please, Mistress Mother."

Herreo's mother looked at her husband.

"If you do not allow it," Isabelle spoke

quietly so Herreo would not hear, "the wound will become infected. Even now he should go to the hospital to have it treated properly."

"If he goes to the main island, he will not come back," his mother said.

"I think he will come back. He is young and he wants his mother and father more than he wants the pleasures of the main island." Isabelle looked at Herreo's father. "Would you rather have him die here or live there?"

"He can go if the master gives permission." Esmé made her announcement from the door of the cottage. "Go ask him now."

"Have you been watching me?" Isabelle did not care if her outrage showed.

"Don't flatter yourself. I was coming to tell you that the master wants to speak with you and saw you walking here."

"All right." She calmed a little. "I'll go ask him but let me cut the stitches open first."

"No. Go to the master."

It was the worst of medical protocol to argue in front of the patient's parents, so Isabelle hurried to the castle wondering why Sebastian would send his message through Esmé when he usually used Cortez as a courier.

At the *castillo,* the servant was welcoming,

410

but when she asked for Sebastian, the man shook his head. "He is busy now, mistress. You can sing, but he is busy."

"I have to see him. Right now. This is an emergency."

"An emergency?" the man said as though he did not know the word.

"Someone might die if I do not speak to him quickly." That was a lie. It would be days before Herreo's injury was life-threatening. She would ask forgiveness for her dishonesty later.

With a troubled nod, the servant let her in and, despite his urging that he would "bring the master down," Isabelle ran to the steps and up to Sebastian's quarters.

She knocked on the door of his study and waited. No one answered. She opened the door and called, "Sebastian. Where are you? This is important."

He came then, from his bedroom, barefoot, his shirt open, his pants unbuttoned, as though he was about to undress. "What is so pressing that you have to interrupt me?"

He could have slapped her with less insult. For, as he asked, a woman came out of his bedroom. She was fully dressed but there was something proprietary about the way she put her hand on his arm. "What is it,

Sebastian?"

Isabelle wanted to scream, yell and throw things. With the greatest of effort, she prayed for wisdom and focused on her errand. She could deal with this insult later. "Herreo is badly hurt and should go to a hospital. Esmé said if I got your permission, I could take him."

He did not react at first, but then nodded. "You have my permission. Leave, and, Isabelle, I do not want you to come back."

This verbal sucker punch caught her where it hurt the most. He spoke with such command that she knew he was serious. If she was not coming back, she would leave him with one last truth. "You know, Sebastian, you can have sex with a dozen women, but none of them will be me."

"I thank God for that," he shot back. "I do not want your heart and you cannot have mine. I do prefer variety. I thought I made that clear."

Numbly, Isabelle left his room, unable to think of anything that might convince him. Her patient was her first priority, but as she reached the courtyard a hymn came to her, one that summed up all the longing she felt. On impulse, Isabelle Reynaud sang to Sebastian Dushayne one last time.

"Come back to me with all your heart. Don't

let fear keep us apart. Long have I waited for your coming home to me and living deeply our new life."

Hosea's song had always been one of her favorites. It was true on so many levels. From God to his lost children, from a couple who are estranged even though they were meant to be together, to a family longing for their prodigal son. For Sebastian Dushayne. She wanted him to be happy and fulfilled, but as she let go of her ego and her pride, Isabelle realized that his choices were not in her control.

Father Joubay had said that one person could change the fate of the world. Isabella had taken that to mean that one kindness would make change possible. But there was more to it than that. The one in pain had to accept the act, accept the love, and build on it. She had given all that she could, but Sebastian had rejected it.

Isabelle left the courtyard, wishing that she could see Sebastian again before she left for the hospital, just one last time.

Sebastian gave the woman a handful of coins and moved as far away from her as he could. "Take this and give Esmé her share." He could feel anger building and did not care what story this woman took back with her. "I know she sent you here to discredit me with Isabelle. And I allowed it for my own reasons." That there would be retribution he left unsaid.

The woman's fright showed in her hurry to leave the room, and Sebastian realized he had never once seen fear on Isabelle's face. For all his cruelty to her she had never been afraid and had almost always managed to mask her hurt. He did not know if that was weakness or virtue.

Forbidding her return was the most unselfish action he had ever taken. His love for her made her as fragile as an orchid. If she came back, she would surely die, be taken from him as Angelique had been. Better to send her away than risk that.

Weariness stole his strength and he sank down on the sofa and wondered if Isabelle's God would listen to him. *Protect her,* he prayed, feeling awkward and stupid. *Please.* "I am begging." He shouted out loud and then whispered, "I love her."

Isabella's hymn reached him even as he heard a voice whisper, "Tell her."

"Come back to me with all your heart. Don't let fear keep us apart. Long have I waited for your coming home to me and living deeply our new life."

Sebastian struggled into his boots, and ran

from the *castillo*. A train of people followed him. The master never hurried anywhere unless it was very important.

"Who is dying?" one asked.

"Has he found something?" another wondered.

"He can't run far," a woman observed.

He found Esmé in her house with a bottle in her hand.

"She has already gone to Herreo's house. She said she is leaving and told me that I have built my entire life around vengeance and for the curse to end, both you and I have to make the right choice. Isabelle insists that I have suffered as much as you."

Esmé looked at the spirits in her mug. "She is right. I am a healer. Doing my best to see you in pain is destroying me too."

She poured the bottle of spirits into the sand.

"Will she come back safely if I tell her I love her?"

"Am I seeing the master ask a question?"

"Yes, you poisonous woman. If you have found wisdom, stop needling me and give me an answer."

"You stupid man. End the curse. Follow her. Your love for her and hers for you will see you to safety."

He found Isabelle halfway across the strip

of land that connected the *castillo* with the main island. Herreo's father carried him and the mother walked quickly to keep up with them.

"Isabelle!" he called.

She turned and when she saw him, after a word with Herreo's parents, ran back to him.

Isabelle leaped into his outstretched arms, and he spun her around and around. "I love you," he shouted.

"And I love you." She slid from him to stand as close as she could. "Could anything be more perfect? I promise I will come back as soon as they are settled in the hospital."

"No one will bring you back, Isabelle. After what happened when you came, no one will take the risk. I will come with you. Esmé agrees with you that love is the key that will unlock the curse."

"The healer? She told me that her mission in life is to see that you are cursed for eternity. How can you believe what she says?"

Sebastian took her hand and began to cross over to the big island. "Silly woman. You're the one who taught me that you have to learn to trust."

EPILOGUE

Some Years in the Future
Isla Perdida
Lesser Antilles

"I swear this island never changes." Sebastian stood at the entrance to the *castillo,* his back to the door, and watched as the villagers returned to work after their very enthusiastic welcome.

"It never changes because that's the way you want it."

Sebastian conceded the point with a half nod. "There has to be one place where I am still the master."

"The only place," Isabelle reminded him.

"Admit it, dear wife, you don't want to have computers in every cottage and generators polluting the air here any more than I do."

"No, so I guess this is our escape from reality."

"Or our return to it."

417

They walked into the *castillo* to find the courtyard a beehive of activity. The usual welcome-home celebration was planned for the evening, and benches and tables filled the space.

Everyone stopped to welcome them back, to ask where the children were and promise a party "even better than the last one."

"Where *are* the boys?" Sebastian asked their mother.

"I wish I knew," Isabelle countered and began to walk back toward the entrance.

"Mom! Dad! We can't wait to go to the beach."

With a glance at Sebastian, Isabelle answered, "All right, but take an adult with you."

Herreo popped up behind them, his shy smile a welcome that was always one of their favorites. "Am I adult enough, mistress?"

He was tall and strong and one of their dearest friends.

"Yes, Herreo, and thank you. Will we see your parents tonight?"

"Of course. Mistress Healer is coming too. Her newest nurse will be with her."

There were times when Esmé did not come and times when she could not stay away. Isabelle was glad they would have a chance to see her.

418

"We can't wait, Herreo," the boys shouted. "We can't wait to go to the beach." They pulled on Herreo's hand and were out the side door before anyone could say good-bye.

Sebastian turned to his wife. His dimples had deepened with age, his hair showed just a little gray and the smile lines around his eyes were more pronounced than ever. He often told her he felt wonderful for a man more than two hundred years old, and she assured him he looked wonderful too.

"I can't wait either," she said, pulling on his hand like a little girl.

"To go to the beach?" he asked, teasing her.

"No," she answered, laughing. "If you will come with me, master, I'll remind you why this is our own corner of paradise."

AUTHOR'S NOTE

My original intent in using singing as a key part of the story was to include words from hymns I sing in church regularly. I thought that would illustrate that the message of love in the hymns has a meaning beyond their spiritual context.

When it became clear that using most of the hymns I chose would not be possible, I wrote my own words with the exception of the use of one line of the hymn "Be Not Afraid," with permission of OCP, and words from the hymn "Hosea," which are from the Bible and therefore not subject to copyright.

If you will take a moment to read the words of the hymns you sing, I know you will see, as I did, that many of them are about love. While the composer certainly had a spiritual view in mind, the meaning of the songs can be expanded to include the kind of love we encounter in dealing with people we are closest too, people we meet by chance and friends.

At the heart of "Lost in Paradise" is my belief that love is why we are here, and accepting love can redeem even the most hardened of hearts. Isabelle convinces Sebastian to accept love and frees him from his curse. I hope that they will convince you.

■ ■ ■ ■

LEGACY
RUTH RYAN LANGAN

■ ■ ■ ■

To those still searching for family.
And for Tom, the heart and soul of ours.

ONE

"Miss O'Mara?" The young man's voice was thick with Irish brogue.

"Yes." Aidan O'Mara watched him doff his cap.

"The car is waiting. Right this way. I'll take your luggage." His big hand clamped around the handle of her overnight bag, and he tucked it under his arm as though it were a toy. He shouldered his way through the crowd at Dublin Airport, slowing his pace whenever she fell behind.

"Here we are." He helped her into the backseat of a vehicle the size of a small boat before stowing her bag.

As he started the car he glanced over his shoulder. "There's a bottle of water if you'd like. We've a bit of a drive ahead of us."

"Thank you." Aidan watched the flow of traffic, the passing scenery, with the fascination of one who had never before been to Ireland. Not only was she out of her own country for the first time, but completely out of her element.

How was it possible that just a week ago she'd buried her mother and watched her whole world unravel? Yet here she was, an ocean away from all that was familiar, being transported in a vintage Rolls by a red-haired, freckled lad in a jaunty cap who looked like a model for a travel brochure, on her way to meet a perfect stranger who hinted of secrets from her family's past.

She was so weary, both physically and emotionally. So much had happened to her in the past few days. Too much for her to take in. The steady flow of traffic, the moving river of humanity inching along the streets of Dublin became a blur.

Drained, she leaned her head back and closed her eyes, allowing herself to drift back.

"Aidan. I'm sorry for your loss." Father Davis handed the young woman a small wooden cross from her mother's casket before turning away from the gravesite. He paused. "You know, of course, our church pantry can assist you with some meals until you're back on your feet. If you need anything at all . . ."

"Thank you, Father. I'll be fine." She

could feel the stares from those who were standing nearby, and could hear their whispered comments about her mother's long illness and the drain on her finances.

She thanked the friends and neighbors who had come to offer their condolences, holding herself together by sheer force of will.

She experienced an odd sense of relief when she was finally alone. Dropping to her knees, she let out a long, deep sigh and looked at the headstones of her family members that surrounded her mother's fresh grave. Thankfully her parents had bought the sites many years ago, in order to be buried near their own parents. If Aidan had been forced to buy a cemetery plot along with all the other funeral costs, she could never have afforded it.

These past months had been so hard. At first she'd been able to juggle her work at the bank and the care of her mother. As the illness progressed and things became more difficult, a neighbor suggested a private nursing facility. Aidan had looked into it, only to learn that the cost was more than she could manage. She spoke with her supervisor at work, hoping for a leave of absence, but that was denied. Ultimately forced to choose between quitting her job and putting her mother in a public facility, she'd stayed home and tended her mother to the end.

She hoped that all these months later her position at the bank would still be available. Her meager savings were now depleted.

Because she'd sold her car, she walked the six blocks to the tidy house she'd shared with her mother, after giving up her apartment. As she entered she picked up the mail and carried it to the kitchen. She made a cup of tea and sat at the table, carefully opening each envelope and adding to the pile of unpaid bills. The medical bills were bad enough, but the unpaid taxes meant that she would soon see her family home go up for auction.

"Oh, Mama." She buried her face in her hands, refusing to give in to the desire to weep.

How had her life taken such a turn? She'd been raised in a lovely, middle-class family, and had a good education and a fine work ethic. Though it was true that her grandfather had squandered a good deal of his savings on land speculation that hadn't paid off, Aidan's mother and grandmother had picked up the pieces and paid off his debts. Her father had saved enough for a decent retirement, at least until his prolonged illness drained his income. With her mother's illness following on the heels of his death, Aidan's life savings were quickly gone, as well.

Her fingers moved over the calculator, tallying the debt so far. She studied her negative bank balance and felt a sudden panic. In her line of work at the bank she'd counseled many people who were one paycheck away from financial disaster. Unlike them, she had no paycheck to depend on. She was already ruined.

She glanced at the clock. Too late to phone her old supervisor now. But first thing tomorrow she would make that call. Mr. Saunders had to hire her back. Had to.

When the doorbell rang, she thought about ignoring it. She was too drained to deal with well-meaning neighbors. But good manners had her doing the right thing regardless of her feelings. She opened the door and forced a smile to her lips.

"Aidan O'Mara?"

The man was dressed in an impeccable suit and tie, and carrying an attaché case. He handed her a business card. "Philip Barlow, with Putnam, Shaw and Forest."

At the mention of one of the best-known legal firms in town, her smile fled. Which of her creditors had turned her debt over to a law firm?

"I'm Aidan O'Mara." She squared her shoulders to hide the feeling of dread at what was to come. A lawsuit on top of everything else would be the final humiliation.

"Ms. O'Mara, I'm sorry about the timing of my visit. But it was your mother's obituary in the newspaper that brought me here. You are listed as her next of kin."

Aidan nodded. "Her only kin."

"Maybe not." At his words, her head came up sharply.

"My firm was contacted by a legal firm in Ireland. Mr. Cullen Glin, from the town of Glinkilly, in the county of Kerry, Ireland, has spent years searching for his long-lost child. We have reason to believe that your mother was his daughter."

Though relieved to know that his visit wasn't about a debt, Aidan was already shaking her head. "I'm sorry. You're mistaken. My mother's parents lived right here in town. I've known them all my life."

"I'm sure you have. But Mr. Glin's sworn statement says otherwise. There are . . . extenuating circumstances that will question certain claims that you have accepted as fact for a lifetime."

"But I . . ."

"Mr. Glin's arguments are very persuasive." The young lawyer glanced around the small foyer, noting the well-worn carpet, the faded draperies. "When I reached his solicitor by phone, I was instructed to relay his request that you fly to Ireland and meet his client face-to-face. If, after that meeting, either of you is not persuaded of the relationship, your visit will be terminated at once." Seeing that she was about to refuse, he added, "Needless to say, all your expenses will be covered, and you will be given a generous stipend for your inconvenience."

For a moment she was taken by such surprise, she couldn't find her voice. At last she managed, "This is all very tempting, but I know without seeing your Mr. Glin that we couldn't possibly be related."

He merely smiled. "Then think of this offer as a gift to you. A chance to get away from your life as you know it and spend a few pleasant days in Ireland."

"Sorry . . ." Her hand went to the door.

"Before you refuse, perhaps you should read this." He reached into his briefcase and withdrew a sheaf of papers. "You have my card. Call me when you've come to a decision."

She watched him turn and walk down the sidewalk to his car. She closed the door and

433

carried the documents to the table, where she sipped her now tepid tea and began to read.

When she finished, she stared into space, trying to make sense of it.

There were detailed reports about a family named Fitzgibbon, who had emigrated from Ireland fifty-five years ago, the same year her mother had been born. There was a map of the town of Glinkilly, in Ireland, where Hugh and Caitlin Fitzgibbon had been born, the date of their marriage and the birth date of their only daughter, Moira, as well as the name of the ship that brought them to the United States and the port where they'd disembarked. It would seem that their lives had been carefully documented, but as far as she could see, none of this could be used to link these strangers to her, or, in turn, to link her to this stranger, Cullen Glin.

Aidan thought about her mother's mother, Maureen Gibbons, a sweet, quiet, rather sad woman who had been married to stern Edward Martin for more than forty years before her death. She rarely spoke about herself, preferring to talk about her beautiful daughter, Claire, on whom she doted.

Aidan's mother, Claire, was the only child of Maureen and Edward. There were no others. Not even a stillbirth had been recorded in their family Bible. Cullen Glin had no claim on her. As tempting as it was to consider an all-expense-paid trip to Ireland and a fat check for her inconvenience, her conscience wouldn't permit it. She had no right to lead some desperate old man on in his quest to find his lost child. His time would be better spent locating his true heirs.

She would phone Mr. Barlow in the morning, right after she phoned the bank to retrieve her job.

That morning call, however, changed everything.

"Well, Aidan." Walter Saunders, her former supervisor, used his best customer-relations voice over the phone. "Good to hear from you. I'm sorry about your mother. Everyone here at First City sends their sympathy."

"Thank you, Mr. Saunders." Aidan had seen and heard her supervisor in action, using that oh-so-warm voice while staring into the distance with absolutely no emotion at all.

She took a breath. "Now that I'm free to work, I was hoping I might be able to come back."

There was a momentary pause. "You were

a fine employee, Aidan. The best."

She waited. When he offered nothing more, she jumped in to fill the silence. "If it's a problem, I'd be willing to start at a reduced salary. I realize that I wouldn't be qualified for the pay scale I'd reached before leaving. Or the benefits." Now she was babbling, but she couldn't seem to stop herself. "I'm not asking for full benefits, just enough to help with any medical situations that might arise. As you can imagine, I'm feeling overwhelmed by medical crises at the moment."

Silence.

She closed her eyes, hoping he couldn't hear the desperation that crept into her tone. She hated that she was begging. "I need this job, Mr. Saunders."

"Yes. Well." His tone sharpened. "I'm afraid we have no openings just now, Aidan. You realize we had to fill your position as quickly as possible. You left us with no other choice."

"I gave you two weeks' notice. I thought that would be enough to train my replacement."

"And you did train her. Very well, I might add. She's become a valuable employee." He cleared his throat. "I have your personnel file. If anything becomes available, I'll be certain to contact you."

"You have nothing now?"

"Nothing. As you well know, these are hard times in the banking industry."

Numb, Aidan heard the phone disconnect while she was muttering, "Thank you, Mr. Saunders. And have a nice day."

Then, because she'd pinned all her hopes on this call, she burst into tears. Once unlocked, the tears she'd been holding at bay for days, for weeks, ran unchecked down her cheeks, soaking the front of her shirt.

She hadn't realized how desperately she'd needed that job. Now that it was being denied her, she couldn't seem to think beyond it. What would she do? What could she do?

Without a quick infusion of cash, she would lose her family home and would find herself out on the street.

Seeing the papers left by the lawyer, she picked up his card and, without giving a thought to the consequences, dialed the number. When she heard his voice, she spoke quickly, so she wouldn't lose her nerve.

"Mr. Barlow? Aidan O'Mara. When can you book that flight to Ireland?"

■ ■ ■ ■

"Had a bit of a nap, did you?" The young lad's voice had her looking up to see him watching her in the rearview mirror. "We're passing through Glinkilly." A note of pride crept into his tone. "Our wee town was built near the site of an ancient abbey, which dates to the twelfth century."

"Such a pretty town." And it was, with its tidy houses and clean streets. The shop windows were bright with goods, and the people walking about looked friendly and prosperous.

"You'll soon have your first glimpse of Glin Lodge."

They left the town behind and started along a lovely country road, wide enough for only one vehicle at a time. On either side of the car were hedgerows of deep pink flowers so thick Aidan couldn't see beyond them.

The hedgerows gave way to a meandering stone wall with an occasional door painted bright red or sky blue or sunny yellow. She wondered where the doors led, but the wall was too high to see over.

The car was climbing, climbing, as though scaling a mountain. When they reached the top of a hill and turned onto a wide, curving ribbon of road, she saw acres of perfectly sculpted grounds. Ancient flowering trees with branches that swept the grass before lifting high in the air. Fountains set among lovely rose gardens, with stone benches set about to enjoy the view. Sheep dotted a distant hillside, adding to the pastoral setting.

They rounded a curve and Aidan's jaw dropped at the sight of the stone mansion glinting in the late-afternoon sunlight.

"There's Glin Lodge, miss."

"This is where Mr. Glin lives?"

"Aye. Indeed." He shot her a glance in the mirror and smiled at the look on her face.

The word *lodge* had planted an image in her mind far removed from this. She'd been expecting a rustic house, with a few barns and outbuildings. It had never occurred to Aidan that Cullen Glin lived in such luxury. The lodge was actually a mansion. The kind of place she'd seen only in books.

They drove past a reflecting pond where a pair of black swans circled, leaving barely a ripple in their wake.

As they pulled into the circular drive and came to a halt at the foot of high stone steps, a pair of massive Irish wolfhounds came bounding up, setting off a chorus of barking.

The lad circled the car and opened the passenger door. When Aidan hesitated, he gave her a wide smile. "They're big and noisy, but they won't bite."

He helped her from the car. Before he could admonish the dogs, a man on horseback came up behind them.

As he dismounted, the man's deep voice called, "Meath. Mayo."

The two dogs sat, tails swishing, tongues lolling. Aidan would have sworn they were grinning.

She turned for a better look at the man.

He wore a charcoal jacket and denims tucked into tall leather boots. His dark hair was wind-tossed, his eyes deep blue and piercing as they boldly studied her. Though not handsome in the classic sense, his rugged good looks and casual elegance gave him a commanding presence. He looked like the hero in every classic novel she'd ever read. The sight of him took her breath away.

He spoke first to the driver. "Sean, you can take the lady's luggage inside. Mrs. Murphy will tell you where to put it."

As the lad hurried away, the stranger turned to Aidan. "You'd be Miss O'Mara."

"Aidan O'Mara. And you are?"

"Ross Delaney, Mr. Glin's solicitor." He gave her an appraising look. "Your pictures didn't do you justice."

"Pictures?"

"As you can imagine, Mr. Glin was more than a little curious to see what you looked like. He won't be disappointed." He glanced toward an upper window. "I'm sure by now he's heard the commotion and will be itching to meet you. Come." With his hand beneath her elbow, he walked beside her up the stone steps.

Aidan became aware of a tingle of warmth where their bodies connected. She shot him a sideways glance, and saw only a stern, handsome profile that seemed chiseled in stone.

The double doors were opened by an old woman who wore a spotless apron over a black dress that fell to her ankles. White hair had been pulled back in a severe bun at her nape. Little tendrils had slipped free to curl damply around her plump cheeks. The woman seemed distracted and slightly out of breath, as though she'd just run a marathon, but when she smiled, her entire face sparkled like sunshine.

"Bridget, this is Miss O'Mara, Mr. Glin's . . . guest."

Aidan shot him a glance. Was it her imagination, or had he stumbled over what term he should use to describe her?

There was no time to mull as he continued. "Here at Glin Lodge, Bridget Murphy is the housekeeper and all-around miracle worker. If you need anything, just ask Bridget."

"Aw, go on with you now." The old woman was positively glowing at his praise.

And why not? Charm that smooth had probably been learned at his mother's knee. No doubt he used it on women of all ages.

Aidan offered a smile. "It's nice to meet you, Bridget."

"As you can imagine, we've all been eager to welcome you, too, miss." The woman took a breath before turning with a brisk nod. "If you'll follow me, I'll show you to your rooms."

Ross Delaney remained at the door, watching her with more than casual interest.

As Aidan walked away and began to follow Bridget up the stairs, she could feel that cool blue stare following her. It gave her a tingle of awareness. Like the hounds, Meath and Mayo, she felt like wriggling all over with delight and was already scolding herself for such foolishness.

Two

After climbing to the second floor, Bridget opened a set of double doors and stepped aside. "These will be your rooms, Miss O'Mara."

Aidan caught her breath at the luxurious setting. She was standing in a parlor that was bigger than her parents' entire house. The floor was an expanse of white- and gold-veined marble, softened by a rug in tones of white and gold and pale green. In one corner was a grand piano. A fire burned on the hearth, with a fireplace surround of the same marble, flanked by two gold chairs and a white sofa. Tossed over two footstools were throws embroidered with a gold crest bearing an eagle and an intertwined monogram with the letters *C* and *M.*

She crossed to the bedroom, which was as elegant as the parlor, with a king-sized bed covered in a white comforter bearing the same crest.

A teenaged girl dressed in faded denims and a T-shirt was busy hanging Aidan's clothes in a closet. She turned as Aidan and Bridget entered.

"Miss O'Mara, if you need anything, just let Charity O'Malley know your pleasure." The frazzled housekeeper gave the little housemaid a meaningful look. "You'll not be dawdling, girl. Kathleen needs your help in the kitchen as soon as you've finished here."

"Of course." Charity seemed completely unfazed by the older woman's attempt to be stern. With a smile, she picked up yet another piece of clothing from the suitcase and transferred it to the closet.

"There's tea." The housekeeper nodded toward the silver tea service on a large tray set on a writing desk across the room. "With the long journey, you'll be wanting a bit of sleep before dinner. Himself wanted to come charging in and meet you right this minute, but I told him that traveling drains a body."

"Himself?"

"Cullen Glin. Your . . ." The old woman stopped, then sputtered, "He's pacing his room like a caged tiger. I told him he'll just have to wait until you've had a nap. He'll get to meet you by and by. You rest now. I'll have Charity wake you when it's time for dinner."

"Thank you, Mrs. Murphy."

"It's Bridget, dear. Everyone here calls me Bridget."

"Thank you, Bridget." Aidan gave up trying to follow the old woman's words. They were spoken nonstop, and her head was spinning. But this much she'd caught. Bridget, and probably everyone else who worked here, knew why she was here. And had already formed an opinion about her.

A glance at the bed had her wondering how she could bear to disturb that perfect picture, with its mounds of pillows and creamy white linens. She looked toward the cushioned window seat beneath the tall leaded windows, thinking she might curl up there for a quick nap.

When the housekeeper left, Aidan poured a cup of tea and nibbled one of the biscuits nestled beneath a linen napkin. The flaky pastry melted in her mouth.

"Do you live here, Charity?"

The girl barely paused in her work as she continued hanging each item with meticulous care. "Oh no, miss. I live in Glinkilly, just down the road."

"Sean pointed out your town when we passed through. It's lovely."

"It is, yes. We're all very proud of Glinkilly. Sean and I are old school chums."

"How long have you worked here?"

"This is my second year. I'm hoping to save enough to attend university in two years."

"What do you hope to study?"

"Medicine. My two older sisters, Faith and Hope, are both studying to be doctors."

Faith, Hope and Charity. Aidan couldn't help grinning. "How grand. That's a fine goal. Is your father a doctor?"

"He's a farmer. He said he's weary of dancing to the whims of nature, and wants better for his children."

That had Aidan laughing aloud. "A wise man. I see you've heeded his advice."

"So far. Of course, he wants us all to marry wealthy men, too, but as our mum says, money can't buy love."

Aidan sipped her tea in silence. There was a time when she would have agreed with Charity's mother. Now she wasn't so sure. Maybe, if a person were desperate enough, she would even trade love for the chance to escape the burden of debt.

"Not that I wouldn't be tempted, if the rich man happened to look like Ross Delaney."

At Charity's words, Aidan snapped to attention.

The housemaid touched a hand to her heart. "Now, there's a man who can make a girl's heart race with just a look or a smile."

"I'm sure," Aidan remarked dryly, "he knows just how to use that kind of charm."

"Then I wish he'd use some of it on me." Charity covered her hand with her mouth to stifle the laughter that bubbled. "My older sisters told me they did everything but dance naked in front of him when they worked here, and he never once noticed them." She wrinkled her nose. "The woman hasn't been born to suit Ross Delaney. 'Tis said he'll never marry. All he thinks about is pleasing the old man. I think if Cullen Glin asked him to lie down in front of a moving train, he'd do it."

"Such loyalty. He must be paid very well for his services."

"I don't think he does it for the money. Those who know him, and they're few indeed, say he genuinely loves the old man. But who really knows? Ross Delaney is a bit of a mystery." Charity lowered her voice. "Something happened between him and the old man years ago. Though there are a dozen variations of the story, nobody knows for sure. Whatever it was, the old man treats him more like his son than his barrister."

"Speaking of sons, does Cullen Glin have any children?"

Charity closed the suitcase and stowed it in the closet. "He never married. He lives all alone in this mansion, which my father calls a mausoleum. Of course, if I had his money, and could live in such digs, I'm sure I could survive a little loneliness. Or buy whatever company I craved."

"Doesn't Ross Delaney live here with him?"

"He may as well live here, for all the time he spends doing the old man's bidding. But he calls the guest cottage down the lane his home. According to Bridget, he told the old man that he needed his own space." She gave a dry laugh. "His own space. Can you imagine? Half our town could live here and it still wouldn't be crowded."

She looked over to see Aidan stifling a yawn. "Oh, here I am prattling on about all this foolishness when you're probably dead on your feet." The girl removed a robe from the closet before drawing back the elegant comforter to reveal snowy sheets. "I'll leave you alone now and let you get some sleep. I'll see that you're awake with plenty of time to dress for dinner."

"Thank you for everything, Charity."

The girl left, closing the door behind her. A moment later Aidan heard the parlor doors close.

Slipping out of her denims and sweater, Aidan picked up the robe. It was soft as a whisper. A look at the label confirmed that it was cashmere. With a sigh, she slid it on and sashed it before walking barefoot to the window to stare down at the scene below. All around were acres of rich green lawn, studded with rose gardens, statuary, wildlife. A garden of paradise.

It all seemed too good to be true.

Wasn't there always a snake in paradise?

She climbed into bed, hoping she could turn off her thoughts and just relax. But she kept thinking about all the things she'd learned. A rich old man who lived here all alone, and believed her mother to be his long-lost daughter. That would make him her grandfather.

Of course it wasn't possible. But what if . . . ?

And then there was Ross Delaney, the mystery man. When they'd first met, he'd been studying her much too carefully. If any other man had looked at her like that, she'd have felt violated. But there was no denying that she'd felt something very different in his presence.

She'd sensed his curiosity and something more. If she didn't know better, she'd think it an instant attraction.

The woman hasn't been born to suit Ross Delaney. 'Tis said he'll never marry. The old man treats him like a son.

He was probably just curious about her, and protecting his turf. Not that it mattered. Once she and Cullen Glin had their meeting, she would be on her way home, with a fat check that would, hopefully, cover the worst of her debts.

Clinging to that thought, she drifted into sleep.

"Miss O'Mara."

The thick brogue penetrated Aidan's consciousness and she opened her eyes to see Charity standing beside the bed.

She sat up, feeling as though she'd been drugged. Sluggish and vaguely disoriented. "How long have I been asleep?"

"Only an hour or so. Bridget sent me to fetch you. It's six o'clock. She said dinner will be at seven."

"Thank you."

"Do you need help? I could run your bath."

"Thanks, but I believe I'll just grab a

450

quick shower. How will I find the dining room?"

"No need to worry." Charity lowered her voice for dramatic emphasis. "Ross Delaney himself will be up shortly, to take you there."

"Up here?" Aidan glanced around.

"Not here. Next door, in the parlor."

"Oh." She shared a laugh with the girl. "All right. I guess I'd better get ready so I don't keep him waiting."

As soon as Charity was gone, Aidan hurried to the shower. Half an hour later, with her dark hair freshly dried, falling long and straight to her shoulders, and her makeup applied, she stood before the open closet doors, trying to decide on the appropriate attire. She'd overpacked for a single night, but she hadn't been certain just what would be expected of her. And, of course, there was the fickle Irish weather to contend with. After much dithering, she'd brought one of her old business suits, a dress that she thought would work for warm or cool weather, as well as the comfortable denims and sweater she'd worn on the flight.

Since they would be eating here, she didn't need to worry about the weather. She settled on her one dress, of aqua silk with a slim, straight skirt, square neckline and long sleeves. She added her grandmother's small

451

pearl earrings and a pair of strappy high-heeled sandals.

With a last glance at her reflection in the full-length mirror, she stepped into the parlor.

"Oh." She stopped in midstride when she caught sight of Ross standing by the fireplace. "I didn't know you were here."

"Sorry." He seemed to pull himself back with an effort from some dark thoughts that had him frowning. "I knocked before letting myself in. I heard the shower running, and decided to make myself comfortable." He picked up a crystal fluted glass. "Champagne?"

"Yes, thank you." Though it irritated her to know that he'd been here without her knowledge, she forced herself to put it aside. He was, after all, much more entitled to be at home here than she was. Still, it rankled that he'd been just outside her bedroom for all this time, listening as she'd taken her sweet time getting ready.

He handed her the glass.

She noted that he was drinking water from a crystal rock glass. "You don't care for champagne?"

"No. What do you think of your first glimpse of Ireland?"

He had a definite way of changing the

subject when it suited him.

She looked up. "How do you know this is my first trip here?"

His lips curved in the faintest hint of a smile. "It's my job to learn as much about you as possible."

"And you're very good at your job."

"I am. Yes."

His brogue wasn't as pronounced as that of the others she'd encountered, but it was there in that simple phrase.

"Then you know that this visit will end as quickly as it began."

"Is that your plan?"

She sipped her champagne to avoid his eyes. "I came here to satisfy an old man's curiosity about me. And, in all honesty, to satisfy my own curiosity about him. But more than that, I came here for the promised check for my inconvenience. Once I've met Cullen Glin and heard what he has to say, I'll be on my way in the morning."

"I wouldn't be so certain."

She looked over. He wasn't smiling. There was no hint of a joke in his tone. And yet . . . Her tone sharpened. "If, as you say, you've done a thorough investigation of me, you have to know that I'm not who he thinks I am."

"I know only that Cullen Glin has spent

years searching for his long-lost daughter."

"I'm sorry for him. I'll be happy to meet him, and then accept his check for the inconvenience. But I won't pretend to be what he wants me to be."

"Nor would he ask that." Ross' tone remained deceptively even. "If you've finished your drink, I'll take you to him and you can tell him what you've just told me."

She handed him her empty glass and he set it beside his on a sideboard.

As they stepped into the hallway and started down the stairs, Ross lowered his voice. "I do hope you'll be polite with Cullen, and at least express your gratitude for this opportunity. Further, I'd appreciate it if you'd take care not to tire him. This is an extremely emotional time for him."

"For him?" Aidan could feel her temper rising. "What about my emotions? If you know all you claim to know, then you realize I've just buried my mother, I've come halfway around the world, and I'm being lectured on how to behave with a stranger who wants to make me into someone I'm not."

He paused to put a hand on her arm. "I'm only trying to help you through an awkward meeting."

She drew away as though burned. "I'll

behave as I damned well please, Mr. Delaney. And when this meeting is over, I'll be more than happy to leave you alone with the old man you're trying so hard to protect from the big, bad American."

For a moment he merely stared at her. Then, unexpectedly, he laughed.

It was the most amazing transformation. His face, which had moments earlier appeared to be carved from stone, was now warm with animation. His eyes, which she'd sworn were ice blue, now glinted with humor. His voice, so stern and self-righteous, now softened with merriment.

"I see you have a temper, Miss O'Mara. A very good sign indeed."

He paused before reaching a hand to the ornate door handle. Leaning close, he added, "I pray you keep it in check until the evening ends. Otherwise, you may find in Cullen Glin its equal."

Before she could form a retort, he had the door open and heard him saying in a clear voice, "Sir, it's my pleasure to introduce Aidan O'Mara. Aidan, your . . . host, Cullen Glin."

THREE

Aidan's temper was forgotten as she stared in surprise at the man facing her. She had expected to meet a frail old man, perhaps in a wheelchair, his lap covered with a blanket. That was her last memory of her stern grandfather in the years before his passing.

There was nothing frail about the man who strode across the room and offered a firm handshake. If anything, he resembled an aging lion, with a mane of white hair, a handsome Irish countenance, and a commanding presence. In his day, Aidan decided, Cullen Glin would have easily rivaled Ross Delaney as the most handsome man at any gathering.

"Aidan. Welcome to my home. Forgive me for staring." He took a moment to compose himself. "I hope you'll excuse my lack of manners. I got momentarily sidetracked. You're much lovelier than your photographs."

"Thank you." She found herself beginning to relax in this man's presence. "Your home is spectacular. My first glimpse of it took my breath away."

"How refreshing." He glanced beyond her to smile at Ross. "Isn't she delightful?" Without waiting for a response, he turned that charming smile on her. "How are your rooms, my dear?"

"They're grand. And, oh, that view of the gardens. I could sit and look at them for hours."

"They've been at their best this season. I hope you were able to rest after that long flight."

"I can't remember the last time I slept so soundly."

"Good. Good." With his hand beneath her elbow, he led her across the room to a grouping of furniture positioned to take advantage of a cozy fire on the hearth.

Like her suite of rooms, the dining room was cavernous, with a table that could easily seat thirty or more people, and a crystal chandelier above it winking with hundreds of lights. Mahogany floors were polished to a high sheen, and softened with an enormous rug in shades of emerald and ruby and gold.

Despite the size, it felt easy and comfortable. Like the man of the house, Aidan thought, who seemed bigger than life.

Bridget entered bearing a silver tray on which stood a crystal decanter and three glasses. Cullen handed one to Aidan and took one for himself before handing Ross a tumbler of water.

"Before we begin dinner, I'd like to offer a toast, my dear. To you, for humoring an old man." He touched his glass to hers, and then to Ross'. "And, as always, to those we've loved and lost."

Aidan was caught off guard by the depth of pain she could hear in his words, and the sudden flicker of it in his eyes.

Her own loss was still too fresh, too deep. She thought of her mother, and how she would have enjoyed this.

To hide her pain, she sipped and looked away. When she looked up, he was watching her closely.

"I was devastated to learn that you'd only just buried your mother, and that you were her sole caregiver during her illness."

She nodded, unable to speak over the sudden lump that clogged her throat.

"Thank heaven she had you. There's nothing like family to see us through the hard times." He glanced over at Ross, who was studying Aidan through narrowed eyes.

"Those of us not blessed with blood kin create our own families. Take Ross. He's as precious to me as any son."

"Then you're lucky to have him." Unable to turn away from that icy stare, Aidan shot Ross a challenging look.

Reading her irritation, his lips quirked in a hint of a smile, further annoying her.

"Sit here by the fire and enjoy your drink, my dear." Cullen indicated a comfortable chaise and waited until she was seated, before choosing a chair beside her.

Ross walked to the hearth to poke at the fire before turning to face them. His hand rested along the mantel, drawing Aidan's attention to the exquisite detail of the sculpted white marble.

"That fireplace is stunning, Mr. Glin."

"Please, call me Cullen."

She sipped her champagne. "Has your family lived here for generations?"

That brought a laugh from both Cullen and Ross.

Seeing her arched brow, the old man explained. "In my youth, I was considered an outsider, despite my name, because I grew up in the poorest section of town. There are hundreds of Glins in Glinkilly. In those days Glin Lodge lay in ruins, as did most of the town and the ancient Glin

Abbey. If you look out your bedroom windows, beyond the gardens, you'll see the ruins of the abbey, which was originally built in the fifteenth century. If I live long enough, I hope to restore it as I restored this place."

"You did all this by yourself?"

He smiled. "I'd love to take all the credit, but it took hundreds of tradesmen hundreds of hours to turn this into the place you now see. All I did was hire good people."

"Not to mention spending a considerable fortune," Ross added.

"Money well spent. I was happy to add to the town's economy, since I make it a rule to hire as many local workmen as possible. Now the people of Glinkilly can take pride in what they accomplish, while enjoying the wages they earn."

"What spurred you to do all this?"

He ducked his head and sipped his champagne in silence. When he looked up, his smile was back. "Ross made me realize that it was necessary to restore not only my land, but my name, as well. Both had gone to ruin, and it shamed me."

He glanced over when Bridget entered, followed by Charity, pushing a serving cart. "Ah, here's our dinner now."

Instead of the large table in the center of

the room, Cullen led her to a small, round table in one corner, set with snowy linens and fine silver and crystal.

The old man held her chair. "I thought this would be cozier."

"It's perfect." She smiled at Charity as the girl paused beside her, offering a tray of tender roast beef slices and an array of vegetables. She helped herself, and waited as Cullen and Ross did the same.

Bridget placed a silver basket of soda bread in the middle of the table, along with a platter of various cheeses.

"I hope you'll try the cheese." Cullen placed several wedges on his plate. "They're all made by the farmers here in Glinkilly."

She tasted first one, then another, before nodding. "Wonderful. They must be very proud."

"And well they should be. Since we've made them available throughout the country, they've become one of the most popular dairy products in Ireland."

"Do I see your hand in this, as well?"

"It was Ross who recognized a highly marketable commodity and suggested we try packaging them on a small scale first, to test the waters. Once the consumers began buying in quantity, I knew we had a winner. The rest was up to our local farmers,

461

who've proven to be more than up to the task."

"Do you own the company that markets the cheese?"

He gave a firm shake of his head. "I suggested the farmers form a cooperative. With some seed money from me, they took over completely. They raise the dairy cows, make the cheese, market it under their own brand, and all members share in the profits."

"No wonder the town looked so prosperous."

He smiled. "A high compliment indeed. Some years ago you'd have thought Glinkilly the poorest of places in all of Ireland."

"And now, thanks to you, it prospers."

His tone lowered. "May it continue, through good times and bad." He brightened. "How is your dinner?"

Aidan laughed. "What little I've tasted is excellent. I'm afraid I got too caught up in your narrative to do it justice."

"You'd best eat or Kathleen, who oversees our kitchen, will think she made a dreadful choice, and probably have Bridget's and Charity's heads in the bargain."

"We can't have that." Aidan took another bite of beef that nearly melted in her mouth.

By the time they'd finished their meal, Bridget and Charity were back, this time with coffee and a tray of assorted cherry and blueberry tarts.

Cullen polished off one of each before sitting back with a sigh. "The perfect ending to a perfect meal. Bridget, be sure to give my compliments to Kathleen."

She smiled and took her leave, shooing Charity ahead of her.

Across the table, Ross refused dessert and sipped his coffee. It occurred to Aidan that he'd volunteered nothing during the course of their meal. Maybe he was on a mission to see that she didn't offend her host. Or maybe, she thought, he found her company too dull to bother with something as inane as small talk.

Still, despite his silence, she'd been acutely aware of him watching, listening, studying her like a specimen to be dissected. It gave her an uneasy feeling. If Cullen Glin was warmer than she'd expected, his legal counsel was behaving like a bodyguard keeping an eye on a trained assassin.

He needn't worry that she would try to worm her way into this very wealthy man's life by some pretense or other. She had every intention of informing Cullen of his error in bringing her here. But not tonight, she decided suddenly. Tonight, seeing the eagerness in the old man's eyes, hearing it

463

in his voice, she would let him have his fantasy for a little while longer.

She sipped her coffee, warmed by the fine food and the fire on the hearth, and the pure pleasure of her host's charming personality.

Just for tonight she would pretend that she was merely a guest in this lovely mansion, invited to partake of all the pleasures such a place could provide.

Tomorrow would be soon enough to deal with the unpleasant realities of her situation. Tomorrow she would firmly, without leaving any room for doubt, let Cullen Glin know that she was who she had always believed she was, the daughter of John and Claire O'Mara, and the granddaughter of Maureen and Edward Martin.

Cullin Glin would have to search elsewhere for his long-lost kin.

"Come," the old man said, suddenly getting to his feet. "Now that we've been fortified by Kathleen's fine food, it's time you had a tour of my humble abode."

"And this was once the library. It's now my office."

Their first stop had been the formal parlor, decorated with a lovely mix of antiques salvaged from the original lodge, and comfortable pieces put together by a local decorator.

This room, however, seemed perfectly suited to her host. Floor-to-ceiling shelves were stocked with leather-bound books. A stone fireplace soared to a second-story gallery that ringed two walls, showing more bookshelves. A massive desk was positioned in front of French doors that opened to a brick-paved patio and the gardens beyond.

"I'm afraid this is where Ross and I spend most of our time." With his hand beneath Aidan's elbow, Cullen led her across the floor.

"It's a lovely room."

Ross moved to a side table and poured coffee liqueur into two small glasses. As he handed her one, she thanked him before nodding toward the patio. "Though I think I'd be more tempted to work out there, to the sound of birds and the scent of all those roses."

"Not at all conducive to work. I doubt we'd get much done out there." Cullen smiled as Ross handed him a similar glass.

Aidan moved about the room, running a finger along the smooth wood of his desk, pausing to study a framed pen-and-ink drawing of the town of Glinkilly that hung on the wall.

The signature of the artist caught her eye. "You did this, Cullen?"

He nodded.

"It's excellent."

He couldn't hide his pleasure. "In my misspent youth, I toyed with the idea of being an artist. Then I was persuaded to put aside foolish dreams and get to the business of making money."

She turned. "What do you do when you're not working?"

He glanced at Ross. "Now, there's a question that hasn't been put to me before. In the years you've known me, can you think of anything I've done except work?"

Ross shook his head. "Not to my knowledge."

The two men shared a laugh.

"What is it you do?"

"I study spreadsheets, cost analyses, profit-and-loss reports. I buy and sell companies, make money for the investors, sit on the boards of several corporations."

Aidan merely stared at him. "It sounds . . . complicated. Do you enjoy your work?"

He took a moment to sip his after-dinner drink. "In that misspent youth I spoke of, I was a laborer. And had the aching muscles to prove it. It took me some time to uncover this other talent, but I've more than made up for my lapse. So the answer to your question is yes. I enjoy my work very much."

"I'm sure the people of Glinkilly are glad, too, since they've been the beneficiaries."

"There is that. It gives me pleasure to improve their lives, especially when I see how hard they're willing to work to continue to grow and prosper. Long after I'm gone their children and grandchildren will keep the legacy going."

"And legacy matters to you."

He met her look. "It does, yes."

He saw her stifle a yawn and was immediately contrite. "I've been having such a grand time showing you my home, I forgot how exhausting travel can be. Please, my dear, go up to your bed now, and we'll have another visit in the morning."

Aidan set aside her glass. "You're right. I really need to sleep now. I'm afraid the flight and time change are defeating me."

He walked over to close her hand between both of his. "I hope you sleep well and late into the day. Whatever time you wake, we'll share one of Kathleen's fine big breakfasts."

"Thank you, Cullen." She glanced past him to where Ross stood, silent and watching. "Good night, Ross."

"Ross will walk you to your suite."

"There's no need."

Cullen ignored her protest. "I insist."

After saying good night to their host, Ross followed Aidan from the room and up the stairs.

Because he remained one step behind her, she couldn't see his face. But the prickly feeling along her spine had her achingly aware of those steely eyes watching her.

At the top of the stairs, Aidan stood back while Ross opened the door to her suite of rooms.

She shot him a weary smile. "Good night, Ross."

"I'd like a word with you." Seeing that she was about to protest, he stepped into the room and pulled the door shut behind him. "Just a word. No more."

She sighed. "What's wrong? Didn't I follow your instructions carefully enough? Did I say too much? Too little? Did I keep frail old Cullen up past his bedtime? Or did you decide that I wasn't grateful enough for this fine opportunity to glimpse the good life?"

A half smile touched his lips as he leaned back against the closed door, arms folded across his chest, regarding her. "Ah. There's that fine Irish temper again."

"I'm tired. I've had a long day, and a longer week. Say what you came here to say and let me get to bed."

"I want to thank you."

The unexpected words had her eyes rounding in surprise. "For what?"

"For using that charm on the old man. I haven't seen him this animated in years."

"You thought I was pretending? That I was heeding your advice?"

"Weren't you?"

Her tone lowered with feeling. "I didn't need to pretend to be charmed. I was honestly responding to Cullen's warmth and goodness."

"You liked him."

She nodded. "How could I not?"

"What's more, he likes you. I can tell that you're all he'd hoped you would be."

"Not all, I'm afraid." Her chin came up. "He's hoping for a blood relative, a grand-daughter, and that's something I can never be."

"You don't know . . ."

She held up a hand. "It's late, I'm tired, and this can go nowhere."

As she started away, he clamped a hand on her shoulder and turned her to face him. "I just wanted to say . . ."

A look of astonishment crossed her face before it turned to anger. "Take your hand off me. Don't you ever put a hand on me without permission."

He lifted both hands in a sign of surrender. "Sorry. Reflex."

"So is a slap across the face, which is what you'll get if you ever dare to do that again." She took a step backward. "Good night, Ross."

A dangerous smile teased his lips and crinkled his eyes, which only fueled her temper.

Before she could say a word, his hand shot out. The smile remained as he touched a finger to her cheek. Just a touch, but she felt the heat of it all the way to her toes.

"You have very soft skin, Aidan O'Mara."

She was about to make a sharp reply when he dipped his head and covered her mouth with his.

She had every intention of slapping his arrogant face. But all her good intentions fled the moment their mouths mated. She was mesmerized by the feel of his lips on hers. By the hunger in his kiss that spoke to a like hunger in her. By the hands, strong and sure, that moved up and down her spine, pressing her to the length of him, testing, measuring. By the slow heat that built and built until she could feel it pulsing through her veins like liquid lava.

When at last he lifted his head, she stood very still, trying to get her bearings. Her head was spinning, and she would have sworn the floor had actually tilted.

He looked equally stunned, and kept his hands firmly on her shoulders, as though anchoring himself while a storm raged within him. After some moments, he took a step back.

His deep, rich voice, with just the faint trace of brogue, washed over her. "Good night, Aidan. Sleep well."

She watched in silence as he opened the door, stepped from the room and closed the door without so much as a backward glance.

She listened to the sound of his footsteps along the hall.

Only when his footsteps faded did she move, on trembling legs, to the bedroom.

She undressed and turned off the lights before walking to the windows. Dropping to the window seat, she stared down at the gardens, silvered with dew in the moonlight.

She drew up her knees as she sat, deep in thought. What had she gotten herself into? Nothing here was familiar. And yet nothing felt strange.

She ought to be feeling at loose ends, and yet she felt an odd sense of peace, as though she'd come home.

Home. Now, that was a joke.

It was all this luxury, she scolded herself.

It would be very easy to get used to a life of such ease, and turn her back on the problems she'd left behind. But the debts would still be there when she returned. As would the unpaid taxes and insurance, and the medical bills, which would probably take a lifetime to pay.

Spying a movement in the garden, she watched as the two wolfhounds leapt from the shadows and scampered along a path. Trailing slowly behind was a tall figure.

Though still in shadow, she recognized him at once.

As she watched, Ross paused beside a stone bench and turned to look up at her window. Even though she knew he couldn't see her in the darkness of the room, she ducked her head. A moment later, feeling foolish, she peered out the window, but he was gone.

She crossed the room and climbed into bed, determined to put him out of her mind. But try as she would, he was there, with that mocking smile, those piercing blue eyes. The press of his hand at her shoulder had brought a flood of anger. But that heart-stopping kiss had been her undoing, sending shock waves rippling through her.

Had it been a spontaneous gesture? Or had it been calculated to elicit exactly the emotions she was experiencing?

She had the feeling that there was nothing innocent about Ross Delaney. From his deliberate aloofness to the way he seemed to be always studying her, he appeared to be every inch a worldly man. No doubt he took this life of luxury for granted, and felt it was his due. A man like that would probably be amused by her small-town reaction to Cullen's lifestyle. Not to mention her reaction to his kiss.

Still, worldly or not, he had no right to intrude in her private life, and even her sleep. Damn Ross Delaney, she thought angrily. He was certainly doing everything he could to keep this from being easy.

She'd envisioned a quick trip to Ireland, an overnight stay in a rustic lodge, and a doddering old man who would offer his apologies for wasting her time, while presenting her with a check for enough money to make a dent in her growing mountain of debt.

Now she would have to deal with a successful, sharp-minded old businessman who seemed genuinely fond of her, even if he was confused about her lineage.

Not to mention having to deal with the very handsome, very irritating self-appointed bodyguard, who was behaving as though she had deliberately come here to break the old man's heart.

She touched a finger to her lips. She could still taste him. Could still feel the jolt when he'd put his hands on her, as though she'd dropped off the edge of the world into some strange new realm.

She found herself wondering if his reaction had been as volatile as hers. If so, there was bound to be a violent explosion of cataclysmic proportions before she took leave of this place.

FOUR

Aidan slept badly. Another reason, she thought, to resent Ross Delaney. Not that it was entirely his fault, but his touch had left her entirely too unsettled. Added to that were the strange dreams. Dreams of her mother and grandmother as young girls, dancing along the garden path with the wolfhounds, Meath and Mayo. They'd been close together, heads bent while sharing secrets, and when she'd tried to hear, they had climbed onto the dogs' backs and disappeared high in the branches of the trees. But they had been so real, she woke from sleep, and found herself weeping furiously because she missed them so.

There had been way too many tears these past days. Time, she thought, to toughen up and get on with life.

As she showered and dressed, she renewed her determination to be perfectly honest with Cullen Glin. He'd been such a charming host, she owed him that much. It wouldn't be easy, she realized. She'd begun to care about him, and hated the thought of bringing him any more pain.

Pain. She'd seen it in his eyes. Heard it in his voice when he spoke of having no kin. Still, she wasn't responsible for his pain. She had her own to deal with.

There would be no dancing around the truth today. She needed to be candid and admit that she had come here out of curiosity, and for the promised money, because of the debts incurred during her mother's long illness. No need to sugarcoat the truth.

Because she intended to be businesslike today, she wore her charcoal business suit and a simple white blouse. She took her time with makeup and hair, and noticed that her hands weren't as steady as she'd like. No matter. It was time for complete honesty.

She descended the stairs and followed the sound of voices until she came to a sunny breakfast room, with a wall of windows overlooking the gardens. Along one wall was a sideboard with several steam tables. The smell of coffee, bacon and freshly baked bread had her mouth watering.

Charity was chatting up Bridget, talking on and on about her father.

"Oh. Good morning." Charity placed a bowl of fresh snapdragons in the center of the table. "Mr. Delaney instructed us to be as quiet as mice today. He thought you'd sleep 'til noon. Did we wake you?"

"Not at all. I simply woke and knew I'd slept long enough." Aidan paused. "Did I overhear you say your father was having trouble with his ledgers?"

"You did." The girl blushed. "As part of the Farmers' Cooperative, he's obliged to balance the books, but the poor dear is having fits over all the numbers. He said he'd rather muck a hundred stalls than tally any more numbers."

Aidan shared a laugh with the girl. "I wish I were going to be here long enough to lend a hand."

"You're good with figures?"

"That was my job when I worked at the bank. I love balancing books."

"Oh, my." Charity touched a hand to her heart. "If you could be here long enough to help my poor father, he'd bless your name forever." She clapped a hand to her mouth. "Here I am babbling, and forgetting my duties."

Aidan watched as the young woman danced away, returning moments later, trailed by Cullen and Ross.

"Good morning, my dear." Cullen greeted her with a smile. "I instructed Charity to let me know the moment you came downstairs."

"I don't want to take you from your work."

"I can work anytime. Right now, Ross and I will join you for breakfast." He nodded toward the steam tables. "There's ham and bacon already prepared. Kathleen will make any kind of eggs you prefer. And she's already baked fresh scones."

"I'll start with coffee. Would you like some?"

"I prefer tea in the morning, but I'm sure Ross would like another cup. Ross?" He turned and the younger man gave a nod.

Aidan filled two cups and handed one to Ross before lifting the other to her mouth and drinking deeply.

Cullen held her chair, then took his place at the head of the table, with Ross to his left and Aidan to his right.

Charity paused beside him. "What is your pleasure, Mr. Glin?"

"Just bacon and some of Kathleen's fine scones."

"Miss O'Mara?" She paused beside Aidan.

"I believe I'll have the same."

Charity glanced at Ross. "Mr. Delaney?"

"Nothing, thanks. I'll just drink my coffee."

Within minutes Aidan and Cullen were enjoying their meal, while Ross, as usual, watched and listened in silence.

When at last Aidan sat back, sipping a second cup of coffee, Cullen folded his napkin. "I didn't want to push you last night, because I knew you had to be feeling somewhat overwhelmed by the stress of your flight, but I hope now that you've had a chance to rest, you'll speak candidly about your grandmother and mother."

"I'd be happy to. What would you like to know about them?"

"What was your grandmother's life like in America?"

"As far as I can recall, she lived an ordinary life in Landsdown." Aidan glanced over. "That's a small town in upstate New York."

"I know of it," Cullen said simply.

"Of course. You researched it for those documents I was given."

"They were carefully researched, not only by Ross and the American legal firm, but by me, as well."

"Then you'll understand my reluctance to give you any hope that we could be related. There is the matter of different names . . ."

She paused when Cullen lifted a hand. "We'll get to that. Please, tell me about your grandmother's life in America."

Aidan took a breath. "She was married to my grandfather, Edward Martin, for more than forty years before he died after a long battle from a stroke. Most of my memories of him are in a wheelchair."

"Was he a wealthy man?"

Aidan chose her words carefully. "He came from a wealthy family, and inherited great wealth through the family business. But he was careless in business and made some unwise investments, losing nearly everything. If it hadn't been for my grandmother's diligence, they would have been left with nothing."

Cullen looked surprised. "Your grandmother became a businesswoman?"

"Out of necessity. She took over his company, paid off his debts, then took over the books and made enough money that they would be comfortable in their old age. Of course, my grandfather didn't live to an old age."

"What did she do after his death?" Cullen had gone very still, as had Ross.

"She talked endlessly about a trip to Ireland. It seemed to be her reason for living."

Cullen sat a little straighter in his chair, his gaze fixed on Aidan's face.

At his unspoken question she explained. "But then she fell ill, and a trip was out of the question. Within the year she was dead."

He stared at his hands for long moments. At last he looked up. "And your mother? What of her life?"

Aidan smiled. "She married my father, John O'Mara, when she was twenty-nine."

Cullen arched a brow. "So old."

That had Aidan chuckling. "I suppose it is, though I'm twenty-five, and don't feel like an old maid just yet."

"I wasn't implying . . ." He spread his hands. "Your grandmother was only seventeen."

Aidan gave him a steady look. "I never mentioned her age. Was that in the documents you sent me?"

He shrugged. "No matter. Tell me about your mother."

"She and Dad were married twenty years when he passed away. His illness ate up my mother's savings, but we were still getting by, until she became ill."

"I understand you quit your job to care for her."

Aidan set aside her cup. When she looked up, her eyes were steady on his. "I went through all our savings. Sold my car, gave up my apartment and moved in with my mother. I'm not proud of the fact that I'm in debt, but I'm not ashamed of it, either. It is what it is, and I'll figure out what to do next. But this much I do know. You desperately want to find your daughter, and I'm sorry that my mother can't be the one you're seeking. As I told you, her parents were Maureen and Edward Martin. I have a copy of their marriage license, and a copy of my mother's birth certificate. Now, I hope this will put an end to your claim that we can somehow be related. Obviously, you can't be the father of my mother, when that honor belonged to my grandfather, Edward Martin."

When he started to speak, she shook her head. "Wait. Let me finish. This isn't easy for me to say, but I have to say it." She looked from Cullen, who showed no reaction, to Ross, who was scowling at her as though she were pointing a gun. "I came here for two reasons only. To satisfy my curiosity about a man who would fly a stranger all the way to Ireland, and to collect the check you promised me for my inconvenience. I'm not proud of this, but I am desperately in debt, and I saw this as an answer to my problems."

Drained, she sat back, prepared for whatever explosive reaction he might have.

Instead of the expected anger, or frustration, he merely leaned forward and placed a hand over hers. "It pains me to hear about your debt, though it was certainly beyond your control. You've had your say, Aidan. Now humor me as I tell you my story."

She nodded, then purposefully removed her hand from his grasp and sat back. She wanted no connection with him while he spoke. She needed to make this quick and painless. Or at least as painless as possible.

Cullen's face grew animated. "When I was just seventeen, I met the great love of my life. Her name was Moira Fitzgibbon, and she lived in the town of Glinkilly. She was the most beautiful girl I'd ever seen, with skin like milk, flashing green eyes and hair as dark as midnight." He shot Aidan a smile. "You look just like her."

"That's not possible because . . ."

Before she could say more, he interrupted her. "Moira's father considered me to be beneath her, because I was a common laborer, while her father made a comfortable living as a landlord who owned a great deal of land in the area, which he leased out to tenant farmers. Moira and I were young and foolish and wildly in love, and we did

483

what young lovers have done from the beginning of time." He waited a beat before adding, "When Moira came to me and said she was with child, I went to her father and asked for her hand in marriage."

Aidan glanced at Ross, who would surely have known all this. But he was watching the old man with a fierce intensity that had her turning back to watch and listen in silence.

"Hugh Fitzgibbon said I had despoiled his daughter, and that he'd see her dead before married to the likes of me."

Though she'd hoped to listen in silence, Aidan was caught up in the narrative. Without thinking, she asked, "Oh, that's horrible. What did you do?"

"I went to our parish priest here in Glinkilly, and begged him to plead my case with Hugh Fitzgibbon. I said I would do whatever it took. I promised to work three jobs for a lifetime if necessary in order to support Moira and the babe. The priest agreed to speak with Hugh Fitzgibbon after Sunday mass. I remember thinking that those next few days were the longest of my life. Little did I know," he mused almost to himself, "that the rest of my life would be even longer."

"So he refused the priest?"

"Worse. On Sunday evening Father Ryan came to tell me that the Fitzgibbon home had been hastily vacated. Hugh and his wife had taken their daughter in the night to Dublin, and from there to America, where, they'd vowed, I would never see my Moira again."

"Did you try to follow her?"

"How could I? I hadn't two coins to my name. Hugh was right. I was a laborer. But not common. Not at all. I spent the rest of my life accumulating the fortune I'd need to find my Moira and our child and bring them back to me. But Hugh was one step ahead of me all the way. When they landed in America, Hugh changed his family name to Gibbons and took his middle name, Francis. For years I searched for Hugh Fitzgibbon, and checked out nearly a dozen or more, only to come up empty. As for Moira, who was now Maureen Gibbons, she was wed to an American almost as soon as she stepped off the boat in New York. Doesn't that strike you as strange?"

"Not at all. You said that your Moira was beautiful. If, and it's a big stretch to suggest that my grandmother Maureen is somehow your Moira, but if it were true, then why wouldn't Edward Martin be equally struck by her beauty? It doesn't sound odd that they met, fell in love and married quickly."

"And less than seven months later your mother was born."

Aidan pursed her lips in a frown. "Don't make this into more than it was. I was told that my mother was premature, and very frail at birth."

He chuckled. "So many babies enter this world before the full nine months. Not all of them frail. It's said that half the population wasn't planned. Many of us are accidents of birth." He looked over. "Did your grandfather strike you as an impulsive man who would marry someone he'd only just met within days of her landing in America?"

Aidan laughed. "Quite the contrary. He was a very stern, disciplined man. But I didn't know him in his youth. Perhaps in his later years he was forced to overcome an impetuous nature."

"Or he was persuaded to marry a dishonored young woman who was in need of a husband in order to hide her shame. Knowing Hugh Fitzgibbon's fury, he would not have been above offering quite a dowry for the right man to take his shameful, headstrong daughter off his hands and spare him and his wife the embarrassment of a grandchild without a father."

Aidan gave a firm shake of her head. "I

simply can't accept any of this. I know what I know, and that is that Edward Martin was my grandfather, and his wife, Maureen, my grandmother. Their daughter was my mother, whom I loved more than life. I'm not prepared to accept that their entire lives have been a lie."

"Not a lie, Aidan. The result of difficult circumstances, perhaps. We do what we have to in order to survive. Your grandmother was no different."

"But to never tell my mother . . ." She spread her hands. "They were too close. There was plenty of time for honesty before she died. She would have had to tell the truth of her parentage to my mother."

"Perhaps she did, and your mother chose not to share that with you." While Aidan was shaking her head in denial he added, "One thing more about your mother. You have yet to say her name." He leaned forward.

"Her name was Claire."

"Have I told you my mother's name?" He paused dramatically before saying, "It was Claire."

Aidan swallowed. "A coincidence."

"Perhaps."

"Or perhaps you're making this up."

"I could be. But there are documents to

prove what I say. My mother, Claire," he added emphatically, "loved Moira like a daughter, and grieved along with me when my great love was taken away to America, never to be seen again. Imagine how my dear mother yearned to see her only grandchild. But it was to be denied her. And yet, though Moira was forced to change her name, live a lie and wed another, she still saw to it that her daughter bore the name Claire, in honor of the woman her namesake would never know."

Aidan pressed her fingers to her temples, where the beginning of a headache had begun to throb. "I'm sorry. This is all so much to take in."

"I know." His tone gentled. "I understand everything you're feeling, for I've struggled with every emotion possible. Through the years I've been angry, sad, defeated, determined, hopeful and, at times, desperately unhappy. After a lifetime of searching, I finally learned the name of the man Moira had married, and was able to put all the pieces together. I don't believe I've ever been so joyful, so filled with hope. Then, just as my legal team was closing in on the one I sought, I was told that both Moira and the child were dead." His eyes were hot and fierce. "But you're alive, Aidan. The daughter of my daughter. Don't you see? My lifetime search has not been in vain."

Aidan scrambled to her feet, nearly knocking over her chair in her haste. "I can't accept this without proof. What you've offered me is a sad story, a few coincidences. I need more."

"Very well." The old man glanced at Ross for confirmation. "We thought you would need convincing. And for the sake of the courts, we'll need more. Ross?"

Taking his cue, Ross picked up the conversation. "With your permission, Cullen would like to order a genetic test. It's simple enough. A technician from our local hospital can be here within an hour to swab both your mouths. Within forty-eight hours a DNA test will offer proof beyond a doubt as to whether or not you two are blood-related."

"Forty-eight hours." Aidan chewed the inside of her mouth, considering. "I'd hoped to be on a plane later today."

"Of course," Ross added, "should the tests prove negative, Cullen will keep his promise to send you home with a first-class air ticket and a generous settlement for your inconvenience."

Aidan looked at the offer from every angle. She could leave now, and always wonder if Cullen's Moira had been her grandmother. Or she could postpone her return for another two days, and know without a doubt.

Two more days in this lovely setting, and a generous check for her time spent.

She looked from Cullen to Ross. "I think it's an excellent idea. And, as you said, it will eliminate any more doubts. You'll make that call to the hospital now?"

Ross nodded.

"Then, if you'll excuse me, I'd like to go to my room."

Cullen stood. "Ross will walk you upstairs."

"No." There were entirely too many emotions bubbling at the surface already. She wasn't up to dealing with the very different emotions Ross evoked each time he got close to her.

She backed away. "I'm used to taking care of myself. Just let me know when the technician arrives."

Before Cullen or Ross could react, she walked quickly from the room and hurried up the stairs, eager to mull over all she'd heard.

FIVE

Aidan paced the length of the room and back, her thoughts in turmoil. It wasn't so much that her mind refused to accept the story told by Cullen, but rather that he had managed to plant a seed of doubt.

What if his Moira were truly her grandmother Maureen? What if the child she bore hadn't been Edward Martin's, but in fact Cullen's?

"Oh, Mama." Aidan struggled to hold on to the image she'd carried of her sweet, stoic grandmother, pouring herself into the intricacies of her husband's business, staving off bankruptcy by the sheer force of her will.

Everyone who had known Maureen Gibbons had been astonished by her strength. Throughout her marriage she had deferred always to Edward. It was he who chose their furniture, each new car, even her wardrobe. Though not in the same category as a tyrant, he had definitely played a dominant role in their marriage.

Had he been chosen, not by her, but by her father? Had their marriage been one of convenience only, to hide the shame she'd visited upon her parents? It would explain so much about that distant relationship. Aidan tried to recall if she'd ever seen a display of tenderness between her grand-parents.

At a knock on the parlor door, she looked up. "Charity?"

The knock sounded again, followed by the door being opened.

Annoyed, Aidan walked to the adjoining bathroom and splashed cold water over her face before hurrying to the parlor.

"I'm sorry." Seeing her look of dismay, Ross paused just inside the doorway. "I suggested that you be given more time to compose yourself, but Cullen refused to wait another minute. He's beside himself and sent me to apologize for having upset you. He begs you to look at some of the things he's been saving."

"I can't. I'm not ready . . ."

He held up a hand. "In all the years I've known Cullen Glin, I've never known him to beg. This means the world to him. You," he said for emphasis, "and your opinion of

492

him have begun to mean the world to him."

"I'm not who he wants me to be."

"So you've said. But you've heard his story."

"And he's heard mine. Just because he wants my grandmother to be the great love of his life doesn't make it so."

"He has documents . . ."

"So do I. A birth certificate, a marriage license . . ."

"Which could have been filled in with any name, especially by immigrants who desperately wanted to hide their identity. You know that's so, Aidan."

"My parents and grandparents lived ordinary lives."

"So do thousands of people who want to blend in."

"Stop." She rubbed at her temples. "You make my ancestors sound like criminals."

"They were good people who thought a baby conceived out of wedlock to be something shameful. They were trying to protect not only their own reputations, but also that of their daughter. You heard Cullen. They thought him unworthy of their only child. So they started a new life in a new country, and persuaded Moira to do the same. Maybe she wanted a new start. Maybe she didn't love Cullen as much as he loved her.

Or maybe her loyalty to her parents was stronger than a tenuous love for an impetuous young man. For whatever reason, whether she was persuaded, or forced, what's done is done. There's no going back. But at least, while you wait for the hospital technician, read the letters Cullen wrote to his Moira through the years. None of them ever reached her. But he kept them, hoping that one day he could give them to her as proof of his love. It is his fondest wish that you read his letters and look over the mounds of documents he's gathered through the years in his search for the love of his life. And then listen to your heart."

She stared at the pile of papers that he set on the coffee table. "What do you get out of all this, Ross?"

He straightened. "I get to see a man I love and respect finally getting the chance to fulfill his dream."

The words were spoken so simply, she knew they came from his heart.

As he started toward the door she said softly, "All right. I'll read his letters and documents. But I can't promise anything."

By the time Ross descended the stairs, she was already settled on the window seat, lost in a young Cullen Glin's declarations to the woman he'd love and lost.

■ ■ ■ ■

Aidan looked up from the last of the letters, her eyes moist. What would it be like, she wondered, to love someone so deeply, and then face the loss of that love for a lifetime?

Cullen had poured out all his feelings on the pages of his letters. Had emptied his heart and soul, until she wondered that he had any passion left. And still he'd refused to give up his search for his Moira. There were piles of requests for information regarding immigrants from Ireland by the name of Fitzgibbon. A thick folder compiled by a private detective agency in New York State documenting every Fitzgibbon who had entered the country legally, and some who had found their way via illegal channels. And finally she found the current file, with her mother's obituary from her local newspaper.

A lifetime search had ended with a death.

Aidan stood, flexing her cramped muscles just as a knock sounded on the parlor door.

She opened it to find Charity poised to knock again.

"Oh." The girl snickered. "I thought you might be napping. Bridget sent me to fetch you. There's a hospital technician in the library waiting to administer a test."

"Thanks, Charity." Aidan followed the girl down the stairs, aware that everyone working at the lodge knew just what was going on. There were no secrets here.

In the doorway of the library she paused. Cullen was seated behind his desk. Ross and a stranger were standing by the windows talking.

They all looked over as she stepped into the room.

Cullen walked around his desk to stand beside her. As though, she thought, to shield her.

"Easiest test I've ever taken," he said with a grin. "A quick comb of my cheek, in triplicate just to be certain, and we were done with it." He turned to the young man wearing latex gloves. "Patrick, this is Aidan O'Mara. Aidan, Patrick is with St. Brendan Hospital. He'll administer the DNA test."

"Miss O'Mara." The young man handed her a long plastic stick with something that resembled a tiny comb at the end. "If you'll comb your mouth for a full minute and place the comb in this vial, please."

"Comb? I thought I'd be swabbing my mouth."

"It's the same. We call it combing." He glanced at the tiny comb. "I'm sure you can see why."

She did as he instructed, pleased that the tiny comb easily detached from its handle as she slid it into the vial. After handing over the vial, he sealed it in a plastic bag, which he carefully marked with a pen.

"And now again," he said, handing her a second.

She swabbed a different section of her mouth before dropping the tiny comb into another vial.

The technician followed the same procedure and handed her a third.

When she'd finished, he turned to Cullen. "The results will be sent by courier within forty-eight hours, Mr. Glin, and possibly sooner. As you requested, we'll give this top priority."

"Thank you, Patrick."

When he was gone, Aidan touched a hand to her middle, and wondered at the feelings churning inside her. She ought to be relieved. The decision was now out of her hands and placed in the capable, unerring hands of science. One way or another, she and Cullen would soon know the truth.

The old man touched a hand to her shoulder, and she wondered if he meant to soothe her or himself. "That wasn't so bad, now, was it?"

"No." She forced a smile. "Easy as pie."

"Indeed." He turned away. "I've ordered Sean to bring the car around to drive me to Glinkilly. Would you care to go along?"

She was about to refuse when a thought occurred to her. "I'd like that. I told Charity that I'd help her father with the figures for the Farmers' Cooperative's books if I stayed here long enough. It seems he's feeling overwhelmed. And since I now have forty-eight hours to do with as I please, it's the least I can do for her."

Cullen arched a brow. "You're good with numbers?"

"It's what I did at the bank. I hope you don't mind."

"Not at all." Cullen turned to Ross. "Would you care to join us?"

"Sorry." Ross started toward the door. "I have things to attend to here."

"I'll just get my purse and meet you outside." Aidan walked away.

"There's the new wing of the school." Cullen pointed with pride to the Glinkilly Academy, bearing his name, where stonemasons had perfectly matched the new stone to the original, so that it was impossible to tell the new wing from the old.

"And this is where the Farmers' Cooperative meets." He glanced beyond Aidan to Charity, who had volunteered to come along and introduce their guest to her father.

The car came to a stop and Sean hurried around to open the passenger door. Aidan and Charity stepped out.

Aidan turned. "How much time do I have?"

"An hour or two. Will that be enough?"

She laughed. "I have no idea the condition of the ledgers, but I'll be ready to leave whenever you say."

"Miss O'Mara, your car is here."

It had been nearly three hours before the ancient Rolls pulled up to the door of the Farmers' Cooperative. Before he could hurry inside to collect Aidan and Charity, the two young women stepped out into the sunlight, accompanied by four men who were all smiles.

As Sean held the passenger door, each man shook Aidan's hand and thanked her for the work she'd done on their behalf.

"If you've a chance to visit us again, miss," Charity's father said in his thick brogue, "we'd be honored to have you to supper."

"Thank you. If I'm ever back in your lovely town, I'd be honored to accept."

One of the men turned to Cullen and tipped his hat. "Such a fine young lady she is, sir."

The others nodded.

"She made it all so easy. A wizard with numbers, she is, and now that the columns of figures are properly tallied, we won't be forgetting what she taught us this day."

Aidan hugged Charity, who had elected to walk home with her father and the others, rather than return to the lodge.

As the car started away, the men were still smiling and waving.

"Well." Cullen turned to study the young woman beside him. "You seem to have made quite an impression on the lads."

"It was all very simple, really. Just columns of numbers. I showed them a few tricks to keep them from getting overwhelmed when the tallies don't match up."

"That was generous of you, Aidan."

She shook her head. "I enjoyed it. It was nice to dip my hand in the work again. I've missed it."

Cullen fell silent as the car moved along the familiar country roads. Then, playing the part of genial host, he began to point out things of interest, until they were once again home.

"If you don't mind, my dear, I have some

work to tend to in my office."

"I don't mind a bit."

As she walked away, there was a spring to her step. She hadn't been completely honest with Cullen. She hadn't just enjoyed working with the farmers in town; she'd been over the moon at the chance to work again.

Aidan sat on a stone bench, watching birds splashing in a fountain. The sound of the water, and the perfume of the roses all around her, brought a sense of peace. She was glad now that she'd sought the solitude of the garden. It was the perfect counterpoint to the chaos in her soul.

So many doubts. So many things she'd taken for granted for a lifetime were now in question since coming here.

On the one hand, she wanted to forget everything she'd heard this morning. The image of a frightened young woman, forcibly separated from all that was comforting and familiar, only to find herself in a new and uncharted existence, was too painful to contemplate. On the other hand, it would explain the lack of tenderness between her grandparents, and the fierce loyalty of her grandmother to her only child.

Had her mother been the love child of

Moira and Cullen? As much as she wanted to deny it, she found herself unable to completely reject the idea. She found herself comparing her mother's smile to Cullen's. The shape of that full lower lip, the merest hint of a dimple in the left cheek, the arch of brow. Despite both her grandparents' dark hair with hardly a trace of silver, her mother had gone prematurely gray. Now that she had met Cullen, she realized her mother's white hair was so like his silver mane.

In less than forty-eight hours she would have the truth.

Too agitated to sit any longer, she stood and began to follow a winding path that led from the rose garden to a wooded section.

As she rounded yet another curve in the path, she found herself standing in front of the guest cottage.

From inside, the wolfhounds set up a chorus of barking. The door opened and Ross greeted her with a smile. "I see you decided to look around a bit. Would you like to come in?"

"Thank you."

He held the door and she moved past him into the most charming cottage.

The dogs circled her, sniffing and curious. With a softly spoken word from Ross, they retreated to the far side of the room.

Dappled sunlight spilled through the wide windows to form patterns of light and shadow on gleaming hardwood floors.

"Oh, this is lovely." Aidan looked around with interest.

Exposed wooden beams ran across the ceiling, giving the room a rustic look. Pale stucco walls added to the feeling of light. The comfortable upholstered furniture had a definite masculine appeal. A wall of bookshelves was stocked with leather-bound volumes.

"Your law library?"

He nodded. "Some of it. I have an office in Dublin, as well." He led her toward a small kitchen, with a wall of glass overlooking a brick-paved patio.

"I was just about to pour myself an iced tea." He indicated a pitcher on the counter. "Will you join me?"

"Yes. Thank you."

While he filled two glasses she looked around. The room, though small, was beautifully appointed, with Spanish tile flooring, marble countertops, and a round glass table and chairs that fit snugly into a bay window.

He handed her a frosty glass before snagging the pitcher. "Let's sit on the patio and take advantage of the sunlight before it fails."

She opened the French doors and stepped out, with Ross following. At a word from him the dogs came bounding outside and ran off.

Several deep, padded chairs had been positioned for easy conversation. The blue of the cushions matched the blue of the ceramic pots holding red roses and trailing ivy.

"I can see that you like beautiful things."

His eyes were steady on hers. "I do, yes. Which is why I can't seem to stop looking at you."

She colored slightly and forced herself to look around. "It's easy to see why you prefer this to the lodge."

"Most people would think me a fool for disdaining luxury for simplicity."

"This isn't simple. It's charming."

He merely smiled and sipped his drink. "Did you read Cullen's letters and documents?"

She nodded.

"Have they answered any of your questions?"

She gave a dry laugh. "If anything, they've just caused more questions. I've tried blocking all these new details from my mind, but it's impossible to stop thinking about them. Each question leads to another."

"Such as?" He was watching her intently.

"Why my grandmother seemed different after my grandfather died."

"In what way?"

Aidan shrugged. "She seemed . . . free. All that talk about a grand trip to Ireland. She was like a girl planning her first dance. And then there's my mother. Why didn't she look like either of her parents? Not just her face, or her body type, though there was that. But also the fact of her prematurely gray hair. Both of her parents were barely gray when they died, with just a few silver threads. She went gray in her forties, and by the time she died she had a silver mane."

"Like Cullen's." He smiled.

"You think it's funny."

He shook his head. "I think it's a family trait, and though you're trying to deny it, you're beginning to believe."

"Maybe." Restless, she set aside her glass on a side table. "But it would take more than gray hairs or a few old love letters to convince me that everything I've held to be true for a lifetime is a lie."

"It happens more often than you think. Adult children are told after the death of a parent that they were adopted, or learn that the woman they called mother was actually their biological grandmother, covering for the mistake of a too-young daughter. Though we may wish it otherwise, life isn't all neat and tidy."

"Knowing it happens to others doesn't make it any easier to accept. I wonder if you'd be so philosophical if this were happening to you. How would you feel about catching your mother in a lie?"

His smile remained in place, though there was a flicker of emotion in his eyes. "I would have had to know my mother to catch her in a lie. And since she disappeared from my life before I was old enough to talk, that wasn't possible."

Aidan felt a rush of remorse. "I'm sorry. I had no right . . ."

He looked beyond her and seemed almost relieved as he got to his feet. "Cullen. Aidan and I are having some iced tea. Will you join us?"

"I will. Thank you." The older man settled himself comfortably in the chair beside hers and began petting the two dogs that rushed up to greet him.

Ross returned with a glass and poured him a drink.

Cullen sipped. "Have you been enjoying the gardens, my dear?"

"I have. Almost as much as I'm enjoying Ross' cottage."

Cullen gave a broad smile. "He and I have enjoyed many a night of heated debate out here. Though I must confess that on my part the heat may have come from a bottle of Bushmill's finest."

"And many a headache in the morning, as you're fond of telling me." Ross laughed.

She could imagine Ross and Cullen sitting here often, debating business or politics or world affairs.

Aidan glanced from Cullen to Ross. "Who most often wins the debate?"

"There are no winners," Cullen declared firmly. "To be Irish is to understand that the joy of a debate is not in the winning or losing, but in the argument itself."

"Ah. So that's where this comes from. My father used to accuse me of enjoying a good argument way too much. Now I learn that it's the Irish in me."

Cullen was still smiling, but his look had sharpened, and she had the distinct impression that he was searching for parts of himself in her face. Wasn't she guilty of doing the same, when she thought he wouldn't notice?

Ross was watching them both, and keeping his thoughts to himself.

"What else do you enjoy, my dear?" Cullen sipped his iced tea and continued to study her.

"Good books."

"Fiction or non?"

Without a thought, she said, "Nonfiction. Usually. I devour biographies."

He and Ross shared a glance. "And what is your taste in music?"

"I love it all, I suppose. But especially classical. Operas in particular."

He arched a brow. "Do you have a favorite?"

"I love all I've seen. But I always cry at *Madame Butterfly*."

He smiled at that. "Do you play an instrument?"

"I never had lessons, so I don't play well, but I play piano for my own amusement. And I've been known to pick up a violin and play a tune or two."

"Any other great loves?" He paused. Smiled. "I should clarify that. Any you can speak of?"

She laughed, enjoying the teasing. "No special man, if that's what you're asking. But I do love to garden. That's something that my mother and I both shared."

He leaned forward. "Your mother was aptly named. Her namesake, my mother, had a garden that was admired by all in our county. I swear she could put a dead stick in the ground and it would bloom for her."

He saw Aidan's smile fade. "Forgive me, my dear. I don't mean to push. It's just . . ." He spread his hands. "When I hear you speak, it's as though I've known you for a lifetime. I forget that this is all new and awkward for you."

She surprised herself by reaching over to take his hand. "You're a kind man, Cullen Glin, and I don't want to hurt you any more than you've already been hurt. I admit that I'm puzzled by all the similarities between my family and the one you've been seeking. But I can't put aside my beliefs of a lifetime because of a few coincidences."

Keeping her hand in his, he drained his glass and got to his feet. "You're right, of course. Forgive an old man's impatience. We'll have our answers soon enough. Why don't we walk up to the lodge and see what Kathleen has prepared for our dinner?"

He turned to Ross. "Will you be joining us?"

Ross gave a quick shake of his head. "Not tonight. I have some work to take care of."

"You can do that later. Come. Join us."

Ross gave the old man a gentle smile. "I suspect that you and Aidan can find plenty to talk about. Maybe I'll walk up later for coffee."

"Your loss." Cullen tucked Aidan's hand in the crook of his arm. "On the way to the lodge I'll show you my favorite roses. Moira and I once planned to fill our yard with them."

Ross watched them walk away, then settled back down in the chair, idly scratching behind Mayo's ears, until Meath nudged her aside. "Jealous, are you?" He glanced toward the old man and young woman, walking along the path arm in arm. "I'd know a thing or two about that."

Six

"Bridget." Cullen sat back as the old woman removed his plate. "Be sure and tell Kathleen that this was the finest salmon I've ever tasted." He glanced at Aidan. "What did you think of it, my dear?"

"I agree." She sighed. "And those tiny potatoes and carrots right out of the garden. You'd spend a fortune for something that fresh in a restaurant."

Once again they'd forsaken the banquet-sized table in favor of a small round one set in a corner of the room near a bank of windows overlooking the gardens. For the past hour they'd talked about books and music, discovering that each of them loved the same authors, and they even described the same scenes from several of their favorite operas.

While Cullen seemed to revel in each new discovery, for Aidan it was an eerie feeling to have such an intimate connection to a stranger. Except that the more time she spent with Cullen Glin, the less a stranger he seemed to be.

"Why don't we take our coffee and dessert in the library?"

She nodded. "But just coffee. I'm afraid I don't have room for dessert after that wonderful meal."

He turned to Bridget with a smile. "Just coffee, Bridget. We'll be in the library."

Once there, Cullen watched as Aidan studied the photographs arranged on a side table.

"Your mother?" She pointed to the plump woman with her arm around a young Cullen.

"Yes." He walked over to stand beside her. "You'd have loved her."

Aidan heard the affection in his voice.

"Is this Ross?" She lifted a framed photo for a better look.

"Indeed. That was taken when he first came to live with me."

"So young?" She glanced up in surprise. "I mean . . . I thought he was merely your lawyer."

"He is. Considered one of the finest in the country now. After university here he studied at Oxford, and then in your country, at Harvard."

She peered at the photograph. "But here he's . . ."

"Sixteen." Cullen chuckled. "You'd be hard-pressed to discern that rough-and-tumble youth as the same polished man who's persuaded judges and juries across Ireland in his clients' favor."

They both looked up as Bridget carried in a silver coffee service and filled two cups before taking her leave.

Aidan and Cullen settled into chairs pulled in front of the fire.

Cullen stirred sugar into his coffee. "What do you think of Ross?"

Aidan shrugged, wishing she could evade the question. "He's charming and smart and funny. And, without question, devoted to you."

Cullen nodded absently. "No more than I am to him."

"And yet you're not related?"

He glanced up. "Not in any legal sense. But without Ross Delaney, I doubt I'd be sitting here."

"What does that mean?"

"Many years ago, Ross saved my life. I was in Dublin on business, and met an old friend at a pub. We drank a bit too much, and when I left, I made a wrong turn and found myself in an unfamiliar neighborhood. I was a perfect target for punks, and a couple of them attacked me." He shook his head. "I fancied myself a pretty good fighter, but I was no match for those street toughs. I was having my hide kicked when suddenly one punk fell, another let out a cry and the lot of them ran screeching like banshees into the night."

"Ross?"

He nodded. "He came out of nowhere and fought them off like a man possessed. I was bloody from head to toe, and this wiry lad, who looked as though he couldn't lift a sack of potatoes, carried me to my hotel, hauled me to my room and cleaned me up before putting me to bed and phoning for a house doctor." He frowned, remembering. "In the morning I was alone. I walked that same street, giving his description to everyone I could find. Nobody claimed to know who the lad was. But finally a girl who plied her trade on the streets said it had to be Ross Delaney. She showed me where he stayed most nights, and sure enough, there he was, asleep in the doorway of an abandoned factory, my blood still on his clothes."

"He was sleeping on the streets?"

"He was, yes."

She thought about what Ross had told her. His mother had left before he could talk. "Where was his family? Who raised him?"

"From what I learned, he pretty much raised himself. He lived with his father until around the age of eight, when, after being beaten nearly senseless in a drunken rage, Ross left."

Aidan thought about the fact that she'd never seen Ross take a drink of alcohol. Now she understood why.

"He just left? At eight? Where could a boy of that age possibly go? How could he survive?"

"He hid out on the streets of Dublin. Learned from other lads where the best scraps of food could be found and where it was safe to sleep."

"What about school?"

"He'd had little schooling when I first met him. I offered him money for saving my life. He refused my money, even though I could see that he was in desperate need of it." Cullen stared down into his coffee. "There was something so noble about the lad, I found myself drawn to him. By then I'd acquired a great deal of wealth, and nobody to share it with. My search for Moira was going badly, and I needed something or someone on whom to focus. Getting the lad out of that miserable existence became my mission."

"How did you persuade him to trust you?"

Cullen smiled. "It took a while, but I can be very persuasive when I've a mind to be. I brought him here and hired tutors to see just what he could do. To their amazement, and mine, we discovered that he had a fine mind and an inquisitive nature, and because he'd been on his own for so long, was far superior to most lads his age. He was soon excelling at academics, and I realized that he could do anything he set his mind to."

"What about his family? Did he ever try to contact them?"

Cullen gave a quick shake of his head. "They'd abused and abandoned him long before he abandoned them. Why should he ever look back?"

Why, indeed? She mulled all she'd just been told about the fascinating Ross Delaney.

"And so, by some strange twist of fate, a street fight brought me the son I'd never had. And like a true son, he now shares my life."

"That's generous of you."

"Not at all. He actually saved a drowning man. I'd been drowning in self-pity. Even though I'd already amassed a fortune, I was drinking heavily, and my life had no direction. At first I thought I was doing this poor down-and-out lad a favor. But in the end it was Ross who was helping me, teaching me. After hearing about his father's abuse, I stopped drinking. Now, on the few occasions that I indulge, I need only think about what some have gone through because of another's drunkenness, and it sobers me instantly. It was Ross who pointed out the poverty of the town of Glinkilly, and how my fortune could be used to make a change. I was too self-centered to think beyond my own pain until Ross showed me the way. So you see, my dear, his love and loyalty have rewarded me many times over. And it was Ross who, because he refused to give up on my search, finally located your mother, and through her death, you."

"What an amazing turn of events . . ."

They both looked up when Ross, accompanied by Meath and Mayo, stepped into the room. His hair was wind-tossed; his cheeks ruddy from the night air. He looked rough and dangerous, and his eyes, when he looked at Aidan, were stormy.

"Bridget said I'd find you here."

"Ah, Ross." Cullen indicated the chair beside Aidan. "Come warm yourself by the fire. Why don't you take that chair next to Aidan."

Was it her imagination, or did the sly old man appear to be pushing the two of them together whenever he could?

"The lass and I have been having a lovely chat. I'm sure you won't be surprised by this, but we've discovered we have much in common."

Including strong feelings for a certain mysterious man.

The thought startled Aidan and she found herself looking from the old man to the younger one.

She was drawn to Ross Delaney. And, she believed, he was equally drawn to her, or as much as a man like him could be.

But that didn't mean they had to act on their feelings. Within forty-eight hours she would be winging back to America.

Why did that fact suddenly leave her chilled?

". . . isn't that so, my dear?"

She looked over. "Sorry. I seem to be dreaming."

She saw Ross watching her a little too carefully and felt her cheeks color.

"Don't apologize. This has been quite a day for both of us." Cullen gave her a gentle smile. "We both need a good night of sleep."

She nodded. "You're right. I'll say good night now."

"Good night, my dear. I look forward to the morning. Ross, why don't you see Aidan to her room?"

"No." She spoke quickly before turning to Ross. "Please stay and visit with Cullen. Good night."

She turned away, needing to flee the dark, dangerous invitation in his eyes, which spoke to a similar need in her heart.

Her legs were actually trembling as she climbed the stairs and fled to the safety of her room.

Aidan stood by the window and stared down at the gardens that looked as though they'd been drenched in liquid moonlight. The fragrance of roses was carried on the breeze, teasing all her senses.

She should be tired. Instead, she felt strangely energized. She wanted to blame it on the stimulation she'd felt while working on the Farmers' Cooperative ledgers, but that would be a lie. It was true that she missed her job. Missed the thrill of adding columns of figures and the satisfaction of making them all balance. But in this case, the cause of this restlessness wasn't a job, but a man.

Ross.

She'd missed him at dinner. Much more

than she cared to admit. Missed him like an ache around her heart that wouldn't be soothed. And afterward, when he'd walked into the library, she'd fled like a coward rather than stay and face him.

She'd wanted to stay. To listen to that deep, rich voice and bask in the glow of that sultry blue stare. Instead she'd run.

And all because she wanted him. Wanted to feel his mouth on hers, his hands on her. Had wanted it since the first time she'd seen him. And when he'd dared to touch her, to kiss her, a storm had been unleashed inside her that was threatening to drown her.

She shivered. There had been men in her life. Friends, coworkers, lovers. Not one had ever aroused her as this man did, with nothing more than a look. Not one of them had ever touched something deep inside her as he seemed to, even though they'd shared but one brief kiss.

She paced the length of the room, then back, feeling oddly disjointed. Again she had the feeling that she was losing control. As though something outside of her was manipulating her as if she were a puppet, and she was helpless to do anything but go along.

Without a thought to the consequences, she slipped out of her nightclothes and into the aqua silk dress. For warmth she picked up one of the cashmere throws from a footstool and tossed it about her shoulders before descending the stairs.

Once in the garden she made her way along the moonlit path and breathed in a jolt of cold, fresh air, hoping to clear her head. Instead, it only reinforced her need to hurry. Hurry.

Her footsteps were quick, her heart racing. She refused to think about what she was about to do. It may be too bold, but there was so little time. And she wanted, needed desperately, to get to Ross.

As she drew near his cottage, the two dogs rose up out of the darkness and gave a welcoming bark. Just as quickly, they dropped down and fell silent.

Aidan looked around. Though she hadn't heard Ross's voice, she knew that he'd been the one to give the command to Meath and Mayo.

And then she saw him. Standing in the shadows, still dressed as he'd been in the library, his hair wind-tossed, his eyes fierce.

Her voice sounded breathless. "I was afraid you'd be asleep."

"I couldn't sleep. I've been waiting for you." He stepped closer and took her hand, drawing her to him.

"You knew I'd come?"

"I sensed it. I prayed you would."

"And if I hadn't?"

"I'd've come to you." He smoothed a hand over her hair, all the while staring into her eyes. "I've been struggling to deny this since I first saw you. Fighting the need for you."

"We don't even know each other."

"True. But there's no denying what we feel."

"We don't have to act on it."

He merely smiled, that dangerous smile that had her heart pounding in her temples.

"Ross, I . . ."

"Shh." He touched a finger to her lips and drew her inside the cottage.

In one smooth gesture he turned her in his arms, pressing her firmly against the closed door.

And then his hands were in her hair, his mouth fused to hers, his kiss so hot, so hungry, he was nearly devouring her. His body was pressed so tightly to hers, she could feel him in every part of her being. His chest rising and falling with each labored breath. His frantic heart keeping time with her own. His mouth, that clever, incredible mouth, moving over hers, taking her higher than she'd ever been with a single kiss.

Her shawl fell to the floor at their feet, forgotten in their haste. When his hands moved to the zipper at the back of her dress, she gasped and stepped away.

"I can't stay. This is madness."

"Don't leave me, Aidan." His mouth burned a trail of hot, wet kisses down her throat to her collarbone.

She was staggered by the flood of sensations that shot through her.

Heat. She was so hot, she couldn't seem to catch her breath.

Light. Behind her closed lids a kaleidoscope of lights battered her senses.

Need. A desperate, driving need gripped her, and she knew that she had to run. Now. This minute. Or it would be too late.

"I can't do this. I don't know what's come over me, but you have to believe that I feel as if I've lost my way."

He pressed his forehead to hers, struggling for breath. "I do believe you, Aidan. It's the same for me. I'm walking a very thin line, and just now I very nearly crossed it."

He opened the door. "Go now. And whatever you do, don't look back."

She ran along the path leading to the mansion. In her haste, she never even noticed that she'd left the cashmere throw behind.

Ross picked it up and buried his face in it, breathing in the fragrance of her cologne, the smell of her skin, and wanting, more than anything, to run after her.

It took all of his willpower to remain where he was.

SEVEN

Aidan stepped into the sunny dining room and watched as Cullen and Bridget, heads bent, quickly looked over at her and stepped apart.

"Good morning, my dear." Cullen walked over to press a kiss to her cheek. "How did you sleep?"

"Fine." She wondered if, up close, he could see the lack of sleep in her eyes. She'd paced the room until, in the small hours of morning, she'd finally fallen into an exhausted sleep. An hour later she'd wakened feeling as though she'd been running for miles across an alien landscape. But she'd wondered, had she been running from something, or to something? "And how did you sleep?"

"Like a baby." He looked up to see Ross in the doorway. "Ah, Ross. Good morning."

" 'Morning."

Aidan knew she was staring, but she

couldn't seem to help herself. He was wearing faded denims and a black turtleneck. His dark hair sparkled with droplets from his morning shower. He looked like a sleek, restless panther about to pounce on an unsuspecting prey.

She wanted to be that prey.

Cullen cleared his throat. "I'm afraid I have some bad news."

Aidan and Ross broke eye contact and glanced over.

"The Farmers' Cooperative is having its annual meeting. With all the excitement here, I nearly forgot. I can't miss it."

Ross was the first to recover. "Of course you can't. Why is that a problem?"

Cullen shrugged. "I was hoping to give Aidan a tour of the property. But now there's no telling how long I'll be tied up." He paused before adding, "Would you mind filling in for me, Ross?"

"Not at all."

Cullen caught Aidan's hands. "I hope you don't mind, my dear. I assure you Ross will be every bit as thorough a guide as I would be."

"Of course he will. We'll be fine, Cullen. But I'm sorry you can't be with us."

"Can't be helped. Well, then." He turned away. "I've asked Sean to bring the car around. I'll probably be gone most of the day."

He winked at Bridget before calling over his shoulder, "I hope you two can make the best of it."

"We'll do what we can to salvage the day." Ross watched him walk to the door.

When Cullen was gone, Bridget wiped her hands down her apron, looking flustered as always. "I hope you don't mind, but Kathleen decided to make omelets and toast with country ham, in order to give you both time to tour the property. She said she'd be happy to make you anything more, if you'd like."

Aidan was busy pouring coffee into two cups. "The breakfast Kathleen already made sounds perfect, Bridget. It's as though she read my mind."

The old woman coughed.

Aidan took a seat at the table, and Ross sat beside her. They were careful to avoid touching, sitting stiffly and looking extremely uncomfortable.

"And you, Ross?" The old woman paused beside him. "Would you be wanting anything else?"

"Not a thing. Thank you, Bridget."

Aidan looked over. "Where's Charity this morning?"

"Himself gave her the weekend off." Humming a little tune, the housekeeper walked from the room, returning with their breakfast. That done, she didn't reappear until Aidan and Ross had finished eating.

As she cleared the table, Bridget glanced out the window. "If you're hoping to give the lass a tour of the property, you might think about doing it as soon as possible, before the rain rolls in."

"Rain?" Ross looked up. "There's not a cloud in the sky."

"Not yet. But trust me. 'Twill rain."

Ross stood and held Aidan's chair. "I'd planned on riding this morning. How do you feel about seeing the countryside on horseback?"

"Oh, could we?" Aidan couldn't keep the excitement from her voice. "I haven't been on a horse since I was a kid."

As the two hurried away, Bridget watched with a dreamy smile on her lips before returning to her chores.

"It's all so beautiful, Ross." Aidan reined in her mount at the top of a hill and stared down at the scene below.

The sprawling mansion resembled a castle, with its turreted roofs sparkling in the sunlight. Around it were the graceful arboretum, green fields of sheep and cattle, and even a bee farm on a nearby incline. "I don't know how you can ever bear to leave this place for even a day."

"It is lovely, isn't it?" Ross brought his horse beside hers. "I once accused Cullen of being a magician. When he first started the renovation, the lodge lay in ruins, the river polluted from an old factory and the fields around it were fallow. The village of Glinkilly was so poor there seemed no hope of ever bringing it back to life. And yet here it is, all of it looking like a sparkling jewel."

He looked up at the clouds beginning to roll in. "Looks like the storm Bridget predicted. It's coming in fast. We'd better get back to the stable."

"I'll race you." Aidan shot him a grin before nudging her mount into a run.

Ross gave a shout of laughter and joined in the race.

By the time they'd turned the horses into their stalls and stepped from the stable, they were feeling the first raindrops.

"Just in time." Ross caught her arm. "I don't think we can make it up to the big house."

They turned and raced through the rain to his cottage.

Once inside, they heard the rumble of

thunder. Minutes later the skies opened up and the storm began in earnest.

They stood together by the windows, witnessing the wind whip the trees into a frenzied dance.

For long minutes they stood watching, each achingly aware of the other. As the minutes ticked by and the storm grew in intensity, Aidan turned toward the door, rubbing her arms.

"I think I'll brave the rain and return to the house."

"Don't go." The words were torn from his throat.

"Ross, if I stay . . ."

He crossed to her in quick strides and gathered her close.

"I'm sorry." Ross pressed his mouth to a tangle of hair at her temple.

"What . . . what are you sorry about?"

"This. I thought I could fight it, but it's too much, Aidan. I want you too much. There's something deeper, stronger here than just my will."

She gave a long, deep sigh. "I know. I feel it, too."

He stared down at her, his eyes so fierce she actually shivered. And then his mouth was on hers, and she was lost in the kiss.

When they came up for air, she touched a

finger to his lips. "I've tried fighting, but the truth is I want you, Ross."

It was true. She had to have this man. She was actually trembling with need for him.

"I want you, too, Aidan."

And then there was no need for words as they came together in a storm of passion. With each touch of his lips, his tongue, his clever fingers, she felt herself growing hotter and hotter until she was engulfed in fire.

Because her legs had turned to rubber, she clutched at his waist for support, and would have surely fallen if he hadn't held her firmly against the cool wood of the door.

His hands found the zipper of her dress, and he slid it from her shoulders. It pooled at their feet as his clever fingers dispensed with the lace that covered her breasts.

She hadn't known how desperately she'd wanted his hands on her. His mouth followed, taking her even higher.

When he lifted his head to catch a breath, she used that moment to tear at his shirt. She heard the buttons pop and roll across the floor as she flung it aside and reached for the fasteners at his waist.

With his help his clothes soon joined hers on the floor around them. In one quick motion her bikini panties were stripped aside.

Now they were free to feast. And did.

She ran her hands over the muscled contours of his chest and shoulders, then followed with her mouth, and thrilled to his low growl of pleasure.

"The bed." She managed the words despite a throat constricted with need.

"Too far." He lifted her, his mouth still feasting on hers, until he bumped into the overstuffed sofa.

He drew her down before stretching out beside her. At last free of any restraint, they came together in a firestorm of desire that rocked them both.

She shuddered as his hands and lips moved over her, taking her on a wild, dizzying ride that had her head spinning, her mind going blank.

"I knew," he whispered against her ear. "The first time I saw you, I knew that you'd be here with me."

"Though I tried to deny it, I knew . . ." Before she could finish, his mouth covered hers in a kiss so heated, she could feel her bones melting.

No one had ever excited her like this. The darkness, the danger of this man had the heat growing until it threatened to choke her.

Desperate, she twined her arms around his neck, dragging his head down for a long, drugging kiss.

Against his mouth she whispered, "I want you, Ross. Now."

"And I want you." He lifted his head. "Look at me, Aidan." His voice was rough with need.

Through the heat of passion that clouded her vision, she struggled to focus. His eyes were hot and fierce, and remained steady on hers as he entered her and began to move.

With incredible strength she matched his rhythm, moving with him, climbing with him.

Heat rose between them, pearling their flesh, dampening their hair as they strained to reach the very top of a high, sheer cliff.

For one precious moment they seemed to hang suspended. Then, eyes steady, hearts thundering, they took that final step into space.

"Ross." His name was torn from her lips as she felt herself soaring high, then higher still, before shattering.

"Aidan."

She heard him sigh her name as though in prayer as she slowly drifted back to earth.

Still joined, they lay in a limp heap of arms and legs on the narrow, cramped sofa.

Ross pressed his lips to her forehead. "What just happened?"

She managed a laugh. "I think we got caught in a storm."

"Sorry I was so rough. Are you all right?"

"I think so. My head's still spinning. You?"

He levered himself above her. "I'm not sure. Guess I'd better check." He brushed a kiss over her lips. "Umm. That works." He ran a hand down her side, then up again, pausing at the swell of her breast. "Everything's still working just fine." He kissed her again, slowly.

Against her mouth, he whispered, "That storm has been building since you stepped out of Cullin's car. But maybe now that we've got that out of the way, we can actually think and talk."

She couldn't help grinning. "You want to talk?"

His smile matched hers. "Not really. But I thought I'd show you that I can be civilized."

"I see. Civilized. I think it's a bit late for that."

He threw back his head and roared. "I guess you're right. All right then, what would you think about joining me in my bed?"

"Is it bigger than this sofa?"

"Much."

"Good." She started to stand.

As she got to her feet he scooped her up in his arms and strode from the room, depositing her in the middle of his big bed.

"Much better." She sat up and watched as he settled himself beside her. "Now, what would you like to talk about?"

"Let's save that for later." He gave her a wolfish grin. "I thought I'd show you that I'm not always in such a rush."

"You have another speed?"

"I do. Yes. Just watch me." He drew her down among the bed linens and began a slow, leisurely exploration of her body with his tongue.

"Where do you think you're going?" Ross snagged her wrist as she started to slide out of bed.

They'd spent hours talking, laughing, loving, until both were sated. Now, with the rain gone and evening shadows dappling the lawn outside the window, Aidan bent to brush a kiss over his mouth and allowed her free hand to stroke his cheek.

"To grab a shower and dress. Cullen will be back. It might prove awkward explaining to Bridget and Cullen why I'm sneaking in, late and mussed."

"To save face, you intend to leave me alone and bereft? I can see where your priorities lie."

The look on his face had her heart stuttering. He looked so inviting, with his hair tousled and his eyes heavy-lidded with passion. Like a man who had been thoroughly loved.

In her most haughty tone, she said, "I live to break men's hearts. Now, like Cinderella, I fear the witching hour. I must flee before I'm discovered, barefoot and in rags."

"Even in rags, Aidan, I'd want you."

Her heart lurched. To keep things light, she simply smiled. "Easy for you. You don't have to face Bridget's wrath."

As she started away he drew her back. "You can't leave me without a kiss."

She brushed her lips over his and was startled when he dragged her close and ravaged her mouth until her heart began tripping over itself.

"Stay, Aidan. I'll show you all the wonders of the world."

"I thought you'd already done that."

"Oh, but there are so many more."

She drew back. "You make it entirely too tempting." She stepped away and this time managed to cross the room.

"All right." He slid out of bed and trailed

her. "The least I can do is scrub your back."

Still laughing, they showered together.

As they dressed, Aidan spotted the cashmere throw which had been carefully folded over the back of a chair.

She arched a brow. "I'd forgotten this."

He merely smiled. "Like Cinderella's glass slipper, it remained after you'd fled. I liked having it here." His tone deepened. "I missed you the minute you walked out the door. Which is why . . ." He linked his fingers with hers and held the door. "This time I'm not going to let you out of my sight."

His words touched her heart and made her so incredibly happy that she couldn't stop smiling as they strode hand in hand from the cottage and made their way to the lodge.

As dusk settled over the land, the storm had blown itself out, leaving the gardens fresh and glistening with raindrops.

Aidan and Ross stepped apart before entering the library.

Cullen and Bridget were huddled in quiet conversation in front of a roaring fire.

The old man looked up with a smile and held out a tulip glass of champagne to Aidan. "I hope you found something to do while I was gone, my dear."

She accepted the glass and sipped. "I had a lovely tour of the countryside by horseback."

"Excellent." He handed Ross a tumbler of ice water. "Thank you for standing in for me, lad."

"It was my pleasure. You had to drive through quite a storm."

"Storm?" For a moment the older man seemed puzzled. Then a wide smile split his lips. "Oh. Yes. The storm. Not quite as fierce in town as it was here, I expect. Did you two have supper?"

Aidan nodded. "And you?"

"Oh, my, yes. We ate at the pub after our meeting. Here, my dear." He indicated a group of chairs in front of the fire. "Warm yourself."

Cullen settled himself beside Aidan, while Ross chose to stand in front of the fireplace where he could watch her expressive face.

"The farmers were impressed by the accuracy of your figures. They claimed that without your help, they'd have had to hire a firm from Dublin, which would have charged them a fortune. Thanks to you, Aidan, they're showing their biggest profit ever."

"I'm so glad." Aidan sipped her champagne and shot a quick glance at Ross, who was openly staring, as though he couldn't get his fill of looking at her.

"The Cooperative would like to pay you for your services."

Aidan flushed. "Please thank them for me, and explain why I must refuse their generous offer. It was such a treat for me to be able to do something that I enjoy while knowing that I was helping them. To me, that's reward enough."

"Indeed." Her response seemed to please Cullen tremendously. "You've a generous heart, my dear. But then, I never doubted it. You come from a long line of generous souls."

After less than an hour of pleasant conversation, Cullen stifled a yawn. "I'm afraid this day has worn me out. Forgive an old man his weariness." He got to his feet. "You two stay and enjoy the fire."

Ross gave a quick shake of his head. "I thought I'd give Aidan a tour of the gardens by moonlight. Will you join us?"

"Not tonight. I'm off to my bed." Cullen bent to press a kiss to Aidan's cheek. "I expect the courier should be here by the time we finish our breakfast."

"So soon?" Aidan's heart contracted and she looked over to see Ross' little frown.

" 'Twill end the suspense for you. For both of us," he added as an afterthought. "Good night, my dear." He straightened and walked to Ross, laying a hand on the younger man's shoulder. "Good night, son."

"Good night, Cullen."

Aidan was touched by the affection between the two men. It warmed her more than the fire.

Ross opened the French doors leading to the gardens. As she was about to follow, she turned to see Cullen and Bridget, heads bent once more in quiet conversation.

The moment she stepped outside Ross caught her hand and drew her deeper into the shadows.

"This is what I wanted." He gathered her close to press soft kisses from her temple to her jaw, before claiming her mouth. "Only this."

When they stepped apart, he started leading her along the path toward his cottage.

She held back. "I thought you were going to show me the gardens by moonlight."

"And so I shall." He gave her a wicked grin. "Look quickly. Drink it all in as you pass through. As soon as we reach my place, I have no intention of letting you out of my arms again until morning."

Their laughter drifted like music on the

night air and carried into the library, where the old man and woman shared a conspiratorial smile.

EIGHT

Aidan crept into the lodge and up the stairs. In the privacy of her room, she undressed and stepped into the shower. When she emerged, wrapped in a huge bath sheet, she sat at the ornate dressing table and dried her hair before dressing for the day.

She'd never felt so alive. So filled with joy. So thoroughly loved.

And all because of Ross Delaney. She felt as though she'd been waiting for this man all of her life. He was fun and funny. Sophisticated, yet as down-to-earth as any man she'd ever known. He had a gentle way of teasing, of coaxing a laugh from her even in the midst of a serious conversation.

Her soul mate.

He'd been so much more than she'd expected. Warm and sentimental. And sexy as hell.

Love at first sight. It was a concept she'd long disdained. But there was no denying, it had happened to her. She felt as giddy as a girl on her first date. Light-as-air happy, and wildly, madly, deeply in love.

Foolish, of course. For Ross, she would be nothing more than a harmless fling.

The woman hasn't been born to suit Ross Delaney. 'Tis said he'll never marry.

Aidan consoled herself that it didn't matter. What she was feeling for Ross was enough for both of them. And he would never know, for she would never admit her foolish feelings. The love she felt for him would be her secret.

At a knock on the parlor door, she hurried over to find Bridget carrying a silver tea service.

"Good morning, miss. I thought, since I heard you up and about so early, you might want a cup of tea before you go down to breakfast."

"Thank you, Bridget. That's so thoughtful." She watched as the housekeeper set the tray on a side table. "Do you have time to join me?"

The old woman smiled at the unexpected gesture. Not that she was surprised. In the short time the lass had been here, she'd proven herself to be kind and thoughtful with everyone, from Himself to the staff to the strangers in the Farmers' Cooperative.

"Afraid not. I've my morning chores to see to." Bridget stared directly at Aidan. "And, as you can imagine, I'll be keeping an eye out for the courier."

Aidan's hand went to her heart as it took a quick dip.

Bridget poured a cup of tea. "Cullen Glin is the finest man I've ever known. It does my heart good to see him so happy, hoping that today may be the day he'll learn that he's a grandfather. Just think, after today, this could all be yours." She set down the teapot and handed the steaming cup to Aidan. "Of course, that will mean he'll have to amend his will."

"His will?" Aidan's head came up sharply.

"When he had his lawyers draw up his original will, he'd planned on leaving everything to the young man who saved his life. Having a blood relative changes everything. Not that Ross will mind in the least. His love and loyalty for Cullen Glin are true and deep, and has never been about fortune or status. Still, it will surely change things between the two."

Seeing the stunned look in Aidan's eyes, Bridget clapped a hand over her mouth. "There I go. Running off at the mouth again. Talking about things that are none of my business. It's always been my greatest shortcoming." She turned away. "Now you just forget everything I said, miss, and enjoy your tea."

She nearly ran from the room in her haste to escape.

When the door closed behind her, Aidan sat, staring into space. Through the open windows she could hear the soothing sound of the fountains and could smell the wonderful perfume of the roses.

Hadn't she called this paradise?

And it was. It was almost too perfect to be real. This could all be hers. If she was indeed Cullen's granddaughter as he hoped, her life as she'd known it would be forever altered. All her debts would be erased. Her childhood home could be saved or sold, according to her whims. Her future secure for all time.

Wasn't this what any sane person would want? Why, then, had her heart suddenly become as heavy as a boulder inside her chest?

Ross.

By rights, this should all be his. His estate. His fortune. His legacy. Without Ross, Cullen would have died that night on the streets of Dublin. Without Ross to carry on the search, Cullen never would have found his lost love, and the daughter he'd never known. Without Ross, Aidan wouldn't be here, sampling a life so foreign to her, it was beyond her wildest imagination.

And now, instead of the reward Ross deserved for his years of love and loyalty, it could be all stripped away. If the DNA tests showed her to be Cullen's granddaughter, Ross would forfeit any right to all of this.

The man she'd come to love would lose everything that was rightfully his, all because of her.

She stood so quickly, the tea sloshed over the rim of her cup, scalding her fingers. She took no notice as she hurried to the bedroom.

She knew in her heart of hearts what she had to do. And she must move quickly, before Cullen awoke and the courier arrived with information that could alter all their lives forever.

Ross looked up when Meath and Mayo barked. Seconds later a knock sounded on the cottage door. He silenced the dogs, then hurried over to find Bridget looking out of breath, her hair spilling out of its neat knot, her eyes wide and worried.

"Good morning, Bridget. What's wrong?"

"Miss O'Mara said I was to give you this." She handed him a folded note. "It must be important, for she said I was not to give it to you until after she was gone."

"Gone? Gone where?"

The old woman shrugged. "She was calling for Sean to bring the car."

"Car?" He looked thoroughly confused. "Whatever for?"

The old woman worried the edge of her apron, avoiding his eyes. "I believe she's planning on leaving for the airport. I saw her suitcase packed."

"Leaving? Now what's this all about?" With a scowl, he started past her.

"Oh. When you see her, be sure to give her this." Bridget reached into her pocket and withdrew a fat envelope. "The courier just delivered it as I was coming to find you."

He stared at the envelope, then slapped it against his open palm before striding away.

The housekeeper watched him go.

As soon as he was out of sight, the frazzled look in her eyes was replaced with a wide, satisfied smile.

Pausing to scratch behind each hound's ears, she said with a sigh, "You may as well come along, too, and watch the fireworks. However it all plays out, it should prove fascinating indeed, with Himself, as always, pulling all the strings."

■ ■ ■ ■

Without bothering to knock on the parlor door, Ross tore it open and strode across the room to the bedroom. Aidan's suitcase was closed and lying on the bed. She was standing by the window, watching for the car.

He crossed the room to stand beside her, tossing her note on the cushion of the window seat. "What in the hell do you think you're doing?"

She closed her eyes, cursing his timing. Another few minutes and she could have avoided this scene. "Just what it said in my note, Ross. I'm leaving."

"I can read. You didn't bother to tell me why."

"I realized that I've been living in a dream world these past few days. This isn't my birthright, Ross. I don't belong here."

"Isn't that a decision you should be discussing with Cullen?"

"He's blinded by the loss of his beloved Moira. He wants so badly to believe, that he's lost all reality."

"Oh, it's reality you want?" He handed over the courier's envelope. "Read this."

"So soon? I was hoping . . ." She stared at

it with a look of dread. "You haven't read it?"

"It isn't mine to read. It's yours. Yours and Cullen's. Go ahead, Aidan. Read it."

Instead of opening it, she shocked him to the core by tearing it into tiny bits.

He hissed out a breath and tried to stop her. "Are you crazy?"

She pulled away, shredding the last of the documents. "I think I was, for a couple of days."

"You're not making any sense, Aidan."

She tossed the bits of paper into a wastebasket before turning to him. Though she longed to reach out and touch him, she dared not, for fear of losing what little courage she had left. "Listen to me, Ross. You and Cullen love each other. And why not? You're his true son."

"And he's more a father to me than my own ever was."

"Without you, Cullen would have never become what he is today."

Ross was shaking his head. "You've got it wrong. Without Cullen, I'd still be a street tough, probably living out my years in prison. Maybe I ought to tell you the kind of life I led before Cullen took me in."

"There's no need. He told me."

"But you don't . . ."

She placed a finger to his lips to still his words. The warmth of his skin beneath her fingertip caused a tiny thrill to race along her spine. "I know that because of Cullen, you've become a better man. And because of you, so has he. You became his reason for living, for growing as a person. That's what family does for family. Whether I'm related or not, I can never love Cullen the way you do. I can never impact Cullen's life the way you have."

"And for that you'd just leave?"

"That isn't why." She shook her head. "Why should I have a claim on his estate? Does it make sense to hand all this over to me because of a mistake that was made two generations ago? Don't you see? You have to let me go."

"There's something else going on here." Ross bit off each word for emphasis. "What you're planning is selfish and cruel, and now that I know you so well, I know that's not something you're capable of being. You're kind and thoughtful and generous, but never cruel."

She looked away, wondering how to make him understand. "It would be even more selfish to claim what isn't mine. I can't be what Cullen wants me to be. I can't stay here. I can't claim any of this, when it's

rightfully yours. If I leave, everything between you and Cullen will remain as it was."

For the longest moment he merely stared
at her, as the truth of her words dawned.
She was turning her back on all of this
because of him.

Ross felt a surge of such blinding love
blooming in his heart, it had him by the
throat until he could barely catch his breath.

She loved him. She was doing all of this
because she loved him. Completely. Unself-
ishly.

Hadn't he truly believed that such love
was impossible in this world?

He fought to speak over the rock that had
formed in his throat, threatening to choke
him. "Aidan, all of this is Cullen's. To do
with as he pleases."

"But he's left it to you. The son he always
wanted." She felt tears sting her eyes and
blinked furiously to keep from weeping.
"And now I've come along and messed up
everything. This is all a big mistake."

"A mistake?" His eyes were hot and fierce.
"Was the love we shared last night a mistake? What about the feelings we have for
each other? Are you saying that's a mistake,
too?"

When she didn't answer he clenched his
hands at his sides. He wanted to shake her

until she came to her senses.

He wanted to hold her. Just hold her. But not yet. Not just yet. They needed to get all of this out in the open and put behind them.

"All of this . . ." She swept her hand. "Ireland. This lovely estate. That fairy-tale town filled with good, hard-working people . . . It's all a lovely dream, but for me, it's just that. A dream. Now it's time for the truth."

"Yes. The truth." He fought to keep his tone even. "Think you can handle it?"

When she said nothing he went on. "I want you to stay, Aidan. Not for Cullen, but for me."

"I can't stay. I told you, I'm . . ."

"I know. Determined to do the noble thing and step aside so that all this can be mine." He fought down the wild swirl of emotions threatening to swamp him. He would have sworn he could hear music playing. An orchestra, the sound growing, swelling in his heart. A heart that had been battered by anger and mistrust, and locked tightly against any hint of trust or tenderness for all of his adult life. "The truth is, you love me. You're ready to step aside because you want what's best for me."

Aidan refused to look at him.

"I need to hear the words, Aidan. Say you

love me."

She looked down at her hands and prayed her voice wouldn't tremble. "Maybe I do. But . . ."

"You do love me." He was finally able to smile. "That wasn't so hard, was it?"

She still refused to look at him. "But I have to go."

"You have to stay."

"Why?"

"Because I love you, too, little fool."

Love. The mere word had all the air leaving her lungs. She could hardly breathe. "But Cullen's estate . . ."

"Is in Cullen's hands. Tell me, does it matter whether or not one of us inherits? Would you be willing to marry me even if I'm penniless?"

"Marry? I thought . . ." She swallowed and tried again. "I was told that Ross Delaney isn't the marrying kind."

"I wasn't. Until now."

"And now? What happened to change your mind?"

"You. And that damnably noble heart of yours. I haven't any defense against it."

Oh, the way her poor heart leapt in her chest. "But what about Cullen?"

"He has to find his own woman."

That had them both chuckling, breaking

the terrible tension building between them.

Finally, with the warmth of laughter, he could take her in his arms. Touch her. Hold her.

He pressed his mouth to her temple and growled. "Aidan, I want it all with you. Love. Marriage. Forever-after. I won't settle for less. Starting right now. Today. This minute."

As his words washed over her, and the reality of what he'd said began to sink in, tears filled her eyes and she was mortified to feel them running down her cheeks. "Oh, Ross. You love me. Truly love me."

"I do. Yes."

"And I love you. Truly love you."

He gathered her closer, needing to feel her heartbeat inside his own chest, keeping time to his. "Thank heaven. At last we can speak the truth. Now, here's my truth, Aidan. The first time I saw you, I felt something so strong, so powerful, I didn't know how to handle it. I knew only that I had to be near you. To see you, to touch you. To have you. I don't even know when lust turned into love. I love you so much I can't sleep or eat or string together a coherent sentence. Now, finally, I understand what Cullen went through. If you left me, I'd have to spend the rest of my life searching for you. Don't you see? We have to be together. I couldn't bear to lose you."

Aidan wondered that her poor heart didn't simply burst with happiness. She took in a long, shaky breath. "I'm not sorry I tore up the DNA results. But what does that do to Cullen's search for family?"

"I'm not sure. That will be entirely between you and Cullen."

"And his estate?"

"It's his to keep or give away. It's not my concern, or yours."

"But do you think . . . ?

"Shh. Don't think." He brushed his mouth over hers to still any further questions. Against her mouth he muttered, "For now, just let me hold you, my love."

Love. Oh, she'd never heard a sweeter, more beautiful word. It filled her up until she was exploding with joy as she gave herself up to his kiss.

Cullen and Bridget stood in the parlor, peering around the open door, listening to every word. When the young couple embraced, they turned to each other with matching smiles of delight.

Bridget shook her head and whispered, "I wouldn't have believed it if I hadn't seen and heard it myself. I was truly afraid she wouldn't be talked out of leaving. But you were right again."

"Nothing like being young and wildly in love." Cullen patted a hand to his heart. "I've never forgotten the feeling."

He crept silently from the parlor, trailed by the housekeeper, and together they descended the stairs to his library.

Meath and Mayo looked up from the rug in front of the fireplace.

Cullen walked to his desk and stared long and hard at the envelope delivered by the courier. It was identical to the one given to Aidan.

Bridget clasped her hands together. "Finally, you have scientific proof of whether or not the lass is your kin."

He nodded, but still he didn't make a move to open the envelope.

Bridget twisted her hands together, her brow knitted in confusion.

After another long pause, Cullen snatched up the envelope and crossed to the fireplace, where he tossed it into the flames.

Bridget sucked in a breath. "Oh, no! What have you done?"

He merely smiled. "I don't need scientific evidence to tell me what my heart already knows. I chose wisely, don't you agree? I knew the lass was unselfish, seeing the way she sacrificed everything to care for her mother. I knew she had a wise, compassionate heart when she agreed to the DNA test for my sake. And when you 'accidentally' told her that Ross would be disinherited in her favor, she reacted just as I'd predicted."

Bridget flushed with pride. "I was quite an actress in my youth."

"And you haven't lost your touch, old girl."

She arched a brow. "But you said yourself you would need the test results for the Courts."

He shook his head. "I can do whatever I please with my fortune. I have no need of a court of law. My heart knows the truth. And now I have even more than I'd hoped for. The son I always wanted, desperately in love with the one I know to be my own." His eyes twinkled with humor. "Oh, I chose wisely. She's the only one good enough for Ross. The only one he'd have trusted enough with that fragile, damaged heart of his. And Ross is the only one who deserves a lass with such goodness, such decency. Each of them deserved to find the best possible soul mate."

The old woman wiped a tear from her eye. "They do make a perfect couple."

He chuckled. "That they do. And together

they'll give me such a beautiful family to carry on this legacy. I'd say my estate, my town, and my world will be in very good hands when I leave it."

As he followed the housekeeper from the room, the envelope and its precious documents turned dazzling white, sending out a spray of glittering sparks that had the hounds backing away.

Cullen turned. Instead of burning to ash, the paper's edges curled up into the shape of a perfect heart. For long moments it gleamed red hot, as though alive and pulsing, before it shot straight up the chimney.

The old man smiled. A magician, was he? Maybe. Maybe not. But one thing was certain. He was a man who'd spent a lifetime seeking perfect love. And wasn't it grand that now, after all this time, it was right here in this very place?

He couldn't wait to see this old lodge filled to the rafters with love and laughter. And babies. Oh now, there was a fine plan indeed.

The thought had him laughing like a loon and rubbing his hands in anticipation of everything that the fine, bright future was about to bring to all of them.

The employees of Thorndike Press hope you have enjoyed this Large Print book. All our Thorndike, Wheeler, and Kennebec Large Print titles are designed for easy reading, and all our books are made to last. Other Thorndike Press Large Print books are available at your library, through selected bookstores, or directly from us.

For information about titles, please call:
(800) 223-1244

or visit our Web site at:
http://gale.cengage.com/thorndike

To share your comments, please write:
Publisher
Thorndike Press
295 Kennedy Memorial Drive
Waterville, ME 04901

LP Fiction
LP Robb J.D.

The lost

4/10